ROMANCING THE REALMS

COURTING THE MOON PRIEST

MIRANDA JOY

ALSO BY MIRANDA JOY

These Wicked Lies Series:

These Wicked Lies

These Wicked Truths

These Wicked Gods (Coming Soon)

Courts of Malice Trilogy:

A Curse of Malice & Mercy

A Dream of Fate & Flesh

A Realm of Fear & Fury

Silver City Series:

Shades of Silver City

Souls of Silver City (Coming Soon)

CONTENT WARNINGS

Blood
Brief drug and alcohol use (fictional, herb-like drugs)
Brief violence
Cutting (self-inflicted wounds)
Language
Sexual content

This is for anyone who learned to thrive in the darkness.
Even on the darkest nights, the moon still shines.
And so do you.

COURTING

THE

MOON

PRIEST

FIRST UNION MONTH

CHAPTER ONE

THE UNION

SORAYA

*E*veryone on the island holds their breath, eyes locked on the night sky. We wait patiently for the twin moons to overlap, forming a single supermoon as they do every thirty days.

"Almost," Mariel whispers, gripping my hand tightly in both of hers.

A few seconds later, the moons cross over one another. The moment the second moon is gone from sight, fully consumed into the other, a roar of appreciation rises from the beach. The conjoined moons' glow intensifies, sending radiant waves of iridescent light streaking through the dark sky.

In response, the jungle brightens, glimmering with the gifted power of our goddesses.

"Praise the moons," I whisper, excitement bubbling up in my chest.

The bright silver light casts an ethereal glow across the

island. The rivers shimmer, running down the single verdant mountain and through the jungle like narrow arteries. They all feed into the ocean around us. The currents pulse softly, as if alive. Along the banks, the plants harbor the same magical light. Their usually vibrant green color now mirrors the ribbons of blue-green streaking through the sky beside the newly formed supermoon.

A smile overtakes my face, and my shoulders soften. Mariel drops my hands, throwing her arms around me.

"Blessed Union, Soraya," she squeals in my ear.

I squeeze her back, and she pulls free. Music starts playing, and the villagers' gratitude is palpable.

Mariel grins. "I'm going to snag us some nectar. I'll be right back."

She bounds off toward the hut at the edge of the sand, waving animatedly at everyone she passes. Most of us were born and raised on the Isle de Lunith, and we're a tight-knit community.

Right as she disappears into the crowd, strong arms snake around my waist, startling me. The scent of salt and earth mixed with a familiar musk invades my nose, and I chuckle.

"This dress does things to me," Joss murmurs into my neck, invading my personal space.

Swatting his arms away, I turn to face him. Moonlight dances on the droplets lining his deeply tanned chest. He runs a hand through his short brown hair, slicking it back. It glistens from his recent dip in the ocean. His lips curl into a teasing grin, and my expression softens, mirroring his.

I playfully roll my eyes. "We're all wearing the same thing."

Gesturing around the beach, I take in the various celestial servants scattered about, mingling with the rest of the island's population. Everyone drinks, dances, and feasts tonight, celebrating the moons' union.

The priests and priestesses are easy to pick out, all dressed in similar wispy, lightweight garments in pale silvers and off-whites. Some don cascading gossamer gowns with thin straps, while others have flowy pants with billowing arms, but they're all variations of the same layered look.

"No," he says, arching a light-brown brow. "You certainly are not." His fingers trail up my covered collarbone until his hand lands on my exposed shoulder. "I like *yours* best."

Planting my hands on his bare chest, I gently push him back. "We talked about this!"

"I thought we were friends." He fake pouts, running his fingers through his wet hair.

I give him a knowing look. "Exactly. *Friends.*"

A broad, charming grin spreads over his features. "And I'm honoring your wishes... by being very friendly."

I can't help but laugh. "You know damn well what I mean, Joss Thalor!"

"It's impossible to keep my hands off you," he groans. "I miss you already."

It's my own fault for blurring the boundaries between us. I might've ended our official relationship, but I haven't kept him out of my bed.

I shake my head, scanning the beach for Mariel. She's out of sight, likely having made her way into the hut for our drinks. But as much fun as Joss is, I ended things for a reason. No matter how handsome, kind, and funny he is, I just don't want *more*.

Not the same way he does.

My eyes flit to the moons. I want a love like *theirs*. Lore says the two moons were previously goddesses who sacrificed their mortal forms and cursed themselves, all to spend eternity together, hung in the skies side-by-side, only kissing once per month.

They're forever suspended overhead, only shifting to touch on Union Night and separating by morning.

I don't necessarily want their fate, but the thought of a passionate, all-consuming, eternal love lingers in the back of my mind. With Joss, things are comfortable, but the thought of being without him doesn't steal my breath or make my heart ache.

When I glance over at him, he's staring out at the dark ocean, all the previous humor gone. My chest tightens at the sight, and I bite my lip. We've been there for each other our whole lives, including when he lost his mother to the very sea he loves.

Guilt gnaws at me, and I step beside him, nudging him with my elbow. "Wanna go find some silverdew?"

The flower, indigenous to the Isle de Lunith, only blooms at night. Though it sprouts in abundance, it's a cherished flower, mainly because it's our primary export and the source of our island's income.

It can be tapped for nectar—the delightful, fruity brew we enjoy for a buzz. It also provides a more intense, euphoric high when the petals unfurl and the pollen is snorted.

Joss shoots me a crooked smile. "How about later? I'm going to catch another quick dip with the other tideborn before they get too nectared."

Squeezing his hand in understanding, I nod. When he leaves, I dig my feet into the cool, packed sand, watching the water gently lick the shore. With my back to the revelry, I take this moment to myself to just *be*.

My lungs fill with fresh, salty air with a fruity tinge. It smells like home, like *everything*.

I love Union Night. Not only for the obvious—the energetically charged revelry, the merriment, the magic—but because I feel as if I'm truly one with the island. Fingering a strand of teal hair, I smile down at the color, feeling less like an outcast because of its unnatural hue and more like I'm an integral part of the ecosystem.

Shoving my hair over my shoulder, I squint, catching the faint ring of the smaller moon as it nestles in front of its larger counterpart. One night a month, when the moons align, the Isle de Lunith comes alive with magic. Even though I've experienced it twelve times a year for twenty-six years, it never ceases to fill me with awe.

Amazement tickles my insides, and my heart pulses in time with the flickering fireflies lighting up the beach.

Familiar faces blow merrily into seashell horns as they sway to the music. Drums and stringed instruments accompany them, blending into a tune that instills a need to move. It's melodic and hypnotic—impossible to resist. A group of celestial servants throw their limbs around as they release pent-up energy in dance. Others chant in groups, leaning into gratitude mantras to thank the goddess moons for their protection.

Every soul dances barefoot on the sand, connecting intimately with the island and celebrating another night, another month, of life-sustaining magic.

Every soul except for one.

I gaze toward the temple atop the tallest hill, which settles into the trees far beyond the village. It's where the celestial servants live and work: the point of the island closest to the moons. Even from this distance, I glimpse a hint of light sparkling from the top where the moonstone lives, absorbing the energy on this powerful night as it does during every Union.

Sparkling waters crest over the stony side, feeding into our rivers.

"You'd think out of everyone, *he* would be down here

celebrating," Mariel yells, thrusting a drink at me as she slips through the crowd to stand beside me.

"Where have you been?" I graciously accept the beverage, wrapping my lips around the bamboo straw peeking out of the coconut shell. The fruity, slightly sour tang of nectar washes over my tongue, and I close my eyes to revel in it for a moment.

"Maybe one day he'll stop thinking he's too good for us," she says bitterly.

A soft sigh escapes my lips as I open my eyes and face my best friend. "You know how he is, Mariel."

"*Reclusive*," she says sarcastically.

My lips press into a thin line as my head swivels toward her. "Hush." I glance around to ensure no one's eavesdropping on her talking poorly about High Priest Raziel Kasper. Granted, I've heard enough whispers to know many of the villagers think the same way. "He's our Moon Priest."

"Exactly." She lowers her voice, but the way she slurs tells me she's already had a little too much fun during tonight's celebration. "With how up the moons' butts he is, you'd expect him to show face during the most sacred night of the month."

"I'm sure he celebrates in his own way." I squint at the temple, unable to understand why he'd choose to skip the Union.

The High Priests before him were known for flashing their magic on this sacred night. He's an enigma for hiding his powers from the islanders.

She snorts. "I'm not the only one who notices his attitude."

Mariel isn't wrong about him being a bit of a recluse, but he's our island's Highest Keeper. *The* Moon Priest. The Goddesses' Anointed. The moons chose him to oversee the magic, and thus, the life of our island.

Yet he snubs every ceremony.

Mariel raises her drink to the moon, and her bracelets noisily clink together. She throws her head back, closes her eyes, and lets out a *whoop*. "To the moons!" she yells.

"To the moons," I say with a soft laugh.

Her eyes flick behind me. "Hey, there's your man." Mariel nudges me with her elbow.

I turn to catch Joss heading toward us. He charges the last few steps toward me, and despite his bare feet sinking into the soft sand, it barely slows him down. His muscular arms wrap around me, squeezing me as he playfully nibbles on my neck.

"Joss," I chastise, swatting at him. "You're getting me wet!"

"I wish," he murmurs before spinning me around, and some of my nectar splashes over the side.

The sheer, wispy bottom half of my gown floats around me, the slits parting to reveal my bronzed legs, toned from my daily treks up and down the temple's archive stairwells. The delicate silver chains crisscrossing my midsection hold the dress in place with effortless grace. The tiny star and moon charms tinkle with the movement.

I laugh. "Put me down!"

He obliges, placing me back on my feet. I stumble, quickly reorienting myself and adjusting my neckline to ensure my chest is fully covered.

"What are you two talking about?" Joss's green eyes twinkle with jest.

I'm glad to see he's swum his previous sorrows away. The grief still hits him from time to time, and though I can't relate in the same way, I know what it's like to miss a mother. Unlike him, I never knew my parents. Where he misses a person, I miss the idea of one.

Mariel, having refocused her attention on us, smirks with amusement. Her dress matches mine, but where mine is high in the front and plunging in the back, hers is the opposite, showcasing her glorious cleavage. The pale color of the garment contrasts beautifully with her brown skin and dark curls.

The outfits are symbolic, marking us as priestesses of the moon—a reminder of who we are and who we serve.

The Moon Priest.

My eyes flick back in the temple's direction. I find it rather blasphemous to talk poorly of him or the moons he protects. That *we* protect. Mariel, on the other hand, loves instigating and stirring up the 'monotony of our island'—her words, not mine.

"We're not talking about anything," I tell a waiting Joss. "Hey, would you mind grabbing me another nectar? Please?"

Joss gives me a broad smile and then glances at Mariel.

"Make that two?" Mariel says, twisting a curl of dark hair around her finger.

Joss offers a thumbs up, then jogs off toward the Nectar Hut, our beach tavern. His muscles flex with power, with only the tiny fabric of his hemp water shorts covering his ass.

"Your boyfriend is a delight," Mariel gushes, grabbing my hand and tugging me through the sand, closer to where the band plays their live instruments.

"You know we broke up." I raise my voice so she can hear me over the melody.

She whirls toward me, rolling her hips to the tempo as she raises a brow. "I saw him sneaking out of your bed this morning."

"Yeah, but we're not—"

"You *always* find your way back to each other." She spins, arms overhead, and her face tilted to the sky with glee.

"This is different, Mar." Shaking my head, I give up and let the music sink into my bones. I move naturally, keeping pace with Mariel's steps.

"He would've bonded with you in a heartbeat," she points out.

I flush at the thought of completing the Union ceremony with Joss, especially on a night like tonight, when such bonding events occur. I'd be lying if I said I hadn't imagined it a thousand times over.

I shake my head, and a few tendrils of hair fall into my face. "I don't want that. We're better as friends."

"No," she says sternly, gesturing from me to her as she dances. "*We* are better as just friends. That man is better as a husband, and you know it, Soraya."

"It was never serious." I stop moving to the music and dig my toes into the sand instead.

She snorts. "He loves you something fierce."

I kick a hearty amount of sand at her legs. She squeals, kicking sand back at me.

Joss appears seconds later with our drinks, cutting the conversation short. Mariel teases him about something, but his eyes stay locked on me. I flush under his attention, hating that I'm letting both of my best friends down with my decision.

Not wanting to think about it, I fiddle mindlessly with my straw and return my attention to the temple, catching the light refracting from the moonstone atop.

Everyone around me is focused on the music, the moon, or the drinks, socializing and dancing in spades. Though the source of the magic comes from the sky, the moonstone nestled in the temple's summit is the true heart of Isle de Lunith. It absorbs the pulsating magic sent down from the goddess moons, after all. Without it, there would be no magic. No island.

Suddenly, the gleaming light flickers out, and the top of the temple goes dark. My heart trips over itself, and I nearly drop my nectar.

"Joss!" I yell, grasping his arm tightly with my free hand.

He stops mid-conversation, turning to me with concern etched into his features. "What is it?"

"The moonstone." I turn back to the temple, raising my hand to point, but the soft glow has returned, wavering hazily above the temple.

"What about it?" The worry leaves his voice, and he gives me a curious look.

"She's obsessed with that thing," Mariel explains as her words slur from nectar. "Overcome by its sheer beauty from time to time."

"I can understand what that's like," he says wistfully, his gaze boring into me.

Mariel giggles.

Sighing, I glance down at my drink, shaking my head. I take a long pull, finishing it off in one go while my friends cheer.

"Never mind," I mutter, blinking stupidly in the direction it sits. But I could have sworn it flickered for a moment. Or maybe I'd had too much nectar, and my eyes were playing tricks. My lips stay sealed, not wanting to rouse unnecessary fear on a sacred night, but sweat beads on my spine.

My hand rises to the center of my chest, mindlessly hovering there.

Joss and Mariel laugh at something, talking animatedly. None of their words stick in my brain. Instead, my eyes stay glued to the temple as if I might catch the moonstone winking again.

"I should check on the High Priest," I say in a rush, interrupting their conversation.

Mariel looks at me as if I've lost my mind.

"Is he sick?" Joss asks with a frown. "We have our island assembly tomorrow."

I shake my head. "Something just feels off." The words are weak, strange, even to my own ears.

"Ooookay." Mariel takes the coconut out of my hand, tossing it onto the beach with a huff. "No more nectar for you. Let's dance it off." She grips my hand and tugs me closer toward the shore, where waves gently caress the packed sand. "Come on, Joss!"

We navigate the merriment, smiling and nodding at everyone we pass.

A pit of dread builds in my stomach, but I don't fight my friends. I can't make sense of my feelings on my own, let alone verbalize them. Instead, I allow Mariel and Joss to sandwich me as we sway our hips in rhythm to the drumbeat.

We drink more nectar, and later, when Joss's hands snake around my waist, threatening to steal me away to the bushes, I let him.

But my eyes continue to flick toward the temple, and the unsettled feeling lingers, even though I try my best to let Joss distract me.

CHAPTER TWO

THE RECLUSE

RAZIEL

*T*he wooden chair groans as I lean back. Tilting my head up, I match the noise, releasing an exasperated grunt of my own as I peer through the gaping window overhead.

The pale, round supermoon twinkles, pouring its silver light over the library. Small waves of power ripple off the moons through the blue-green sky, surging like an ocean current. A fragment of power courses through me in response, and I shiver, quickly refocusing my attention on the book before me.

My antsy fingers tap against the page, filling the air with a soft patter. The *whoosh* of energy in my veins makes it hard to sit still. Adrenaline builds, and my breathing grows quicker. For a second, I think it might linger.

Then it fizzles out.

Just like the previous few months.

This is pointless.

Sitting here like this is getting me nowhere.

My magic is clearly dying... and though I should be thrilled, I know what that means. If it were just *my* magic and not the whole island's, then that would be a different situation.

I finger the broach attached to the front of my cloak, near my heart. The broach signifies me as the goddesses' chosen: Keeper of the Island, Protector of the Moons, the High Priest of Isle de Lunith.

A title I feel ill-equipped to possess these days.

Huffing, I slam the book shut and jump up from my chair. My blood surges, thrilled at the prospect of movement after sitting for hours. I grit my teeth, working to quell my emotions.

I suck in a deep breath, letting the aroma of ink and paper fill my lungs. My favorite scent—that of knowledge, of insight, of *power*. Not the physical or magical manifestation of it, but the kind that matters. The type of power that's readily available to everyone on our island. The kind that's often overlooked and underappreciated.

Once my pounding pulse simmers down, I snatch the book off the table and hurry back to the shelf I borrowed it from. I tuck it away carefully, despite my trembling hands, and quickly leave the library.

A thick blanket of warm, humid air greets me once I'm beyond the temple's threshold. Without the climate control indoors, our books and archives wouldn't survive.

The door thuds shut behind me, automatically locking itself, and I jump at the noise.

My eyes lift to the moons, locking on the soft, iridescent waves of light rippling through the sky. My throat grows thick, and I swallow.

A chorus of distant laughter startles me. I gaze down the hill toward the village and the beach beyond. Lights twinkle on the coast, as they do every month during the Union. A pang of guilt and regret hits me square in the chest, and I grit my teeth. Sometimes, I wonder what it feels like, to be that joyous and free. I recognize that my failure to appear is a disappointment to my people, but it's better this way. They'll never understand how I protect them.

Turning on my heel, my dark cloak flutters around my ankles. It's lightweight but decorative; a symbol of my position on the island. It billows behind me as I speed through the jungle, seeking the River of Rest.

The island is home to multiple sacred rivers, each with a unique significance and purpose. Among them, the River of Rest holds a special place in the islander's hearts. The serene waterway serves as a final farewell to the departed, as their bodies are sent out to sea on pyres.

It symbolizes a peaceful transition into the afterlife. We believe the river retains a connection to the souls, offering a place for communication and remembrance.

Gentle bubbling reaches my ears, and I wind through the lush jungle until I spot the river ahead. Moonlight glints off the gently flowing surface. Once I make it to the bank, I pause. Looking up, I'm greeted by the sight of the moons overhead, their radiant glow casting a mystical aura over the land.

In this moment, the ancient power of the island courses through me.

Usually, it'd be too risky to be out during the Union, but with my power dying, I have nothing to fear.

A harsh, low laugh rips from me, and I shake my head.

The truth is, that's wrong. I have *everything* to fear. My time is running out.

I kneel beside the edge, reaching my fingers into the water.

"High Priest Amos," I whisper hoarsely, hoping the current carries my words to wherever he rests. A sad laugh tumbles from my lips. *"Father...* Ironically, I never got to call you that while you were alive, huh?" I muse.

Hanging my head, I perch on my haunches and try to make sense of the jumbled feelings weighing on my shoulders.

"You were a terrible father. Not a great man at all, really. But you were an okay High Priest." The lie tastes bitter on my tongue. I shake my head, amending my previous statement with, "No, you were a disappointment as a priest, too. You never prepared me for *this*." I pause, clenching my teeth and trying to process my emotions. "I wish I could say I miss you, but that's not true. I miss what we could've been. And I wish you were here to help me with this. Even *your* help would be better than being alone."

I don't have anyone else to seek help. I'm *it*—the leader of not only the temple but the entire island. And I've never felt so alone.

My mother was a priestess. My father, High Priest Amos, got her pregnant when they were barely twenty, and then sent her away to the mainland. He used the moons' magic to sterilize himself after, to prevent it from happening again.

He didn't want additional responsibility, which was so typical of him.

Technically, I was born on the mainland. But when my mother discovered the moons chose me, she quickly brought me back to fulfill my destiny.

I don't know if High Priest Amos knew I was his biological son. But I didn't care to have a father-son relationship with him after how he'd treated my mother, anyway.

It's not a given that the moons will choose from the same lineage, but sometimes they do. Unlike the celestial servants, who choose to serve the moons, the moons choose their High Priest.

I open my left hand, and the dull, iridescent gleam makes me wince. On Union nights, my palm used to gleam like a moonstone, in tune with the magic. It's the kiss of the goddesses, tying me to my role as the Moon Priest.

The faint, swirling magic embedded beneath my skin tugs at my heartstrings. It reminds me of everything I am and everything I will never be.

"You could've at least tried to fix this instead of giving in to your libertine impulses," I mutter to my father, scowling at the river. "Did you know?"

He couldn't have... He would've warned me, right? Or tried to stop it? Instead, he was reckless. All of the islanders and celestial servants know how to party. But Amos was the worst of all.

He passed away when I was ten, leaving me to assume the role prematurely.

I've vowed never to make the mistakes he did.

My promise to myself, to the moons, and to the island is that I will stay dedicated to my work. I will not engage in sexual activity, I will never sire a child, and I will always choose duty above all else. Nothing will distract me from upholding my duty.

A rustling noise rips me from my musings. My head jerks to the left, and I quickly ball my hand into a fist, snuffing out the glow. Slowly, I stand, peering into the darkness.

A low groan and a whisper float by me, and a bush nearby shakes. Is someone spying on me?

The last thing I need is for whispers to circulate about me or my lineage. I refuse to be seen as weak or incompetent.

Storming toward the noise, I round a tree and immediately

lock onto the teal-haired priestess from my temple. It takes a second for the image before me to catch up with my brain.

The woman's back is against a tree, presumably for support, as a man kneels under her delicate skirt. One of her legs is thrown over his shoulder, her foot arched in pleasure.

The sight of such a vulgar act out in the open shocks me. I freeze, unable to tear my eyes away. Her hips undulate as she grips the man's short hair, holding him in place.

I shouldn't be witnessing this. I should turn and go, but I can't.

Her head is tilted back, eyes shut as she moans softly in pleasure. Her thick hair is partially braided away from her face, allowing me to see each inch of pleasure that flashes through her features. The rest of her waves tumble around the soft, tanned skin of her shoulders.

A bolt of heat shoots through my core, down to the base of my spine. Much to my dismay, my pants tighten around my groin. Her thin skirts part, and if it weren't so dark, I'd be able to see her—

"High Priest Raziel?" she squeaks in a tight voice, freezing when she spots me.

My eyes drag back to her face. The temperature ratchets up, practically burning me alive.

What the moons am I doing?

What is *she* doing?

As a celestial servant, this is a disgrace.

"Priestess Nyx," I say, voice rough.

Her eyes widen further, and she nearly tumbles sideways. She drops her leg from the man's shoulder, pushing him backward. He tumbles onto the dirt as she quickly lets her airy dress fall back into place.

Despite the position I just caught her in, she holds herself with a touch of grace, head up and shoulders back. She adjusts the dainty gold chains across her midsection.

The man glances over his shoulder, his nostrils flared. He stands, wiping the back of his hand over his mouth. I grit my teeth, holding his stare as an inferno consumes me.

He's tall, tanned, and muscular, dressed in tideborn shorts. I recognize him immediately as the son of our Chief Warden. My disappointment swells. Celestial servants *and* wardens should lead by example, not engage in whatever reckless nonsense this is.

"Are you planning to watch, or would you prefer to join?" the warden asks snarkily.

"Joss," the priestess hisses, slapping his chest.

This is why I refuse to seek help from the celestial servants. They're shamelessly distracted by pleasure.

The heaviness between my legs only heats my blood further, infuriating me. The erection taunts me, reminding me how quickly my body betrays me.

My purpose is to serve the moons, not to seek pleasure.

My palm burns, the light blazing brighter as it peeks from between my fingers.

Without a word, I whirl away and storm through the jungle. Strong, unexpected emotions stir up the stifled magic within me, provoking it.

"Oh, *now* you make an appearance," I mutter to my glowing palm.

I need to get away.

It was stupid to come here on Union night, regardless of how weak my magic has been.

"High Priest Raziel, please!" The priestess tramples over the flora behind me, eager to catch up.

I pick up my pace, navigating through the towering trees wrapped in glowing vines. Ducking under a low fruit-bearing branch, I step carefully over a clump of freshly sprouted silverdew.

"Wait!" she yells.

The edge of the jungle comes into sight, and I pick up the pace. Once I'm free from the maze of trees, I bolt as fast as possible.

Finally, I make it to the temple. I round to the back, hoping there's still a decent distance between the bright-haired priestess and me.

Her pleasure-drenched face is embedded in my mind, taunting me. It riles me up.

Setting my jaw, I focus on the old iron door before me and yank it open. When I'm certain it's shut and locked securely behind me, I face the darkness.

Lifting my trembling right hand, I open my fist and let the soft glow emitting from my palm light my path. I give myself a second to gaze down at its shocking beauty. The full scope of its opalescent shine causes me to squint, nearly blinding me. The moonstone matches the one atop the temple, embedded seamlessly into my flesh, having always been a part of me. It glows softly, its iridescent light shifting between silver, blue, violet, and white depending on how I angle my hand.

"Why tonight?" I murmur in confusion, if not frustration. It's been fading out consistently the last few months. So why the resurgence?

I run a finger over my magical palm. It feels like skin, as if a thin layer of translucent flesh covers the stone, revealing it beneath the surface.

Letting the light guide my path, despite knowing it by heart, I descend the dark stairs, circling like water in a drain. By the time I meet concrete at the bottom, the prismatic glow grows stronger, pulsing in time with my heartbeat.

The power is too much, even with being so far from the moons.

It's overwhelming.

Suffocating.

I hate it—I've *missed* it.

Gritting my teeth, I force myself through the short passageway into a large chamber. Then I make quick work of locking the door before barring and chaining it.

Far away from the moonstone.

From the moons.

From the *people*—the ones I refuse to let down. The ones I will never truly be part of, for they are merely a distraction from my duty.

And distractions are dangerous.

CHAPTER THREE

THE MYTHS

SORAYA

*T*he next evening, my eyes are supposed to be on the book before me, scanning for signs of wear. Instead, they're locked onto High Priest Raziel Kasper's backside as he bends over, searching for a book on a lower shelf. His cape has slipped to the side, and I can make out the firm muscles of his legs. His black, fitted pants hug him delightfully.

My face heats as a reminder of last night flits through my mind—of the High Priest catching my poor enforcement of *friendship* boundaries with Joss.

Granted, we did nothing wrong, and I should feel no shame.

But for some reason, I feel guilty. Maybe it was how the High Priest had looked at me, with horror and disgust etched into his handsome face.

A hand slaps down onto the table, making me jump.

Jolting, I glare at the smirking priestess sitting across from me.

"Stare any harder, and you'll burn a hole through his trousers," Mariel quips. Her abundance of dark coils frames her face, highlighting her beauty.

"Shhh! I wasn't staring," I lie, forcing my eyes back to the page open on the table in front of me. I briefly make out something about curses and markings. "I was... processing." I quickly flip to the title page, reminding myself of what I'm trying to read. I clear my throat and whisper the title, "Processing the *Myths of the Twin Moons*."

"Processing his ass in those pants." Mariel giggles, and I flinch.

At the sound, Raziel straightens. His shoulders go rigid, and he slowly turns to face us. His dark eyes carry a calm, contemplative depth as they study me.

There's a quiet intensity to them, and it's not often they're directed my way. The permanent, disdainful scowl is etched so deeply into his light brown skin that, despite only being in his late twenties, I'm willing to bet he has frown wrinkles under his scruff.

He's only a few years older than me, not even thirty yet, but that gloriously gorgeous face of his hides an old, tortured soul.

His appearance is effortlessly brooding yet relaxed. His slightly tousled, shoulder-length dark hair is braided away from his face, the waves framing features defined by a neatly trimmed beard and sharp cheekbones.

"What is he doing down here?" I whisper across the table.

In all the years I've worked in the temple, Raziel rarely breaks routine. I'd know since I've tracked his movement since we were children, desperate to know more about the quiet High Priest.

He has his own private library and archives, where the most important texts are kept. He rarely makes an appearance down here among the priestesses.

Mariel watches me with amusement. "Uh, it's kind of *his* temple."

"He's never down here, and you know it." I shake my head.

"Mhmmm… you've always been rather in tune with his routine," she teases.

"He's been acting strange." I wonder if it's connected to the flickering moonstone I saw last night. Something *is* going on; I know it.

She leans back, crossing her arms and arching a brow at me. "You're the one acting like you sniffed one too many silverdews."

"Quiet in the library, *please*," the High Priest mutters without looking up. He turns over a book in his hands, staring at it as if it personally insulted him.

A long strand of raven hair falls into his face, freed from the half-bun with braids he wears. His lips pinch, his irritation growing more prominent as he tucks his hair behind an ear. Then he blows past us, his onyx-colored cloak fluttering behind him.

His scent hits me—an earthy, spicy vetiver—and it sinks low into my belly. My cheeks flare with heat, and I hope I'm not as red as I feel.

Glancing at Mariel, I bite my lip to keep from laughing at her amused stare.

She swats my arm, snorting with laughter.

"I wasn't staring at his ass," I hiss at her. Then, lowering my voice, I add, "He caught Joss and me last night."

She sits up taller, her eyes gleaming. "Caught you doing what exactly?"

My lips press together as I contemplate what to say.

Mariel's smile grows. "Thought you were just friends?"

"We are," I mumble.

"I *knew* you'd get back with him!"

"We're not… Ugh!" I sigh, rubbing the tension in my neck. "I'd had too many nectars, and he was… well, *there*." A distraction—until he wasn't.

"Mhm." She smirks, clearly not believing me.

My eyes wander back to Raziel. What was *he* doing in the middle of the jungle last night? I had chased him back to the temple, hoping to ask about the moonstone, but he was gone long before I arrived.

"So what happened with you two?" Mariel pries, raising a curious eyebrow.

"Not much," I say quickly, knowing she's talking about Joss and not Raziel, despite where my thoughts linger.

She purses her lips thoughtfully. "You sure? Now that I think about it, he seemed rather agitated when he returned to the beach without you."

"Mariel," I sigh, "can we please change the subject?"

She lifts a brow, glancing from me to Raziel. "Would you rather talk about the sexy Moon Priest over there?"

"*Mariel!*" My heart drops, and my cheeks heat. I swat at her, then make a *shushing* motion.

"So you agree, he's sexy."

"Stop trying to provoke me," I warn, squirming under her keen eye. "He's our High Priest. This is ridiculous." I think of the way he glared at me with hatred and judgment last night. He flat-out ignored me, then bolted like I was a venomous reptile. Annoyance chews at me. I narrow my eyes. "Plus, I don't find rudeness attractive."

She taps the table, scrutinizing me before shrugging and returning her attention to her book. "Whatever you say. He might be an ass, but he also possesses a great one."

I groan. "Can we stop with all the ass talk?"

"*Please.*" A throat clears dramatically beside us.

I glance up, catching an unimpressed Raziel standing with his arms crossed over his broad chest. His sleeves are rolled up, and his forearms flex, peeking from beneath his cape. Muscles like that shouldn't be wasted on a grumpy recluse. I can't help but stare. If my mouth wasn't watering before, it certainly is now.

It takes me a second to realize he's speaking, but I somehow missed everything he said.

"What?" I ask, cutting him off mid-sentence.

Mariel's body shakes with silent laughter beside me. I scoot my chair away from her, trying to be discreet. Of course, it scratches the stone floor, making a horrid scuffing noise. I cringe as Mariel laughs harder.

Raziel lifts a single eyebrow in an artfully condescending manner. "Could you please bring that book to my office when you're finished?" he says in a chalk-dry tone.

I swear he doesn't blink as he holds my stare with those deep brown eyes. I wonder what he's seen in his short life that's caused him to be so... stale. Rigid. Methodical.

The complete opposite of me. And of Mariel, too.

Of... well, everyone on the Isle de Lunith, really. We're an island of cheerful people, blessed with abundance and pleasures, gifted by the goddesses. It's a shame the Moon Priest is so... discontent.

The one before him, High Priest Amos, was notorious for leading the celebrations, yet Raziel is a stark contrast to his lighthearted predecessor.

I point to my still-open book. "This book?"

"That would be the one," he says condescendingly.

I blink at the non-descript page, struggling to make out any distinguishable words or images. The paper has a cream hue and is littered with countless minuscule black ink lines, but it's impossible to discern anything at a glance.

Slowly, I turn back to Raziel and squint at him. "What book am I reading?" I test. There's no way he knows what book I have. So why does he claim to want it?

"*Myths of the Twin Moons,*" he says emotionlessly, peering past me at nothing in particular.

I continue to study him, wondering why he's acting even stranger than usual. The other priestesses speculate about Raziel's mysterious power; legend says each High Priest is gifted with magic, but no one has ever seen Raziel's.

"How did you know that?" I ask, eyes widening. Maybe I'll finally find out what his ability is.

Is he a mind-reader? A psychic? Does he have enhanced vision?

"I *heard* you."

Sitting up straighter, I can't help but ask, "The moons gifted you enhanced hearing?"

He frowns as if my question is ridiculous. "No... and clearly the moons didn't gift you intelligence either."

Mariel gasps. All logical thoughts, and ridiculous ones, evaporate from my brain as I stare up at the Moon Priest. If embarrassment could kill, I would die on the spot.

"Oh," is all I can say.

"You are not nearly as quiet as you think," he mutters.

An awkward beat passes between us. My cheeks blaze. Thankfully, Mariel keeps her lips shut and doesn't make a scene. I can't even look at her right now. Breath shoots out of her nose in stilted puffs.

"How much did you hear exactly?" I ask with a wince.

"Enough to know you have a thing for asses," he says flatly. "Unsurprising considering the provocative position I discovered you in last night. Now, please, bring the book when you're finished."

My jaw drops as my heart pounds, but he doesn't give me a chance to reply as he turns on his heel and strides out the door.

As soon as the library doors echo shut behind him, Mariel loses it. She hits my shoulder, gasping out indecipherable words between bouts of laughter.

"It's not funny." I sit, stunned, processing the bizarre interaction.

When she finally catches her breath, she cocks her head at me. "What the hell were you doing to Joss's *ass* last night?"

"Wha—*nothing!*" I lean forward, swatting at her.

"That's not what ol' Razzy implied."

Huffing, I quickly explain what was really going on, finishing with, "Raziel was just making a smart comment at my expense."

"I can't believe he did that." She snorts, her breaths turning wheezy as she doubles over. "Truly, who does that?"

"Oh, my moons," I mutter, tempted to slam my book closed and call it a day. "This can't be happening. I should've just given him the damn thing; now I have to find him later."

"Maybe he's trying to get you alone so you can teach him a thing or two." She winks.

"Knock it off!" I kick her shin under the table, and she kicks me back. "I thought you were angry, not *humored.*"

"Oh, I was pissed off for sure, but if I'm being honest, the hilarity of it outweighs my anger."

I can't help but roll my eyes. "Gee, thanks."

She scrunches her nose, finally realizing her blunder. Guilt flashes through her soft eyes. "Ah, sorry, Soraya." She reaches for my hands, and I give them to her.

"It's fine." I squeeze her and then release, dropping my head down to my book.

I have to face High Priest Raziel again now—likely alone if he's crawled back up to his dwellings.

Except... maybe that isn't the worst thing. Maybe I can bring up what I saw last night—the flickering moonstone. It's my duty as a priestess, after all, to work with the High Priest. We serve the moons and preserve our island's history and magic.

I only hope he takes me seriously after overhearing that mortifying bit of conversation between me and Mariel.

Groaning, I bring the book to my forehead and hide behind the pages. "That was easily one of my top three most mortifying moments."

"What two moments beat *that?*" Mariel asks.

"I don't know! I was just being rhetorical. Maybe it's the top spot contender."

"Well, there was the time you drank too much nectar and tripped into the bonfire, catching your dress on—"

"Stop," I plead, cheeks flushing.

"Hey," Mariel says softly. She reaches up, gently grabbing my wrists and forcing me to lower the book. "It wasn't that bad."

"He knows I was checking him out. He heard us," I insist. "He also saw..." I lower my voice and lean in, "Joss sampling my nectar last night."

Mariel howls at the ridiculous innuendo, and I can't help but chuckle in response.

"I'm mortified on all accounts," I add with a wince.

"First, we could all use the entertainment around here." She narrows her eyes and grins coyly. "Second, I *knew* you were into the priest!"

"Am not!"

"Then why do you care so much about what he thinks?"

"Because he's the *Moon Priest*!" I throw my hands up. "Why do *you* care whether or not I like him? You hate him! And aren't you set on tethering me to Joss? Why the switch up?"

She grins mischievously. "I live for the excitement. Plus, why settle for a tideborn when you could marry the Moon Priest?"

I glance around to make sure no one's listening, my eyes wide with shock. A couple of celestial servants sit at another table across the room, and another is perched high on a ladder, sorting books on the shelves. They pay us no mind, lost in their tasks.

I grip Mariel's arm and lean in. "Knock it off before you start rumors, Mar." She laughs harder, and I release her and step back. "And don't say tideborn like it's a bad thing. Being an island warden is just as important as being a celestial servant."

"Yeah, I mean, the wardens are hot." Her eyes gloss over as she zones out. "Especially the tideborn in those little shorts... with their spears... Have you seen Nyla's abs?" She fans herself dramatically.

An image of said shorts flits through my mind. But it's not Joss I envision in them. No. Raziel and his muscles, usually hidden beneath the layers of his dark clothing, flicker through my mind. What would he look like stripped down to nothing but sea shorts?

I quickly shove the image aside, blaming Mariel for sending my mind there in the first place.

"If you think Joss is so hot, why don't you have at him?" I attempt to redirect.

She sputters, shaking her head. "I never said *Joss* was hot."

"Just like *I* never said the High Priest was. Now get back to work before we get fired," I whisper, gesturing to the books on the table.

Today, we're conducting condition monitoring to ensure nothing is deteriorating. Even with the temple's magically charged environment, which is meant to preserve the texts and archives, the books sometimes require rebinding or restoration. Time, unfortunately, still gets to them.

Considering there are thousands of texts and considerably fewer celestial servants, it takes us a relatively long time. However, I'd choose *this* task over the transcribing and copying that some of our colleagues are currently doing.

Mariel snorts, her eyes glittering with amusement. "Priestesses don't get fired." But then she hesitates, tilting her head. "Do they?"

I grimace. "I'd rather not find out."

CHAPTER FOUR

THE WARDENS

RAZIEL

*D*espite it no longer being Union night, an unshakeable energy buzzes through me. I try to stuff it down, focusing my mind before stepping into my monthly meeting with the wardens, but I'm off-centered.

I grumble to myself, blaming a certain priestess for throwing me off.

Once I reach the assembly hut, I adjust my cloak and broach, steeling my nerves.

The doors loom tall, weathered by years of salt-laden air and whipped-up sand. Reaching for the bamboo handle, smooth from years of use, I pull one of the doors open and step inside.

The conversations within fizzle out as the attention slowly shifts to me. There's a faint hum of energy, which is to be expected at these meetings. The day after the Union, there's always a renewed sense of hope among the people.

As much as I think the celestial servants shouldn't engage freely in pleasures for fear of it being a distraction from their critical work, it indeed serves the people of our island well.

"High Priest Raziel, greetings," a middle-aged man with silver hair and a broad smile says.

I nod subtly at Lachlan Thalor, the Head Warden who oversees both the tideborn and treeborn, despite having an affinity for the sea himself. He stands atop a small dais with his son at his side. A son whom I never paid much attention to until now.

But when he smirks, and his bright blue eyes sharpen knowingly, I go still. He crosses his arms over his broad, sun-drenched muscles, and his small tideborn shorts hug his thighs. This was the one who was fraternizing with the priestess on the day of the Union.

"High Priest," he says calmly, his smile widening as he sees realization strike me.

"What's your name, boy?" I ask, knowing he can't be more than a few years younger than me.

His smile falters, a muscle in his cheek twitching. He won't challenge me in front of everyone. His father might be running the show here, but the wardens still report to *me*.

"Joss Thalor," he grits out.

People continue to filter into the room, quietly finding their seats. Without turning to see them, I imagine they're eavesdropping—nosey folk. I cross my arms, trying to wipe away the image of Joss on his knees under my priestess's skirt last night.

"It's good to see you on your feet instead of your knees this time," I say, hoping to give the villagers something *else* to clamor about. Something other than me, for once.

Hushed whispers rise around the room, excited at the prospect of drama, undoubtedly.

Lachlan's brow furrows with apparent confusion, but then he laughs off the tension. He claps his son on the shoulder. "Inside jokes. I like it. It's well past time the two of you become acquainted, considering my retirement is right around the tide."

Joss's muscles tense further, but he nods at his father. "You know it."

I've always liked Lachlan. He's fierce yet lighthearted, an icon of a warrior, and everything I'd hope our wardens would continue to be. But as Joss and I hold each other's stares, that flicker of annoyance sparks back to life.

It'll be impossible for him to follow in his father's footsteps.

"The day you step down will be a sad day for all," I tell Lachlan. Then, ignoring Joss, I turn and stride to the back of the room, finding a quiet seat in the corner.

Eyes and murmurs follow me as I walk, and I repress a sigh.

"Welcome," Lachlan says, greeting the room packed with people. "Today, we thank the goddesses for their protections— for another month of blessings." His eyes meet mine, and he smiles.

I want to force a smile back, but I can't. Not when I'm unsure of how the upcoming Unions will pan out.

As far as Lachlan and everyone else are concerned, my presence here is merely a symbol. It's the silent acknowledgment that things are going well.

Even though that's not the entire truth.

Things have been... off lately, but I refuse to cause alarm or give them a reason to doubt me.

As Lachlan continues to talk, my attention wanders to his arrogant son.

Wardens and celestial servants work closely. Though we

have a peace treaty with the mainland, providing them with nectar and pollen from the island's magical silverdew, the occasional pirates infiltrate our waters. The tideborn protect the surrounding seas, running trade and offering the first line of defense. The treeborn guard the land, monitoring the silverdew and helping harvest the pollen.

Lastly, the celestial servants guard the archives and magic —the heart and soul of the island.

I had never realized just *how* closely the wardens and keepers worked together until last night...

An image of the priestess's desire-filled face flits through my mind.

Much too close for my liking.

My skin heats up, and suddenly, my cloak is suffocating me despite the lightweight material. I tug on the collar of my shirt, desperate to loosen it.

"We're ready?" Lachlan's question reaches my ears as nearly every head swivels to look at me.

"Excuse me?" I ask, keeping my expression neutral. This is why pleasure is a bad thing—it's a distraction.

"To send a group of wardens to the mainland?" he repeats patiently.

I swallow down my unease, locking eyes with Joss. Yes, I am indeed ready, and I know of a way to solve two problems at once. "Warden Joss can lead this month's expedition."

Lachlan's smile falls as murmurs spread like wildfire around me. "That'll be half the month."

"I'm aware of the timeframe," I say, rising from my seat.

"He'll be head warden soon. He should stay here by my side to—"

"It's best he learns the route and workings of *all* the tideborn roles as Head Warden." My voice is loud, powerful, drowning out the whispering. Everyone falls silent, and Lachlan slowly nods in agreement.

A scowl etches onto Joss's face, betraying his displeasure. The bitterness in his expression is so palpable, I can almost taste it—the loathing a thick, acrid cloud.

Not wanting to indulge the rest of the meeting, I excuse myself and exit the assembly hut.

A few paces away, I hear the door creak open and shut behind me. Someone catches up with me easily, and without turning to look, I already know who it is.

"Why are you sending *me* off the island?" Joss asks, his voice level.

"As I said inside, it's imperative you learn all the roles you'll soon oversee."

He laughs, matching my pace. "That's bullshells, Raziel, and you know it."

The casual way he addresses me infuriates me. Has he no respect? Then again, I did refer to him as a *boy* publicly. To what, humiliate him?

"This is because of Soraya," he says, humor lacing his tone.

"No idea who that is." I feign confusion, although it doesn't take a genius to put two and two together.

"I saw the way she looked at you," he scoffs. "She left me to chase after you."

I halt, turning to face him. "Whatever you think is—"

"Let me finish." His jaw tightens, and he runs a hand through his hair. "I respect your leadership, High Priest, and I love that woman." The way he addresses me is sincere, and it's what keeps me quietly listening as he continues speaking. "This isn't some jealous outburst or a misguided attempt to claim her as my own. If she doesn't want to be with me, I have to accept that. And I'll support her with someone else if they make her truly happy."

He steps toward me, a dark glint in his eye as he lowers his voice.

"But we both know that person won't be you."

We're practically the same height, standing eye to eye. He appears cocky enough to think he can intimidate me. I nearly laugh in his face. He might have a little more mass than I do, but I've trained like a warden for years in secret. I wasn't lying when I said learning all the roles we oversee is imperative.

I practice what I preach.

Just because I'm not supposed to fight doesn't mean I don't know how to.

The mere fact that this man has me so riled up that I'm considering fighting him is precisely what encourages me to de-escalate.

Taking a step back, I narrow my eyes. Annoyance buzzes in my head. "You are waterlogged out of your mind, warden, if you think there's something between the priestess and me."

"Oh, I *know* there isn't," he says confidently. "But I'm warning you that there won't be, either. If you're suddenly deciding to find your way around a body for the first time, it won't be with her. She deserves better."

He brushes past me before I can refute him further. It's probably for the best.

I shake my head, exhaling the unnecessary drama away as I continue my ascent through the jungle and up the hill toward the temple.

The fish-brained warrior thinks his lover is interested in me. Based on what I overheard in the library today, it's not an invalid assessment. But it's certainly irrelevant.

I have no interest in *finding my way around a body* or whatever the hell that tideborn brute thinks.

Unlike him, I'm too busy trying to protect our island.

CHAPTER FIVE

THE MOONSTONE

SORAYA

*O*nce I complete my duties, I stand on the temple's stone porch, gazing at the surrounding jungle. The night air is rich with the scent of tropical fruit and sea salt. I breathe it in, my lungs filling with gratitude.

Canopied trees and vines slowly slope toward the village. In the distance, lights blaze to life, and a bonfire roars near the beach. The wind catches a hint of music and merriment, and I smile, excited to join them shortly.

Although the Union is the largest party of the month, various celebrations are constantly occurring. We work hard, but we also make the most of our lives.

All of us except for Raziel.

My eyes draw up the temple's imposing stone form as it stretches up toward the clouds. He lives up there, alongside the moonstone.

I'm eager to ask him if he saw anything abnormal during

the Union last night, too. Maybe that's why he's acting slightly out of character today. I grip the book he asked me to bring him tightly in my hands. Maybe he's trying to research what's happening.

Craning my head, I study the bright moons overhead.

No longer overlapping entirely, they've already begun pulling apart. I squint at the smaller moon in the back. I swear it doesn't seem as bright as it usually does, its color a little dull.

The door behind me thuds shut. I jump, glancing over my shoulder as Mariel fiddles with the lock. It rattles, and she huffs out a breath.

"Finally—done for the night!" she chimes, crossing the wide porch and darting down the elaborate stone steps. Her eggshell-colored skirts billow out around her, skimming her bare feet as she twirls with her arms up. "Let's go."

I hold up the book clutched in my grip, giving her a pouty face. "I need to bring this to Raziel."

"Be quick. I'll wait for you."

"No need." I shoo her. I need to talk to him alone before alerting her to what might be going on. Moons above, I don't even know that something *is* going on. "Go have fun. I'll be down shortly."

She ceases her dancing and hesitates.

"Who knows how long it'll take?" I add quickly. "Plus, I want to check on the moonstone." It's not a lie, but I won't alarm Mariel if it's truly nothing.

She throws her head back with a laugh, and her dark brown curls shake gleefully. "Maybe he wants to ask you for tips after what he saw last night."

My cheeks heat, and I instantly regret divulging that information to her. Especially since it painted Raziel as the target of more of her jokes. It's a small island, and word would get out quickly if the High Priest were intimate with someone.

And as far as we all know, he hasn't been. Ever.

"That was probably the most action he's ever gotten," she continues as if reading my thoughts. "Do you think he went home to mastur—"

"Moons have mercy, Mar." I give her a gentle shove. "Stop talking about the High Priest that way." She laughs harder, and it's impossible to be irritated with her. The way she loves and laughs so freely is admirable. If only she'd stop doing it at mine and Raziel's expense. "Get out of here. Go find Joss or something."

I wave her away with a smile and turn my back on her before she can protest.

The temple is perched on a high foundation, with a sturdy stone porch encircling it. The public library's doors serve as the grand front entrance, but around the right-hand side are the celestial corridors, kitchen, and recreational rooms. Around the left is where I head.

I reach out, my fingertips grazing the rough-hewn, weathered stone as I stride nervously toward the tower on the east side of the building. Much of the stone is uneven, jagged, and sharp, but some spots are smoothed by rain, wind, and time.

There's a quiet, resolute strength found here at the temple. The energy and history of centuries radiate from within.

Inside the temple are the library and the main archives. The celestial servants' quarters and dining hall are tucked in behind the library. But atop the ancient building, only accessible from outside, is the Moon Priest's sanctum. He lives alongside the moonstone, symbolically protecting the magic.

I soon reach the heavy wooden door at the base of the tower. My pulse flutters as I reach for it. Even though there's no rule explicitly stating I can't visit the Moon Priest, something about it feels forbidden.

It creaks in a whisper, revealing the narrow, winding staircase within. I take the stone steps one at a time, lifting my wispy skirt to avoid tripping. The ascent is almost dizzying. I continue curving upward for what feels like an eternity. The stone is cool on the bottom of my bare feet.

Finally, at the top of Raziel's sanctum, I push open a door to reveal the night sky.

Up above, two full moons gaze upon me, overlapping slightly. Their light brightens the rooftop sanctuary: the temple's summit.

Ornate stone railings rise gracefully around the roof, curving gently to create a sense of enclosure, separating the roof's highest point from the lower levels. A shimmering pool of clear water sits in the center. The floor gently slopes toward it, catching the water during rainfalls. Narrow channels cut into the stone, carrying water down the sides of the temple. The rivers cascade gently, spilling over the edges to form a dozen small, glistening waterfalls.

The melodic rush of water brings me a sense of serenity, and I soften at the sound. Without looking over the edge, I know the waterfalls meet at the bottom, feeding into a river that runs into town.

The giant moonstone sits in the pool's center, its luminescent opal hue glowing in an ethereal manner. It's as wide as I am tall, coming up to my sternum. Moonlight reflects off it, shimmering and changing color.

The moons charge the stone during the Union, which then infuses our water with magic. It's the source of everything— the heart and soul of our community.

Mindlessly, I rub the center of my chest as I take in its beauty. It never ceases to steal my breath away.

On nights like tonight, when the sky is clear, I can see the ocean in every direction from up here. Our island is small, populated by only a few thousand folk, but we're close enough to the mainland to experience an influx of visitors and tourists. Many other priests and priestesses are orphans brought here to serve the moon goddesses. To be of use.

Sometimes, it brings more nefarious types, too, but that's what the wardens are for.

My heart squeezes as I stride to the rooftop's edge, leaning on the stone railing and gazing down. The library's roof is located one level below, and the ceiling is made of glass, offering access to the night sky. It's dark and glossy, reflecting the silver light.

My eyes lift toward the village down the hill in the distance. Modest cottages, cabins, and bungalows sprawl out at the base of the hill, sprinkling into the jungles and to the coast.

Sandy shores stretch out in nearly all directions.

Sighing, I push away from the railing and glance at the abode on the other side of the room. The stone rises into grand archways, dividing the indoor and outdoor space. White curtains billow gently, offering a sense of enclosure within.

Like me, Raziel Kasper doesn't have family here. He was an orphan too, chosen by the moons and taken in by the temple. Despite having watched him closely since I was little, I've never truly *known* him.

In my eyes, he's always been more of a relic than a human. Then again, our paths rarely cross unless they need to.

Like now.

I glance at the moonstone, warily eyeing the soft power that pulses from it, causing the waters to shimmer. I always envisioned it as brighter, more colorful. Regardless, the stone radiates gorgeously, sending shocks of pale color through the surrounding pool.

Clutching the book he requested to my chest, I stride toward his home.

"Hello?" I call as I slip inside the curtains.

I'm greeted by an earthy, spicy scent I recognize from earlier in the library. *His* scent. It's so different than the fruity notes of the jungle or the light, salty scents of the sea. It's deeper, richer, and moodier.

Just like him.

A chuckle escapes me at the thought.

The seating area is empty, and the pillows and couches are stiff with disuse. The doorway beyond sits open, and light spills out from within. I head toward it.

"High Priest? I brought the book." I hold it up in offering as I invade his private space.

Overhead, the ceilings are steepled in many places, with wooden beams crisscrossing in support. The moons peek in through the angled overhead windows, offering a glimmering silver light to see by.

The kitchen is beautiful, with exposed brick, high ceilings, and expansive stone countertops. Many prep tools scatter the counter, crumbs trailing across the island—it's a lived-in mess.

The whispered scent of garlic and onion lingers in the air like the ghost of a once-pungent meal.

Continuing deeper into his dwellings, I peer around through the various doorways. Large windows overlook the jungle trailing down the mountain beside the temple, giving it a wild feel.

Every corner of the space is carefully crafted, with meticulous attention to detail. Small double moons are carved into the arched wooden thresholds separating rooms. The sigil of our island repeats faintly underfoot throughout the hallway.

I can count on one hand how many times I've been here over the years, but it never ceases to send a zing through my spine. Raziel is a private and uptight man, and I find pleasure in seeing this more personal side of him.

Granted, there's nothing personal here at all.

Outside of the prominent architectural characteristics and the messy kitchen, the home is lifeless. It's like he doesn't live here much, which is unfathomable considering he spends practically all of his time here.

Alone.

I frown, glancing around with the added realization. What a lonely—

A door slams, and I gasp, jerking back out of the doorway I was peering into. At the end of the hall, Raziel stands with his arms crossed in front of his dark navy sleep shirt. It's a short-sleeved shirt with loose, matching pants.

I've never seen him in anything so casual, and it throws me off. His nearly black shoulder-length hair is braided back out of his face on either side and tied into a bun, his signature look.

I swallow, trying to ignore the fact that he looks decidedly divine and almost human for once in his simple silk pajamas.

A line creases his forehead as he stares me down. A dark, haunted look takes over his eyes, but it only intrigues me further.

"Why are you in my home?" His gruff voice tickles something low in my stomach, and I push it aside.

"It doesn't feel very much like a home," I say before I can think better of it. My eyes widen, and I shoot Raziel an apologetic look. "I just mean—"

"It *is* my home," he says flatly. My eyes drop to his biceps, which flex against his chest as his muscles tense. "You imposed upon my space at this hour to *insult* me?"

Slowly, I drag my eyes back up to his face. When our eyes lock, illuminated by the moonlight overhead, his mouth presses together into a thin line. I shake my head.

"That was never my intention. I'm sorry."

He frowns, unfolding his arms and rubbing his jaw.

Stepping forward, I hold up the book. "I brought this."

"Leave it," he mutters.

"Okay." Glancing around, I'm unsure of where to set it. So, I awkwardly place it on the ground at my feet and slowly back away. It's eerily quiet, and something about leaving him up here alone, in the dark, doesn't sit right with me. Maybe he just needs someone to make an effort. "So, there's a party down at the beach…"

His scowl deepens, but he doesn't say anything.

"Would you like to come?" My eyes snag on the messy countertop and stove again; it's so at odds with the neat precision of the rest of the home. "There will be food… and it looks like you like to eat."

I inwardly cringe at my words. *Really, Soraya? Everyone likes to eat.*

"I have work to do. Please leave." Without giving me a chance to respond, he turns and reenters the room he exited earlier, slamming the door behind him.

Exhaling heavily, I pinch the bridge of my nose. "Please leave," I mimic.

The door flings open, and he narrows his eyes as he strides toward me. I hold my breath, eyes widening as he stops right before me. He slowly kneels and snatches the book from the ground without allowing his piercing eyes to leave mine.

"Thank you, Priestess Nyx," he mumbles, as if it's hard to say the words.

"It's Soraya," I say softly. "Technically, all of the females at the temple are *Priestess Nyx*. It's the surname we take on when we commit to the moons."

He pauses, pressing his lips together as if contemplating saying something further, but he doesn't.

My cheeks flare with embarrassment. "Obviously, you know that," I add awkwardly. "*You* don't have to take the surname on, though. You keep only your first and middle names. What does Kasper mean, by the way? It's an interesting—"

"Priestess." He clears his throat, arching a brow at me.

"It means priestess?" I ask lamely. My blunder quickly hits me. "Of course it doesn't." Shaking my head, I mentally slap myself. "Excuse me, High Priest. I'm not myself when I'm nervous." I fiddle with the silver jewelry crossing my midsection and holding my dress together.

"Nervous?" he repeats, his brow scrunching as if he truly can't understand why I'd feel such a way in his presence. Then his face softens, and the corner of his mouth twitches as if it's trying to tug into a smile. "My middle name means *treasurer*," he finally says.

My heart thumps faster, thrilled and terrified at being here alone with the High Priest; at finally getting a piece of him. "So, what are you working on so late? What's your favorite food? I saw you like to cook."

Slowly, he lifts his hand and points toward the entrance to his home. "Please leave."

The fragile moment shatters just like that, and we're back to our regular dynamic.

"Are you sure?" The words leave my mouth before I can stop them. "Maybe you'd like some company for once?"

"This is highly inappropriate," he mutters, stroking his jaw.

"What is?" A disbelieving laugh escapes me. "A priestess

offering to help her High Priest? It's quite literally in my job description to serve the goddess moons by assisting you. Kassia trained me to—"

"Don't talk to me about Kassia," he snaps, cutting me off.

The ice in his tone freezes my blood. I study him, wondering why he refuses to call me by my first name, yet he calls Kassia by hers. Technically, we're *both* Priestess Nyx, after all.

"Stop invading my personal space with your... questions." He waves a hand dismissively toward me.

I'm too stunned to speak. After all the times I've stood up for him and demanded that the others respect him behind his back, and *this* is how he treats me. Joss and Mariel are right; he truly is a jerk.

He starts turning away from me, and I step forward, my pulse thundering in my temples. "Wait!"

Pausing, he cocks his head toward me, his face blank.

"Last night..." I chew my inner cheek, trying to think of a way to word it without sounding ridiculous.

"What you do in your free time is not my business." His dark eyes hold mine, unwavering. It's so intense that I'm forced to look away.

"Not *that*," I mutter, my cheeks flaring with mortification. Of all people to witness my lapse in judgment with Joss, of course, it had to be Raziel. Forcing my gaze back to his, I finally spit it out before I miss my opportunity. "The moonstone flickered out." His eyes widen briefly before he clears his throat and neutralizes the shock. "It was only a few seconds, but I saw it from the beach, and I figured if—"

"The moonstone is fine," he says in a low voice.

"It is *now*. And it was very brief, but what if—"

"What if you exit my chambers politely like I asked, Priestess Nyx?" he sighs, shaking his head, and without sparing me another glance, he storms back toward his private room. "I have things under control. I don't need your help."

This time, he doesn't slam the door as hard, but there's a bit of force there.

My brows raise. His brutish demeanor takes me aback. Nowhere in any of the celestial texts does it say the High Priest must be an *ass*. In fact, the High Priests before Raziel were known to engage in acts of pleasure freely. Many even indulged in their celestial servants to assist with... needs.

It's encouraged, for fuck's sake!

Not that I'm interested in that kind of thing. But strangely, he's so... prudish and uptight compared to his uninhibited predecessors.

I used to think that he thought he was too good for us, that he was better than us. That's what Mariel, Joss, and some of the others think.

But standing here in his cold, empty home, that assessment feels off. This home doesn't give the impression of someone who thinks they're better than us. If anything, it's almost like a prison—as if he locks himself away each night to punish himself.

The questions mount.

After a moment of hesitation, I steel my spine. It's my duty as a priestess to serve the High Priest. I stride forward, knocking on Raziel's door. I'll demand he face me so we can discuss what I saw last night. It's my job, after all, and I take it seriously.

Based on the way he reacted, it's clear he knows something is up.

What is he hiding?

Why is he hiding it?

"I think one of the moons is fading!" I shout. But when he doesn't answer after a few minutes, I give up. "You can't ignore me—or *this*. It's only a matter of time before people notice!"

Shaking my arms out, I let go of the weird energy coiling through me and exit his home. I gaze reverently at the moonstone as I pass, grateful to be amidst its beauty and power. My shoulders soften at the sight of it.

Everything is fine. The stone is charged, and the magic is pouring through our island as it should be.

Maybe I'm overreacting, and it's nothing at all.

Except my intuition tells me that something is most certainly wrong.

I'm truly honored to serve the moon goddesses and wish High Priest Raziel would let me help. But I need to respect him and trust that he has things under control.

Right?

The nagging need to help him doesn't fade. If anything, as I descend the spiral staircase, it grows. With a sigh, I try to shrug it off and muster excitement for tonight's party.

But for the first time in... well, *ever* really, the idea of partying doesn't sound all that enticing.

CHAPTER SIX

THE MOONS

RAZIEL

I glance up toward the window overhead, frowning at the moons beyond. A chill skates down my spine when I take in the fading light of the second moon. The sight only serves to confirm my worries.

"What am I missing?" I mutter, running a hand over my face.

I must focus on my task, but my mind keeps drifting back to Priestess Nyx.

Soraya.

The teal-haired beauty who has as much brains and kindness as she does intelligence.

She saw something.

She noticed.

Everyone else was distracted. But she pays attention. Perhaps she could truly help me figure out the issue and rectify it before anyone else catches on.

Groaning, I slap my palms on the table.

I can't ask for help; I'm supposed to be her leader. If she views me as weak or incompetent and tells the others, it could send the island into turmoil. But then again, she could've told them earlier. She waited until I was alone and tried to speak with me privately, even without her curly-haired friend, who is always by her side.

I turn the book she brought me over in my hands, using a finger to trace the embossed title on the leather cover. I place it on my desk, standing over it as I carefully sift through the thin, worn pages.

Incredibly, we've managed to preserve so many texts for so long, not only from our island but from the mainland beyond as well. Though we stay far away from their affairs, they've sent us their historical accounts and literature for centuries, knowing we could preserve it for them. Many wars and conflicts have ravaged their lands while our island remains untouched, protected by the moons and their magic.

The celestial servants are to be thanked for protecting not only our art and history but the mainland's as well. They work harder than I once thought.

The priests and priestesses spend all day in the library and archives, absorbing vast amounts of knowledge and history without treating it with the reverence it deserves. They work hard, but they treat it as a job, a task list to complete.

None truly live in service to the moons, dedicating themselves to the island's magic. Not like me, at least. But some harbor a natural affinity for the temple.

Perhaps I should swallow my pride and recruit the priestess for help, in exchange for her keeping what she saw to herself. It's better than risking her going public with her concerns.

I go rigid at the thought. Time to choose the lesser evil, I suppose.

Having made my decision, I exit my office and continue past the curtains separating my chambers from the night air. The soft trickle of water greets me, and I blow out a heavy breath, relieved that the magic is still flowing. Overhead, the round moons twinkle as if nothing is amiss, overlapping considerably still, even as they begin to part from their monthly Union.

Except I've stared at these moons long enough to see the slight deviation in brightness.

I have a few months to figure out how to stop what's happening.

Intending to seek out the priestess, I tug open the narrow door and enter the stairwell. It shuts silently behind me, plunging me into pitch-black darkness. My feet are light and quick on the stairs, having followed this path countless times over the years.

Yet a sudden burst of fear strikes me as I descend.

If I show up on the beach searching for the priestess, won't that raise the villagers' hackles? I never show my face at their gatherings.

Worse, what if I stumble upon her engaging in activities with that cocky warden? Just the thought of it sends a tremor of annoyance through me, followed by an unexpected bolt of heat below the belt.

This is a bad idea.

I'm about to turn around and head back upstairs when something collides into my gut.

"Oomph," I groan, regaining my balance, but the person who ran into me squeals, falling backward.

Instinctively, I unclench my left hand and reach for them.

A streak of soft, pearly light bursts from my hand. Quick

as a bolt of lightning, it shoots out, wrapping around the falling frame. My body goes stiff as the shimmering moonlight washes over the very woman I intended to seek.

"What is this?" she squeaks, eyes wide.

My magic cradles her, suspending her over the stairwell and confirming that it caught her before she could tumble down.

Soraya stares at me in silence, her cheeks flushed, and her plump lips parted. Waves tumble around her freckled face, the shock of color perfectly framing her beauty. Startled by the thought, I lower my gaze, catching on bare feet.

They hover over the stone steps. The blue-green paint on her toenails matches her hair and eyes almost perfectly, and I can't pull my attention away. Her toes wiggle, and I clear my throat.

Jerking my left hand, I guide the magic stream forward until Soraya regains her footing. The light pulses protectively around her, then slowly unwinds and releases her.

"Thank you?" she stammers, as if unsure what else to say.

Shaking off my shock, I focus on my palm and the invisible string of energy humming there, pulling the light back to me. It obeys immediately, heeding my whim and leaving a trail of fading light behind as it winds back into my hand.

I stare suspiciously at my palm, the iridescent glow swirling like trapped moonlight, teasing me with its shifting colors.

"What... the moons... was *that*?" Soraya whispers, voice tight.

"I don't know," I admit, balling my hand into a fist and effectively snuffing out the remaining light. "I mean, I know what it was, but I don't know why it..."

Shaking my head, I shut my mouth.

It's only been this strong on Union nights, and that was

before my power began weakening, so my shock is as authentic as hers. I've never accessed my magic on any other night, and certainly not like *this*.

"What are you doing here?" I hiss, changing the subject. "*Again.*"

An awkward silence stretches between us. Finally, she shrugs and says, "The party was not nearly as interesting as... whatever's happening here."

"Nothing is happening here," I mutter.

"I meant with the magic—the island," she quickly adds.

"Fine." I rub my forehead, as if I can soothe the ache she leaves me with. Then I reopen my left fist, allowing the fading light from my palm to illuminate the stairwell. It's dim, but just enough to see by. "Come with me."

She eyes me warily. "After you were so adamant that I leave earlier?"

I grimace, running a hand over the braid on the side of my head. Glancing away, I shake out my other hand to snuff out the moonlight. It sputters out, bathing us in utter darkness.

"Well, you decided to come back anyway, didn't you?" I retort.

Her cheeks redden, and she bites her bottom lip, glancing away.

"I changed my mind," I say gruffly. "Come on. Don't trip."

She reaches for my hand, and a shock of energy zings through my palm where our skin touches. I nearly jump out of my skin.

"Ow!" She yanks free. "You shocked me."

"*You* shocked *me*," I point out, my face burning with embarrassment and frustration.

Without waiting for a response, I head back up to the roof.

For a second, I'm afraid she won't follow me. Then

moments later, her bare feet patter quickly on the stone as she hurries to catch up. Relief softens my body.

I push open the rooftop door and make space for her to pass.

"You *do* have magic," she says, shaking her head in disbelief. "I knew you were hiding it!"

I frown, striding over to the moonstone pool. Gesturing for her to sit on the short stone ledge beside the water, I do the same.

Shifting to face her, I quickly scan her for any sign of injury. "Are you okay?"

"Never better, Raziel Kasper." She laughs as if the question is absurd.

She reaches for my left hand again. I hesitate, then sigh and give it to her. She scrutinizes it with a furrowed brow. The moonlight has long receded, the skin soft and wrinkled like a regular palm. Frowning, she turns it over a few times, and then she does the same with my right hand.

Her wavy hair falls around her like a curtain, and for a moment, I have the inexplicable urge to push it out of her face to see her. Swallowing the thickness in my throat, I force myself to look away again.

But when she gently runs a finger along the middle crease of my palm, it tickles. My stomach alights with nerves, and I rip my hand from her grip, scooting further away.

"You almost fell down the stairs. You could've died," I growl, addressing the real issue.

"That's uncharacteristically dramatic of you," she deadpans.

"And how would you know what's characteristic of me?"

She opens her mouth to reply, then shuts it and glances away again.

"What the hell were you doing creeping around my—"

"Creeping?" She blows a heavy breath out, her eyes snapping back to mine. Her brows rise in indignation. "Checking on you because I'm concerned is creeping now?"

My chest tightens. She's concerned? About *me*?

When I don't immediately respond, she mutters, "Maybe if you weren't keeping so many secrets, you wouldn't be so damn jumpy."

"I am *not* jumpy. You're the one who flinched backward and nearly launched herself down the stairs."

"No, you ran into me and made me lose my footing." A flush stains her cheeks. "And you are jumpy. You jerked away from me like I was a piranha about to feast on your hand, for moon's sake."

"I don't like being touched," I grit out.

"I apologize for that." She shifts awkwardly, and when she glances up again, her eyes shine with sincerity. "I shouldn't have been so brazen, High Priest. Truly, I am sorry."

The formal way she refers to me spears my chest. Is that how she feels when I call her Priestess Nyx?

"It's fine," I mumble.

We sit in awkward silence for a few moments. The faint beat of music carries on the gentle breeze, coming from the beach undoubtedly. Other than that, only the soft trickle of water from the moonstone pond fills the air.

I eye it, wondering when the next rainfall is coming. The water level is almost low enough to worry me.

"So, you admit you do keep secrets?" Soraya asks carefully, snagging my attention.

Clenching my jaw, I sift through what to tell her. I wanted her help, right? This opening is the perfect opportunity to seek it.

There's so much I could share, though, and I don't know where to begin. She could be pestering me about my magic, yet she's not. It's arguably one of the biggest secrets the Moon Priests possess. The villagers know we're chosen, that there's moonlight in our blood. They know we're the keepers of magic.

Yet they don't know how literal those statements are. They're more than mere myths.

"Moons, you are the most frustrating... Argh!" Soraya glares at me. She grips her skirt tightly, balling the fabric up as she cuts her statement off. The gap in her skirt's slits widens with the motion, revealing more of her tanned flesh.

Any words that were about to come out of me are long gone as I'm lost in the glory of her thick thighs.

My skin heats, and I tug mindlessly at my shirt collar as if loosening it will help me breathe better.

"This is ridiculous," she growls, shooting to her feet.

It takes me far too long to recognize my mistake. She mistook my silence for a reluctance to answer.

"No..." I shake my head, still grasping for the right words.

Her face goes blank as she watches me struggle.

"No, you're *not* frustrating? Or no, this isn't ridiculous?" A short laugh bursts from her. "I should've known coming back up here was pointless. Goodnight, High Priest." She spins on her bare feet, her skirts sashaying around her toned calves.

"Wait!" I jump up, grasping her wrist loosely before she can flee.

She whirls around, her gaze icy as she stares at where I'm touching her. She pulls free, staggering backward. "I thought you didn't like *touch*."

I interlace my fingers and plant my palms on my head. Moons, this is a mess. "I'm trying to explain."

"Well, you're doing a terrible job so far."

She's right, but the words still hurt. Hearing I'm terrible at anything is a kick to the gut. "I... I'm not good with people."

"Whose fault is that?" she snaps back, and this time, I'm the one who stares in shock at her tone. "Maybe if you put in the effort and stopped avoiding everyone, it wouldn't be such an issue."

The back of my neck heats up, and before I can stop myself, I shoot back, "Because sticking my head up someone's skirt is how I improve my socialization skills, right?"

Her face falls, and I've never regretted words so dearly in my life.

"That was wildly inappropriate. I apologize," I say quickly before she can respond. My hands drop from my head, hanging limply at my sides. "I didn't mean that. And you're right. About everything."

She shrugs, brushing off my insult with grace. "Maybe if you stopped being so judgmental and tried it for once, you might not be so uptight."

My jaw tics. Is she seriously implying what I think she is?

"Not with me," she rushes out as if picking up on where my mind went. "But it further nullifies your initial argument and enforces that *you* are the one with a creeping issue."

My words lodge in my throat.

The wind shifts, causing her hair to whip around her face briefly. The music in the distance grows louder before fading away again.

"Why aren't you at the party?" I ask, needing to regain control of the situation. It's hovering over dangerous territory, which won't do us any favors.

"I already told you." She pouts, crossing her arms over her chest.

The fabric there is thicker than the rest of the dress, rising to her collarbones. It would almost be modest except for how low the back dips and how translucent and wispy her skirts are, the slits rising thigh-high on both sides.

Why am I suddenly so interested in what she's wearing?

Because it would be rather easy to drop to my knees and bury my—

No.

My eyes widen in horror as unwelcome lust unravels deep in my core. I force my gaze back up to hers, and her previous fight has softened. If I'm not mistaken, she's watching me with the same intensity. Her blue-green eyes are sharp, but her freckle-dusted cheeks redden again.

"Why were you coming to check on me?" I force out, again trying to salvage the conversation.

Moons, could this be any more uncomfortable?

"Because if I don't, then who will?" she whispers so quietly that I almost miss it. Squaring her shoulders and brushing her hair over her shoulders, she shakes off the intimate moment and regains her confidence. "Something is obviously wrong with the magic, and I refuse to ignore it."

"You're right," I say after a moment.

She tilts her head, surprise flickering through her features. "I am?"

I almost chuckle at the reaction, but I don't. I force myself to remain blank, portraying calmness and control. "Yes. Did you miss it the first time I said it?" My words are colder than I intended, and Soraya immediately hardens.

Her shoulders go stiff, and she narrows her eyes. "I thought you were merely placating me earlier."

"No." I shift my weight and try to find the words I've been looking for. "I would like to ask for your…"

She blinks a few times, and I still can't get myself to say it.

"Your…" My lips stop working again.

"My what?" she prods. "My help in learning how to pleasure a woman?"

I balk, putting my hand up and waving it aggressively in a *nooooo* formation.

"Oh. Sorry for assuming. A man?"

"Moons save me," I mutter, rubbing my forehead and avoiding her stare.

A genuine laugh erupts from her. "Oh, whew. Mariel mentioned you might try to get me alone to seek advice on—never mind." Pink blossoms on her cheeks. "What do you really need?"

"Help," I finally spit out.

"You haven't said with what, though." She scrunches her nose adorably.

"I need your help with this." I gesture to the moonstone, then the sky, then my palm. This is a horrible idea if our recent interactions are any indication. Still, it's time I confide in someone. "I think there's something wrong with the magic."

"Moons above," she mutters, glancing up at the sky. *"Finally."*

CHAPTER SEVEN

THE SECRETS

SORAYA

*R*aziel sits at his oversized mahogany desk, his elbows on the surface, his hands steepled. Colorful books and belongings fill the shelves, a breath of fresh, chaotic air in the rigid priest's life.

He stares me down with narrowed eyes, as if I'm a book written in an unfamiliar language.

"So, your blood is truly made of moonlight?" I pry, curiously. "If I cut you, would you bleed—"

"You're planning to cut me now?" His eyebrows draw together as he studies me.

"No, but *if* I did, well…?" I raise an eyebrow as I wait for his answer.

Sighing, he opens a drawer in his desk and pulls out a letter opener. With one swift stroke, he slices his palm. Shimmering, pale liquid slowly leaks from the cut. It wells up like blood, but in gleaming silver.

"Holy goddess," I say on an exhale, satisfaction blossoming in my chest. It's confirmation that Raziel is indeed one of the moons' chosen. I'm about to grab and inspect his hand before remembering what he said about not liking being touched. Catching myself, I freeze and eye his hand in wonder.

The cut slowly begins stitching itself back together, leaving unblemished skin behind. He pulls a rag out of his drawer and wipes the remains of his shimmering blood on it. Then he cleans the blade and stows it away.

His movements are rigid, as if he's working to contain his anger.

A muscle in his cheek twitches as he clenches his jaw. Then, with a sigh, he says, "There you go—confirmation of your initial theory."

"It heals you? Does it heal others, too?" I dare to ask.

He nods, cupping the back of his neck. He looks like he wants to say something else, but he doesn't.

"Then why don't you use it to help others?" I prod, ignoring the guilt that flickers to life inside me.

Mindlessly, I rub the spot on the center of my chest, just below my collarbone. Everyone else I've ever met bleeds red. He truly is goddess-blessed to protect the moons and their magic.

He scowls. "It's not that simple."

It never is.

"So, you have magical healing blood, and you can wield moonlight in your palm... You know, the islanders were starting to think you don't have magic at all," I point out. There are many documents and archives recounting the various powers bestowed upon the High Priests, and not all are the same.

All have *some* version of moon magic, but not *this*.

Why is he hiding his magic from us?

"No." He squirms, adjusting the neckline of his shirt, as if the conversation makes him uneasy. Without his cloak and broach, he appears much less intimidating. Almost... dare I say, normal.

"Why do you keep it a secret? The other Moon Priests didn't keep theirs hidden."

A scowl twists his features as he crosses his arms and strides over to the large, arched window overlooking the dark jungle behind the temple. "I'm nothing like the others," he spits.

If the words were said with less attitude, I'd understand. Instead, irritation flits through me at his arrogance. He's right that he's not like the others. He's withdrawn and moody, keeping everyone on the island far from him.

"You're right. *They* didn't think they were better than us," I mutter, staring at the back of his head.

Slowly, he turns to face me, and lines of regret mar his forehead. "That's not what I think."

"Isn't it? Even now, you could barely ask for my help, and you're not giving me enough to help you."

"You don't need to know the details about my life."

Flustered, I throw my hands up. "You just said something's wrong with your magic. How am I supposed to help if you won't give me anything?"

He grinds his teeth, staring at me for a long, tense beat. "All you need to know is that it's been behaving strangely."

Well, that confirms my observation that *he* has been acting odd, too. "Fine, if you want to keep your secrets, then I'll keep mine, too."

His arms drop, and he steps closer to me, pausing halfway. "What secrets?"

I smirk at his interest. "If I told you, that wouldn't be a secret, now would it?"

"It's different," he says, his tone authoritative. "I'm your High Priest, and you're my priestess."

I flinch. That slimy feeling takes over my chest again. "I thought they were wrong about you," I whisper, hurt.

"Who?"

Anger scorches my chest. "A lot of the villagers. Some of the celestial servants." *Joss. Mariel.*

He stares me down from across the room. "What do they say?"

"They talk about how you look down on us all—thinking you're better than us, how you refuse to partake in our traditions and ceremonies, and how uptight you are."

His brows flick up. "That's why you made that comment a moment ago." Running a hand over his face, he sighs. "And what do you think?"

Squirming, I wish I had kept my mouth shut. Now, I've gone and ruined a perfectly good evening. "I—I don't know. I've always stuck up for you. You *are* my High Priest, and I respect you. But I don't know you."

Striding to his desk, he plops into his chair and steeples his hands in front of him. "Sit, Soraya."

I narrow my eyes at the command, but the fact that he said my name instead of calling me Priestess Nyx has me obeying him. Perched in the chair across from his desk, I hold his stare. Thousands of secrets swirl in those rich brown irises of his.

It's irritating that he won't trust me and let me in.

"What initially alerted you to something being amiss?" he asks, leaning back in his chair casually as if I hadn't just insulted him by implying that most of the island dislikes him.

Shaking off the discomfort, I focus on his question.

I recount how the moonstone flickered, how I think the smaller moon is fading, and how *he* has been acting out of character lately. His frown deepens at the last bit, but he lets me talk without interrupting.

"I've noticed the same," he mutters, running a hand over his hair. A dark tendril loosens from one of the braids on the side of his head, falling across his cheek.

I try not to focus on how soft his hair looks when it's not secured into a bun at his nape. Or how round the muscles in his shoulders and arms are beneath his silky sleep shirt.

But it suddenly hits me how quiet it is here, how alone we are in his private chambers. As much as he might keep things to himself, he *is* letting me in, in his own way. Maybe it's selfish of me to demand more when it's clear he's trying. He has invited me into his home, to his private office, and he called me Soraya for the first time ever. Those things hold a lot of weight.

Softening my posture, I focus on those wins instead of the minor irritations. He's meeting me halfway for the sake of our island, so I can do the same.

A heavy exhale leaves his mouth. "The past few Unions have been... different."

"How so?" I ask.

He shifts in his chair, eyes flicking to the large overhead window. I follow his gaze, scrutinizing the moons. When it's clear he's not going to reply, I swallow my disappointment and redirect the conversation.

"Do you think what they say is true? About the moons being goddesses?" I ask.

This earns me a chuckle. My eyes lock onto his, and he lifts a brow. "Perhaps it is. Or perhaps it's a ridiculous story to explain the otherwise unexplainable."

I gasp, jolting straight up in my chair at the blasphemy. "The goddesses were made of sky and sea previously. Is it so far-fetched to imagine they've changed form into *moons*? You, of all people, should believe!"

His eyes twinkle. "I never said I didn't believe; I'm just pointing out that it might not matter what's true because the truth changes nothing for us." Before I can reply, he continues, "But yes, I believe the lore and the *curse* are true."

His admission satisfies me, and I relax back into the chair. "I was starting to doubt you, High Priest."

The way his face tightens makes me think I've said something wrong.

Until he says, "Raziel is fine."

I don't bother fighting the smile that takes over my face. The fact that he's inviting me to address him by his first name is a gift that I'll cherish.

"Is that why you wanted to read that?" I point to the book I brought him earlier this evening.

Sighing, he reaches for the cover and gently fingers it. "Yes, but I found nothing about waning magic, flickering moonstones, or fading moons."

"So, what can I do to help?"

"For now, keep this between us."

"Agreed. I'd rather not worry anyone unnecessarily."

His rigid shoulders soften, and he regards me carefully before nodding. "While you're in the library, perhaps you can scour for anything that might be of use. You're much more familiar with the public texts and archives than I am."

I preen under his compliment. Well, maybe it's not quite a compliment, but it feels like one compared to his usual prickly commentary.

"What will you be doing in the meantime?"

He goes rigid again, shutting down before my eyes. "I have a few things I'm exploring on my end."

Gripping the chair's arms tightly, I work to keep the

frustration off my face. "Fine. You can keep your secrets so long as you acknowledge that it only makes our collaboration harder."

His jaw clenches. He's smart enough to know I'm right.

Again, when he doesn't reply, I decide his confirmation of the wonky magic is enough. For now. Standing, I level him with a serious stare. "But maybe one day you'll realize I truly want to help, and you'll trust me enough to share."

Without giving him a chance to reply, I whirl around and head to the door, slipping out and leaving him to his quiet home.

Alone.

CHAPTER EIGHT

THE CUT

RAZIEL

*L*ong after Soraya leaves, I sit back in my chair, staring at my palm. Lined, light brown flesh stares back at me with no hint of the moonstone or the magic simmering within.

How—why—did it explode out in the stairwell? I'm glad it did, as it saved Soraya, but never in my twenty-nine years has that happened before.

"Another sign of my impending doom," I mutter, rubbing my tense neck.

At least asking for help went better than I expected. Soraya didn't judge me or view me as weak or incompetent. She did, however, irritate the living shells out of me.

Must she ask so many questions?

After I give myself another moment to replay and dissect the conversation, I open my drawer and pull out the letter opener again. I twirl the thin hilt between my thumb and forefinger, and the moonlight overhead glints off the shiny blade.

"Just to see," I mutter to myself.

Pressing the blade against my palm, I suck in a breath. Then, I add pressure. The skin resists for a heartbeat before splitting open, revealing an angry, red line. The cut deepens, and blood wells up, richly red.

My breath hitches, and I freeze, staring at the crimson seeping into my palm. "What the *fuck?*"

Tossing the letter opener onto my desk with a sharp clatter, I release a growl. Then I snatch the cloth and squeeze it in my hand to stop the bleeding.

The sting lingers. "Now you have to heal the old-fashioned way, you erratic nuisance."

This is what I had expected initially when I cut myself for Soraya. I bleed red twenty-nine nights a month—except for the thirtieth night, when the moons overlap and the rest of my magic appears. It's a package deal. I hadn't expected tonight to be any different.

Yet the moonblood startled me.

I chuckle bitterly to myself. "Why am I even surprised at this point?"

Gritting my teeth, I hang my head. It was a mistake to be so vulnerable with Soraya. Her questions are endless, and I don't need the distraction of trying to evade them. I've made it this far alone, and either I'll succeed in making it past my thirtieth birthday, or I'll succumb like the Moon Priests before me.

Except this time feels different... There's no replacement child with a moon marking yet. And the moons themselves seem to be affected.

I still have a slew of journals I'm slogging through, anyway. They'll keep me plenty occupied. We have four more weeks until the next Union, though, and I'm nervous it won't be enough time to find an answer.

Standing, I make my way to the bathroom to locate a bandage. But when I catch sight of myself in the mirror, I double-take at the layer of scruff coating my jaw. I should clean myself up.

Taking my time bathing, I wash my hair. Afterwards, I dry it and braid the sides away from my face, tying it off into a bun at my nape. Then I bandage my sliced hand.

Locating my steel razor, I tackle my beard next. I much prefer to keep it neat and short.

As I'm trimming my facial hair, a glimmer of light distracts me. My eyes shift up, meeting my own in the mirror. A glow conceals my brown irises.

I jerk, dropping my steel razor.

"No," I gasp, gripping the counter and leaning forward, inspecting my eyes.

Warm, dark brown irises stare back at me. Unwrapping my hand, I check the cut. It's unchanged, unhealed. Which means the magic is still at bay.

But it doesn't matter. The damage is done; the fear is instilled.

I hadn't even thought about the deeper repercussions of my magic acting erratically. If my moonlight blood and magic can appear on non-Union nights, that means…

"No," I repeat, willing my voice not to waver. "You're in control."

With a trembling hand, I pick up the razor once more. I force a few deep breaths until my heart rate slows and my hand stills, and then I continue with my grooming.

I pray to the moons that I figure out what's going on before it's too late.

CHAPTER NINE

THE TEACHINGS

SORAYA

*T*he next couple of weeks fly by uneventfully. Joss has been gone, saving me the stress of navigating *that* dynamic.

Raziel locked himself away in the temple's summit. I've tried to visit him twice, and both times, the stairwell was locked. At first, I was angry. Then I realized that without any new insights into what's happening, I have no reason to visit him.

After the second failed visit, I took the hint and decided to push the grumpy priest to the back of my mind.

A task that proves challenging.

At least I have Mariel to distract me in the afternoons. Luckily, I can mask my research under the guise of analyzing the old books without her noticing.

However, it's my week to take over the children's morning temple teachings, which cuts my investigation time in half.

A dozen children between the ages of five and twelve sit in a semicircle in the colorful classroom. I plop down in front of them, my skirt billowing gracefully around my legs, the thin fabric a light whisper, catching the breeze. A snug band with tiny moons and gemstones wraps my midsection, matching the headband and keeping my hair out of my face.

"Priestess Nyx," a little voice says. A girl with blonde hair and a big frown raises her hand. "Is it snack time yet?"

I chuckle. "After this story, we'll take a break and have lunch."

The children light up, their gleeful noises overlapping and ratcheting up the volume of the room.

"Okay, okay, simmer down."

"I like your stories, Priestess Nyx," another child says. He scoots closer to me, chewing on the neckline of his shirt. He pauses long enough to say, "You're my favorite priestess."

A smile tugs at my lips as other children clamor in agreement. All the celestial servants take turns teaching the children, as each of us has different perceptions and experiences. It's good to expose the children to the teachings and history of our island in as many ways as possible, since everyone learns in different ways.

I'm honored that the children connect with me and that I can make a positive impact in their lives. When I was young, I had a favorite priestess as well.

Kassia.

The priestess who raised me. The one who knows *everything* about me.

Snapping myself from my thoughts, I reach for the colorful, oversized book beside me. The glossy pages full of illustrations are sleek and thick, satisfying to turn.

Locating the story's start, I hold the book up so the kids can see. An image of two beautiful women fill the page—one with rich, black skin and short, coily hair. The other with alabaster skin and a flowing silver mane. They hold hands, gazing at one another with such intensity that my stomach tumbles.

Smiling down at the pages, I begin to tell the story.

"Once upon a time, there were two goddesses, Neridessa and Celandria, who were sent to protect the sea and sky, respectively—"

A hand shoots up, and I point to the child to call on them.

"What does *spectifly* mean?" she asks.

"Respectively," I repeat. "It means in the same order just given. So if I say Lillie and Max got a toy and a book, it would mean Lillie got the toy and Max got the book."

"Oh." Her nose wrinkles.

I point to the dark-skinned sea goddess first. "This is Neridessa, the Goddess of the Sea." Then I point to the fair-skinned woman. "This is Celandria, the Goddess of the—"

"Sky!" the girl finishes, her eyes lighting up.

"Yes! Exactly."

"But they're *people* like us," another child adds. "Not moons."

I smile, loving the way the kids ask questions and make statements freely. It's important to me that they feel comfortable speaking up.

"You're right," I say. "But we're not quite at that part of the story yet."

The kids watch me with eager eyes, some sitting stock-still, others bouncing around, but they all remain quiet, so I continue.

"The goddesses were able to remain in their human forms for many years." I turn the pages as I speak, glancing down at the art depicting my words. "But when the humans needed them, the goddesses had to return to their sea and sky forms."

I continue the story, detailing how the goddesses were separated. The children's version of the lore remains relatively innocent, leaving out the most gruesome and cruel details. It's honest enough to tell a watered-down truth of the story, but not heavy enough to haunt their little dreams.

The adult version depicts the goddesses lashing out, angry with the humans' misbehavior, which forced them apart from their true love. So, they created a whirlwind of storms that devastated many of their cities.

Clearing my throat, I continue the more innocent version of the story. "Not wanting to remain apart, the goddesses made a deal with their creator—the source of their magic."

"Who was that?" a little boy squeaks out.

"Not a who, a *what*," one of the older kids supplies. "Source."

"Source." I nod. The powerful entity attributed with creating the many realms, their gods and goddesses, and the magic.

"Oh," the little boy says. "Priestess Mariel told us about Source last month." He sticks a finger up his nose, and I gently gesture for him to remove it.

"Priestess *Nyx*," the older kid chastises. "Not Priestess Mariel." She looks at me. "Sorry about my brother."

A hearty laugh bubbles up. "Nothing to be sorry about. Now, where was I?" Looking down at the upside-down page, I perk up. "Yes, right. So, the goddesses made a deal to return to one another. But in doing so, they condemned themselves. No longer bound to the mortal realm, they became moons."

"Why *moons*?" someone asks.

My teachings flit through my mind. It's said their essence was sealed in immortal form high above our realm as punishment, so they were forced to forever watch over humans, sharing their magic with them instead of using it against them. They send it to the Isle de Lunith, where the moonstone absorbs it and spreads it through the land.

The lovers only meet once per month on the Union, but to them, that was better than the alternative, which was never. They were offered a chance to remain in the sky and sea, sacrificing their love instead, but they refused.

They were stripped of everything—their forms, their magic, their duties—all in the name of love. They weren't tricked; they *chose* such a fate. That's how powerful their love was.

"Because moons are beautiful," I say softly, closing the book.

The overlapping moons each month symbolize their union, strengthening their power and allowing them to recharge the island's moonstone, sharing their magic with the humans.

"We honor the moons each month to thank them for sharing their magic with us," I continue. "The moons represent love and balance and trust."

"No," a deep voice says, sinking straight to my core. "The moons represent the importance of *duty*."

"It's him! The Moon Priest," one of the children whispers.

My chest flutters, and my head jerks up. Raziel stands just inside the door, and the sight of his imposing form and stoic stance steals my words. His intense, liquid brown eyes lock with mine, and for a moment, we simply stare at one another.

His posture is rigid and confident, but his arms are crossed across his chest. The black cape sits on his shoulders, connected at his collarbone by the moon broach. My eyes drop down his fitted pants to his dark leather slippers.

He moves like a panther. No wonder I hadn't heard him enter the room.

But then his words repeat in my mind, and I clench my teeth. "Duty is another symbol, of course."

"The most important one," he says in a monotone voice, raising a brow.

My jaw goes slack, and my cheeks heat. Did the High Priest seriously barge in here to argue with me in front of the children? Of all people, I never expected that from him.

I force a smile for the children's sake, but none of them are paying attention to me. All of their curious little eyes are locked onto Raziel. They squirm with excitement, not knowing how to react in the presence of their idol.

He was my idol, too, until recently. But I won't spoil that for the kids.

Quickly gathering my wits, I force a chuckle, addressing the kids again. "And that's why we must talk about these stories together so that we can learn all the different interpretations!"

My eyes narrow on Raziel. He raises a brow.

"Excuse me, littles," I say sweetly. "I need to speak with the High Priest."

They babble excitedly, jumping to their feet around me. I weave through the group, smiling at them as I reach Raziel.

"A word?" I grit out, tempted to grab his arm and yank him out the door. But annoyed or not, he's still my High Priest.

He follows me from the classroom, and I whirl around to face him. We stand silently until the door thuds shut beside us.

"*Duty?*" I spit at the same time he says, "*Romantic?* That's what you're teaching these kids?"

Fury burns my face. "It *is* romantic."

Disbelief rings through his tone, loud and clear. "They turned their back on the roles they were *created* for, permanently disrupting both the skies and seas and forcing humans to serve them eternally. Their position is punishment for disobeying their duty. It's the opposite of romantic."

I grit my teeth together, my fury sparking hot and fast. "Sacrificing their physical forms to be together, forever frozen in the sky alongside one another, is the most romantic act of all."

"Did we learn the same story?" he scoffs.

I don't speak it aloud, but it's a kind of love I crave deep down. Being so wholly desired that someone would give up everything to be beside you for eternity. "Clearly we see things differently. I believe it's the ultimate sacrifice for love."

He grunts, staring down at me with disdain. "It's a tragedy —that's what it is."

Taking another step forward until I'm in his face, I say, "What's a tragedy is how absolutely miserable you are. I thought you were..." I stop myself and shake my head.

"Thought I was what?" he says quietly, his warm breath fanning against my cheeks.

I square my shoulders and keep my eyes locked on his, only a few inches of space separating us.

"I've always respected you—stood up for you against the others." His expression shifts, a cloud of bewilderment briefly obscuring his features, but I keep going. "I thought you were selfless, kind, and loving, despite everyone saying you think you're too good for us. You'd have to be to hold your job title, right?" A sad laugh slips from my lips. "I was wrong. No wonder you hide yourself away from everyone. You *do* hate us. Just like you loathe the moons and your role."

His mouth pulls into a frown, and he shakes his head. "No, it's not—"

"The goddesses would be ashamed of you." I lean up, so my mouth is angled right in front of his. "Just because *you* don't believe in romance and the beauty of our lore doesn't mean you can steal it from those who still dare to hold onto hope."

He sucks in a sharp breath, and his eyes flit to my lips. A tense moment passes between us, filled with something fiery. Something more than merely passionate conflict.

The door creaks open, and we jerk away, putting space between us.

"Priestess Nyx?" a small voice asks.

I turn, smiling at the dark-haired child. "Yes, sweetie?"

"I have to use the bathroom."

"Oh, honey, you don't have to ask. Do you need help?"

She shakes her head, and I smile, gesturing for her to go on. When I turn to Raziel, the space is empty. He's already gone—the infuriatingly silent bastard.

Something slick like disappointment slithers through my chest.

I almost wish I'd never pushed to learn more about him, because so far, all it does is disappoint.

CHAPTER TEN

THE BOOK

RAZIEL

J exit the residential wing of the temple and rush past the dining hall. My left hand clenches under my cape, concealing the magic that threatens to surface. My magic has been eerily quiet these last couple of Union cycles.

Until I began arguing with *her*.

Until she stepped so close that I could've tilted my head down and tasted her.

The thought hits me hard and fast, sending a wave of shame down my spine.

What was I thinking, challenging Soraya in front of the children like that?

I just couldn't keep my mouth shut. Seeing her romanticize the magic, and the moons, set me on edge.

They should teach the truth.

Her words echo in my head, a taunting ghost: *Just because*

you *don't believe in romance and the beauty of our lore doesn't mean you can steal it from those who still dare to hold onto hope.*

The truth sinks uncomfortably into my gut. Again, she's right. My entire existence is based on the idea of hope. It's what I symbolize for the people here. Who am I to take that from them?

"This is why you need to stay away," I scold myself.

I had intended to seek her out about that damn mythology book I read, and instead, I ended up frozen, listening to her sweet voice recount the myths of our island to those eager children. Something about the way she looked, so peaceful and *happy*, awoke a part of me.

If only it wasn't too late…

The persistent heat has mellowed out, so I carefully pull my hand from beneath my cape and unclench my fist. My hand looks as it should, and I exhale. Wiggling my fingers, I roll my eyes and mutter, "*Now* you're back to normal? Keep acting up, and I'll just chop you off myself, you little—"

Someone squeaks, and my head snaps up.

A pair of celestial servants in their teens freeze a few paces away, their eyes wide.

Awkwardly, I lift that same hand in a wave. "Hello."

"H-High Priest," the boy mutters, his pale cheeks blazing red. He throws himself aside, flattening against the wall, even though the corridor is plenty wide enough for us all to pass.

"Priest Nyx," I greet, dipping my chin. Then I glance at the girl. "Priestess Nyx."

She squeaks again and scurries alongside the boy, bowing her head as she moves aside. She clutches her books to her chest, then slowly draws her gaze back to mine.

My feet stick to the floor, and I freeze, studying them. They practically wither beneath my stare, their eyes unblinking. The boy's throat bobs as he swallows heavily.

Are they *afraid* of me? I study them, unsure of why that'd be the case. I've avoided them to protect them, not to terrorize them.

Is it because I was muttering to myself like a maniac?

I point to my left hand. "He acts up sometimes."

They nod rapidly, seeming to understand my plight. I relax, offering what I hope is a peaceful smile to ease their minds.

As I continue down the hallway, I hear the girl whisper, "They're right—he *is* insane!"

"What was that face he just made at us?" the boy whispers back. "I almost pissed my britches!"

My face scrunches in confusion as I glance back over my shoulder, but they're no longer in the hallway. Shoving the strange encounter out of my mind, I veer into the public library. My cape flutters out behind me, ridiculously announcing my presence.

Just like the last couple of times I showed my face here, the celestial servants grow quiet, watching me curiously.

I don't bother trying to wave or smile again. Clearly, that's not my thing.

Soraya's closest companion, the curly-haired priestess, bounces over to me with a blinding smile. "Hello, High Priest Raziel."

"Priestess Nyx," I mutter, not particularly wanting to socialize after my last few attempts.

I make a move to go around her, but she sidesteps in front of me. "It's Mariel."

"Okay. Will you please move?" I go left, and she mirrors my movement, once again cutting me off.

Her smile grows, looking a little too mischievous for my liking. "What are you doing down here?"

I sigh. "Locating a book."

"Perfect!" She claps her hands together, and I flinch at the sound. A half-dozen sets of eyes lock onto us with interest. "What can I help you find?"

I scowl, rubbing my tense jaw. "I'll find it on my own. Thanks."

"Nonsense. We're all just here to help *you*, after all."

The overeager smile and too-friendly tone strike me as feigned, but I nod, so long as it gets her to stop drawing attention to us. Something tells me she's fond of the attention.

"Fine, I'm looking for a follow-up to the mythology book Soraya was reading the other day."

Mariel's smirk grows as she scrutinizes me. "She wasn't actually reading it."

I nearly choke on air, not wanting the reminder of what she was *really* doing.

"Hey!" a cheery voice calls from behind me, and at the sound of it, I turn instinctively. Soraya bounces in, a smile on her face.

"Priestess Nyx," I greet with a nod. "Will you assist me?"

"Oh, I see how it is," Mariel drawls before bounding away with a sly glance at her friend.

Soraya sighs heavily, tucking a strand of hair behind her ear. "Was that really necessary?"

"Yes, I need you…" I shift my weight, clearing my throat. "Need you to help me find a book. The follow-up to the one you gave me."

Her sweet, fruity scent fills my nose, temporarily distracting me.

"You pulled me from my friends for that?" Her nose scrunches, and she stares at me, bewildered. "You could've asked anyone in here for help."

"And…" I run a hand over my hair, pushing the few freed strands out of my face. "I wanted to apologize."

She narrows her icy eyes. "For what exactly?"

"For not knowing how to do whatever this is,"—I gesture between us—"and for challenging you in front of the kids." Before she can reply, I continue, "I'm trying to do the right thing, Soraya, but I'm different from all of you. Not just in that I'm the High Priest, but I don't know how to interact."

Her lips curve up, and she uncrosses her arms with a laugh. "It's entertaining to watch you try, though."

Adjusting the collar of my cape, I shift uneasily beneath her penetrating stare.

"Come on." She reaches for me, but I hesitate before taking her hand.

I've always hated touch, but with her, it's natural. It comes without thought. And it feels right.

She leads me up a winding set of stairs to the second floor and doesn't stop moving until we've weaved in and out of a few rows of books. It's impressive how intuitively she can navigate the thousands of tomes stored here.

"I think it's in this section," she murmurs, biting her lip as she glances upward. "Hold on."

Scurrying forward, she reaches for the rolling ladder and pushes it a few shelves over. Then she nimbly climbs it, barefoot and all. I glance up at her, wondering how high up the damn book is.

My sights snag on her dirty feet, and I grimace. "What's wrong with wearing slippers?"

"Hardly anyone wears shoes," she says distractedly.

"We should change that."

"Or *you* could try going barefoot sometime."

Her skirts swish with the motion, the slit that runs up her thigh parting obscenely. Lacy white garments peer down at me from her apex.

"Soraya," I hiss, quickly averting my gaze. But it's too late.

The intimate sight of her sends blood rushing below my waist, and my cock hardens in record time. The betrayal of my own body repulses me.

She thuds down beside me a second later, having jumped from the ladder. She smiles sweetly as she holds out a book for me. Instead of reaching for it, I turn to the side, hoping she can't see the apparent lust pressing against my pants.

"Why do you wear this?" I hiss, scowling at her.

Her eyes widen, surprise rippling across her features. "You mean the same thing we all wear and have worn forever?" she scoffs.

I grind my teeth back and forth, closing my eyes and willing myself to get it under control.

"Because it's lightweight and breathable," she continues. "We're constantly running errands around the village, going up and down the stairs and ladders—"

"I saw that," I growl.

"Then what's the issue?" she challenges, a hard glint in her eyes when I face her again.

"It doesn't have to be so… revealing."

"Why are you such a prude? Everyone other than you celebrates skin." Leaning forward, her warm breath tickles my ear. "And pleasure."

My skin heats, and a lump forms in my throat. Her nearness causes my blood to rush south again, and I quickly jerk away. I've never ached to be touched before, not like this. The newness of the emotion threatens to drown me.

"I don't need the distraction," I mutter, my voice rough.

She tips her head back and laughs. "I promise you, if you weren't so obsessed with control and let yourself indulge regularly, it wouldn't be a fraction of the distraction you currently find it to be."

I clear my throat, glancing away.

"What a conundrum!" Her eyes widen. "You've never..."

"Don't go there," I warn, side-eyeing her.

"You're so touch-starved and deprived that seeing up my skirt got you hard?" she whispers, smiling scandalously and tipping her head up in pride.

"No," I lie.

She stares at me, her freckled cheeks flushing. When her tongue darts out to wet her bottom lip, it takes everything in me not to groan.

Where the hell did this come from?

This... unrelenting need.

"The more you try to stifle your desires, the harder you make it for yourself." Her eyes drop to my cock, startling me.

My disobedient member twitches at the innuendo, and I wrap my cloak around my front, hiding from her.

"If you want to touch me, you can," she whispers, tipping her head down and biting her lip. A lock of hair falls into her face, and my immediate response is to reach out and tuck it behind her ear for her.

So I do.

And her softly freckled cheeks light up pink as she smiles at me. Quickly, I snap my hand back.

"That's not what I mean." Her voice is breathy, filled with a need that mirrors the one blazing within me.

"Priestess Nyx," I warn through gritted teeth. Glancing over my shoulder, I ensure no one else is here to witness this misbehavior. "This is highly, highly inappropriate."

She smiles coyly, stepping closer until our chests brush, and then she glances up at me. "So is stalking me. In the jungle... in the classroom... When else do you watch me, High Priest? Apparently, that's what you're into: watching but not touching."

"I—no! That's not what I was—" I sputter, unable to spit the words out.

"Here's the book you're looking for." She drops the leather tome at my feet. Then she whirls around, her chin tilted up haughtily as if she has just won a battle.

Stunned, my eyes track her movement as she gracefully flits away. Just before she disappears out of sight, she pauses and turns back to me with a coy grin.

"And don't worry, High Priest Raziel, your voyeuristic secret is safe with me." She winks, then leaves me there gaping after her.

It takes a full minute to process the interaction. Snorting my displeasure, I finally reach down to adjust myself in my pants. Then I stoop and snatch the book.

"Voyeur," I mutter with a scowl. "That's the last thing I am."

After all, I don't want to watch someone else pleasuring her.

No… I want to be the one tasting her.

The realization sends me fleeing back to my chambers, holding the book in front of my crotch the entire time.

CHAPTER ELEVEN

THE FRIENDS

SORAYA

The next day, after dinner, I stalk to my chambers. I'm exhausted, annoyed, and relieved. Raziel didn't make an appearance today, and I wonder if I scared him away with my forward approach yesterday.

But I haven't seen Mariel either—not for lunch nor our afternoon shift in the library—which is highly unusual.

I reach my door, wondering whether I'll find her inside. But I'm extra disappointed when the small, shared room sits empty and quiet. Only the empty beds and tall, wooden armoires greet me.

My eyes linger on Mariel's disheveled green sheets. Her priestess gown hangs haphazardly off the edge, as if it were abandoned in a rush. Golden evening light pours in through the single oversized window between the beds. It shines off the bamboo floor, highlighting dozens of footprints. Tiny particles of dust and sand dance in the sunlit space.

I stride to my armoire and fling it open. After rifling through my options, I settle on a camisole and shorts to sleep in. After changing, I rehang my gown with a yawn.

The day is still young enough to do something, but I opt to lie in bed and sift through my thoughts instead.

Somehow, I lose hours to my own mind.

Shortly after the sun sets, the door creaks open. My head snaps up as Mariel steps inside, tracking sand behind her. A strip of moonlight highlights her frame. Her curls drip water onto the floor, and she gives me a sheepish grin. Her sea wear, a pale bandeau and revealing, high-waisted bottoms, is still damp.

"You ditched me to go swimming?" I tease, throwing myself onto my bed and leaning against the wall. "You've been gone all day!"

She laughs. "It wasn't like that."

"You missed lunch *and* library shift." I scrutinize her, narrowing my eyes in jest.

"I didn't think you'd notice with how distracted you've been lately." Her eyes glitter, a teasing smile tugging at her lips.

"Is that why you ditched me? Because I've been busy?" I hope she'll keep talking; anything to get my mind off the High Priest before I get angered all over again about the shenanigans he pulled yesterday in my classroom.

Shaking her head, she drops the few items she's carrying at the foot of her bed. "Of course not. I've just been so bored." She groans, fake pouting at me. "Especially without you in the library this week. Can you blame me for wanting to get out and take advantage of the open air instead of inhaling dusty books?"

"I would've gone with you," I say with a frown.

She laughs, arching a perfectly shaped brow. "No, you

wouldn't have. You'd never abandon the temple."

"You don't know that."

Crossing her arms, she cocks her head. "I've known you for our entire lives, Raya."

"Okay, fine," I retort, grinning at the nickname. I pull my braids out, shaking out my hair, and I flick one of my hair ties at her. "I wouldn't have gone *during* work, but I would've gone after."

Shaking her head, she begins to strip out of her wet sea wear. "I'm not like you," she says quietly. "I can't sit still and do the same thing every single day. It drives me insane."

She pulls a satin robe out of her armoire, wrapping it around her body.

Guilt prods at my insides. Mariel loves the temple, but she's always struggled with archival and library duty. She wasn't made to pore over books in a quiet library for hours at a time. She was born for thrill, adventure, and socialization. She thrives whenever she's on ceremony duty, teaching, or doing island tours during tourist season.

"Who'd you go with?" I ask, infusing my tone with extra joy so as not to make her feel bad.

She tilts her head, staring into space as she recounts. "Nyla! Annnnnd a few others from the temple—"

Gasping, I grab my pillow and playfully whack her with it. "*That's* why the library was so quiet today!"

A laugh erupts from her as she digs through her armoire, pulling out articles of clothing and laying them on the bed. "I thought you'd be more appreciative."

"That you kidnapped half the celestial servants during working hours?"

She shrugs a shoulder. "Better for your focus, no?"

"How very scandalous of you, Mariel."

Perched on the edge of her bed, she faces me. Only a few

paces separate our beds. If we both stretched out our legs, we could just barely touch.

We used to do it when we were younger, waiting to see if one day we'd grow tall enough to connect. She's been my roommate, my friend, my *sister*, since we were first assigned rooms in the temples. And though we've moved from the children's rooms to our current hall, our bond hasn't changed.

The moonlight trickles in through the open window, and I gaze out at the twinkling sky.

"You work almost as hard as the High Priest himself," Mariel says quietly. Before I can reply, she continues, "Have you seen Joss yet?"

My attention snaps back to her face. "He's back?"

She nods, tucking a damp curl behind her ear.

"You talked to him?" I study her.

"I saw him in the village when I visited my ma for lunch," she says quickly.

My heart softens at the mention of her mother. She's a kind, welcoming, albeit handful of a woman at times. A healer with a habit of drinking too much nectar.

"How was he doing?" I whisper, needing to know if Joss is okay.

"Joss being Joss, as always," she says with a laugh, and the tense breath I was holding escapes.

"And Delores?"

"You know, she's Delores. Still high as a pufferfish on pollen and terrorizing the tideborn daily, per usual."

I snort, shaking my head at her shenanigans. She's been an asset to the island for years, working as a healer for the wardens. "You should visit her more often, Mar," I say softly.

"You're one to talk!" She playfully swats me with her book. "When's the last time you've seen her?"

"She's *your* mother." I don't want to scold Mariel, but if my own mother were around, I'd visit her as much as possible. "But you're also right, I should. Maybe we can visit her for lunch sometime this week?"

Mariel smiles, but it's stiffer than usual. "Yeah, she'd like that." She gestures to her hair, changing the subject, "Anyway, it's a wash night now."

She pops up from the bed and then pulls open the drawer at the bottom of her armoire, snatching up a basket with her bathing supplies. A wide-tooth comb, coconut moisturizer, a silk bonnet, and other various care items.

She sets it on her bed with a yawn. "I think I'll soak for a bit to let the moisturizer sink in."

I nod, knowing it means not to wait up for her. She cares for her curls diligently, especially since the saltwater tends to dry them out. "A lavender soak kinda night?"

She pulls a small jar out of the basket and shakes it at me. The tiny bath salt beads rattle. "You know me too well. Can we talk after, though?"

"Of course." We haven't gotten much time together lately to catch up.

A few minutes after the door shuts behind her, while I'm fluffing up my pillows and getting ready to slip into my sheets, a *psst* reaches my ears.

I crane my neck, scanning the window between the beds. Fingers grip the windowsill, and a second later, there's a groan. Joss hoists himself onto the ledge and swings his feet into the room. He lands with a graceful thud, running his hands through his damp hair and smirking down at me. The smell of salt and sand hits me, the scent clinging to him even more potent than it was to Mariel.

Then again, it's a part of him. He's a tideborn warden meant to guard our waters.

"This window gets higher and higher, I swear," he jokes, cracking his knuckles.

"Joss!" Jumping out of bed, I wrap my arms around the cocky brute. He squeezes me tight, and I breathe him in. The sea and Joss. Two of my favorite familiar staples.

His lower half presses against me, his tiny shorts chilled and damp.

Pulling free from his touch, I shift awkwardly. Things are different now, and I haven't set boundaries well.

"You don't have to use the window," I murmur. "We're not kids anymore." And we haven't been for almost a decade.

He laughs. "It's more fun that way." His light scent, jovial tone, and easygoing nature are the opposite of Raziel in every way. I never meant to consciously compare the two, but now that I've thought about it, I can't unsee it.

"Are you okay?" I search his face, desperate for a hint of his feelings.

"*Me?*" he says, forcing a broad smile. "Of course!"

"I can't believe you went to the mainland." My hand rises automatically, cupping his cheek. "Oh, Joss."

"None of that." He turns from my touch. "It's my job, and I did it. If I'm going to be an even better Chief Warden than my father, I can't let sailing stop me."

"How was the trip?" I ask quietly.

"The journey itself was peaceful. No pirates." He groans. "But the mainland is polluted and stinks like rotten fish and seaweed. The people don't ever slow down, and there's so much *crime*." His jaw tenses, and his eyes darken.

The teachings from this morning flit through my mind. The Isle de Lunith was said to be a sanctuary; a place of peace to preserve the magic. It's all I've ever known. Though we can visit the mainland at any time, I've never had an interest in doing so.

One season per year, we welcome tourists, showcasing the beauty of our island. It's a vacation destination for the richest of the mainlanders. From what I've heard from others—and now, Joss—I can see why they'd want to escape to our beautiful homeland.

"I'm glad the sea was calm," I say, offering reassurances.

The very sea that once hosted the turmoil that stole his mother.

He sighs, rubbing his brow, letting me see the vulnerable side he hides from everyone else. "Awful."

"Why did you even go? Why now?"

"The High Priest chose me." He clenches his teeth, and I know he wants to say more, but he's decent enough not to talk poorly about the Moon Priest under the sacred temple's roof.

It shows what kind of man Joss is because I know how he feels about boats. The water is a part of him, but after his mother's ship was attacked by pirates during one of the treks to the mainland almost a decade ago, resulting in the loss of her life, he refused to ever journey by boat himself.

"Why did Raziel choose *you* to go?"

He stares at me, his brows slowly drawing together. "You really don't know?" After a dramatic pause, Joss scoffs. "It's because he likes you."

The absurdity of it makes me squeak. But then guilt makes my chest tighten; Joss was sent to the mainland because of *me*?

"Don't worry, I don't blame you," he quickly adds, reading my expression. "The Chief Warden can't be afraid of the water, after all." Another bitter laugh escapes him.

"Joss…"

"Stop saying my name like that. With pity. I'm a big boy." He winks at me, and I roll my eyes. "I'll show you if you need a reminder."

"Joss." This time it's said in warning. I give him a stern look.

He puts his hands up. "Like I said, I don't blame you. Nor do I blame *him* for wanting you to himself. You're a catch, Soraya."

My face heats. "How much silverdew did you snort before coming over here?"

His mouth tightens into a grim line. "I'm serious, Raya. Why else would he make a slick comment about our nighttime activities and then kick me off the island for half the month?"

I shake my head at the ridiculousness. "I've barely seen him over the last couple of weeks." And when I *did*, he managed to irritate me thoroughly.

"Sure," he says flatly.

"You're wrong."

He rolls his eyes. "If you say so."

"We're working on something together. For the temple."

He lifts a brow. "He interacts with you. Willingly. That's telling."

"Oh, stop. He's my High Priest.

"I'm going to say two things, then I'll drop it." He holds up his fingers, counting as he says, "One, he is definitely into you." A *pfft* of disbelief leaves me before I can stop it. "Two, I came through your window because he was lurking in the hallway, pacing outside your room like he was on the verge of a life-altering decision."

"What?" My back goes ramrod straight as his words hit me like a comet. "What do you mean?"

"Exactly what I said, Raya." He gives me a smug look. "Since he's not in here, I assume he didn't have the balls to knock."

If Raziel was coming to find me, does that mean he learned

something new? My blood blazes with curiosity, and I straighten up, glancing toward the door. I should go find him.

Joss makes a pained noise in his throat, and when I turn back to him, there's a shadow haunting his features.

"Don't tell me you're into him." His tone is hollow.

I shake my head vigorously. "Of course not. I told you, we're working on something together. You said you'd drop it, Joss."

"Fine." His gaze roams my bare legs, then flits to Mariel's empty bed. "Where's your other half tonight?"

"Bathing."

Slowly, his lips spread into a mischievous smirk. He prowls toward me. "So, we have the room to ourselves for a bit?"

My hands fly to his chest, stopping him before he can wrap his arms around me. "Joss…"

"Don't say it," he warns. With a sigh, he steps back and shoves his fingers through his hair. "It's been two weeks, and I've missed you, Soraya."

"I've missed you too," I whisper.

When he turns back to me, pain shimmers in his piercing green eyes. "Not the same way I've missed you, though."

My heart spasms painfully, but I don't refute him. He's not wrong. I just hate hurting him.

"Come on," he says, striding to the open window. He pauses, reaching an outstretched hand for me.

"Where are we going?"

"Anywhere," he says. "The jungle."

Hesitating, I bite my lip. I really need to speak with Raziel, but I don't want to clue Joss in on it being a big deal. "Now? Why?"

"Because I want to spend time together but staying near a bed with you wearing *that* is simply unbearable."

I roll my eyes with a sigh. "Well, when has a jungle stopped you from touching me?"

He cocks his head. "It hasn't before, but I promise to behave tonight. I mean it. Let's go find some silverdew."

"Fine." Glancing at the door one last time, my shoulders slump. Raziel could've knocked if he really wanted to speak with me. Goddesses know if I push him to share, he'll close up like a dehydrated clam guarding a pearl anyway. Plus, I haven't seen Joss since before his trip.

As for Mariel, she'll understand. I'll talk to her when I get back later.

I meet Joss at the window. He plants his hands on my waist, lifting me with ease. I swing my legs over the windowsill one at a time, and he releases me. I bend my knees, landing in the plush grass with a soft *oomph*.

Joss lands beside me a second later. "Thanks for coming," he says, giving me a crooked grin.

He won't admit it, but he needs me right now. The journey to the mainland was a bigger deal than anyone else can imagine. I hate that he had to spend the last couple of weeks on his own, suffering the pain of losing his mother all over again.

From what I remember, she was a wonderful woman. Strong, vocal, intelligent. She and Lachlan Thalor were a perfect pair. Until her death, *she* was the Chief Warden. She wasn't a tideborn like Joss and Lachlan, though; she was a treeborn with a natural affinity for the jungle and mountains rather than the sea.

When Joss reaches for my hand, I let him take it.

We run toward the jungle behind the temple, giggling like children.

As the warm air pricks my skin and moonbeams light my

path, I relax. Ever since I saw the moonstone flicker during the Union those couple of weeks back, I haven't felt like myself. Tonight, I'll enjoy the company of one of my best friends, indulge in pollen, and forget about it all.

Just for one night.

CHAPTER TWELVE

THE POLLEN

RAZIEL

*P*acing in front of my office window, I glance out into the trees sloping down the mountain toward the jungle below.

A flicker of movement catches my eye far below, and I home in on it. My breath catches as I lean forward. Two figures race off, hand-in-hand, toward the canopy of trees. There's only one person I know with hair as bright as the Union sky.

I can't make out the person with her, only that it's a male figure, mostly nude, save for those ridiculously tiny shorts.

The meddling, moon-cursed warden.

Balling my hand into a fist, I try to redirect my focus back to my original musings. But it's no use. I'm distracted. By her. *Again.*

This is precisely what I've worked so hard to prevent.

My legs move before I can logically process why. They

carry me out the door and to the stairwell. I spiral downward, so light on my slippered feet that I'm practically flying.

My silk pajamas allow me to move efficiently, and I catch up to their laughter in no time.

Relief settles in my bones when I catch sight of them. Moonlight glints off the sparkling silverdew meadow. I pause behind a tree to watch them for a moment.

The silverdew flowers stand tall and ethereal, about knee-high. With nightfall upon us, the silver petals unfurl like delicate drops of moonlight. Each petal shimmers with a dewdrop sheen, glistening with pollen. It's as if they've bloomed from the moon's magic rather than the soil.

Soraya and Joss bend over at the waist, burying their faces into the silverdew's blossom, which is about the size of a fist. The air is quiet enough that I can hear their thick inhales as they drag in breaths of the delicate powder. When they lift their heads, they giggle.

A silver glitter clings to the lower half of their faces. The moonlight catches on it, causing them to shimmer with each movement.

It's reckless—gluttonous.

Joss leans forward, tucking a strand of Soraya's hair behind her ear, and I grit my teeth. Her gaze is soft, her eyes half-lidded and dreamy.

She's so… comfortable with him. It makes the inside of my skin itch.

I need to put a stop to this behavior.

Making my presence known, I stomp out from behind the tree and lock my glare onto Soraya. She giggles, nudging Joss and pointing in my direction.

A comical play of emotions spreads across his face. First, his eyes widen, then his brow furrows, and his mouth goes into a grim line before spreading into a grin. He lifts a brow at me.

I clear my throat. "Are you two done?"

She giggles again, bouncing on the balls of her bare feet. I frown at her dirty toes. She hates shoes more than anyone I've ever met.

"Done what?" she asks, genuine curiosity invading her tone. "Having fun?"

"It's called enjoying life," Joss interjects. "You should try it sometime."

"I enjoy life plenty." I cross my arms, narrowing my gaze on Soraya. "This is reckless. You realize that, right?"

"Oh, here we go," Joss mutters, rolling his eyes. He leans back down and sniffs another flower, smothering himself in the silvery powder.

"You should try it," she says, beckoning me forth. "There's no harm in letting go sometimes, Raziel."

The way she says my name, so tenderly, has my tense muscles relaxing. Joss's head whips up, scrutinizing her. I ignore him, stepping closer to Soraya.

"Being high doesn't appeal to me," I mutter. "I like to be in control."

"The silverdew barely affects mentality," she says, scrunching her adorably freckled nose. "It gives you a sense of euphoria and enlightenment. It's a very joyous, calming experience."

"Given our recent... *project*, you should keep your wits about you," I say through gritted teeth.

She sighs, tossing her head back and closing her eyes. "You're ruining my high, Raziel."

"What does he have you doing?" Joss asks, frowning at her.

She gives him an apologetic look. "I told you I can't tell you details. It's official celestial work."

"That's never stopped you before," he mutters.

"This is different."

His eyes flit to mine, narrowing. He glowers at me, though he addresses her. "I'm sure it is." Then he turns to her, grasping her hand and interlacing their fingers. With a lowered voice, he says, "We don't keep things from each other, Raya."

The nickname and soft tone he addresses her with cause my stomach to pitch. A sharp, unusual pain settles in my gut. I glare at where their hands connect.

Slowly, she pulls from his grip and gives him a conciliatory smile.

"You have an early start tomorrow," I say. "You should go to sleep."

Her forehead scrunches as she studies me, but she doesn't challenge me in front of Joss.

Instead, she sighs. "I'm hungry anyway."

Pride and satisfaction replace the previously uncomfortable feeling, and I try not to let it show on my face.

"Sleep at my place tonight," Joss says, quickly erasing my short-lived joy. "I'll make you fish tacos."

"Celestial servants are to reside at the temple," I say, narrowing my eyes at him. "Go home, Thalor. Alone."

In response, the warden laughs, leaning toward Soraya. "I told you."

Soraya flushes, her mouth dropping open. She plants her hands on Joss and pushes lightly. "Knock it off!"

He stumbles, laughing. "He's as rigid as his unused cock," Joss continues, cracking himself up as he finds his footing. "I'd wager he wouldn't even know what to do with it if he got the chance."

He studies her, lifting a brow as if waiting to see how she responds.

"Enough," Soraya says, her face dropping in horror. She turns to me. "I'm sorry." But then she snorts a small laugh of her own, quickly stifling it with her hand. "Sorry, sorry—it's the pollen, not me." She breaks out into another fit of giggles.

Anger blazes through me, and my jaw tics. "Walk away now, Thalor."

He rolls his eyes, wrapping an arm around Soraya's shoulder and kissing her head. Visceral jealousy washes over me. Is he trying to provoke me?

"Don't make me tell you again," I threaten, emboldened by his attitude.

Soraya pierces me with a glare. "Leave him alone."

The unexpectedly protective tone catches me off guard, intensifying my envy. My palm burns, and a liquid warmth spills through my veins. I glance down at my balled-up hand, catching a hint of light seeping from between my knuckles.

Great.

"Come with me," Joss murmurs to her. "I want to be as tangled in you as these vines are in each other."

She pulls away from him, shooting him an apologetic look. "We shouldn't," she says softly. "You know we—"

"Don't say it." His face falls.

"You should go home," she whispers as if trying to keep the conversation from my ears.

With a stiff nod, he plucks a silverdew flower and dramatically salutes her. He turns an unimpressed gaze on me, then he laughs sarcastically and swaggers toward the trees, slanting down to the village.

"Be safe, Joss," she yells after him. "Please."

"Take your own advice, darling," he calls back.

Once he's completely out of sight, Soraya turns her attention back to me. Her mood is unreadable until she crosses her arms and tilts her head, clearly displeased. "What was that about, Raziel?"

My jaw tenses. "Exactly what I said. The future Chief Warden and Moon Priest's second shouldn't be gallivanting through the jungle, snorting pollen in the middle of the—"

"Second?" she parrots back, her brows flying up.

I flush. "Yes."

"So you admit you need me."

I swallow, glancing at her feet again. The admission sticks in my throat. Why is it so damn hard to tell her I need her? Just the thought of her perceiving me as weak and incompetent sends a tremor of unease through me.

"The temple needs you, yes."

"But *you* don't?" she challenges.

A thick tension blankets us as we stare at one another, the silence punctuated only by the rapid pounding of my pulse in my temples. My throat clogs with unspoken words and unnamed emotions.

I genuinely don't know how to put my feelings into words, to answer her effectively.

Instead, I stay silent.

Her gaze hardens, but she refuses to look away. The longer the silence stretches, the taller and prouder she stands. Each passing second feels like an eternity as we engage in the standoff.

Finally, I exhale the anxiety away and shrug.

She huffs a breath. "Why are you so…"

"So, what, Soraya? Say it."

Her lip trembles as if she can't bear to speak the word. Finally, she whispers, "Unfriendly."

I feel the hint of a smile threatening to tug at my lips. Of everything I thought she'd say, I hadn't expected that.

"I'm not here to make friends," I say. "I'm here to protect the magic and the island."

"Yeah, I know," she shoots back. "It's your *duty*. Well, you're not the only one around here fulfilling their obligations."

What have I done now to upset her so deeply?

Sucking in a deep breath, she stomps up to me, glaring into my soul. The air around us stills, and for a moment, I'm afraid to breathe—afraid to shatter the fragile connection between us.

"Maybe if you made an effort to know the people here, you'd know that they make their own sacrifices and face their fears every single day." Her hot, angry breath fans across my face, and my skin burns with the need to be closer. "Joss is a good man."

Hearing his name is like an icy wave crashing into me.

I step back, putting space between us. Her careful attention to him and protectiveness suddenly make sense. She's *concerned* about him for some reason.

She's right; I know nothing about him, or anyone else for that matter. I couldn't even begin to guess what grave sin I've committed.

"Noted," I say stiffly. There's no point in telling her that I don't care for Joss Thalor beyond my general responsibility to the islanders. But for her, I'll make an effort to be... nicer, I guess.

"Raziel..." she sighs my name exasperatedly. Then she advances again, invading my personal space.

Glancing down at her, I allow myself a moment to get lost in her sparkling sea-blue eyes.

"What do you want from me, Soraya?" I murmur. I've been the same way for years, and she never made an effort to reach me before. So why now? I feel like it's more than concern for the moons and magic.

"Something I can't have," she whispers, confirming my intuition. Her soft, sweet scent mixed with silverdew pollen lures me in, and I find myself tilting my head down toward her.

My eyes flit to her nose, then to her sparkling lips still tainted with pollen. I can't help it—a tiny grin tugs at my mouth.

"Will you try pollen with me sometime?" she asks.

I blink a few times, processing. It wasn't what I had expected her to say. But right now, with her this close, every nerve ending in my body begging to reach out to touch her, I'd agree to anything.

So, I whisper, "Yes," before I can think better of it.

The space between us slowly disappears. She presses her soft lips against mine. A feeling like magic zings through the air, and my stomach bottoms out.

Externally, I don't react.

Internally, a burning desire unlike anything I've ever felt before nearly sends me to my knees.

My dick hardens so painfully at the mere feel of her soft, innocent kiss that I'm fearful I'll come in my pants if I allow this to continue. Unsure of what I should do, I stay rigid and unresponsive.

My carnal desires war with my logic. But as quickly as the kiss starts, it stops.

Soraya sighs against my mouth. "I thought so," she murmurs, blowing a soft breath.

Then she chuckles. Pulling back, she pats my chest.

Stunned and silent, I gape at her. Instead of recoiling at my rejection, as I'd expected, a look of glee overtakes her face. She reaches up, using the back of her hand to wipe the kiss from her lips.

I frown. Was it that horrible?

I mean, I guess it was—I froze. I didn't touch her or move or react in any manner.

Her soft laughter draws me back to the present. She wavers slightly, an aura around her brightening. The colors of the jungle grow more vibrant, the trees swaying gently around me.

"What's happening to me?" I choke out, causing her to laugh harder. My voice sounds strange, deep and warbly. My heartbeat ticks up, and I plant a hand on my chest, gasping for breath.

I lick my lips, tasting an unfamiliar sweetness. Too late, I realize Soraya wasn't wiping away my kiss—she was wiping away the pollen.

The pollen she just shared with me.

"Am I... *high?*" I whisper, still clutching my chest and breathing deeply.

"Lighten up, Raziel," she says with a smirk. She rubs the spot just below her collarbone. A mindless, self-soothing tactic I've noticed she does often. Her shirt has no sleeves, but the collar rises to her throat. It's an interesting contradiction, almost like she's dressing modestly, but the rest of her clothes are flimsy and barely there.

Saturated ribbons of turquoise, from the deepest teal to the brightest aquamarine, and glowing silvers, like molten metal, caress the land. I stare, mesmerized, until my eyes are dry and gritty. I'm forced to blink.

"You can see the island's magic on pollen?" I murmur, awed by the rare sight. It's like Union night, only more intense and widespread. "Wow... It's so..." Beautiful. Unexpected. *Magical.*

She nods, satisfied by my response.

Her stomach rumbles violently, like lightning tearing through the quiet night. It's so loud and absurd that I can't help but chuckle. The noise distracts me from my internal panic.

"Moons," I say, sounding a thousand seas away. "When's the last time you ate?"

"I…" She bites her lip, zoning out as she presumably tries to recall. "Yesterday?"

"For the love of the goddess." I drag a hand over my face. Unlike the island, which is now pulsing with magic, my palm no longer glows. I feel a sense of renewed serenity. "Come," I say, offering a hand.

She stares at it, hesitating before slowly reaching for me. Just like that day in the stairwell, a soft shock flows through us at the contact. She gasps, and I know she feels it, too.

This time, I don't release her. Encouraged by the soft, flowing energy of the pollen, I allow my fingers to interlace with hers. We practically glide through the trees, up the stairs, and to my chambers.

Wordlessly, I lead her to the kitchen.

"Sit," I say softly, gesturing toward one of the chairs at the island counter.

I stride to my sink, turn on the water, and wash my hands thoroughly before patting them dry. Focused on the task, I pull out a loaf of freshly made saltbread and the bowl of jackfruit I cooked this morning.

"Is a sandwich okay? Jackfruit sandwiches are my favorite food."

Delight crosses her face as she lifts herself onto my counter and swings her feet. "Oh, he's sharing now."

I turn, chuckling to myself silently as I locate a plate, cutting board, and bread knife. "*This* isn't a secret."

"Tell me a real secret, then?" she asks coyly.

My hands pause, the knife hovering over the loaf. Then I

shake my head, slicing the bread into even pieces and assembling them on the plate. "Your effort is futile."

A soft huff comes from behind me. I smile, still facing away from her so she can't see the effect she has on me.

"I told you the pollen won't ruin your control," she says. "Do you believe me now?"

I allow myself to *feel* the emotions coursing through me. They're soft and mellow, like the sea before a storm. Nothing like the usual invasive turmoil I experience. "You have made a point, yes."

Using a serving spoon, I scoop a bit of the meaty, shredded jackfruit and let the excess sauce drain before plopping it onto a slice of bread. The savory, sweet scent makes my mouth water.

She makes a sound of quiet appraisal. "Did you make that yourself?"

"This morning. Yes. It's been marinating." I usually cook it with various spices, then let it simmer in sauce for maximum flavor.

"Of course you can cook, too."

"What do you mean by that?" My eyes flick to her.

"You're good at everything you do," she murmurs with a little laugh.

"That's not true," I say, my cheeks heating.

"Yes, it is." She nods animatedly. "You might not be the most warm or open person on the island, but I do think you care about it with a ferocity not many understand."

"But *you* understand?"

She smiles, biting her lip and glancing down. "I do. Because I care too, Raziel."

I turn to her, taken aback by the comment. Her face is sincere; she truly seems to mean it. She thinks I'm good at everything? I don't know how to respond, because my brain shouts that she's wrong. That I'm a failure, an impostor.

But I stay quiet and observe her instead.

She's so pretty sitting in my kitchen, relaxed. She leans back, her palms on the counter behind her. She kicks her feet, and my eyes trail down her skimpy sleepwear to her smooth, bronzed legs.

They land on her dirt-caked feet. Normally, the sight would irritate me. But under the influence of pollen, I simply shake my head and return to my task.

She's right... Without the distraction of my immense feelings, I feel *more* in control rather than less. Not that I'm about to admit that. Snorting pollen is a slippery slope. That's how it starts. First the pollen, then the nectar, then the ceremonies... and then I'm losing myself to the pleasures of the jungle rather than sacrificing myself to servicing the moons.

"Raziel?" she asks sweetly.

For a second, I debate ignoring her, just to hear her say my name again. But instead, I turn, handing her the plated sandwich.

"You really are a good Moon Priest. I hope you know that." She accepts the plate, smiling widely at it, totally oblivious to the way her compliment rocks me. "Thanks for this."

Her scent, rich like the jungle and sweet like silverdew, invades my space. It's heady and attractive. I *like* it.

I like *her*.

"You're welcome," I mumble awkwardly, my head buzzing with the pollen still.

"Who taught you how to cook?" She sniffs the sandwich before hopping off the counter and moving to a stool. "I only know two people who can make jackfruit like this—Delores and Kassia."

The second name washes over me with a sense of nostalgia and familiarity.

"Oh," she quickly adds. "Delores is Mariel's ma, and Kassia is the priestess who—"

"Raised you," I finish. "Yes, I'm aware. Now, eat your food."

She shoots me a surprised look. Keeping her eyes locked on me, she slowly bites into the sandwich. As she chews, she leans back and makes a noise of contentment. After she swallows, she says, "Makes sense why I never see you in the dining hall. Or in the village." She laughs lightly. "If I could cook like this…"

I glance at her, taking in the faint sheen of pollen still shimmering on the tip of her nose. She doesn't seem to care as she continues eating.

And moons above, so she's so damn pretty that I can't look at her a second longer. Instead, I excuse myself, locking myself away in the bathroom. I'm hard again just from the scent of her—her proximity.

Something roils in my veins alongside the desire… the familiar buzz makes the hair on the back of my neck stick up.

Magic.

How?

With a shaking hand, I reach for my letter opener. I hover the blade over my palm, afraid of confirming what I already feel. Steadying my hand, I press into the skin and drag the blade down until the skin splits. Moonlight pours from the wound.

Turning my hand, I watch in awe and terror as the glittering liquid drips down my wrist. The pain quickly dissipates, and the edges of the wound begin to draw together. The skin threads itself together again, leaving no indication that it had been split.

I don't—*how?*

Part of me wants to cling to this as a glimmer of hope. I wish I could believe it's a revival. But I know the truth about my magic *and* the curse. My time is drawing swiftly to a close.

Pausing, I take inventory of my body. Nothing threatens to surface from the depths. Despite the magic awake and coursing through me, I feel calm and in control.

Is it because of the pollen?

Or because of *her*?

None of it makes sense.

Even though things seem okay right now, I won't take any risks. The moment she's done eating, she needs to go. If the magic grows unruly, I'll head below the temple to my safe space.

I wash my hands and quietly return to the kitchen.

Soraya tips her head back, eyes closed, as she sways gently, her feet still swinging and skimming the ground beneath her. A soft *hmm* of pleasure bubbles up as she takes another bite, chewing carefully. Once she swallows, her eyes flick open and lock onto mine. A smile graces her lips.

The lust inside me grows, and I ache to reach out to her. Very little is stopping me right now.

"You need to leave when you finish," I force myself to say, cutting through the mellow energy of our night.

"What?" Her forehead wrinkles with confusion. She sets down her empty plate and stands. "You invited me up here."

"It was a mistake." I swallow the regret in my throat, striding past her.

"Wait." Her fingers wrap around my wrist, stopping me. She tugs until I turn to face her. "What did I do?"

My skin buzzes where she touches me, and I come alive.

This is exactly the distraction I'm trying to avoid. Yet somehow, she continues to get under my skin.

The sadness in her eyes slices deeper than my letter opener

ever could. Instead of responding, I shake my head. "You didn't do anything."

"But—"

"*I* made a mistake," I repeat. "It was inappropriate to bring you up here at this hour." The lie is bitter on my tongue, but it's easier than opening up and explaining the truth.

"Not even the pollen can help you, Raziel Kasper," she says sadly.

I watch her go, fighting the urge to call out to her.

When she leaves, I plop into her abandoned stool and hang my head in my hands. "You idiot."

CHAPTER THIRTEEN

THE STAR

SORAYA

*T*he next day, Mariel doesn't meet me for lunch, so I visit Kassia in the village. It's been far too long since I've seen the elder priestess, and Raziel's jackfruit last night reminded me so much of hers.

Her wooden screen door opens with a loud creak, announcing my visit. Instantly, the scent of fresh-baked cinnamon bread fills my nostrils, and I smile at the nostalgia. Before she left the temple, she used to always bake snacks for the celestial servants. I miss having her closer, but I'm glad she was able to retire and has since found her peace in the village.

"Kassia?" I call out, scanning the sunroom.

All light, natural wood and furniture woven from branches and reeds cover much of the floor space. She has *so* many plants that it feels like part of the jungle. The sun lights it up from windows overhead.

I wipe my bare feet on the grass mat beside the door, then

stride to a wicker chair with bright yellow cushions. I tuck my feet underneath me and revel in the familiar comfort of Kassia's home.

"Soraya, is that you?" she shouts from the kitchen just out of sight.

"Hi, Kassia!"

A second later, she appears in the open doorway. Her white-grey hair settles in loose waves, stopping at the tops of her tawny shoulders, kissing the thin straps of her pink dress. It's loose and flowy, so long that it hides her feet.

"Darling, let me put tea on," she says, quickly settling into our routine without giving me grief for the lapse in recent visits.

A short while later, she reenters the room, passing me a steaming mug. She settles into the chair at an angle beside me, her face wrinkling with a smile.

"Thank you," I murmur, lifting the cacao tea and inhaling the rich, chocolatey steam. "How'd you know?"

Cacao tea is for when I'm feeling down and need my spirits lifted. I shouldn't be surprised at her keen perception after all these years, but I am.

She gives me a knowing smirk. Her hands tremble as she sips her kava tea from a coconut shell. It's the only thing she drinks—to soothe her aches. It's on the tip of my tongue to ask if she knows Raziel can heal. Maybe she'll let him heal her.

But it's not my secret to share, and he's awfully protective over his personal life.

Then again... his magic is a gift from the goddess moons, meant to be shared. It's not a dirty little secret.

I sigh into the dark brown liquid in my mug.

"Spit it out, little star," she says, pursing her lips at me as she takes another sip. "I can see the mist leaking from your ears."

Her old nickname for me makes me chuckle. She's called me that since I was young, claiming I was the brightest star in her sky. It's also the origin of the name she picked for me: Soraya.

Despite my fondness for the old woman who raised me, I find the words about Raziel stick to the roof of my mouth. I'll convince him to help her later, but for now, I'm unwilling to betray his trust.

I switch to another topic I wanted to ask her about. "The night you found me…"

Her face softens, and she sets the coconut on the wicker table. "Yes?"

"You've always said I was a gift from the goddesses."

"You certainly are, darling girl. I stand by my words."

I've never had a pressing urge to know more about who left me or why. It never mattered to me; it's always been more of a factual recollection versus an emotional event. I figure whoever left me had their reason for doing so.

Kassia and the other celestial servants have always been my family. Joss and Mariel, along with their families, have been there my whole life, too—loving me unconditionally.

"Why are you asking?" Kassia says softly, her rich brown eyes studying me with warmth. "You've never given it much voice before."

"I know." I pick at the cushion beneath me, my gaze averted. "It doesn't matter, I guess."

My thoughts flit back to Raziel. Last night, he supposedly lingered at my door. Then he came after me and Joss in the jungle. He brought me to his home, cooked for me, and then sent me away.

Instead of angering me, it makes me hurt for him, for how lonely he must be.

I sigh, rubbing my chest. Kassia's eyes track the movement, and she softens, leaning forward to plant a hand on my knee.

"You're right where you're meant to be, little star. Be patient."

"I've dedicated my life to helping the islanders," I whisper. "But the one person I want to help most, I can't." I don't bother telling her *who* I'm talking about. "What if... I was wrong? What if I'm meant to do more?"

Raziel and I have much in common; more than he can even imagine. We're both orphans with a prominent role serving the moons, and we care about the island immensely, yet he closes himself off.

What happened to make him this way?

I'm not ignorant enough to think it's about me. It's more than that. It's about *him*, but I don't know how to help.

Drawing my gaze back to Kassia's, I ask, "What do you know about our High Priest?"

She was there when he was raised, and I remember her being relatively close to him until Amos passed.

Her smile falters, and when it resumes, it's pained. "He's a very tormented young man. I fear he's rather detached. Perhaps even a bit hollow."

Hollow? I frown at the word.

Hollow isn't one of the many things I'd call Raziel. If anything, he's the opposite—*full*. Stuffed to the brim with knowledge, magic, and responsibilities.

I bet if we threw him into the ocean, the weight of his secrets would sink him.

"That's not true!" My voice raises an octave. An inexplicable instinct to protect him rises to the surface. He's just hurting; why can't anyone else see it? See *him*? "Just because he's reserved doesn't mean he doesn't feel."

Kassia gives me a knowing look, sipping her kava tea, and I continue.

"We both know quiet waters run deep."

I swear I catch a hint of a proud smirk on her face, but she hides it behind her coconut again as she drains it.

"What about his parents?" I ask.

Her eyes flit to the left before shooting to the ceiling. She blows a heavy breath and shakes her head. "What about them?"

"Did they ever return to the island?" I heard Raziel was born on the mainland, brought to the island when his marking appeared.

She chews her lip, and a mist settles in her eyes. "That's not my business to share," she finally says, tone wistful. "Why do you ask, dearest?"

Shaking my head, I step forward and kiss her cheek. "No reason, Kassia. None at all."

Hawkish eyes track me as I stride to the door. Right before I exit, her voice reaches my ears.

"You misunderstand me, little star." My head swivels back to her. "I said he's hollow, not *shallow*."

"What's that supposed to mean?" I frown in confusion.

"Someone hollow can be filled, but someone shallow can never run deep."

I understand the message behind her tone. I nod, my throat too thick to speak through.

She adds, "You know, little star, you might be more charming and gregarious than he, but you're equally opaque."

A scoff escapes me, and I glance at my feet. Her implication that I'm secretive sends a chill down my spine. Slowly, I turn to her. "Kassia," I mumble, "you know it's different."

"Is it? You two have much in common." Her eyes twinkle

with the promise of something she's not saying, but I shake my head. And as I wave goodbye and leave, she whispers, "Take care, Soraya, and tread carefully. If you carve out any more of his heart, there won't be anything left to save."

My lungs squeeze as I exit the hut, pretending not to have heard that last bit. I should've known Kassia, of all people, would see through me... despite being *opaque*, as she put it.

Her words make me snicker to myself. The elder woman is rarely wrong.

I haven't even admitted it aloud yet, but I care about Raziel.

And it's more than him simply being my High Priest.

I stride through the village, lost in thought. My feet drag over the packed dirt path, my body heavy. Villagers smile and greet me as they wave, and I force myself to respond in kind.

Bells chime as the various shop doors open, with people bustling to and fro. There are only a few hundred of us who live on the island, but it's up to us all to keep everything running effectively. Which means we're constantly busy. When we're not working, we're celebrating.

At the edge of the jungle, the rough texture of Delores's hut comes into sight.

Nestled between two similar structures, the small structure, built of driftwood and palm bark, sits sturdy in the gentle breeze. The palm trees around sway casually, like old friends greeting those who visit.

Part of me longs to say hello to Mariel's ma, but the other part is too exhausted to fathom more socialization.

I pause, weighing my options. Before I can decide what to do, I hear Mariel's familiar laugh.

A smile crosses my lips, and my decision is made for me. I start toward the hut. Halfway to the door, she rounds the house into sight, with Joss at her side.

They laugh, deep in conversation as they stride up to Delores's door together.

Somehow, they don't see me. Panicked, I hurry off the trail and into the jungle. Peering out from behind a tree, I watch the two disappear into the hut.

Is this why she's been avoiding me?

The shock of the betrayal stings my eyes. I pick up my pace, hurrying up the hill toward the temple. It's not that I wouldn't be happy for them as a couple. Of *course* I would be. They're two of my favorite people.

But what hurts the most is that they're keeping this from me.

Then again, I'm keeping things from them, too.

CHAPTER FOURTEEN

THE EFFORT

RAZIEL

*T*he old wooden chair creaks as I sit back, huffing a breath. I roll up my sleeves and loosen the neckline of my shirt. The crisp material suddenly feels stifling. To ease the suffocating, I undo the broach holding my cape together and lay the fabric over the back of my chair.

I stare at the words in front of me, but they don't stick in my brain. Instead, images of the priestess in my home replay, pulling my attention away from the task at hand.

It's been a week since I invited Soraya to my home and made her a snack. I haven't seen her at all since that night.

Well, that's a lie, actually.

I've seen her every day this week, but from afar. However, I haven't interacted with her.

Her kind words continue to replay in my head. All I've ever wanted was to be a capable Moon Priest, to carry on the legacy of our island, protect the people, and serve the moons and their magic.

It's the first time since I became High Priest that someone said I was doing a good job.

And I panicked and hurt her feelings, making a fool out of myself once more.

As much as I want her words to be true, they're not. Bringing her into the fold has distracted me and proven that I *am* incompetent.

But I need her help because it's been another week of getting nowhere.

Staring blankly at the journal on my desk, I groan. The books I've been analyzing have taken me on a wild hunt, so I've opted to read the private collections of the High Priests before me. Not all of them kept journals, but Demetrius did.

His handwriting stares up at me, referencing a book I've never heard of:

The Curse of the Moon Priest.

Of course, it sounds like exactly the book I need. And of course, I don't have it in my possession. I'm certain I'd remember coming across such literature.

"That would be too easy, wouldn't it, Demetrius?" I sigh, rubbing my head in frustration.

After checking my shelves twice for good measure, I debate my options. I could waste time checking a third time, hoping it makes a magical appearance, or I could visit the bubbly priestess downstairs and ask *her* for help.

And hope I don't run into her feisty friend instead.

"Damn it," I mutter, flipping the diary closed with a huff.

Demetrius was a Moon Priest over a century ago, and his penned thoughts mention a curse, but he couldn't speak of it.

Allegedly, none of the High Priests could.

The entries are vague, puzzling, and the more I read, the

more I'm convinced he went utterly mad. I speculate that his magic went awry, consuming him. His entries stopped just before his thirtieth birthday, as I suspected, which further confirms my theory.

Amos also perished on *his* thirtieth.

My father dying unexpectedly when I was only ten came as a surprise. We're gifted with moonblood, and lore says we are meant to lead longer-than-average lives. So why were the Moon Priests cursed to die young?

It shouldn't be this way... There must be a solution, something I'm missing.

Not wanting to waste any more time, I decide to push my emotions aside and seek Soraya out. I stand, stretching my arms overhead. The first few steps are slow, and my legs are rigid, tingling with disuse. Shaking them, I allow the blood to return before organizing my books and heading out.

Maybe I should tell Soraya my other truth: it's not necessarily obligation that keeps me dedicated to my role, it's fear of the repercussions if I don't appease the goddesses.

It's why I refuse pleasures. No silverdew, no nectar, no intimacy, no friends. None of it.

Perhaps if I lead a different life from Amos, fully dedicated to the moons, I will be spared an early death. Part of me hopes the *curse* is simply punishment for failing as Moon Priest.

Downstairs, inside the temple, I pause outside of Soraya's classroom. Her soft voice carries out into the hall, and it instantly soothes me.

"—and that's why the goddesses were split into two separate moons instead of one."

"But why can't the magic just make them one?" a squeaky voice asks.

"Magic must always have balance, darling," Soraya

responds. "Legend says their magic was much too powerful for a single moon, so it was divided into halves."

Peering carefully into the open doorway, I watch her roam around the room. Her kids are spread out at a long table, scribbling furiously on the papers in front of them.

"So why are there not two Moon Priests?" a child calls out.

Soraya chuckles lightheartedly, stopping to place a hand on their shoulder. "Because we only need one."

"Why not one for each moon?"

Soraya continues to speak in an encouraging tone as she circles them, her head bowed. Small braids on either side of her temples pull the strands from her face, connecting in the back into one large braid before merging with the free-flowing blue-green waves.

That's my favorite color.

Teal.

The night sky on Union night, when it's lit up by magic once per month. The rivers and plants as they dance under the moons on that same special evening.

And *her* hair. Every single day.

It looks as soft as she is, and I wonder what it would feel like to run my fingers—

"High Priest!" a child gasps, having noticed me lurking.

Heart lurching, I pull my head out of the doorway and flatten against the wall. Soraya says something, but I can't hear it over the pounding in my temples. Holding my breath, I beg her not to come looking for me.

The last thing I need is another reason for her to accuse me of creeping. Even though I know that's exactly what I'm doing.

A second later, the door snicks shut, and I exhale, my body softening.

Confident I've averted a minor crisis, I leave Soraya to her job and head to the library to find *The Curse of the Moon Priest*.

Searching the library did not yield the book mentioned in Demetrius's journal.

Hungry, and with Soraya's soft voice echoing in my mind, I decide to break routine and eat in the dining hall. The heavy doors of the library close behind me with a thud as I step into the cavernous corridors of the west wing. The glossy, painted floor provides a softer atmosphere, contrasting with the rest of the temple's unyielding stone. The goddesses, depicted in the stained-glass windows, seem to follow my every move.

Deeper into the temple, a clamor of voices echoes around me.

I hesitate a moment, then enter, allowing the dining hall's wide mouth to consume me. As soon as I'm spotted, the chatter begins to cease, and my throat closes.

What was I thinking?

Despite the enormity of the space, it feels as if the walls are closing in. I stay focused on my breath, ignoring the dozens of eyes locked onto me.

Soraya had commented on never seeing me in the dining hall. That, combined with the desire to try and make an effort, brought me here before I could think better of the idea.

Once my pulse steadies, I scan the room. The long, dark tables sit in neat rows, with the kitchen and food station on the opposite side of the room. Chandeliers flicker overhead, offering a surprisingly soft lighting. Rich, hearty scents wash over me, relaxing me even further.

Food is a language I speak well.

Immediately, I spot Soraya's bright hair. My heart beats relentlessly, and I sputter, choking on air.

How incompetent am I that I suddenly forgot how to fucking breathe?

I pause to steady myself, placing my hand on my chest to will it to calm down. My gaze slides from the back of Soraya's head, instantly locking with Mariel's coy brown eyes.

She pins me with the same curious stare she did in the library. Her mouth moves rapidly as she addresses Soraya.

When the latter slowly turns, locking eyes with me, I raise my hand in an awkward wave and will my feet to move. I stride up to their table, trying to choose my words carefully, when a deep sigh reaches my ears.

"High Priest Raziel," a low male voice says from beside me.

Instantly, I tense up, turning toward the frowning warden. Disappointment and annoyance gather in my chest as Joss slips onto the bench beside Soraya, placing a plate in front of her before turning his attention to his food.

"Warden Thalor," I say flatly, not the slightest bit thrilled to see this man bringing my priestess food.

"It's Joss," he says casually, giving me a fake, toothy smile. "Good to see you in the temple rather than the trees for once." He winks.

The sight of his mere face offends me. I've never been a particularly violent man, but I'd like to hit him just once.

Ignoring him, I nod a brief greeting toward Mariel and Soraya. Then, not wanting to speak with her in front of Joss, I rise from the table and make my way toward the far side of the room, toward the meal stations. Marble countertops boast polished brass warming trays and stoneware. A vibrant mural of the night sky and twin moons is painted along the wall, a way to honor the meal.

I try not to glance over my shoulder, but it's useless. Joss throws his arm over Soraya's shoulder, and he talks animatedly, leaning halfway across the table. Mariel laughs loudly, her head tipping back.

Soraya smiles, her eyes lighting up as she shakes her head. As if she can sense my gaze on her, she glances up. My pulse skyrockets again, thundering in my temples.

Slowly, the smile melts off her face, and she drops her attention back to the plate before her.

I go through the motions of securing food and finding a seat, not registering anything around me other than *her*.

"High Priest," a quiet male voice says.

Tearing my gaze from Soraya, I spot a tall teenage boy giving me a wary look. I nod, taking another bite of my jackfruit sandwich.

"How's your hand?" he whispers.

I freeze, nearly choking on my food. When I swallow, I ask, "What?"

"The other day…" He looks flustered, reaching up to scratch his neck. "Never mind."

Oh, the hallway. The boy who caught me threatening the damn finicky moonstone.

"My hand is fine," I say carefully. "The part about cutting it off… was a joke." It lands flatter than my tone.

But to my surprise, he smiles. "Ha!" He laughs, and it's so loud and unexpected that I nearly drop my sandwich.

Is he… pretending I'm funny to placate me?

Do these people really tiptoe around me out of *fear*?

My eyes flick back to Soraya's table, and she and her two friends stare openly in my direction. Suddenly, I'm that much more grateful for her group. They might hate me, but at least they don't pretend to like me.

SECOND UNION MONTH

CHAPTER FIFTEEN

THE SILVERDEW

SORAYA

*T*he beach blazes to life with a bonfire, music, and flowing nectar. Soon, the two moons will merge, powering our island with their blessing as they do every month.

Or so they should. The lingering doubt of the magic failing haunts my mood. Raziel and I still haven't figured out what's going on or how to fix it. I only hope this month goes smoothly, and that *if* something is awry, no one notices.

But the magic isn't the only thing acting strange.

I swear, everyone I know is hiding something. I mean, at this point, I *know* they are. Joss and Mariel are both acting on edge, distancing themselves from me. Joss refuses to look me in the eyes, and Mariel seems more glum than usual.

They're two of the most jovial people I know, yet they wear matching frowns.

Other than that, Raziel has been avoiding me again. The

library erection was unexpected but rather delightful. Knowing he's attracted to me, that his body wants mine, fills me with a sense of satisfaction. If he ever chose to give in to his carnal needs finally, I want to be the one he indulges with.

My cheeks grow hot at the admission, and I nearly run into the ocean to cool myself down.

I sip my nectar, desperate for the buzz to fill my veins. Joss plants his interlaced hands on his head, huffing a breath as he stares at the waves lapping at the shore.

"I need a drink," he sighs before bolting off.

Mariel watches him go with a frown, then she turns to me.

"I know you two are seeing each other," I say at the same time she says, "I have to tell you something."

We stare at each other for a second, and then an incredulous laugh leaves her lips. "*What?*"

"You and Joss. I saw you at your ma's house last week," I admit, quickly chugging the rest of my drink. "This doesn't have to be weird—"

She laughs harder, cutting me off, and then loops her arm through mine. "Oh, my moons, Soraya. I'm not dating Joss!"

"But I saw you two at Delores's house."

"Yes, we've been having lunch with her." She pauses. "And Lachlan."

"His dad?" My brows tug together in confusion.

"They're planning on going through with a bonding," she explains. "My ma and his dad."

I rip free from her grip, spinning to face her. "What?" I shriek, the shock prickling my chest. "Why didn't you tell me?"

Guilt flickers across her face. "They didn't want anyone to know... not until we digested it."

"What does that even mean?"

"Apparently, they've been seeing each other in secret. The

four of us had a couple of *family* meals to test out the dynamic and see if this is a viable situation."

"And?"

She smiles, and it's heartfelt. "They really want to complete a bonding ceremony, but they wanted to ensure Joss and I were okay with it first."

My stomach twists. "You could've told me, Mar."

"I wanted to. *Joss* wanted to. But our parents made us keep an oath of silence. You know how the island is; they didn't want outside opinions weighing in and making it even more complicated for us. Lachlan is the Chief Warden, and Joss is set to take over in the next couple of years..."

"I know," I say, giving her a weak smile. "Are you happy about it?"

"Yeah." Her eyes light up. "I am. He's a good guy, and Ma deserves that, you know?"

My eyes flick to Joss, who has secured his nectar from the bustling hut. He chats animatedly with his father and a few other wardens. "I can't believe Joss is going to be your brother."

She shrugs, making a face. "That's the weirdest part, but at least it's not like we're sharing a home. We're not *really* siblings."

I think about how I'm keeping Raziel's healing ability from Kassia—from everyone—and my sourness evaporates a little. I'm not entitled to anyone's private business, just as they're not entitled to mine. I'd be a hypocrite not to recognize that.

"Are we okay?" Mariel whispers with a frown, pulling my attention back to her.

I wrap my arms around her. "Of course we are, Mar. You're like a sister to me."

She blows a breath out, squeezing. "Moons, it feels good to talk about."

"Is that why you two have been acting so strange lately?"

"Girl, do you know how hard it is to keep things from you?" She pulls back, eyeing me carefully. "You've been so busy assisting Raziel that I didn't want to add more to your plate. It's hard as shells to watch what I say. Joss thought for sure I'd crack."

I roll my eyes playfully, not bothering to contest the comment about my secrets. She's not wrong.

"Sweetie beans!" A warm, familiar voice washes over me.

I turn to see the woman in question. Delores walks toward me with her arms open wide and a broad grin on her face.

"Ma!" I say cheerfully, greeting the woman I've loved most of my life.

She wraps me up in a big hug, shifting me from side to side. I nearly lose my footing in the sand, and we laugh as she rights us. The sweet, pungent smell of liquor washes over me. I share a look with Mariel.

"You stink like sour nectar, Ma!" Mariel chastises, scrunching her nose. "The ceremony hasn't even started yet."

Delores laughs. "Hush, girl, and have a drink with me." She turns back to me. "You too, miss stranger. Who do you think you are, ignoring this old woman for so long?"

"You are *not* old," I retort with a laugh.

We trudge toward the hut, and as we pass, I notice the way Lachlan's eyes soften as he watches Delores pass by. How did I miss that?

Next to him, his son observes me with a similar fondness, and my smile wavers. I quickly break eye contact, my mind flitting back to the dark-haired enigma up in the temple. Why is he so adamant about avoiding us? He says that he doesn't think he's better than us, but it sure seems that way. Otherwise, I can't make sense of his aversion to the very island he claims to cherish.

We secure another round of drinks, and as the moons finalize their approach, the villagers simmer down. Only the crackle of the bonfire and the chittering of nighttime insects in the jungle fill the air.

Everyone gazes admirably at the moons, while my attention flits to the temple in the distance. I tell myself I'm watching the moonstone for any signs of flickering, but really, I'm thinking about *him.*

What is he doing all alone up there?

And before I can even register it, the moons must've successfully settled into one supermoon, because the island quickly flickers to life, startling me. The aqua and sea-green luminescent glow washes over every plant in sight. The resounding roar of excitement is deafening.

I force a smile, trying to find it in me to be happy, but for some reason, it's harder tonight.

The jungle buzzes with vitality, a faint vibration that prickles my skin. Joss and Mariel lead the way, joking amongst themselves. I stay quiet, trailing behind as I soak up the ethereal beauty around me.

I've always been more in tune with the island and its power than the others. I was young, probably around ten, when I realized not everyone feels the magic like I do. It's a subtle, melodic hum deep in my skull, a steady thrum of energy waking every cell within.

Even so, I'll never not be stunned by the magic of the island during the Union. It is fleeting, after all.

A harsh, "Ha!" grabs my attention, and I refocus on the conversation taking place in front of me.

"All you do is stand around by the water in little shorts,

showing off your muscles," Mariel says, puffing up her chest and deepening her voice to imitate Joss. "I'm a big, tough warden—I protect the island from seaweed and clams."

He swats a vine out of the way, looking amused at her. "Says the woman who reads books and twirls around in a nightie like an aloof faerie."

She gasps. "You did not call me aloof."

"A nightie?" I snort, eyeing the asymmetrical hem of Mariel's dress. "That's a sacred priestess gown, fishbrain."

We're dressed in the same outfit, with a flowy skirt and snug, thin-strapped top. Her cut showcases her full cleavage, but I have an extra layer draped across my collarbone, like a wispy scarf, for additional coverage.

Our waists are cinched with delicate chains and a moon-faced belt.

"It's timeless," Mariel mutters, sharing a look of solidarity with me.

"Elegant," I add.

Joss shoots me a crooked grin, his eyes roaming down to my bare calves and feet. "Stay out of this, Raya. We're fighting right now."

Mariel groans. "Why are we even arguing about this? Don't you have fish to fight or something?"

"It's a serious job," he insists. "You never know who or what might stumble upon our sanctuary. I need to always be prepared for battle."

"Yeah, battling waves," she mutters.

"Look at me," he says in a ridiculous, high-pitched voice. Snagging a large, leafy palm frond off the ground, he holds it over his front, pretending it's a skirt. He swishes his hips, using his thumb and forefinger to grip the material daintily. Then, he spins. "Weee, I'm just a pretty little priestess. Protecting the island from those wretched dusty tomes."

"Impressive impression. Uncanny, really," she deadpans. "I'd rather sit in the library than stare at the sea all day, waiting for nothing."

"Would you, though?" he teases. "Sounds like a real adventure—warming your chair every day."

"Okay, shells for brains." Mariel grunts, and I watch the duo with keen interest. It's not unusual for them to bicker like this, but knowing their parents are marrying each other makes it more amusing.

"You fight like siblings already," I remark with a laugh.

She makes a gagging face, sticking her tongue out. "Gross."

"He's not wrong, though, Mar," I add. She glances over her shoulder at me, a look of betrayal etched into her features. I laugh. "About your *boring* job. You weren't born to be a priestess."

"Gee, thanks," she mutters, returning her gaze to the path before us.

Joss smiles smugly, pushing ahead to lead the way.

"I think you should've been a tideborn."

"A *warden?*" Her mouth drops into an O as she slows until we're side by side.

I wave a hand with dramatic flourish. "You need the excitement, the adventure. You *love* the sea."

"Yeah, but this hair doesn't." She snorts, but her eyes gloss over in longing.

"Admit it, Mar," Joss calls to us. "You wouldn't last a day in a warden's life."

"Oh, that's bullshells, and you know it, Thalor!" She scurries back to his side, a challenge in her tone. "I'd be damned good at it."

"I bet you a month of doing laundry that you wouldn't last a week."

"I can't just leave the temple for that long!"

"You could ask Raziel for a release, you know," I call out, egging her on. "Just a week—to make Joss eat his words."

The two continue to snark at one another while I chuckle to myself.

Each leaf, vine, and blade pulses with a soft, radiant glow, like tiny, living stars illuminating our path through the trees. Their branches are woven into a dense canopy above, sealing us off from the night sky. There's a distinct sense of intimacy, almost like being enclosed in the jungle's welcoming arms.

I trip over a root and nearly go sprawling. My hands lash out, grasping onto the closest vine. A sharp pain shoots through my thumb, but I ignore it, quickly regaining my balance.

"Are you okay?" Joss is at my side in an instant, and Mariel stifles a laugh.

I roll my eyes at her, chuckling at the ridiculousness myself. After all these years in the jungle I still manage to make a fool of myself. I'm not nearly as nimble as Mariel is.

Glancing down at my thumb, my heart stalls as a small slice stares back at me. Panic overtakes me for a second.

"What is it?" Joss reaches for my hand, but I quickly bring my thumb to my mouth to suck the blood away.

"Nothing," I lie, mumbling around my thumb. "I thought I cut it, but I'm fine."

He hesitates, clearly debating whether or not to press it. His eyes flit to my feet, which, like his and Mariel's, are caked in dirt and grime. We're used to navigating barefoot; our feet are used to the abuse at this point.

"Watch your step," he murmurs, frowning at me.

Shortly after we continue, the jungle opens, spilling us into a mossy opening beside a river. Joss and Mariel halt so suddenly that I nearly crash into their backs. The air is silent other than the river's soft gurgle, neither of them speaking.

"What is it?" I plow past them to get a closer look.

Hundreds of silver-stemmed flowers sway beside the riverbanks. They sprout in abundance, giving the impression of being a weed rather than our island's most valuable asset.

"The silverdew," Mariel whispers, her tone bordering on panic.

The sight of them isn't unusual.

At first.

I quickly realize their petals are still furled into a ball, like a transparent dew drop. By this time, they should've opened, their petals unfurling to free the pollen within.

My lungs compress, leaving no room for air to enter. "Oh *no*."

CHAPTER SIXTEEN

THE ASSEMBLY

RAZIEL

*T*he rushing water spray greets me as I emerge from the temple's basement.

I wince at the bright morning sun, my slippered feet settling on the soil for the first time since last night. Holding up a hand to block out the worst of the rays, I squint and give my eyes time to adjust.

Beside me, the thin waterfall trickles down the temple's side, spilling into the stream before me. It carries the magic-infused water away, feeding it into the rivers that wind down the hillside. We can't see the magic, except during the Union when the supermoon lights everything up... or, apparently, when you're high on pollen.

I glance down at my hand, flexing it.

What would happen if the jungle lit up, the magic flaring to life outside of Union Night, like mine has been?

Then *everyone* would know I'm failing as Moon Priest, that

the island's magic is sick. I'm lucky no one else has noticed yet.

My muscles stay tense, the prospect concerning me. Bright blue skies stretch overhead, adding to my unease. It needs to rain soon. If the moonstone's pool gets any lower, the falls will stop flowing, so the magic won't be distributed throughout the island.

I don't know what's worse: the magic flaring to life on its own or the magic not flowing through the island at all.

They're both ominous in their own way.

However, I don't have time to worry about that right now; I need to change and arrive at the village in time for the Assembly.

I round the front of the temple, eager to head to my sanctum, when the sight of a small crowd stops me.

Soraya rushes down the steps toward me, a look of fury blazing in her face. Her glittering silver and white dress billows around her calves. Today, it ties around the back of her slender neck, showcasing her toned shoulders. Her brilliant hair is piled high with braids and cascading curls.

Even angered, she's so beautiful it hurts.

Her presence is the last thing I should be focused on, but it's the first thing I find solace in.

"Where were you?" she hisses.

I frown, glancing past her at the silent celestial servants watching us. "What's going on?"

"The silverdew." She lowers her voice. "It didn't open last night."

Fear washes over me. I run a hand along my jaw, contemplating what this means. "Do the others know?"

"Where were you?" she repeats, narrowing her eyes at me. "And don't lie and say you were *home*. I went up to the sanctum to warn you before everyone found out. You weren't there."

"I need to change and get to the Assembly," I say, keeping my face carefully blank as I avoid her question.

Her eyes drag down my body, taking in my wrinkled clothing. I thought I would have time to change before running into anyone like I usually do. The day after the Union is generally quiet, with most people sleeping off their indulgences or waiting in the village for the assembly.

When I glance back at Soraya, she's pale. Something akin to hurt flashes across her face as she studies me.

"Who were you with?" she asks quietly.

I glance toward the temple, not the least bit interested in speaking about this here. Or now. But at the same time, I harbor an inexplicable need to reassure her.

"I wasn't with anyone, I promise, but I need to get to town."

She flushes, nodding her head. "It's not my business anyway." A tense moment stretches between us, and questions flit through her bright blue eyes. Eventually, she sighs. "You should get ready for your meeting. I fear it'll be... eventful."

Spinning on her heel, she walks gracefully back to her fellow priests and priestesses.

"Come on, then," she commands loudly, gesturing toward the temple. "Stop gossiping and get to work."

The priests and priestesses loitering around the steps turn and file into the temple. Before entering, Soraya turns to me.

"You owe me a conversation later, High Priest," she says before slipping inside.

I exhale in gratitude, glad she didn't press me. The other celestial servants respect her, and I'm grateful she dissuaded their prying eyes.

Once I'm alone in my sanctum, I change my clothes and tie my hair back into a neat bun. I slip my cape on, fastening it near my collarbone with the Moon Priest emblem, and slide back into my leather shoes.

Before I leave, I grab my letter opener. The handle is smooth and cool to the touch. I press the tip of the blade into the tip of my finger, just enough to draw blood and see its color.

I hold my breath until a bead of red appears. A mixture of relief and disappointment flits through me.

I don't know whether to be grateful the magic is at bay or be scared for what that means for my fate.

The assembly hut is rife with tension when I enter. It's thicker than the humid air outside. An alarming level of overlapping voices fills the space, floating up the high ceilings. The tight room is packed with more bodies than usual. The rows of benches on both sides of the walkway are packed, with people standing along the back wall, too.

"—we have no export," a panicked voice says.

"Does this mean the moons are sick?"

I clench my jaw, striding to the front of the room. My head is up, my shoulders are back, and I hope I exude confidence. They need a leader right now, so I refuse to let them see me crumble.

Their fears are beyond warranted.

They're right. Without silverdew, we lose our key export. It's native only to the Isle de Lunith, blossoming under the moons' magic. We're able to distill it into nectar, harvest the pollen, or sell the plant whole for medicinal purposes.

Subsequently, this loss means we lose our bartering tool for peace with the mainland.

Nodding in greeting at Lachlan, he returns the gesture

grimly. I swing my eyes to his son, who crosses his arms, glowering at me.

"Warden," I say to the elder Thalor.

"High Priest Raziel," he says respectfully. "I fear the people need to hear from *you* today."

My neck heats at the thought of all eyes on me, judging me. But he's right. The people need their leader. They need *me* to simmer their fears.

When I don't reply, Joss steps up to us.

"Do you even care?" he challenges, chest heaving. "You hide away on Union night, avoiding everyone. For all we know, it's *your* fault! Maybe if you didn't hoard your magic—"

"Enough," the elder Thalor scolds, placing his hands on his son's chest. "He's still the Moon Priest."

"Yeah? Well, he's doing a fantastic job leading our island to the wasteland," Joss snaps, taking a step back. "Maybe he should let someone else take over."

A flurry of murmurs rises, and panic claws at my throat. I wish I could refute him, but it's no use. He's right.

"The moons chose the boy for a reason," a familiar voice says, and it's like a balm to my heart.

A second later, Kassia appears by my side. She plants a hand on my shoulder, and I fight the urge to flinch under her touch. The only thing different about her now from the woman I remember all those years ago is that she no longer wears the pale priestess garments. Instead, she dons a bright yellow slip that grazes the floor.

I can't even look her in the eye.

My heart beats wildly, and something inside me softens. It means something—that she stood up for me. That she's beside me, reaching out to me, quite literally. Instead of recoiling, I force myself to endure the pain of her affection.

"You know nothing of the sacrifices the High Priests make

for our island, and you're all the better for it," she says sternly. "You should be ashamed of yourself, Joss Thalor, for speaking blasphemy."

"Apologies, Kassia," Lachlan says, voice smooth. "High Priest Raziel." He sighs, rubbing his forehead before turning to his son. "This isn't how we do things here, and you know it. Your mother wouldn't—"

"Don't you dare," Joss threatens, his cheeks reddening. "You never even talk about her, and *now* you bring her up?" His jaw tenses, and he shakes his head. His piercing green eyes land on me. "Kassia is right, *High Priest*. We know nothing about you, even after being raised alongside you. Yet we're supposed to put our blind trust in you and believe that you're looking out for us all." He scoffs. "Well, faith only lasts for so long."

"*Jossidian Murr Thalor,*" Lachlan hisses, his normally tranquil features darkening.

"Something's wrong with you, Raziel," Joss insists, ignoring his father's warning. "And I'm going to be the one to figure it out." He storms past me, and I turn to watch him navigate the clamoring crowd and exit.

"I'm sorry about him," Lachlan says when he's gone.

"No." I shake my head. "He's right." My sights shift to Kassia. "I'm not doing a good enough job, and I'm letting everyone down."

The door opens again, and Soraya slips inside. She sneaks to an open space along the wall in the back, standing awkwardly. I've never seen her at the Assembly before.

Kassia pats my shoulder again and shuffles down the hallway toward the back of the room. She stands beside Soraya, murmuring to her. Then the old woman reaches out to grasp her hand in unity, and a strange jealousy flickers through me.

Kassia raised her; it shouldn't be surprising how close they are.

But it's the pain of what could've been.

Averting my gaze, I give Lachlan a solemn nod and climb the few steps of the wooden dais at the front of the room. The chatter quickly dies down, and everyone turns their attention to me.

"Greetings, Isle de Lunith. We meet after another blessed Union—"

"*Blessed?*" a man sputters, jumping to his feet in the middle of the room.

Chatter flares back to life, and I grit my teeth. A surge of anxiety builds in my chest. My instinct is to retreat and distance myself from their scrutiny to preserve the illusion of my competency.

But I've stayed hidden for so long. Right now, they need to hear it from me.

"Enough!" I roar so loudly that a muscle in my neck tenses. The room quickly dies out, going so silent I can hear my blood whooshing in my head. "I understand you're frustrated, and I'm aware of the situation. If you'd let me speak, we can dive into your concerns momentarily."

I pause, waiting to see if anyone will challenge me again. To my relief, no one speaks. The villagers gape at me with various expressions of surprise, intrigue, and wariness.

"I stand by my words: Yes, it *was* a blessed Union." My heart thuds violently, but I keep my voice steady. "The moons merged, the moonstone absorbed the magic, and our little island is *alive* to see another month."

"But the silverdew," someone murmurs.

"The silverdew didn't open. Yes, I understand the gravity of the situation." *More than they know.* "However, panicking will do us no good. We need to act strategically until we figure out what the issue is. We might not have pollen for trade this month, but we *will* have silverdew flowers and nectar. As long as the flowers continue to grow, we can work around this minor obstacle."

"What if they don't grow back?" another villager yells.

"Then we will deal with it then. Right now, I'm focusing on the present, not hypothetical concerns."

Hushed whispers spread like wildfire through the group.

I raise my hands, silencing them again. "Rest assured, I am doing everything I can to investigate this. I'm looking into—"

"Are you?" the initial man who challenged me asks, crossing his arms. He narrows me with a dark gaze. "Joss Thalor was right. You hide in your temple and keep your magic from us."

Lachlan interrupts, trying to get the crowd to settle down. But it's no use; questions begin to crop up around the room from every direction.

"Do you even have magic?" someone else asks, causing speculation to erupt. "How do we even know you're the High Priest?"

"Where were you last night?"

"He was hiding because he doesn't have magic!"

"The island is dying because he's not a real Moon Priest!"

The villagers' frantic voices take over, hurling accusations that I don't possess magic or the approval of the goddesses.

Pressure builds in my chest, and heat creeps up my neck. They're waiting for answers, expecting me to share more than I'm willing. Worse, they want me to have it all figured out, and I—*I don't*. My voice sticks in my throat, and I freeze.

I can feel their eyes on me, sharp with judgment.

I'm failing them.

I'm dishonoring the moons.

Sweat beads on my brow, and the panic continues to rise.

What if I can't fix this? It'll only get worse.

A loud whistle cuts through the noise. My head snaps up. Soraya gestures for someone to move off a bench, and she climbs atop it, a fierce look overtaking her face.

Her hands are balled into fists, and her cheeks are flushed. My gut sinks. She's had enough of my elusiveness. I should've realized she'd choose the village over me. I don't blame her.

Sucking in a deep breath, I steel my spine and brace myself for what she has to say.

It's my own fault, after all.

I'll take the backlash.

"High Priest Raziel is *not* a false prophet," she yells, her voice admirably steady. The energy of the room shifts, and everyone turns to face her. She meets my gaze, inclining her chin. "He *does* have magic."

Whispers erupt like a swarm of restless bees buzzing. I wince, knowing I've officially failed at my role.

"How do you know?" the same skeptical man yells.

"Because..." She smiles. "I've seen it myself."

"Bullshells!" a woman yells.

Pausing, Soraya waits for the excitement to die down before she says, "The reason you don't see it is because you're all too busy partying on the beach during the Union. While High Priest Raziel is sacrificing his free time, his life, to absorb the magic we thrive on."

Confusion rumbles through the room.

"It's not the moonstone that absorbs the magic during the Union—it's Raziel. *He's* the conduit, and without him, our island would wither."

The lie takes me by surprise, slamming into my chest with a force I hadn't expected. I'm paralyzed for a moment, my mind racing to catch up. Something resembling warmth spreads through me, unexpected and unwelcome.

She's covering for me. She lied for me—publicly.

It's a strange feeling, and I can't quite explain it. She holds my stare, her face softening as she gazes at me with something akin to reverence.

But why?

I'm failing her and letting everyone down.

"He gives his *all* to you, to the island!" Soraya's voice rises with conviction.

Slowly, the villagers turn their attention back to me. This time, many of their expressions match Soraya's. For the first time in a long time, I'm greeted with a sign of respect as the villagers bow their heads and murmur their blessings.

CHAPTER SEVENTEEN

THE KISS

SORAYA

*a*fter the assembly calms down, I'm tempted to follow Raziel back to the temple immediately. Instead, Mariel invites me to her ma's house for lunch. Already feeling guilty about the rift between us, I accept.

The modest two-story hut greets me like an old friend. The sweet, nearly overpowering scent of nectar and Delores's coconut cream brings forth a wave of nostalgia.

The dining room is decorated as it's always been, with a table fit for six nestled neatly in the center. Abstract art of waves and whorls lines the walls, making the space feel even tighter.

"Thanks for inviting me for lunch," I say to Delores across the driftwood table.

She and Lachlan swap tender smiles. Her chair groans as she reaches over to grasp my hand. Her soft skin is warm against mine. "Stop with the formalities. You're as much a daughter to me as Mar is."

Mariel kicks me gently, shooting me a told-you-so look. Joss, having picked up on it, laughs from my other side. We pile our plates with salt-crusted fish, roasted breadfruit, and stuffed plantains. The savory scents cause my mouth to water. Delores is a damn good cook.

We eat in silence, all of us too busy appreciating the meal.

"Oh, let me get the nectar," Delores says when we finish, causing Mariel to sigh. "I also made a loaf of cinnamon bread for you, Soraya."

She smiles widely at me, wiggling her brows, and I chuckle. "I knew I loved you for a reason."

"I'll help you prepare it." Lachlan rises to his feet, offering Delores a hand. He's so tall that he ducks through the threshold into the kitchen at the back of the house.

"I wish she'd lay off the juice," Mariel mutters.

"She'll have to with the silverdew dying," Joss says flatly, and I frown.

I can feel his gaze burning into the side of my head, so I turn. Sure enough, his bright green eyes bore into me, his brows drawn together in frustration.

Sighing, I hold his stare. "Just say it, Joss." He's been in a mood since the assembly.

"I need water." Mariel shoots up from her chair, causing the table to rattle with the movement. She vanishes into the kitchen before I tell her not to leave.

Joss leans back, putting space between us as he crosses his arms. "You defended him."

Annoyance buzzes like a gnat inside me. "You weren't even there, Joss, and yes, I did. He's our High Priest."

"He certainly doesn't act like it."

"You don't know anything about him!" I catch my voice

rising, and I rein it back in. "You're supposed to be our next Chief Warden, and you're certainly not acting like one right now," I hiss.

Hurt flashes across his face, and a muscle in his jaw twitches. "I just want the best for the island."

"So does he," I insist, refusing to back down.

He shakes his head. "I hope you're right, Soraya. We've known him our entire life, but have we ever really *known* him?"

"Then maybe make the first effort, Joss, instead of waiting for him to be something he's not."

"Why don't you take your own advice and stop pretending, Soraya?" He reaches for me, but I swat him away.

"Joss—*don't.*" I lower my voice, leaning toward him. "Not here."

"Why not?" He cracks a cocky grin. "Because you know that if they knew the truth,"—he gestures toward the other room where Lachlan, Delores, and Mariel laugh and converse together—"they'd agree with me."

I stand, tossing my napkin down on the table. "Tell Delores thank you, but I need to get to the temple. I'm late for work."

"Don't go," he says as he makes to follow me. "I'll leave instead."

"No. This is your home now."

"Raya—no. Don't run away."

I pause, giving him a sad smile. "I'm not, Joss. I just don't have time to bicker." Not when the island's magic is dying. It's up to me and Raziel to fix it before the villagers notice. They're usually oblivious, having complete faith in the Moon Priest.

The thought of leaving cinnamon bread behind pains me, but ignoring my responsibilities to the island for leisure time is worse.

It's only a matter of time before it starts to affect the people I care about, too.

———

The air is thick and muggy. My legs are heavy by the time I get back to the temple. Instead of entering the library, I round the building and climb the endless stairs to the sanctum.

The moment I step onto the roof, I'm met with an angry grunt.

I freeze, searching for the source.

At first, I don't see Raziel until I hear a splash of water.

He stands in the shallow pool, with his hands on the moonstone and his eyes closed. His forehead is wrinkled, and the muscles in his body are tense. He shifts his hands, pressing his palms flat against the giant gem.

Nothing is happening, and I'm unsure of what he's trying to do.

I quietly make my way over to him, watching with burning interest. After a few seconds of him mumbling and grunting to himself, I can't hold back anymore.

"What are you doing?" I blurt.

He jolts and locks his scowl onto me. It would be haunting if I didn't know him well enough to know he's annoyed at the intrusion. "What are you doing here, Soraya?"

"Why are you in the water?" I peer over the pool's edge, frowning when I see how low the level is.

Usually, the water is deep, up to my waist, and is replenished frequently through rainfall. But that's not the only thing unusual. The moonstone's colors are duller than they were last time, fading into a smoky grey.

My heart clenches. "What's wrong with the moonstone?"

Without an answer, Raziel splashes through the shallow

water. He's still in his leather slippers and pants, the water soaking his calves. He hoists himself onto the pool's ledge. Without his cape, I can make out the way his muscles strain against his dark shirt. A few tendrils of his hair fall free around his face, framing his trimmed scruff and endlessly deep brown eyes.

My cheeks heat, and I turn away to give him privacy, like I'm invading a personal moment.

When he settles onto the wall and sighs, I face him.

"I've never seen the water level so low," I murmur.

Sometimes it rains above the temple's pool only, the clouds drawn to the moonstone late in the night, as if summoned by the pull of magic, so it's unlikely the villagers would be aware of this situation.

Regardless, it's incredibly concerning.

"If it doesn't rain soon..." He pushes his hair back out of his face and hangs his head. "It'll be worse than the silverdew."

"The clouds are rolling in." I point toward the beach, where grey gathers on the horizon.

"Yeah, but it never goes this long without raining up here. Things are changing, Soraya. The island's magic is sick. Look at the stone!"

I lean against the pool's stone wall, and for a few moments, we simply exist, simmering in the shared dread. I can tell he doesn't want my optimism; he's sharing a sliver of his emotions with me, and I'll honor the space he needs to process.

"Yeah," I finally say, "it is. Do you think that's why the silverdew didn't open? The moonstone doesn't have enough magic to feed the island?"

He sets his jaw, staring straight ahead.

"What were you doing in there?" I ask a second time, unwilling to let him keep avoiding my questions.

"Trying to infuse my magic into the moonstone," he mutters, glancing away as if embarrassed. "Since I'm the *conduit* for magic and all."

"Is anything happening?"

His gaze snaps to mine. A shadow brews in his irises. "Of course it isn't."

"But you tried." It tells me that he's desperate, perhaps out of potential solutions.

A few beats of tense silence pass before he says, "Why'd you lie at the Assembly?"

"Did I?" Raising a brow, I hold his stare without backing down despite the hyperawareness of how close we are. It sends a flurry of butterflies through my stomach, but I don't react outwardly. "I thought that's what your magic did," I say carefully.

My tone is coy and full of implications, but he knows as well as I do that I exaggerated the truth in front of the villagers.

He stares, unblinking. "Really, Soraya."

"Fine." I fiddle with the silver chain around my midsection to distract my hands. "I believe in you, and contrary to their assumptions, you're a good High Priest. Maybe I don't need to know all the details to know that."

His body goes still, and for a second, I think he might not be breathing. Then, he slowly exhales and turns his head to me. "Not good enough."

"Let me help you then," I command softly. "You need to let me help you so you can help all of us."

"No."

"That's unacceptable." I grow increasingly annoyed at his refusal to budge. "We're going in circles, and there's only so much I can do—"

"You can continue going through the texts, like I requested."

There's no point in arguing. I've been more than content to sift through the archives, which I'm wholly familiar with from over the years, because I thought he'd eventually share more with me.

I tilt my head, studying him. "What happened to you? To make you so... distrustful."

"Soraya..." He says my name like a prayer. Then he sighs and hangs his head. His shoulders slump, and my heart does the same, wilting.

Striding closer, I hesitate right before I reach him. "Raziel?"

He stays perched on the pool's wall, legs dangling. When he finally looks up, his eyes shimmer.

"May I touch you?" I whisper.

His muscles tense, then he nods once, stiffly.

Cautiously, so as not to frighten him away, I draw closer, stepping between his legs. I rest my hands on his shoulders, and my palms buzz to life. "You're not alone anymore."

"You don't understand..." he says hoarsely.

"I do, though. I understand more than you think."

"No. None of you do." Fury flashes in his eyes, and I see him shutting down before me. Any traces of vulnerability are washed out to sea. "You have no idea what it means to be Moon Priest, to need—"

I swiftly move in, pressing my lips to his and cutting off his words. A powerful surge, like liquid lightning, zaps through me. I gasp into the kiss, my eyes flicking open to catch him staring back. He doesn't give in to it, but he also doesn't pull away.

We're frozen, our mouths touching and hearts beating erratically.

Suddenly, thunder claps through the sky, and I jerk

backward. I barely have time to glance up before the sky breaks and fat raindrops splatter down on my skin.

"See?" Raziel clears his throat. He closes his eyes, tilting his face up as he murmurs, "Maybe it's fixed... Maybe I don't need help after all."

I laugh, first in shock, but it quickly turns bitter. A foreign, unwelcome pang surges through my heart.

"What's so funny?" he asks, turning his attention back to me.

"This!" I gesture between us. "The difference between the two of us."

"I don't understand."

"*I* took the rain as a sign that the two of us working together is right..." My lungs constrict as I stare at him, wearing all my vulnerability on my face. "And *you* took it as a sign that you don't need me." My voice cracks, and I hate how small I feel.

I should've known Raziel would never let me in, never want me. Not the way I've wanted him for longer than I care to admit.

Perhaps he's onto something with his dedication to avoiding distractions. Because so far, all I've managed to do is become distracted by him.

When I stand, I incline my chin and stare him down. He looks past me, purposely refusing eye contact. After a long, drawn-out moment, with only the pattering rain filling our ears, I sigh.

"You get your wish," I whisper. "I'm done, Raziel Kasper."

CHAPTER EIGHTEEN

THE TURMOIL

RAZIEL

*O*ne week.

It's been a whole week since she pressed her lips against mine, and still, her taste lingers. Soft and sweet, just like her.

I stare at the moonstone pool, listening to the steady trickle of water as it flows over the edges of the temple.

One crisis averted.

However, the moonstone is still a sickly, faded version of its usual glimmering beauty, and the silverdew still hasn't opened. It's growing, at least, and we've harvested extra for nectar instead to make up for what we'll miss in pollen for the trade. As a result, the wardens had a late start on trade this month.

Everything is messed up and out of order.

My routine is botched.

My heart is in knots.

I stare down at my left hand, cursing the marking that condemned me to this position. My magic is increasingly erratic. Is this because I'm nearing the end? The magic will soon burn out, consuming me as well.

I feel like a prisoner, threatened by the fickle status of the moonlight within me. I want to leave my sanctum and mingle with the villagers for the first time in many years.

With *her*.

But now, ironically, I'm trapped—a prisoner to my magic.

If Soraya knew the full truth, she'd flee far away and never look at me again. Moons, she'd probably inform the village, and they'd lock me away in the temple's dungeon permanently. But I don't want that.

My head falls, and I shake it, exhaling a heavy breath.

I've barely been able to focus. All I can think about is that kiss with Soraya. It broke me, yet it was somehow healing. Every day since, I've cut myself, hoping to see red again so I could chase after her, desperate for something I can't name.

Reaching into my pocket, I pull out the letter opener that stays glued to my side these days. I press the pad of my finger to the tip of the blade. Adding a little pressure, I grit my teeth, begging to see red.

A small silver drop trickles out. My shoulders fall. The blade slips from my hand, clattering on the stone floor. Panic shoots through me.

Why is it lingering for so long?

I *feel* okay—in control. But if the moonblood is coursing through me, it's only a matter of time before…

I can't do this. Not now.

I need to get it out. I don't know how or if it's even possible, but I need to try. Maybe now that the pool is refilled, the moonstone can absorb my magic.

My heart races, panic building in my throat as I rip off my

cloak and shirt. Unbuckling my pants, I slip them down my ankles and kick off my shoes.

Anxiety propels me forward, and I climb over the stone wall around the pool, plunging into the lukewarm water. When I emerge, I suck in a deep breath and smooth my hair back out of my face. The water comes up to my chest now, and the rain continues each night, refilling the pool.

Why can't everything else go back to normal, too?

I don't know what I'm doing wrong.

Wading over to the moonstone, I press my palms against its glassy surface, desperate to infuse my magic into the vessel.

It absorbs the moons' magic, so why can't it do the same for me?

I've never tried this before last week, when Soraya caught me. I never needed to. It was her little lie at the assembly that gave me the idea. Maybe I just need to get the magic *out*. Perhaps that's how I'll survive this damn curse.

The island needs it more than I do, anyway. I do nothing with it.

Maybe Kassia—

No. I grimace at the thought. I'm not selfish enough to bring her into this mess.

My mind flits back to what happened *that* night.

Blood. So much blood.

The scent of copper, the sound of her pained cries.

Images flicker through my mind, causing nausea to roil in my stomach. My hands tremble, and I keep them on the moonstone. My head hangs between my arms, and I focus on not letting the past catch up with me.

There's a reason my life is empty and lonely.

My chest wells with emotion, and it builds so quickly that I fear I'll explode. The magic churns inside me, refusing to come out. But it responds to my feelings, as if excited at the prospect of losing control. The steady thump of my pulse in my temples intensifies; adrenaline urges it to beat faster and faster.

Why couldn't I have magic like Amos's? His was a calming wave of energy he could send outward, to relax others.

Every Union, he'd give me a blast of it large enough to knock me out for the night. Part of me blames him for what happened to Kassia. If he had taught me how to control my magic instead of subduing me, maybe this wouldn't be happening now.

If he had chosen *me* over his selfish indulgences—

A creak grabs my attention. My head lifts, my eyes locking with Soraya's across the roof. She stands hesitantly in front of the door, like she's not sure whether to turn back around or approach me.

The sight of her stirs my insides, and my left palm heats in warning.

"Soraya," I say, my voice cracking. I slowly back away from the moonstone and wade toward the pool's edge.

Carefully, I lift myself up and over the wall. She stays rooted in place, watching me with her head tilted and lips parted. When my feet hit the stone, I freeze.

Her eyes drag down my body, her cheeks flushing when they land on my shorts. They're no more revealing than the warden's sea shorts, but it's more skin than I usually show.

"Raziel," she whispers, voice strained. Her cheeks turn pink, and she sucks in a long breath. She snaps her eyes back up to my face.

There's so much I want to say to her. Instead, the thoughts of *that* night—of Kassia's wounds—replay in my mind. Except now, it's Soraya's face I envision instead.

It's Soraya I see lying in her own blood.

The rage, the terror, it stirs up the magic within me.

"You shouldn't be here," I say flatly.

Her features distort, and she pauses. "I was just coming to see if you... Never mind. I'm sorry for bothering you." Her voice is strained, and she shakes her head.

"Just go," I mutter, clenching my hand into a fist.

She squares her shoulders and gives me a nod. Even with her pride hurt, she's something fierce and confident. *Special.* That's what she is.

Calmly and quietly, she turns and heads back to the stairwell, disappearing out of sight without a single look back.

A long, steady exhale pours from my lungs. I unclench my hand, taking inventory of my palm: no sign of magic. The noise in my head quiets, and my pulse calms down enough that I debate going after her.

I'm not sure I can trust myself, though, so I shake it off and trudge to my chambers.

After poring over Demetrius's journal for the third time this week, I gently close it and push it aside. Reading between the lines won't magically provide me with answers.

Instead of doing the same thing I've been doing and getting nowhere, perhaps it's time to try something new.

I exit onto the roof, striding past the moonstone. I try not to let the stone's dimming light raise my blood pressure. Instead, I reach the edge of the roof and lean my elbows on the stone barrier. Even with the sun slumbering, the stone is warm beneath my skin.

Sucking in a breath of sea-tinged air, I glance toward the village at the base of the mountain. Small, orange torch lights flicker along the beach. Faint musical notes reach my ears. Joyous squeals send a pain of longing through me.

Is Soraya down there? Is she happy?

Did she escape to the trees with the warden again?

The last thought, a viper's strike to the heart, sends a surge of white-hot jealousy through me.

Before I can talk myself out of it, I'm trudging through the jungle down to the beach. I take a detour, passing by the River of Rest.

When the tree where Joss and Soraya were all those weeks ago stands silent and empty, my muscles loosen.

I follow the river, trailing to the end of the jungle where it meets the sea. Dozens of people spread out on the beach. Some are in the water, partaking in a competition. Others root them on from the shore.

People pour out of the Nectar Hut, standing in line as they eagerly await their drinks. They stand two or three deep, lining up around the side of the old shack and down the beach.

I can't help but frown. How can they drink so carelessly, even after knowing the precious resource is threatened? How can they party and dance and celebrate, even after the palpable rage of the assembly last week?

Either the villagers are even more careless than I imagined… or they're more trusting and resilient than I've given them credit for.

A flash of blue-green, like a tropical bird's feather, catches my attention, and my gaze fixates on Soraya. Her graceful twirling mesmerizes me, and all other thoughts fade. Her bare feet dig into the sand, yet she manages not to stumble.

Even from afar, with her eyes closed, the bliss on her face is clear.

She's comfortable in her skin, in nature. She's free, encompassing, and loving—everything I'm not. She moves with the effortless grace of the tide. Her ethereal beauty is blinding, as if she's made of magic and moonlight.

She's *beautiful*.

No, beautiful doesn't quite capture the stunning quality of her being.

I've always thought she was miraculous, ever since we were children. She was a teal-haired curiosity with the most beautiful eyes I'd ever seen. It was like she was made of the sky and sea, wielding an essence of each in physical form.

Kassia raised her, and I used to watch them from afar. At first with envy, then with a renewed dedication to doing my job well.

It was the two of them, combined with my father's frivolity, that inspired me to commit myself fully to being the best protector the island ever had.

My eyes shift, meeting Kassia's. She tilts her head, and her face drops as if she's seen a ghost. Instantly, I'm brought back to that night. Guilt floods me. I turn and flee back to my safe space. Away from everyone I could hurt.

CHAPTER NINETEEN

THE STORM

SORAYA

*T*he next Union is only a week away. That's two whole Union cycles since I first noticed something was wrong with the moonstone.

And I was right: the magic is sick. Raziel's power is erratic. The smaller moon is dimmer. The silverdew still hasn't opened.

And I have no idea where Raziel's head is at or what he's even discovered, if anything.

At least it's raining. I mean, it's raining a little *too* much, soaking the entire island through, but it's better than no rain at all.

Lightning flashes through the window, followed by the rumbling crack of thunder. I perch on the edge of my bed, sighing at the sight beyond. I'm off today, given a day of rest, and I want to see Kassia. The elder priestess usually has just the advice I need.

Everyone's on edge lately, Mariel and Joss included, and Raziel is as elusive as ever.

When lunchtime rolls around, I head to the cafeteria. I perk up when I spot Mariel and Joss, but they greet me warily. After snagging my food, I approach their table with caution.

"Hi," Mariel says quickly, averting her gaze to her plate.

We've barely spoken lately. Things have been strained, and I know my leaving her ma's early didn't help things. To make matters worse, Joss continues to have an attitude with me.

"First the silverdew, now the rain," Joss mutters, stabbing his coconut noodles aggressively with a fork. "Signs the moons are unhappy, clearly."

I sigh, bracing myself as I slide into the seat beside Mariel. "I see we're still on that."

"Don't start," Mariel warns, side-eying me.

Her tone causes my chest to ache something fierce. Tears form in my eyes, but I blink them back. I hate how fractured our group has been lately.

"I said I was sorry, Mariel," I whisper. I even returned to Delores's home and apologized to her in person after Joss left that day. *She* wasn't at all upset with me.

"It's disrespectful," she says without looking at me. "Ma went through all the trouble to host lunch *and* make your favorite treat, and you left without so much as a thanks."

I scowl at Joss, even though I know it's not entirely his fault. He glowers at me, stuffing a forkful of noodles into my mouth.

"Joss is right," Mariel says, finally turning toward me. "All this time with the High Priest is affecting you poorly."

"I haven't even seen him all week," I say defensively.

"Yeah, and we've barely seen *you* all week," Joss mumbles. "I don't like who you're becoming."

"Maybe Raziel should've sent you back to the mainland again this month," I mutter, pushing my plate away.

"Soraya!" Mariel gasps, staring at me with disappointment.

I instantly regret the words, my gut churning with shame. "Joss, I'm so—"

"It's fine," he says quickly. "Maybe you're right." He gets up and leaves while Mariel continues to frown at me.

"He didn't deserve that," she chides.

I sigh. "I know."

"I don't know what's going on with you lately, but I want my friend back," she whispers. Following Joss's example, she stands, taking both of their plates and putting them on the dish cart before leaving me behind.

Ironically, all my life, all I wanted was to feel normal—loved and accepted by my friends. Yet despite everything I've done to prevent it, here I am, feeling more alone than ever.

On my way to Kassia's, rain pelts me. The cool drops are a welcome reprieve. They snap me out of my head, bringing me to the present. The storm can't hurt me any more than my own feelings already have.

I head down the mountain's gentle slope toward the village. My bare feet slide in the mud, and I think about Raziel's comment on footwear. It makes me frown harder. I plant my hands on a nearby palm tree to steady myself and cast a scathing glance upward.

"Where the hell are you going in this storm?" The stern voice sends a shiver down my body.

A very angry and very soaked Raziel stomps his way toward me. Mud swallows his slippered feet, splashing onto the bottom of his fitted pants, yet he pays it no mind.

"Why are you following me again?" My words are almost lost to the torrent of raindrops falling around us.

"You shouldn't be out here in the storm."

"Said like someone who cares." It's petty, but I can't help it. After Mariel and Joss, I don't have the patience or energy for this. I'm letting everyone down lately.

Seems it's all I'm good at these days.

"I do care, Soraya." He's suddenly at my side, squinting at me through the rain. His hair is matted to his head, and droplets cling to his thick lashes. His mouth twists into a frustrated frown.

"No, if you cared, you'd let me in. You only care about what I can do for you." The ache in my chest grows. I rub the wet fabric sticking to the spot, wishing there was something I could take to make it go away. But not even all the silverdew in the world could fix the pain.

Balling my hands into fists, I stomp away from him, intending to continue my trek down the hillside through the trees.

"Why are you so utterly infuriating?" he yells after me.

I whirl around, raising my voice so he can hear me over the rain. "ME? *I'm* infuriating?"

"Beyond!" He grips his hair, his eyes flashing with desperation. "You're downright maddening."

"I've only been trying to *help* you, and now my friends are mad at me!"

"That's your own fault. I've said I don't need your help."

"All that time alone must've melted your brain, because obviously you do." I flick my wrist toward the sky. "Take a look around, Raziel! The damn rain wouldn't come, and now it won't stop."

"No, that time alone is what helps me think clearly. Being around *you* is what's thrown everything off."

I stumble backward, his harsh words a blow to my chest. "Is that how you really feel?"

Only the relentless patter of rain on the jungle plants around us fills the air. My chest heaves as I sit with my emotions. What's the point of all this?

"Tell me, Raziel, why are you such an uptight prick?" The fight leaves me, and my voice is defeated. "Why can't you ever loosen up and have fun? What's the truth there?"

"Because I'm the one keeping you all safe while *you* live carefree!" he roars, shoving his soaked hair out of his face. His chest heaves, and he looks so wild, so unlike his normal self, that it takes my anger down a few notches.

"Then let me help you at least," I say quietly.

"This island is *my* responsibility." He slaps his chest, the wet material squishing at the impact. "I'm responsible for everyone and everything here; I can't afford to get distracted. I can't let the goddesses down. I can't let you down."

His voice cracks at the end. The way he says *you* tells me he's not only referring to me but to the island as a whole.

"Raziel," I whisper, my voice barely audible above the rain. I take a step forward and then another until I'm in front of him. Reaching up, I gently cup his cheek. "You deserve as much as you give everyone else."

His eyes flit shut, and he leans into my palm, his anger evaporating. Whatever this is, I know he feels it too.

"You don't have to be perfect to be valued," I say, my thumb stroking his scruff. "You're enough as is. You give us your all. We all see how hard you work, and nothing could ever erase your dedication to this island, to the moons."

His eyes whip open, and a storm brews within those dark irises. His hand comes up and covers mine, holding it there. "I wish it were that simple."

"It can be." Only a few inches separate our faces, barely

enough room for the raindrops to fall between us. I swallow down my nerves and take a risk. "If you could do one thing without fearing vulnerability, irresponsibility, or whatever it is that haunts you, then what would you do?"

His eyes drop to my lips, and my breath stutters. He swallows, his throat bobbing heavily with the movement. His hand drops from mine, and disappointment floods me.

"This," he murmurs, catching me off guard as he grips my face in his hands and brings his mouth to mine.

His lips are soft and gentle, and they move hesitantly against mine. My insides burn with urgency. There's a frenetic energy within me, begging me to take charge, to kiss him with all the hidden passion I've stuffed down. But I force myself to slow down, to live in this moment.

It's his choice to kiss me, and I want him to set the pace since I'm not sure how much he's comfortable with. Plus, this might be the only piece of Raziel I get, and I want to relish it for eternity.

When he continues to explore my mouth, with no sign of letting up, I allow my arms to snake behind his neck. In a surprising move, he groans against me, hoisting me up with ease. I wrap my legs around him, and he stumbles back until he hits a tree.

We're soaked to the bone, our clothes sticking to our bodies. Raziel's strong hands grip my bottom firmly, squeezing me tightly to him. His erection prods my core, impossible to ignore between us. My hips move of their own accord, grinding down against him.

He hisses, quickly pulling his lips from mine and setting me down on my feet.

"I can't," he says, whirling away from me and leaning his forehead against the tree. His arm comes up overhead, and he slaps the bark.

"Raziel," I whisper, placing a hand on his shoulder.

He shakes me off, and the rejection slices deeper than I expect. I blink in confusion at the unexpected withdrawal.

"You shouldn't have kissed me like that then," I mutter, cheeks flaming with embarrassment.

"I know," he says hoarsely, refusing to look at me. "I'm sorry." Then he whirls around, sadness glinting in his deep, brown eyes. "You asked me what my one thing would be. That was it."

"Yeah, but I didn't mean that it literally had to be—"

"That was my *one* moment," he reinforces sternly. "That's it, Soraya."

Tears well in my eyes, and I thank the goddesses for the pouring rain so this man can't see me cry. I've never cried over a man before, not even Joss. I guess it's a day for many firsts.

Nodding in understanding, I turn and leave Raziel alone in the jungle, drowning in both his sorrow and the rain.

One day, he'll realize it's more exhausting to push me away than it is to just let me in.

I only hope that it's not too late by the time he finally succumbs.

"I knew something was going on between you two," a familiar voice calls. Hurt laces his tone. "That's why you broke things off with me, isn't it?"

I turn to catch Joss studying me carefully. The frown looks out of place on his normally jovial face. Rain sluices down his naked chest. I glance down at my own body, overly aware of how the thin material is plastered against my curves. The normally pale material is stained with mud, betraying my tumble through the mud.

"It's storming," I say lamely. "I should go change."

"You kissed him."

I sigh as Joss crosses the small strip of grass between us. "Yes, Joss, I did. And he rejected me. Are you happy now?"

His frown deepens as he peers down at me. "Why would that make me *happy*, Soraya?"

Shaking my head, I open my mouth to speak, but the words lodge in my throat. My eyes well with tears again, and I choke them back.

"Is that what you think of me?" he says quietly. His voice is barely audible over the slap of rain around us. If I thought he was hurt before, it's nothing compared to how his features fall now. "If it is, then it's no wonder we never stood a chance."

Without waiting for me to respond, he turns and strides toward the trees.

"Joss, wait," I call after him.

He pauses, turning back toward me. "I loved you, Soraya. I still do. I'm not selfish enough to wish for your misery. I only want you safe and happy."

"Then stop being the cause of my pain, Joss."

He flinches at my words, then he runs a hand over his short hair. "Fuck, I'm sorry, okay?"

"You owe Raziel an apology, too."

"After he made you cry?" He crosses his arms with a scoff.

I narrow my eyes, squinting through the rain. "Were you eavesdropping?"

"Moons, no," he says with such sincerity that I believe him. "I just… I don't know about him, and I wanted to make sure you were okay. You're still my friend, Soraya. Truly."

"If you're really my friend, just apologize to Raziel and stop interfering in… whatever's going on between us."

"Fine. I know I was an ass at the assembly," he admits,

surprising me. "With the silverdew issue, it's more important than ever that we have a united front."

I nod, unclenching my jaw. "He's been training for this role ever since he was a child," I say. "Our childhoods were rigorous, but his was downright stifling. Imagine what a pressure that must be, knowing you've been chosen by the moons—that your destiny is to live for everyone else." I rub my chest, that same spot growing warm again. It's been irritating me more than normal lately. "He cares a lot, Joss. Too much."

Which is why he pushed me away and hurt me. As much as I hate it, I can understand it. I can't change him.

"Shells," Joss groans, pinching the bridge of his nose and briefly shutting his eyes. "We just... I just... Where do we go from here, Soraya? The silverdew is *everything* to our island."

That sinking feeling threatens to drag me under. He doesn't even know all of it. If he did...

He continues, "Maybe Raziel isn't the right person to protect our magic. Maybe it's supposed to—"

"Joss. *No.*"

"Think about it," he presses. "You know I'm right."

"It'll be okay," I murmur, the lie rolling off easily. Maybe it's because deep down, I genuinely believe it's the truth. "If anyone can fix it, it's Raziel."

Thunder booms through the sky again, causing me to jump.

Joss glances over his shoulder, then back to me. "Look, I have to go. We'll catch up properly later, right?"

Despite the productive conversation, Joss's face is pinched in pain. It sends a surge of guilt through me, knowing that I've contributed to it.

I step toward him, wanting to give him further reassurance that things are fine between us, but he shakes his head, brushing me off. He turns and picks up into a jog, his bare feet splashing through the puddles.

"I'm sorry," I mumble pointlessly, even though he's out of sight.

My heart hurts for both Raziel and Joss, but for different reasons. One man is great but doesn't see it, and the other is great, but *I* didn't see it. If Joss felt even a fraction of this after I rejected him, then he truly is a great man to stick around and be my friend.

Why couldn't I love Joss the way he loves me?

Instead, my stupid little heart thumps harder at the thought of the High Priest, even after his rejection. I don't think I could ever be just friends with Raziel, not after seeing the bits of his fractured soul and wanting to glue them to my own.

The thought tastes like ash on my tongue, but I swallow it down and head toward the temple to dry off.

CHAPTER TWENTY

THE PUNCH

RAZIEL

*L*ong after Soraya leaves, I stand among the trees, staring in the direction she went. She deserves better. Why can't I give her what she wants?

My lip aches where her teeth nipped me. I swipe it away.

Red.

The rain quickly washes it from my hand, so I tilt my head up as if it can wash all my sins away.

The relief is short-lived because something moves in my peripheral, and my eyes widen as I spot an enraged Joss Thalor stomping toward me. I haven't seen him since the assembly, and it's clear he still hasn't let it go.

"I'm working on the silverdew problem," I yell in exasperation. "Back off."

He doesn't slow his momentum. "It's not about the silverdew!" he roars. "I warned you not to fuck with her."

I groan, not in the mood for this. He cracks his knuckles,

eyes locked onto me with vengeance. It doesn't take a genius to realize his intention.

"Hit me and get it over with, Thalor—"

I see spots as his fist flashes out and cracks against my cheekbone, and surprise zings through me. Part of me underestimated him, not thinking he'd actually go through with it. Spitting blood, I'm relieved that it's red and not silver.

Joss is the *last* person I'd want to explain that to.

I find my balance and meet his eyes. Rage simmers beneath the surface, and instinctively, I know he's not done with me.

"One hit—you get one hit in, and then I'm fighting back." I grip the neckline of my shirt, yanking it until all the buttons pop off, leaving my chest as bare as his. I toss the fabric, discarding it in the mud.

Joss's brows flick up animatedly, then he smiles, taking on a fighting stance. I mirror him, staggering my feet and lifting my fists.

His eyes drop down my chest. I might not be quite as broad as him, but my muscle mass rivals the warden's. It's clear he didn't expect that, and it gives me a sick sense of satisfaction.

"Ahhh, so the priest fights," he says appraisingly.

"And the warden picks the fights," I shoot back, decidedly less amused by our predicament. "With the *High Priest*, no less. Your father would be disappointed."

He smirks, circling me like a keen predator. "Good thing the mellow bastard isn't here to spectate this ass-kicking then, eh?"

"Good thing he taught me how to fight, eh?"

Joss falters, unable to hide his surprise. It quickly morphs into hurt. "What?"

A smile buds on my lips. Normally, I wouldn't enjoy causing pain, but Joss got himself into this. All I'm doing is telling the truth. "You didn't know? Lachlan has been training me since I was a boy."

He unclenches his hands then balls them into tight fists, his jaw hardening as he stares me down. My smirk grows.

Instantly, it's clear neither of us plans to hold back.

With an agility I recognize from the elder Thalor, Joss shoots forward and throws a fist toward my face. I duck left, evading the blow. Before he can process, I send my fist into his gut. He grunts, taking it impressively as he regains his balance and catches the breath I knocked out of him.

The fight progresses quickly after that. My responsiveness only fans the flames, and soon we're throwing reckless punches, matching the tempo of the storm. Between the mud and the rain, we're slick and sloppy, less focused on defense and both going for offense.

Skill falls to the side, and we tumble through the mud, taking turns dominating. It's clear we're evenly matched in effort and rage, both of us having something to prove.

We exchange blows until we're out of stamina. The rain lets up, subsiding to a soft patter as we lie in the mud, side by side, panting.

After a few minutes of merely trying to breathe, Joss groans and turns his head to me.

"I came to apologize," Joss mutters, spitting blood.

"Most people don't apologize with their fists," I shoot back, clutching my aching ribs.

"That wasn't the apology, ass-clam. *This* is."

I surprise myself by barking a laugh. It's not funny. Nothing about this is. It's absurd.

"Can you just accept it so Soraya will forgive me?"

"Oh, *that's* what this is about."

"Of course it is," he mutters.

I sigh, too exhausted to care about Joss's intentions. "Fine. Accepted."

"You know, you'd make a good warden if you decide to step down from the Moon Priest thing." He shoots me a cocky grin. "You have a killer left hook."

"I'm not stepping down, Thalor. That's not how it works."

"Just saying. You could have a future elsewhere on the island."

I roll my eyes. Yet somehow, his compliment cracks an icy layer within me. Is it possible he's not as horrible as I've thought?

I chuckle again at the absurd timing, at how it took us fighting for me to respect the damn guy. It sends a zing of pain through me, and I wince, sucking in a deep breath through my teeth.

We lie side by side in the mud, both battered and bruised. I almost feel bad for the poor sucker. I'll heal quickly, thanks to my moonstone blood.

Except, I can't anticipate *when* that'll happen.

My magic used to only appear on Union Night. Spontaneous healing is a nightmare. If anyone discovers what my magic does, they'll see it as a miracle and want me to share it with them.

But they don't understand that it's not as miraculous as it seems. They don't know the darkness it brings along with it— the harm it can cause.

I'll need to hide until enough time passes.

My chest heaves as I catch my breath.

"Are we good now?" Joss asks.

"Yes, Thalor. So long as you don't intend to hit me again, we're fine."

He chuckles. "Your jaw is made of steel." The amusement fades out. "I can't believe my father trained you."

"I asked him to when we were little."

"Why?"

Gritting my teeth, I debate evading the answer. Finally, I sigh and figure I can practice the whole opening up thing. "Amos used to drink a lot of nectar…" I pause, loathing the oily feeling in my gut at this admission. "Sometimes he'd hit me, then he'd use his magic to keep me calm, so I just took it."

"*What?*" Joss sucks in a sharp breath.

I force the rest of the story out. "Your dad walked in on him one day. There wasn't much he could do to stop Amos; he was the High Priest, after all. But he taught me how to fight instead, to protect myself. Your mother was still alive at the time, so Lachlan wasn't Chief Warden yet. He had the time to mentor me."

"I had no idea…"

"No one did, Joss." I swipe a hand over my face, tasting blood and mud. "He stopped after that, though. Amos, I mean. I don't know if Lachlan ever said anything to him, but Amos only used his power rather than his fists after that day."

We're silent for a few moments as the admission chokes the air. After Joss's mother died and Lachlan became Chief Warden, he had less time for me, but I continued to train on my own.

"Your father is a good man. I respect him deeply," I say.

"That explains why he's so fond of you," Joss mumbles. "I always questioned why my father was so blindly trusting of you."

"I asked him not to tell anyone." I didn't want them to perceive me as weak.

Joss rolls onto his side, spitting blood before collapsing onto his back. "Her favorite color is silver." A broken laugh escapes him. "It's not even a color. It's a shade."

Turning my head, I frown at him, not following the segue. "What?"

He stares at the sky, still chuckling silently. "Soraya's."

"Look, Joss, I—"

"Her favorite food is cinnamon bread," he continues. "She likes cacao tea but usually only drinks it when she's sad, which isn't often. But if she lets you see that she's upset, then you're special to her because she tends to hide her emotions to make the people around her comfortable."

Jealousy washes over me. The vigor of it catches me off guard. These are the little details I haven't been able to learn about Soraya yet, but the warden has been there for much of her life.

Her face flickers through my mind. I might not know her favorite things yet, but I know how to read her expressions.

If she chews her lower lip, it means she's deep in thought. She tends to do it when reading intently. She cares so thoroughly for those around her, cautious to keep them at ease, but she somehow does it without sacrificing herself. She's unapologetically Soraya.

She's kind and patient with the island's children, taking her duties seriously. Yet she's also free and uninhibited, twirling in the sand while drinking nectar during the Union.

She's a conundrum of responsibility and pleasure—the perfect mix I've never been able to find.

Even Kassia adores her.

"Why are you telling me all of this?" I ask grimly once I find my voice.

He sighs. "To help you."

"I don't need—"

"Yes," he says flatly, "you do. You wouldn't have fought back like that if you weren't willing to fight for *her*. And these are the details that'll help you win a proper battle."

After a long silence, I swallow my pride. "Sorry," I mutter. "About the eye. And the jaw. And the—"

"I'm not the one you should be apologizing to." He smiles smugly. "Moons, the irony of it all. How can such a small island harbor so many secrets?"

Guilt gnaws at me. As much as the bastard irritates me, he's defending Soraya's honor. It's admirable, unfortunately. And our irritation for one another aside, he has many redeeming qualities.

"You should lay low until that heals," I say.

"Why?" he asks skeptically.

I fight the urge to roll my eyes. "Because the villagers don't need to see evidence of our scuffle."

A surprised laugh bursts from him. "Or you can own it and wear your wounds like a man, Raziel Kasper."

Glaring at him, I say, "Because seeing their High Priest and future head warden battered will go over real well with the villagers."

Joss pushes himself up, hissing at the pain. "You make a good point."

"I'm not a complete idiot," I mutter. "Not usually."

Joss flashes me a bloody smile. "It's what love does—makes a damned fool of us all."

"Love?" I scoff, shooting him a piercing look. "I'm not in *love*."

"So you beat me up for the hell of it?"

"I defended myself. That is all."

"No." Joss laughs. "That was two men in love with the same woman beating the barnacles out of one another."

"Whatever you say," I murmur, not wanting to start another argument.

"It felt good, admit it." He leans toward me, and I swat him away.

"Nothing about this feels *good*." Except, deep down, there's a tear in my loathing. It reveals a sliver of relief underneath. Maybe he's right; it does feel marginally better to let the rage out. Not just the rage, but all of the emotions, really.

I've locked them away for so long that I've forgotten how human it is to *feel*.

"If I admit it, what does that say about me?"

"We're having a cordial conversation for once," he says. "I'd say it went well. Very productive."

"If you say so." Snatching my ripped shirt from the mud, I stuff it in the waistband of my pants and storm away. "See you at the next assembly."

"Sure, Raziel," Joss calls after me. "And hey?"

I pause, glancing back at him.

"Next time you kiss her, don't make her cry. I might just feed you to the fucking sharks."

I continue walking, making a rude gesture over my head, and he roars with laughter.

"There won't be a next time," I mutter to myself.

Later, after hours of ruminating on my next steps, I head down to the village. Luckily, the rain has let up. The descent through the jungle is slippery and muddy, so I'm careful to take it slow.

I stop in front of Kassia's. Sucking in a long, steady breath of humid air, the salt and seaweed taste fills my lungs, renewing me. I glance down at my knuckles again. When I see they're still battered and cut from my fight with Joss, I relax.

The magic is quiet, dormant.

It's now or never.

Finally, I step inside the small hut, pulling the door shut

behind me. The pungent, peppery scent knocks the breath from my lungs. It transports me to the past, reminding me of the kava tea she loves.

"Who's there?" a familiar voice calls.

I scan the room, but she's nowhere in sight. The place is light and airy, with abundant natural light despite the grey day, decorated with pale wood and wicker furniture. Two archways on the far wall lead into other spaces, but I can't make out much from my position. A large potted palm blocks much of my view.

Plants are *everywhere*—hanging overhead, crawling up the walls, sitting on every surface. The room is small, and the abundance of things makes it even more suffocating.

"It's... me," I finally reply.

Something clatters in the distance, and I hear shuffling.

Glancing down at the bamboo slats underfoot, I debate taking off my shoes. Most villagers go barefoot since it's better to connect with the land that way, but I don't like the feel of things sticking to my skin, so I opt for leather slippers.

I stand there awkwardly, not wanting to take them off, but also not wanting to track mud and wet sand into her home. My cloak sits heavily on my shoulders, but I refuse to part with it. The weight is reassuring, safe.

She appears in the doorway, and our eyes lock. The coconut shell she was carrying clatters to the floor, and a dark puddle blooms beneath it.

"Raziel Kasper." Her face pales as if she's seeing a ghost. Those bright brown irises of hers widen, the depths unfathomable. The eye contact fills me with a surge of discomfort, so I lock my eyes on her chin instead. "In my home."

I freeze. My mind takes me back to that night, and my throat closes up.

No.

I concentrate on Kassia as she is now, before me, pushing away the haunting memories of the past.

Half her grey hair is in a tightly woven braid, starting at her crown and securing the top half while the rest flows loose and free around her shoulders.

"Both of you in one day," she whispers, a smile caressing her lips. She shakes her head. An abundance of wrinkles in her light brown skin marks a life of laughter, joy… and stress.

"Kassia," I say, choking on the nostalgia of it all.

Slowly, I reach up and pull my hood back.

"What in the moons' light happened to your face?" She rushes toward me. Her hands tremble as they come up to cup my cheeks. She inspects me, her frown growing deeper.

Regret claws at my chest, and there are a thousand things I should say—that I *want* to say. But I don't know how.

"I'm fine." I clear my throat, pushing the rising emotion away. "What's this?" I grasp her hands carefully, gently pulling them from my face. My brows pinch together as tremors continue to wrack her paper-thin skin. "Why didn't you tell me?"

Pulling free of my grip, she scoops up the abandoned coconut shell and sets it on a small wicker table. "There's nothing to tell."

"Kassia—"

She exhales a long, slow breath. "Why are you here now… after all this time?"

I shift, embarrassed that I barged in unannounced, not considering how she might feel. I've seen her from a distance, so her aging hasn't caught me off guard, but the state of her health has.

Despite knowing what I could do for her, she never bothered to ask for my help.

When I don't reply, she disappears into the kitchen. She returns with a cloth and blots up the spilled tea. Then, she tosses the rag down atop it and abandons the task.

A hefty sigh escapes her as she drops into a chair facing me. "Well? The High Priest doesn't do house calls, so we both know you came for a reason."

My hands itch to fiddle with my cloak, to wither under her studious glare, but I do neither. Instead, I stay rooted in the spot. "I apologize for barging in like this. But I need—I came to ask for cinnamon bread and cacao tea."

Embarrassment flares in my cheeks.

This was a mistake. Deep down, this was meant to be more than asking for help; it was supposed to be an opening to make amends. My way of trying to let her in after all this time.

Kassia grips her armrests, leaning forward. Her grey brows dip, then rise to her hairline.

"All these years, Raziel Kasper, and you finally come by for bread and tea?" Her tone is admonishing, and I wince. "Boy, I ought to…" Then she trails off, laughing.

Slowly, I turn back to face her.

She grins at me, her eyes narrowed knowingly. "For the little star with bright hair?"

I cup the back of my neck, giving her a shrug. This is not the response I'd expected. "How'd you know?"

"An old woman has her way of knowing things." She rises and reaches for my hand. With a tight squeeze, she gives me a look of appraisal. "Now, come. Sit. I'll prepare your treats."

Once I'm settled into a stiff chair, still in my shoes and cloak, she nods contentedly and shuffles into the kitchen.

My fingers itch to reach for the letter opener, to dig it into my flesh and ensure my blood runs red still. But there's no need. The collection of cuts, scrapes, and bruises I'm currently sporting reassures me plenty.

I'm safe.

She's safe.

This time.

After a few long minutes, she returns holding a bundle wrapped tightly in palm leaves, tied with plant fibers, and a small clay pot. "You're lucky. Her visit earlier inspired me to make a fresh loaf of cinnamon bread."

I smile, remembering how Kassia always had a variety of treats on hand. Now that she's retired, I'd imagine she bakes even more than she used to. It was always her passion.

"Thank you," I say earnestly, standing and accepting the items. My eyes remain locked on her shaking hands. "Will you let me help you in return?"

"Absolutely not," she says, swatting at me.

"But I promise, I won't hurt—"

"It's not about *you*." Her tone is much softer. "Moons, you two are so alike." My brow furrows, and I open my mouth to ask what she means, but she keeps going. "I've paid my dues and accepted aging naturally, as the goddesses intend."

"You don't have to suffer though, Kassia."

"The only one suffering here is you, Raziel, and because of your own stubbornness."

Not wanting to go down that route, I give her an exasperated look and head to the door. I pause to pull my hood up, then turn back to her.

"I'm trying," I mutter.

"I know, darling. I know." Her smile is so sad that my ribs squeeze in response. "That is precisely why I'm giving you space to seek me out when you're ready. I'd like to hear all about our little star."

I want to ask why she calls Soraya *little star*, but I don't. Just as she's respecting the fragile ground between us, I'll do the same.

After a second, her eyes begin to water.

Gripping the goods to my chest, I shift my weight. The tears are seconds away from falling, and I'm unsure how to react.

"You've always loved that girl," she says, catching me wholly off guard. I open my mouth to respond, but she puts a hand up, effectively silencing me. A wistful smile lights up her face. "You can argue till the moons turn blue, but it'd be a waste of breath. You always had your eye on her since you were a little boy."

My face heats, and I drop my gaze to the floor, grateful for the hood to hide beneath.

"Why didn't you say anything?" I mumble.

"You, my darling, cannot be pushed. We all wait for you to come to us—when you're ready." She clears her throat. "Off you go now. Preferably before you make this old woman blubber. I do hope to see you again soon, Raziel."

CHAPTER TWENTY-ONE

THE APOLOGY

SORAYA

"*I* can't believe the silverdew still hasn't opened," Mariel sighs as she taps her fingernails on the book before her. She stares at the page, but I feel like she's absorbing about as much as I am today. Which really isn't anything. "Do you think the mainland is going to understand?"

"I don't know," I murmur.

When we were little, around ten, I vaguely remember there being an issue when High Priest Amos died. Trade was disrupted, and the mainland didn't take it too well. It wasn't their officials that came for us, but the rebel pirates who made a dishonest living off others' addictions. Without pollen, their livelihood was threatened.

Luckily, from what I remember, the issue was short-lived and resolved before it escalated.

"At least it stopped raining," I say, glancing at the window above us.

Bright blue sky peers back, and the two moons sit high above in their usual spots. Forever suspended overhead.

Instead of dusting the shelves like we were scheduled to do this month, we've been scouring the texts for insight on the silverdew—the magic. Part of me is relieved to have the other celestial servants on this.

If Raziel had stuffed his pride away and asked for help, the entire village could've rallied around him long ago.

Instead, he created a tangle of lies and shut himself away. Secrets, I understand. Those I can forgive. But it's the blatant disregard for my feelings that guts me. How can he push me away when I know he feels this thing between us, too?

Tears fill my eyes, and I quickly blink them back, not wanting them to fall here. Not in front of Mariel. Last night, we finally talked. I told her about Raziel and me, minus the bits about his magic. She listened without judgment and held me when I cried. We both apologized for how we've been acting lately, and things are lighter today.

The library door groans open, and hope surges through me as I turn toward the noise.

Joss enters the room, running a hand through his hair as he scans the faces within. I'm disappointed it's not Raziel, even though I shouldn't be.

Our eyes meet, and he strides toward our table.

"Your brother's here," I whisper, nudging Mariel with my foot under the table.

"Oh, moons," she groans, tilting her head back. "Please don't call him that."

As Joss draws closer, I make out the dark shadow of a black eye. His cheek is bruised, and he looks on edge. My blood runs cold at the sight.

I jump up, nearly toppling my chair with the movement. "What the hell happened to you?"

"I tripped," he lies, not even wasting the effort to come up with something halfway believable.

"Yeah, into a fist," I scoff.

Mariel gasps when she sees what I'm referring to. "The village—"

"Is fine," Joss quickly adds, settling fears about a hostile invasion. He tugs on his ear as he tells Mariel, "Training was rough today."

I narrow my eyes, recognizing the small tell that he's lying. But Mariel seems to accept it as she stands and reaches for his chin, tilting his face to inspect the damage.

"You should go visit my ma. She can take a look and make sure it's healing well," she mutters. "She's good at that."

Joss rolls his eyes, batting her hand away. "I'm fine."

"It doesn't *look* fine, Joss."

"See, I told you being a warden isn't for you, princess." He smirks, glancing down at her wispy dress and then her fingers, which tap anxiously. "You might get those clean little nails of yours dirty."

"Fuck it," she says, crossing her arms. "Simmer in your pain, Jossidian."

He cringes when she says his full name, his face falling. "Can I speak to Soraya, please?"

Mariel arches a brow at me, and I nod. Shrugging, she scoops up her book. "You know, just because I like pretty things doesn't mean I'm not tough as seashells," she mutters, bumping his shoulder as she passes.

Joss chuckles, turning after her. "I crush shells like they're nothing, darling."

"You know what?" She whirls around. "A second black eye might even out your look."

At this, he laughs outright. "I'd like to see you try."

She narrows her eyes, then shakes her head before walking off. When Joss turns his attention to me, I plop back into my chair. He does the same in Mariel's vacated seat.

"You lied," I say flatly. "What really happened?"

"*Me* lie? Never." He touches his chest, feigning a look of hurt.

"You told her that happened in training."

"No," he says carefully, "I said training was rough today, which technically wasn't a lie."

Squinting at the old bruises on his face, my suspicions are confirmed. "Those aren't from today."

"Never said they were." He grins.

Yesterday, when I ran into Joss after my *incident* with Raziel, he didn't have those wounds. I'm a second away from asking if Raziel did that to his face, but the High Priest doesn't fight. It's the reason he wears his cape, after all—a symbol of benevolence.

Raziel takes his duty beyond seriously. He wouldn't give me more than a fleeting kiss, for moon's sake, so there's no way he could've done this to Joss.

"You should speak with him, Soraya," he says quietly, all signs of humor drained away.

I go rigid. "Who?"

"You know who." He gives me a pointed look.

Gasping, I lean forward. "Joss, no... Tell me you didn't fight Raziel."

He grimaces. He looks like he wants to say more, but he doesn't. "I might've misjudged him a little."

My brows fly up to my hairline.

"I think... I think you might actually be good for him."

"How?" I whisper.

"I don't know how to explain it." He shakes his head.

"You've been more reserved and moody, like him. But he's been slightly more open and social, like you. It's almost like the two of you balance each other somehow. It's weird, but it works, I think."

Sighing, I drop my forehead into my hands. I don't bother arguing about there not being anything between us this time. He *saw* us kissing, after all.

"Just... maybe don't give up on him?" he suggests.

At this, my head snaps up. "Who are you, and what have you done with Joss?"

He leans back, tilting the chair onto two legs as he gives me a cocky smirk. He drags his hands down his bare chest. "I'm right here, baby."

At this, I roll my eyes, chuckling.

He adds, "You could've had all this, but instead, you chose a moody loner who wears a blanket on his shoulders."

"It's a cape," I scoff, rolling my eyes. "Traditionally, all the High Priests have worn it, and I didn't *choose* him."

"You're right." He smirks. "You can't choose who you fall for."

I study him, wondering why he seems so much calmer than yesterday. Whatever happened between when I saw him in the storm and now has certainly changed his attitude. My eyes roam over the bruises on his face, not making sense of it.

"I have to get back to work. Just go talk to the guy, eh?"

"I've given him plenty of time to *talk*, Joss. It's exhausting trying to get through that impenetrable wall of his."

"Keep penetrating. You'll get through." He snorts. "Or maybe he just needs to penetrate *you* finally."

My face burns in embarrassment. "Oh, my moons. Shut up, Joss!"

He laughs, standing and shooing me away. "Go figure out your issues so I don't have to get hit again."

My jaw unhinges as that last statement settles. I rush out of the library and to the temple sanctum, if only to verify what Joss implied—that Raziel was responsible for the condition of his face.

The soft scent of cinnamon reaches my nose when I enter Raziel's kitchen. Candles sit on every surface, the soft orange light flickering. In the center of his counter is a loaf of bread on a palm leaf; I immediately recognize Kassia's handiwork anywhere. Beside it are teacups.

A throat clears beside me, and I spin toward the sound, my breath catching.

Instead of his usual proper attire or the pajamas I love so much, he's dressed in soft, low-hanging black pants, with a bare chest and feet. His hair is unbraided, hanging in dark waves down to his shoulders. Bruises and cuts line his face and chest.

I don't know what surprises me most: the fact Joss looks worse than he does, or that he hasn't healed.

"Raziel," I murmur, flying toward him. I tenderly cup his jaw, and he winces when my thumb coasts over the shadow of a bruise. "You idiot."

Tension seeps from him, and his lips twitch as if fighting a smile. "You're right," he says softly. "I am the biggest idiot of all." His hand comes up, cupping the back of my head. His fingers intertwine in my hair and tug gently, forcing me to look up at him. "For letting you walk away yesterday."

My heart stalls, and the room closes in around us. "What does that mean, Raziel? I need to hear it from you."

His eyes drop to my lips, blazing with desire. "It means I want to kiss you—more than once."

"So do it," I dare, heart pounding.

He pulls me toward him, ever so slowly, leaning down to meet me halfway. As our mouths barely brush, he whispers, "I'm scared."

"What are you afraid of?"

"I want you... more than I've ever wanted anything." He sighs against my lips, and I want to breathe in all of him. "If I let you in, you'll see everything, Soraya. Every flaw I try to hide, every mistake I've failed to correct. And if you walk away after that... it'll destroy me."

I smile, wrapping my arms around his neck. "I stand by my initial assessment: you're an idiot, Raziel Kasper."

He pulls back slightly, frowning at me.

I roll my eyes, chuckling. "I'm going nowhere. I'm not here for perfection; I'm here for *you*. But you need to stop trying to sabotage us."

His eyes brighten slightly. "So, there is an us?"

"It depends on how good you are at groveling."

Releasing me, he carefully drops to his knees, staring up at me with a vulnerability I rarely see worn on his face. He grips my hands tightly in his, caressing them with his thumbs.

"Soraya Nyx, I've been a fool." He swallows, his throat bobbing dramatically. "Will you please forgive me for being slow to let you in? For being a wholly incompetent man and underestimating your ability to handle... this?" He squeezes my hands, and I can't help but smile softly and shake my head.

"Is that cinnamon bread from Kassia's?"

"And cacao tea."

I gasp. "Who told you?"

"Joss," he admits, and there's no animosity in his tone.

I continue to stare down at him, stunned. "You *fought* him, which I'm still trying to wrap my head around by the way, and now you're friends?"

His nose wrinkles. "Friends is a stretch."

"Maybe people really can change," I murmur. "Okay, you can get up now."

I try to pull him up, but a wicked grin takes over his face. "There's something else I wanted to try while I'm down here. Something that might show you how I feel about you."

My heart skips a beat. "Oh?"

"I meant it when I said I want to kiss you,"—he licks his lips, his eyes dark with lust—"but I never said *where*."

Before I can reply, his hand reaches through the slit in my skirts, wandering up my thigh. Goosebumps immediately break out on my leg, and it feels like I'm being touched for the first time.

"Raziel," I gasp, reaching out to grip his hair as his fingers explore my skin.

"I love the sound of my name on your lips," he croons.

His fingers tickle me as he explores my inner thigh. I squirm, liquid heat blazing through me. "You don't have to do this," I whisper.

"You underestimate my desire, Soraya." He freezes. "Is this okay? Do you want this?"

I nod enthusiastically. "Yes—as long as you're sure *you* want this."

"I don't want it," he says, pausing to give me a stern look. "I *need* it." He punctuates his words by pulling my panties aside a little more aggressively than I expected of the inexperienced priest. His thumb brushes my entrance, and he sucks in a sharp breath. "I don't have much time."

Pausing, I grip his wrist. "What do you mean?"

He shakes his head. "Nothing. I just… I should've done this a long time ago."

Satisfied, I lean back and open my legs a little wider,

inviting him in. He runs the pads of his fingers over me, gathering moisture and spreading it around.

I whimper, excited by the uptight Moon Priest's forbidden touch.

"Are you always so wet?" he murmurs.

"No." My pulse races, and I need him to touch me more. "This is all for you."

"Can I taste you?" The way he looks up at me, with unbridled desire, clogs my throat with affection.

"Please," I choke out.

He leans forward, tilting his face up to meet the apex between my thighs. Still holding my underwear to the side, he tenderly licks me as if tasting a snack for the first time.

"Soraya…" he groans, and his hot breath flutters across my clit. It sends a surge of heat through me, and I shift my hips forward, needing more.

"Do you like it?" I ask, afraid of his response.

He shakes his head, smirking up at me. "I *love* it."

Then, his mouth descends on me again. He explores me, experimenting with different positions and tempos. I let him play, giving him feedback when he hits the right spot.

The pleasure in my core builds as I grip his hair tightly, riding his face. He reaches for my ankle, lifting my foot and placing it on his shoulder. I gasp, and he grips my hips, steadying me while continuing his onslaught.

"I'll never let you fall, beautiful," he murmurs, and the soft words combined with the thrill of *him* beneath my skirts sends me spiraling.

My breath hitches, and he seems to notice—ever the perceptive learner, and he chuckles darkly. He might be new to this, but he's quick to master it. When he slips a finger inside me, I pull his hair, a low moan escaping me. His mouth sucks at my clit, and my legs tremble as I reach the peak of my climax.

"Raziel!" I yell, my hips undulating against his fingers and tongue as hot, powerful pleasure pulses through me. My walls clench around his fingers, and a growl builds deep in his throat.

Gently, he removes my leg from his shoulder and sits back on his haunches. His mouth and scruff glisten, highlighting a wide smile.

The sight is so rare that I can only stare wordlessly.

"Was that okay?" he asks, his smile faltering like he's suddenly unsure.

I lunge at him, knocking him backward as I press my mouth to his. He groans, meeting me greedily in return. His cock is hard between us, and it would be so easy to free him and let him slip inside.

But being with him is so beautiful and powerful, I don't want to rush. I want to take all of our firsts slow, to relish each moment.

"I told you," I whisper, "you're good at everything."

We continue to kiss lazily on his kitchen floor, lost to each other.

When I pull back, I freeze. "Raziel…"

"What is it?" He sits up, alarmed, with me still on his lap. His arms wrap around my back, locking me in place.

Reaching up, I caress his jaw. The scruff tickles my hand. He doesn't pull away or wince this time, because the ugly bruise that was on his cheek earlier is gone. The purple and yellow marks have disappeared entirely. I pull back, trailing my fingers down his neck, across his chest, and to his abs.

Not a single scratch or marking is left behind. Not even a scar.

"You're healed," I whisper.

Instead of looking relieved, like I expected, fear flickers in his eyes.

CHAPTER TWENTY-TWO

THE MONSTER

RAZIEL

I grip the steel hilt of the letter opener and press the blade to my inner forearm. With one slick slice, I split the skin and silver wells.

It's been days since I gave in to my pleasure with Soraya. My moonblood made a sudden comeback, and it hasn't gone away. This is the longest it's lingered, and it's perilous with the Union tonight. I've been far too risky, trusting myself when I know I shouldn't. Nothing about this is routine or usual.

The magic of the moons fusing will send me over the edge. I'll need to lock myself away in the chambers beneath the temple tonight.

I've managed to avoid doing it for quite some time—the magic simmering out before it tips me over the edge… but *this* spark inside me is hotter, brighter. It's on the verge of creating an inferno that blazes through everything I've worked for.

The other day, getting intimate with Soraya was beyond

anything I've experienced. All it took was one time, and I'm already addicted to her taste. Burying my head in her skirt was better than I could've possibly imagined.

What surprised me most was that I didn't panic and push her away even though my magic flared to life. Luckily, it only healed me, and beyond that, it stayed tame. We still spent a beautiful night together, snacking and laughing, tasting each other's lips.

But I need to tell Soraya the truth soon.

Committing to her is both harder and easier than I could've prepared myself for. Being around her is so naturally easy, but the realization that I can't keep things from her anymore scares me.

It should scare her, too. If she knew the truth, she wouldn't want to be with me.

Wiping the gleaming silver blood off my blade, I toss it down on the counter beside the sink. It clatters against the porcelain. I trace my fingers over the smooth, healed skin where I cut myself. The wound healed at a remarkably accelerated rate.

Gripping the counter, I lean forward, eyeing myself in the bathroom mirror. It's too much. Iridescent silver rings my irises, and they flash briefly before returning to their normal brown.

"Silver shells!" I slap the counter, turning and fleeing.

I can't wait until tonight. I need to get downstairs now.

Descending as quickly and quietly as possible, I glance down at my left hand. It gleams brightly, taunting me. I clench it into a fist, tucking it beneath my cloak before exiting my tower.

The door creaks open, and I glance both ways to ensure no one is around. It's midday; the celestial servants are working indoors.

In a rush, I fly across the uneven stone porch. The warm morning air kisses my skin as I hurry down the temple's steps and around the back to the rear. At the back of the foundation, with only the trees standing witness, I approach a door. It's nearly indistinguishable from the weathered stone, its aged wood worn and dark.

"Raziel, wait!"

My hand pauses on the doorknob. I grit my teeth. She can't follow me. It's not safe to engage with her right now.

I need to get down there.

Pretending not to have heard her, I throw the door open and surge into the darkness. Before I can pull it shut behind me, she's there, yanking it back open with a force I would've never expected from her small frame.

"Soraya, go!" I order, even though sending her away again cleaves my heart in two.

"What's going on?" She's taken aback. Her curious blue eyes roam my face, her forehead wrinkling with concern. Then they drop down to my hand, which blazes with light. She squints. "Why is it so bright?"

"This used to only happen during the Union," I explain, voice thick. "It's been so long. I thought I was... It's not safe. It's never safe. You need to go."

"I'm not leaving you while—"

"You need to go!"

"Your eyes," she whispers.

Magic roars to life within me, causing my head to buzz. I don't need to see myself to know my irises are glowing as brightly as my palm. But for some reason, she doesn't seem surprised. Or scared.

"I'm coming with you." She ushers me forward, then tugs the door shut behind us.

I suck in short, sharp breaths through my gritted teeth.

The magic surges, and I groan at the force of it. Every last bit of my willpower fights to hang onto my dwindling sanity.

"I'll hurt you, just like I did her," I choke out.

The light emitting from my hand and eyes is so bright that it guides my path down the stairs. I bolt, moving as fast as possible, hoping desperately to outrun her.

I must get to the chamber and lock myself away before she reaches me.

The echo of our footsteps is deafening as we run, each footfall a thunderclap in the confined space. My lungs burn from the force of my breathing.

By the time I reach the room, my entire skin is glowing with an iridescent sheen. I'm sweating. My hands are shaking. I attempt to throw the door shut, but she's there.

"FUCK!" I roar.

Again, with a brutal strength I'm unprepared for, she flings the door back open and steps inside. I can no longer find my voice to argue with her. Dropping to my knees, I writhe and groan as the power consumes me.

"Raziel," she says softly.

"Lock—lock it!" I cry, squeezing my eyes shut.

Please shut and lock the door.

And be smart enough to be on the other side when you do.

Faintly, over the thunder in my skull, I hear the sound of the door shutting and a chain being locked. But when I look up, she's still there, watching me without a flicker of fear present on her face.

Instead, she squats beside me, watching me sadly like I'm a wounded animal. Growling, I close my eyes. I'm not what she thinks I am.

I'm a predator.

And I'm going to kill her.

Amos won't be here to help like he did the last time I lost control.

"Raziel," she whispers. "Look at me."

I do.

Not because I want to, but because the monster living in my skin does. He's hungry, desperate.

As I try to fight it, a silent scream echoes in my mind, but the magic thrashes against me. It grips Soraya by the throat.

It's that night all over again. Instead, this time, it's so much worse.

Fight it! Fight me! I want to yell, but I have no control over my physical body. *Why aren't you fighting?*

I'm forced to watch as a roar escapes my mouth. My skin glows like the supermoon, and my nails shift into claws, stretching into points as sharp as my letter opener.

"It's okay," she whispers, reaching for me and clutching my hair. "I forgive you."

And the emotional pain of knowing I'll be responsible for her death is enough to cause my vision to go spotty. Everything moves in slow motion as the last of the shift happens, and my canine teeth elongate. A roaring in my ears drowns out all other sounds.

I'm lost to my monster as he spills the blood of the only woman I've ever loved.

The last thing I see before sinking my teeth into her soft throat is a flash of fear and sorrow in her eyes. A metallic tang fills my mouth—sweeter than I remember. My muscles strain, taut and powerful, yet a hollow ache spreads through my chest.

Somehow, even in this moment, grief tries to claw its way out.

Then it all goes black, and a piece of my soul dies.

CHAPTER TWENTY-THREE

THE TRUTH

SORAYA

I sit on the corner of the small mattress, my legs tucked close to my chest. I rest my chin atop my knees and continue to watch Raziel. A dim glow flickers from beside the door, bathing him in pale light.

He's sprawled out on his back in the corner on the dusty stone floor. The steady rise and fall of his chest indicates he's still asleep.

This space is so unlike the grandiose architecture up above. It smells of musk and earth, having been built deep into the mountain beneath the temple.

My eyes flit from wall to wall, taking in the grimy dungeon. Because that's what it is—a prison cell.

The thick chain lock crossing lopsided over the door confirms it. Instead of being locked in by someone else, Raziel is a prisoner of his own making.

Is this where he goes every Union?

Watery sorrow pricks at my eyes as I gaze at Raziel. No wonder he's felt so detached, so alone. In his slumber, his thick, luscious hair sprawls out around his head, framing masculine features: his sharp, stubble-lined jaw, dark lashes, and sturdy nose. Instead of being turned down in irritation, his lips are relaxed; there's a softness to his mouth that's usually not found when he's awake.

The spot on my chest tickles, and I scratch at it mindlessly. When my fingers hit bare skin, I freeze. My eyes drop, noticing the large rip in the front of my dress. My collarbone is bare, my breasts and the skin between exposed.

Gently, I finger the brightly glowing spot between my curves, the one usually hidden away behind the material of my gowns.

"Soraya?" Raziel croaks, and my head snaps up.

He's cautiously pushing himself to a seated position with one hand, his other coming up to rub the back of his head. When he pulls his hand away, his fingers are coated in dark brownish-red.

I wince. He must've gone down a little harder than I intended.

"You're okay," he says on an exhale.

Slowly, he tries to stand.

"Wait." I jump up, lunging for him and gripping his arm to help steady him.

He pulls away from me, quickly stepping out of my hold. That single rejection is sharper on my heart than his claws were on my skin. My eyes flood with tears again, but I blink quickly to shove them down.

Then his face twists into confusion as he glances at my bare chest. "You're glowing... what is...? A moon marking?" His pupils dilate, and a faint blush marks his cheeks before he quickly turns away.

A muscle tics in his cheek, and he tugs his dark tunic up and over his head.

"Here." He thrusts it at me.

Understanding washes over me. I might be comfortable with exposed skin, but he's not.

"Sorry," I whisper, gently accepting his shirt and slipping it on.

What was snug on him hangs loosely to my upper thighs.

He turns back to me, relief and gratitude flitting through his face. My fingers hover over my moon marking, lightly brushing the barrier of fabric.

He paces beside me, his hand repeatedly stroking the soft stubble on his jaw.

"How are you alive?" His tone is more accusatory than relieved, and that stings even more. His usually warm brown gaze is cold, and it drops to my neck, then my arms. "I attacked you... I hurt—"

"I'm fine." I paste on a smile, hoping he'll see the truth behind my words. Physically, I *am* okay.

"That marking..." he asks, avoiding eye contact. His left hand balls into a fist on his lap. "The marking of a Moon Priest."

Sighing, I reach into my hair and pull a small starry hairclip free. Pointing the sharp edge at the meaty flesh of my arm, I prepare to drag it down.

"What the hell!" He lunges for me, but it's too late.

I press hard and split the skin on my arm. Shining silver blood pours out, freezing him on the spot.

"Moonblood?" he whispers in awe.

I nod, biting my lower lip, terrified of sharing the truth with him. "Here." I thrust my arm to his lips. "Drink."

He recoils, maneuvering out of my reach.

"Raziel," I say sternly. "You hit your head when you went

down. Please, *drink.*" A faint warmth radiates from the wound as the skin on each side, soft and pliable, swells and stretches toward one another.

The edges begin to stitch themselves together. A viscous, pearly luminescent blood, warm and slick, oozes from what remains of the gaping wound.

"Now. Before it heals," I demand.

Reluctantly, he steps forward. I offer him my arm, and he gazes at it with warring emotions.

A grimace twists his mouth as he stares, transfixed, at my skin. He mutters something to himself gruffly, then slowly leans forward. His head descends toward my skin, and when his tongue gently laps at the liquid gathering on my inner forearm, my knees nearly buckle.

My skin prickles with awareness, a sudden chill causing gooseflesh to rise. It's an incredibly unerotic moment under normal circumstances, but because it's him—*his* touch, *his* tongue—it's everything to me.

"Raziel," I whisper, nearly trembling beneath him.

He laps gently, then plants his mouth on my arm and sucks from the small opening that remains. "Soraya," he whispers against me as he pulls back. "You're my replacement for Moon Priest."

"I was born with the marking, Raziel," I finally say, shaking my head. "I'm only a few years younger than you. We've both had our markings this whole time. Kassia says it's why I was left on the temple stairs—"

"*Kassia* knew?" Betrayal is etched into his face. He shakes his head, running a hand over his hair. "That's the mark of a Moon Priest, Soraya."

My face falls, regret pinching my features together. "I know."

"I don't…" He picks up his pace, striding the room's length

and repetitively running a hand through his hair. "Start from the beginning, Soraya, because I'm confused. I was terrified— *petrified*—thinking my secret would harm you this whole time, yet here you sit, unharmed and unbothered, as if you somehow knew?"

"I told you that you could keep your secrets if I could keep mine," I whisper, fiddling with the hem of the shirt he gave me.

But the words taste bitter on my tongue. It was a cheap way to avoid telling him things I wasn't ready to, despite my pressuring him to open up with me. The hypocrisy, the irony, isn't lost on me.

He's too smart; it won't be lost on him either.

He narrows his eyes at me, and I hold his stare, unwavering.

"You hid your secrets, Raziel, and I hid mine."

I finish showering and head down the hall toward my bedroom, clutching the toiletry kit. My hair drips down the back of Raziel's shirt. It was delightfully comfortable, so I put it back on, tucking it into the waistband of one of my flowing, frayed skirts.

Raziel immediately began to retreat to his shell after my revelation. I could see a thousand questions burning in his eyes, but he clamped his mouth shut and swiftly exited the chamber. Instead of following him up to his sanctum, I'm flexing my patience. He needs to process... alone. It's what he does best. As much as it hurts, I have to accept that's what he needs.

Raziel and I should feel closer now that we've started to reveal our truths to each other. So why do I feel farther away from him than ever?

And how, *why*, does my magic respond so dramatically to his? I've known my whole life that my moonblood could heal myself and others. I've taken special care to keep it secret; I begged Kassia not to tell anyone. She never pressured me to.

The island already had a Moon Priest, after all. They didn't need another. It would've only invited unwanted attention and made me different than my friends.

I've spent much of my life in the library, playing it safe. Avoiding swimming in a suit, so no one sees my gleaming marking. Taking care not to wound myself in front of anyone, lest they see my healing potential.

On my period, I wear double undergarments to avoid any potential leaks. How would I explain silver stains instead of the red and brown ones that other girls have?

Now, it feels like all of that was for nothing because, ultimately, the Moon Priest still discovered my secret.

"Where were you?" Mariel practically pounces on me the moment I enter our room, causing me to gasp. "You *never* skip a Union, and you didn't come to the room last night."

A smattering of abandoned silverdew flowers lies on the floor before us, their petals still curled into balls.

"What's going on?" I toe a flower, then glance back up at her. "Why aren't you at work?"

"Okay, now you're freaking me out. Seriously, where the hell were you?" She picks up a stem, twirling it in her fingers. "Last night, Joss and I went searching through the silverdew. None of them are open anywhere on the island, but they're blooming everywhere."

With urgency, she pushes me toward the window. I peek outside, and my jaw drops. How did I miss that?

I was so distracted by Raziel on my way back from the basement that I failed to see the canopy of silverdew spread across the jungle floor, weaving between the trees and cresting up the side of the mountain.

"What the hell?" I murmur.

What is going on?

Why are the flowers sprouting faster but without opening?

"Oh, my moons." Mariel's voice drops into a scandalized whisper. "Is that... *Raziel's* shirt?"

The spot on my chest hums softly, and I stroke it. It tickles, feeling a little lighter than usual.

"Yes." The admission causes my skin to heat. Even though he was under my skirt days ago, it's last night's events that make me flush furiously. "I ripped my dress and needed something to wear."

"You skipped the Union, spent the night with the Moon Priest, and you come home in his shirt?" she squeals. "You showered and put his shirt back on." She points to the toiletry kit I'm still awkwardly holding.

Sighing, I stride over to my armoire and drop the kit on the floor. Then I flop onto my bed. Raziel's shirt felt like a safe choice. With my moon marking blazing a little brighter than usual, I thought the dark fabric might hide it better than my dresses.

Or is that a lie?

Kassia had helped me sew extra fabric to the front of all my clothing to hide the marking purposely.

Maybe I just like the way it smells. Without thinking, I pinch the neckline and pull it up to my nose, inhaling greedily.

"You got horizontal with the Moon Priest!" Mariel claps her hands, bouncing over to my bed and throwing herself down.

My skin heats, and I shake my head aggressively. "I promise I didn't."

She gives me a pointed look. I groan, smooshing my face

into a pillow. I can't tell her everything, but I'll need to share something with my best friend, so she doesn't think I'm pulling away from her.

As much as I want to nap, the Assembly is starting soon, and I should get ready.

"Okay, fine, I spent the night with Raziel," I admit, quickly putting a hand up before she can say anything. "But it wasn't like that!"

"Joss is going to lose it," Mariel says, lifting a brow.

I nearly roll my eyes at that. "First, it's not his business. Second, he already thinks something is going on between us. Third, we were..." I try to pick my words strategically to avoid outright lying to her. "Trying to figure out a problem, and it ended up being more complex than we expected. We were both exhausted and lost track of time."

"Was the problem trying to get your dress off?" She snorts, pointing to the discarded fabric hanging off the foot of my bed.

"No—that's not how it happened. *That* was an accident. He was gentlemanly enough to give me a shirt."

Mariel pats my hand gently. After a beat of silence, her face grows serious. "I'm sorry for being a snot lately, Soraya. I've just missed you. I felt like you've been pushing me and Joss away—"

"No, it's not—"

"Seriously. I'm sorry." She sighs, hanging her head and picking at a cuticle. "We've been hard on you because we're worried about you... You've been consumed by the High Priest. I get it; he's divinely handsome and intriguing, but don't lose yourself to him. Please."

"I won't," I murmur. Reaching out, I grab her hand. She gives me a watery smile and squeezes it.

"Before you say it, because I know your people-pleasing

ass will, no, we're not going to stop worrying about you." We both laugh at that, and warm comfort spreads through my chest.

This is why she's my best friend. Even when things are rough or we're imperfect, we look out for each other at the end of the day. We love each other like sisters.

"Come here." I scoot closer, opening my arms and wrapping them around her shoulders. She hugs me back, sighing into my hair.

"Damn," she mutters, inhaling deeply. "No wonder you wanted to keep his shirt on. High Priest smells *good*."

"Mariel!" Laughing, I rip free from her and playfully swat her away.

"Do you want to skip work and go swimming with me?" she asks, hope sparking in her eyes.

I shake my head. "I really need a nap."

She stands, heading back to her side of the room. "Okay, but when you're ready to talk, *really* talk, I'll be here. In the meantime, remember you're not alone, Soraya. And if he makes you feel alone, then he's not the one for you."

CHAPTER TWENTY-FOUR

THE BATTLE

RAZIEL

*S*oraya's soft voice echoes in my mind: *You hid your secrets, Raziel, and I hid mine.* I should've asked her outright what she meant, but her marking and magic caught me off guard. My mind spun, and I needed time to let it sink in.

She has moonblood, like me, and Kassia knew.

The elder priestess is exactly who I need to talk to. The Assembly is starting soon, but I have just enough time to stop by her house first.

"Kassia!" The hut door swings shut behind me, and I pause at the entrance, arms crossed. Without my cape to tuck myself away beneath, I feel exposed. My eyes drop to my bare feet.

I also forgot shoes.

I'm missing my armor.

At least I remembered my pants and shirt.

What does that say about my state of mind?

A half-grunt greets me from the kitchen, and a moment later, the elder priestess pops her head through the archway. Her grey hair is piled haphazardly in a tangle of braids.

"Raziel, dear!" She smiles at me. "Let me grab some tea, and I'll be right out!" Her head withdraws back into the kitchen, and I sigh, pinching the bridge of my nose.

It's nearly impossible to be angry with the woman. Nearly, but not entirely. I quickly swipe my dirty feet on the grassy mat beside the door, flinching at how it tickles.

How does Soraya go barefoot so damn much?

It's not *as* horrible as I expected, but there are still so many sensations. Dirty feet unsettle me.

A moment later, Kassia reappears with two coconuts. She hands one to me, and the shell vibrates with her trembling hands. It sucks some of the gusto out of my lungs. Accepting it graciously, I fall into one of her chairs.

"I don't know how you take it," she says wistfully, staring at one of her dangling pothos. "Don't know much about you at all these days."

That anger burns in my throat again. All this time, I've blamed myself for scaring Kassia away. But that wasn't it, was it? She knew Soraya had the marking. She took *her* under her wing—a replacement granddaughter and a replacement Moon Priest.

Right?

"You could've visited me, Kassia." I sip my tea, and the kava goes down like dirt. I've never liked the tea, especially not now.

"Darling, I didn't come to visit you because I couldn't handle the stairs to the sanctum…" Her face falls, marred with guilt. "You never really came down, and these days, I can't even climb the mountain to get to the temple."

Another bout of guilt blazes through me, and I put the coconut on the table and bury my face in my hands.

Kassia clears her throat daintily. "It's nice to see you not hiding in your tower… or beneath your cape for once."

"You and Soraya…" I start, unsure where exactly I'm going with it. "You know about her marking, the moonblood. Why did you care for her and abandon me?"

I glance up, and Kassia's face falls. She sets her coconut down beside mine and reaches out to pat my knee. "You pushed everyone away, Raziel. I had no idea you wanted… a relationship. Anytime I tried—"

"I turned my back on you," I finish, "because I was afraid of hurting you. Again. I almost killed you that night, Kassia!" Jumping to my feet, I pace to give the furious energy within me an outlet. "If anyone knew the truth of that, they'd never want me as their leader. For good reason. Without my role as Moon Priest, who would I be? Nothing but a monster."

My voice cracks, and I wince at the display of weakness.

"Then you should understand why Soraya and I kept your secret," Kassia whispers.

My head snaps in her direction. "What do you mean?"

Her frown deepens. "After she healed me that night—"

"Amos healed you."

A flicker of surprise crosses her expression, then she sighs and purses her lips. "No, darling. Soraya did."

My heart squeezes, and I fall back into the chair. My lungs ache for air. She knew what I did. What I am.

Suddenly, it makes sense why she wasn't shocked by my transformation last night. I was too busy reeling from the secrets I'd learned about her that I didn't even recognize that *she* wasn't surprised by mine.

"We agreed to keep it between us. She begged me not to tell

anyone about her marking. At first, I kept it secret until she was old enough to make the decision herself. We already had a Moon Priest; she had no reason to share unless she wanted to."

"Why did she choose to keep it secret?" I ask.

Kassia doesn't meet my eyes. "Perhaps this is a conversation you should have with her."

"No, Kassia. Tell me."

She sighs, rubbing her forehead. "From the time you were young, she saw how... dedicated, obsessed, you were with the role. She never thought the island needed another Moon Priest when they already had the best one for the job."

My body goes numb as the revelation sinks in. She knew about me... my monster... and she protected my biggest secret. Not out of fear, but because she believed in me?

Warmth spreads through my chest, quickly melting away the numbness. I need to talk to her, hear this from her—

A chorus of panicked yelling cuts through the air, and the hair on my neck stands up.

"Moons," Kassia exclaims, slowly standing. "What's going on?"

A blur of color passes the windows as people run past.

"Stay here," I tell her.

Without hesitating, I bolt from the hut, following the direction of the screams on the beach. My feet practically fly down the dirt-packed path as I weave through the handful of small buildings between Kassia's home and the Nectar Hut

Once the path gives way to sand, I halt, taking in the ruckus.

A dozen or so wardens crouch behind the large wooden rack used to store the tideborn's seaboards. They take cover, with Lachlan furiously spewing instructions. Joss moves quickly, handing out spears while his father briefs the group.

A boat bobs just off the coast, slowly growing larger as it comes toward us.

Arrows line the beach, some abandoned and some protruding out of the sand.

Villagers stand near the Nectar Hut talking in a rapid cacophony. I recognize Mariel and bolt to her.

She stands in just a seasuit, with her arms wrapped around her body. Her dark curls are sopping wet and slicked back out of her face, which is a shade paler than normal.

"High Priest," she says quickly. The group around her grows quiet upon my approach.

"Where's Soraya?" I ask, my heart jackhammering with fear.

She shakes her head. "Sleeping in our chambers."

The relief that floods my blood is so immense I nearly drop to kiss the sand. "You should go up to the temple." I scan the faces of the nervous villagers. "All of you—go!"

Much to my surprise, they heed my advice and scamper toward the mountain. Mariel furrows her brow at me but doesn't listen. I don't have time to argue with the stubborn priestess.

"Don't be stupid," I tell her. "If something happens to you, it'd crush Soraya."

Before I spin away, I catch the hint of a smirk on her face. Without waiting for a response, I dart toward the group of wardens.

"Same goes for you, Razzy!" Mariel yells after me.

The strange nickname distracts me briefly, but I push it away and pick up my pace. The sand slows me down, stealing my stamina faster than I expected.

How the hell do the wardens run through this?

Lachlan spots me, and his words trail off.

"Take cover!" he yells, and the wardens turn to face me, their expressions tight.

An arrow whizzes by, landing in the sand with a soft explosion of dirt. Heart pounding, I dive behind the stack of towering, weathered planks, joining the wardens in their nook of safety. A succession of relief-filled sighs litters the air.

I take a second to catch my breath, eyeing the rack filled with old, sun-bleached boards, which casts a shadow over us. It leans crookedly from days of sun, wind, and sea beating on it, and the boards are cracked and chipped, but it successfully protects from the approaching arrows.

"High Priest Raziel," Lachlan greets, voice tight.

"What's happening?"

"Mainlanders," he says. "They want our silverdew—the pollen they didn't get last month for the shipment."

"Can't we just show them the flowers, let them see they truly haven't opened?"

Lachlan grits his teeth. "Doesn't seem like they're interested in docking peacefully."

"This concern should've been brought up sooner," I say in a calm tone. "If the mainland officials are unhappy—"

"They're not officials," Joss cuts in. He points through a gap in the wood. "See that flag?" I squint, vaguely making out a red flag with a black bow and arrow image on it, fluttering high above the boat. "Symbol of the insurgents."

"Rogue pirates?" I ask, frowning.

"We can fight back," Lachlan says. "It's not a declaration of war on our end to defend ourselves, and if they're not official soldiers of the mainland, then our ties are not broken."

My eye catches Joss's, and my gut twists. He was right; I didn't take the issue of the silverdew seriously enough, and it's spread to the mainland and beyond. Our island is under attack, threatened for our most valuable resource.

This happened once when I was young, and I remember thinking it was Amos's fault for being a reckless leader.

Now, I see the truth.

It wasn't him, it was the curse. Our dying magic, our impending death at the thirty-year mark.

This is my fault. And I can't fix it.

Instead of looking smug like I expected, Joss grimaces, and then he gives a small nod of acknowledgment that takes me aback.

"They can't get too close," Lachlan insists, a sharp edge to his tone. "Their boat is too big. They'll get stuck on the sandbar."

The group exchanges uncertain looks. We crowd together, moving closer to the board racks, peeking through the small cracks in the wood. A large wooden ship bobs just off the sandbar, its plethora of flags waving ominously high above. Shouts carry on the breeze, raising my hackles.

"I don't see dinghies to bring them in," another warden says with certainty. "They'll be forced to swim to get ashore."

Murmurs of relief go up around me. It'll be an advantage in our favor.

"They can't use their bows while they swim," someone else says.

Joss grunts. "If they're smart, they'll split up and keep shooters on the boat."

"What do we do?" I ask.

"Wait for them to get close enough," Lachlan mutters, eyes narrowing. I follow his line of sight. The boat appears larger than it was a few minutes ago, quickly growing closer.

"There's at least twenty on deck," Joss says.

"That we can see," someone else adds.

"We'll use the jungle cover to our advantage." Lachlan straightens up, turning to the blond warden beside me. "Nyla, instruct the treeborn to stay where they're at, hidden in the trees, and once the ship hits the sandbar and they begin to disembark, nock the arrows, set them aflame, and shoot in synchronization."

"Yes, Chief." She nods, checks the beach, then bolts toward the jungle beside us. A few delayed arrows rip through the air, none finding their mark.

"They're ignorant, out of their element, and have poor aim," Joss murmurs.

"Never underestimate your opponent," Lachlan warns.

Joss grimaces, his gaze flicking to me. "Learned that lesson the hard way," he mutters.

Lachlan turns back to the wardens around me. "You are all tideborn, gifted with an affinity for water. They cannot outswim you. Once the ship catches fire, they'll be forced to abandon it. We will attack while they're in the sea, before they set foot on our island."

He clears his throat, barking a few more specific instructions to various wardens.

"Joss and I will stay on the beach as a safety net. The treeborn will stay in the jungle, attacking at long range. We won't let them near our silverdew or the temple."

The temple.

Soraya.

My nerves alight, and suddenly I realize why the wardens are so protective of the island. It's more than saving our land or history; it's about protecting our people. Now I know what it's like to have someone to fight for.

"I can fight, too," I insist, stoking a flurry of whispers.

Joss nods. "He can. He's damn good," he confirms.

"No," Lachlan orders. "The High Priest stays back."

"But Dad—"

"No. And you stay with him—guard him." Lachlan moves away from his son, swiftly ending the conversation.

Lowering my voice, I speak to Joss. "We won't let them touch our island."

He tips his head in respect, pride sparkling in his eyes. He glances from his father to me, then surprises me by giving me a small nod. I return it.

There's no room for pettiness or emotion here; it'll only distract us.

I force thoughts of Soraya, of the temple, to the back of my mind.

Right now, we need to be a team.

Shortly after the roles are assigned, havoc erupts. Everything happens so fast. The ship hits the sandbar, sticking just off the coast. Flaming arrows fly from the jungle, courtesy of the treeborn hidden there. The boat quickly catches fire, causing the incoming mainlanders to panic and dive into the sea as violent flames shoot up, angrily devouring their transport.

Once they're all in the water, distracted by their panic, our first line of tideborn rip their seaboards free of the wooden rack and charge toward the waves.

A few enemy soldiers stand in the knee-deep water of the sandbar, nocking their arrows. They let them rip through the air. Joss, Lachlan, and I crouch behind the remainder of our cover, watching in silence as the wardens use their boards as shields to block the incoming arrows.

In response, our treeborn let more arrows of their own rip, swiftly meeting with their targets with sickening thuds. Cries ring out through the air as people on both sides are hit.

"Moons have mercy." Lachlan lurches upward, tearing a seaboard free and charging toward the water. He releases a battle cry, leading a group of wardens into the waves.

I stand, unwilling to watch this bloodshed any longer. Joss reaches for my wrist, tugging me back down. He gives me a stern look.

"You can't. You're the Moon Priest."

"I thought you wanted to replace me."

He rolls his eyes. "Soraya would murder me if I let you get yourself killed."

I grit my teeth. He's right.

"Trust me, I want to be out there fighting just as badly," he mutters, his whole body practically vibrating with the need to move. It mirrors my own.

Joss is forced to stay back as the next in line for Chief Warden. That way, should anything happen to the chief, his successor is protected. The chief and the successor never fight in the same battle together.

I glance at my palm, remembering how the moonlight shot out to help Soraya when she almost fell down my stairs. If only I could access that magic, I could wield it against our enemies. But I have no idea how or why that power appeared.

If Soraya were here...

Someone else joins us, crouching behind the remaining boards.

Joss glances over his shoulder, his eyes immediately darkening. "What the hell, Mariel?!"

"I couldn't just leave you," she says, out of breath. "If something happens to you or Lachlan..." She shifts her gaze to me. "Or our High Priest..."

"No," he says sarcastically. "If anything happens to any of us, it'll cause a ripple effect that destroys the whole island, so don't do anything stupid." He huffs. "Anything *else* stupid."

A deep scream cuts through the air. My heart stalls as I peek through the boards again.

"I can't sit here and do nothing," I hiss, jumping to my feet.

Another scream rips through the thick, humid air, and I take off toward the shore.

"Shells—*Raziel!*" Joss curses at me, but I don't turn to see if he's following.

The sand slows me down as I dart toward the scuffle happening in the shallow water, but I pump my arms and use my upper body momentum to carry me faster. I barely know how to swim, so there's no hope for me in the water, but I can help here.

Sitting by and doing nothing isn't an option.

A red-haired warden collapses a few paces in front of me, falling onto his side in the shallow waves. A pained cry tears from his lungs as he grips his leg. The dark wood of the enemy's arrow protrudes from his thigh.

He groans, tumbling onto his stomach with a splash.

Instinctively, I reach for him, pulling his face from the water. He gasps, blinking at me in shock. An inky crimson stain spreads out around us, tainting the normally pristine waters.

"High Priest," he croaks, eyes widening. "Leave me—run, *hide.*"

Ignoring his protests, I scoop him to my chest and sprint toward the seaboard storage. My lungs burn by the time I make it back and gently lower him to the ground between Mariel and Joss.

"Can you help him?" Joss asks, looking at me expectantly.

My chest tightens, and I glance at my palm, where dried *red* blood lingers. I shake my head, and a shadow crosses Joss's face.

Damn unreliable moonblood.

"We need to keep the arrow in place until we can properly staunch the bleeding," Mariel says. The warden's eyes flit shut, his face turning an unnatural shade of green. Mariel reaches for a pulse. "We need to create a tourniquet so I can remove the arrow; I think the tips are poisoned."

She glances down at his leg, growling. I follow her line of sight to where the arrow protrudes, and my heart stalls at the sight of black, web-like veins spreading across his skin.

Without hesitating, I reach for the hem of my shirt and tug it off, thrusting it at Mariel, and her mouth drops into a surprised O.

Joss grunts, and Mariel snaps out of it, quickly getting to work and ripping the fabric. She winds it around the sick warden's leg, tugging it tight before tying it into a knit.

"I'm going to have it push it straight through," Mariel whispers, face grim.

Glancing down at my palms, I silently curse the moonblood for not showing up when I need it. The burning desire to help consumes me.

"I need to get back out there," I say, jumping back up. "There might be others hurt."

Joss is on his feet in an instant. "I'm coming with you."

"You need to stay—"

"If you're going, *I'm* going," Joss snarls. "I've sworn to protect Isle de Lunith with my life."

I nod, not wanting to waste time arguing. Admittedly, his persistence in protecting our people is admirable.

We work in tandem, pulling our wounded back to shore and narrowly avoiding arrows. Between our treeborn and tideborn, we've managed to keep the enemy mainlanders off our coast, but there were nearly double the number of people we initially counted. The others must've been stowed away, hidden beneath the deck.

Flames shoot from their ship, consuming the wood whole. With it turning to ash in the distance, the pirates have been flushed out, backed into a corner, and forced to attack.

"We never wanted a fight," Joss murmurs as he pulls a dead enemy soldier ashore. My gut churns, and I force the nausea down. "They attacked us first."

"I know," I say through gritted teeth. "We're protecting our people, our island. Our moons."

My mind replays the lore of our goddesses, Neridessa and Celandria. The violent nature of humans was the catalyst. This exact behavior incited the goddesses' rebellion, resulting in their moon-curse.

After a while, the cries die out as our enemies are cut down.

Is this how Neridessa and Celandria felt? Their hands forced into a violent response in a desperate attempt to protect their peace?

It's the cruelest of ironies, and it breaks my heart.

Perhaps we're not that different from the goddesses after all.

"Father!" Joss's hoarse voice rips me from my musings.

I scan the carnage around us. Splintered wood drifts past, still smoldering. Bodies float face down. Arrows line the beach. Wardens lie on their backs along the wet, packed sand, their chests heaving violently.

Joss hovers over a body in the sand, his back to me. I join his side, crouching down.

Lachlan lies unmoving, an arrow protruding from his chest.

"Don't remove it," I instruct Joss, working hard to keep my voice steady. "We haven't lost a single warden today, Joss, and we're not about to now."

Choppy breaths come from Lachlan's open mouth, and I know it's not too late... yet. But the small trickle of blood seeping out of the corner of his lips warns me of his impending fate.

My uselessness overwhelms me. If my magic wasn't broken, cursed, I could save him.

It hits me: Soraya can.

She should be leading this.

"Where's Soraya?" Joss yells, as if reading my mind. His eyes are wide with panic. He runs a hand over his hair frantically, scanning the beach. "She can help."

"Help how?" I ask quietly, challenging his knowledge.

He grunts like a wild animal. "She just can—it doesn't matter! We need her!"

A bolt of jealousy spears my chest. He knows her secret. It's not the time for envy, or other distracting emotions, yet I can't push it away.

Until I take in the sight of Lachlan, unconscious and bleeding on the sand.

I can't help him.

But Soraya can. If the villagers see what she can do, if they learn the truth, they'll undoubtedly want *her* as our leader. She's kept it secret for this long for a reason.

Yet as my eyes flit from Joss to his father, I know she'd expose herself in a heartbeat if it meant saving someone that matters to her.

The other issue is what it means for me. My life's work will be null and void, and none of my history as the Moon Priest will matter.

Without my role, who will I be?

I've tried so hard to be a competent leader, and for what? To lose it all because when it truly matters, I failed my islanders?

No… failing them would be letting my own fears of incompetence prevent me from asking for help. Joss has lost enough; this island has lost enough. We need Soraya's help.

We must save Lachlan, no matter what that means for me. It's not about me.

Throat thick with emotion, I turn toward the wooden stack of seaboards. "Mariel!" I yell.

She pops up a second later, a thin sheen of sweat lining her face.

"Get Soraya," I command. "Please. Tell her I *need* her, Mariel."

She nods briefly and spins away, pumping her arms as she darts across the beach toward the mountain.

Joss releases a choppy breath and drops to his hands beside his dad. His body sinks into the sand as he cradles Lachlan's still form.

"Thank you," he mutters without looking at me.

CHAPTER TWENTY-FIVE

THE HEALING

SORAYA

"Get up, Soraya!" A shoulder on my arm shakes me violently.

I gasp, jolting upright from my sleep. Mariel releases me and steps back, her eyes wide with panic. At a glance, I can tell something is amiss. She sucks in a deep breath, steadying her shaking hands.

"What's going on?" Alarms blare inside me as I take in her bloodstained hands and tear-streaked face.

"Come!" She turns and shoots toward the door.

Without another question, I'm out of bed, following her out the door.

"The village was attacked," she yells over her shoulder as we run.

My chest caves. A thousand questions flit through my mind. Raziel, Kassia, Joss, Lachlan… everyone else I've grown up with and love come to the fore of my thoughts. Instead of voicing any of my fears, I save my energy and bolt as fast as my legs and lungs will take me.

We reach the beach in record time, my knees and shins screaming at me. But the pain is short-lived. Once I stop running, the healing properties of my moonblood catch up, swiftly rectifying the source of my pain.

Instantly, I realize the source of Mariel's shocked state.

Mangled bodies lie all over the beach—mostly people I don't recognize, dressed in strange swimming suits that cover most of their bodies. The relief is short-lived, though, as I spot a familiar warden with a bandage around her head.

I start for the injured warden, but Mariel grabs my shoulder.

"Raziel told me to get you," she says, voice wavering.

"Where is he?" The trepidation in my chest builds, constricting so tightly around my lungs that I fear I'll suffocate.

Her face is somber as she looks past me, pointing further down the shore. I spot Raziel's dark hair and broad, light brown shoulders. Instantly, gratitude washes over me, and the worst of my fears are alleviated.

He's okay.

He kneels beside Joss, who stares down at the sand, at the body they're hovering over.

Panic grips my throat.

I take off, sand shooting up around me as I move as quickly as I can. At my arrival, the men's heads whip up toward me, both donning equally somber expressions.

"Soraya." Raziel pops up and wraps his arms around me.

I'm stunned silent by the display of affection, but my body responds to his, molding against his bare chest. His hand cups the back of my head tightly.

"Thank the moons you're okay." His scruff scrapes my skin deliciously, sending a shudder through me.

"What happened?" I gasp, pulling back to look at him. He grimaces.

My gaze moves to Joss, whose eyes fill with tears and an unspoken plea.

"Joss?" I reach for him, but the sight of Lachlan on the ground, unmoving, freezes me.

"Please," Joss whispers. "For me, Soraya."

He needn't say another word. I drop to the sand beside Lachlan. His chest rises and falls with shallow breaths, but an arrow shaft protrudes unnaturally. Crimson rivulets drip from the wound, staining the pale sand around him.

Panicked, I say, "I need a—"

"Here." Raziel hands me a letter opener with a glinting blade.

I pause, wondering why he had it on him. Brushing off the concern, I accept the blade, nodding in thanks. My eyes roam Lachlan's chest, wincing at the black ink-like webs spreading out beneath his skin. "Poison."

Joss grinds his teeth. "I'll need to push the arrow out the other side."

My face softens as I study my friend. "Are you okay to... should we have someone else—"

"No." He grips his father's shoulder, carefully rolling him onto his side. "I'll do it."

"Okay."

Sucking in a deep breath, I line the blade up with my palm. In a swift motion, I drag it across the skin. Mariel gasps, but Raziel blocks her from coming closer. Faintly, I hear her cursing at him, but I stay focused on the Chief Warden.

Joss wraps his hands around the arrow's shaft and meets my eyes.

I nod. "Now."

With a little force, he snaps the fletching off the end of the arrow. He begins pushing the wood through his father's chest, holding him steady on his side. My stomach roils at the squelching sound. There's a sickening pop as the point digs free through his back.

I squeeze my eyes shut. "Hurry. Get it all the way out so I can heal him." My voice is strained, but I focus on taking deep breaths to stay steady.

The wound in my palm tightens, already stitching itself together.

"Done," Joss says hoarsely a second later.

My eyes flick open, and the silver blood on my palm gleams in the sunlight. I quickly bring it to Lachlan's lips, forcing it to drip into his open mouth before the cut can mend fully.

The crowd around us is still. My skin prickles with the awareness of onlookers, but none of that matters.

Joss tilts his head toward the sky, muttering a prayer to the moons under his breath.

I told Kassia I wanted to keep my power a secret unless there ever came a time when someone needed it. She warned me against interfering with natural life cycles such as old age, prohibiting me from using my magic on her ever again, but there's no way I'd refuse to help Lachlan.

He's in his late forties, still young and full of life and vigor. Joss needs him.

Our island needs him.

Slowly, Lachlan's lips begin to move as he responds to my moonblood. The dark, inky web spreading across his chest fades. The jagged hole grows smaller, mending itself together flawlessly.

I don't have to see his back to know it's healing just the

same. A cry rips from Joss's throat as he whispers a slew of gratitude to me.

The only proof left of his brush with death is the drying blood streaking his body.

Gasps rise around the beach, and the crowd pushes closer.

Raziel warns them to give us space.

"Dad?" Joss asks, a tear sliding down his cheek.

With a sputtering cough, Lachlan sits up, his eyes flicking open. I sit back on my heels, giving him space. He touches his head, then drops his hand to his unblemished chest.

"Soraya?" he asks, confused, as he glances from me to Raziel to his son. "Joss."

The two wardens crash into an emotional hug, and I stand, giving them space. Privacy, however, doesn't seem to be an option based on the dozens of stunned stares locked in our direction. The many islanders place a hand on their hearts, bowing their heads deeply in a sign of respect.

The sight stuns me, and I nearly lose my balance.

"Secrets out," Raziel whispers. My cheeks blaze under the excessive attention. "I'm sorry."

I cup his cheek gently, and a pulse of energy zaps my skin and causes me to jerk back. "You should be—for not getting me sooner."

He blinks once, twice, then furrows his brow. "You're not mad at being forced to reveal your magic?"

I laugh softly. "Of course not. I'm mad that you let all these poor wardens suffer for so long."

My eyes shift to Mariel's, who are marred with hurt, and I know I'll have to explain everything to her as soon as possible. Then my gaze washes over the various bruised, battered, and bloodied wardens.

Turning back to Joss and Lachlan, I begin to instruct them. "Chief, you need to head to Delores's hut and rest—"

"No, I need—"

"Listen to her," Raziel commands, voice low.

"Yes, Soraya," Lachlan says, his lip tilting up in amusement.

"Send her here with any supplies she has." I turn to Joss. "Identify which wardens need immediate care. Sort them by priority so I can help them."

"Are you sure?" he asks, brows furrowed.

I nod, then turn to Mariel before he can say more. "I know you're angry with me—"

"Bitch," she whispers before reaching for me and drawing me into a hug. "I'm downright *pissed* at you, but holy moons, you're incredible!"

Pulling free with a chuckle, I say, "Can you please find Kassia? We need to feed these wardens. They need to get their strength up for recovery, even with my... magic." It feels weird to say it aloud, but when Mariel giggles, I smile in return.

"How can I help?" Raziel asks.

For a moment, I stare at him, considering the question. The spot on my chest tingles, as if roused by his proximity. Mindlessly, I rub at it.

"I have an idea. Give me your hand." He does as I say, and once again, my skin prickles when it meets his, the magic beneath buzzing with excitement.

I tug the hem of my—*his*—shirt down, revealing the faint outline of my moon marking. Away from the Union, the bright iridescence light has nearly faded away. Taking Raziel's left palm, I plant it flat against my chest.

The magic inside me roars to life, erupting in response to his touch—bright, blinding rays of dazzling, opalescent light seep from the cracks between our skin. In response, the beach goes quiet. The islanders watch in awe, undoubtedly surprised by the unexpected display of power.

My skin comes alive, humming with magic. I can feel it

churning, tickling my insides, as it melts away into Raziel's hand. He shudders, keeping his palm flat against my skin.

His eyes meet mine, telling a story of reverence and adoration.

"Soraya," he whispers, eyes flitting to my lips. His fingers curl slightly, tickling my collarbone.

The intensity subsides as quickly as it started, and he cautiously removes his hand. Both of our markings continue to glow, and for a moment, I stare at his hand, mesmerized by the swirl of colors.

I'm no stranger to the sight, having stared at my own in the mirror on many Unions, but the fact that his moonstone responds to mine is magic of its own.

"There," I whisper. "Now, you can help me by healing our people."

"How'd you know that'd work?"

I chuckle. "Honestly? I had no idea it would. Intuition told me to try."

We work in tandem, flitting from warden to warden and feeding them our moonblood. Mariel and Delores work to patch up minor wounds, distributing coconuts to keep the villagers hydrated.

Joss and Kassia get a big spitfire going. Soon, the beach air is a blend of sea, smoke, salt, and sweetness. The scents dance on the air as the sun sets in the distance. Coconut meat and fish roast, slowly feeding everyone.

I close my eyes and inhale deeply, taking a moment to exist in the warm, intoxicating scents. *This* is what it means to be alive: community.

Lachlan wanders back down to the beach a short while later. Our eyes meet over the blazing fire, and he offers me a bashful smile. I nod my head in understanding.

Despite him needing to rest, I knew he wouldn't stay away for long.

Later, when the twin moons twinkle high overhead, the sun long gone, Joss approaches Raziel and me. He throws his arms around both of our shoulders, pulling us in tight. A maniacal laugh escapes him, and Raziel and I share a concerned look.

"My dad survived because of you," he says, the laughter fading. "All the wardens are okay. The island is okay. And you know what? Everything is going to be more than okay."

I pat his hand. "We'll be fine, Joss."

"I'm sorry I ever doubted you," he says to Raziel.

Raziel stays quiet, studying the warden. They share a long, tense look.

"I see it now, the truth," Joss says.

"What's that?" Raziel asks.

"Two moons but *one* Moon Priest?" Joss laughs in a self-deprecating manner. "We're all idiots."

CHAPTER TWENTY-SIX

THE TIP

RAZIEL

"*D*o you care to elaborate?" I ask, frowning at Joss.

He drops his arms, looking from me to Soraya.

"Source loves balance, right? Well, there are two moons and one curse." He points to the sky. "Why wouldn't there be two Moon Priests, too?" He cocks his head, that stupid grin appearing on his face as he gestures from Soraya to me. "Maybe that's why you two balance each other so well."

He saunters off in those minuscule little sea shorts as if he didn't just rock my world to the core.

Sighing, I clench my hand into a fist. I've been looking at this all wrong.

Instead of searching for insights into the other Moon Priests' curses and magic, I should've been studying the goddesses and their original curse.

My head spins as the thought I had earlier comes roaring

back to me: the irony of Neridessa and Celandria. Cursed lovers.

I need to get to my library.

Now.

The immediate need to unravel this thread consumes me, and I flee from the beach, sprinting toward the mountain.

"Raziel!" Soraya calls from behind me.

I can't stop, can't explain it right now. We're so close to the answers, the solution, that I can't see anything else. I *need* to get to the bottom of this.

Joss's words replay, spiraling in the drain that is my mind.

I don't stop running until I make it to my sanctum, exploding into my private office. Crazed, I begin to pull down all the books I have on the goddesses and the moon curse—historical accounts, lore, legends, or anything relevant.

By the time Soraya catches up with me, my desk is covered with books for us to comb through.

"Raziel!" she yells so loudly that my spine goes rigid. Slowly, I turn to face her.

She heaves, her face red and flushed, and I don't think it's because of exertion. Her mouth is pinched into a tight line, and she narrows her eyes at me. It catches me off guard, and I open my mouth to apologize, but she cuts me off with a scathing look.

"After everything, how *dare* you abandon me again."

"No, I swear it's not—"

"Hush!" She stomps toward me, the hem of my black tunic caressing the tops of her thighs as she moves.

My mouth waters at the sight of her in my shirt. I force my eyes back to her face. It does little to help, though, because every bit of her is magnificent. My skin buzzes, drawing me toward her like she's a lighthouse and I'm the ship she's leading home.

Heat pools low in my core, my body responding with carnal need, something I've tried for so long to suppress.

Now is decidedly not the time to get aroused.

Suddenly, she stops, tilting her head and smirking. "You like this shirt, don't you?"

I swallow, trying to clear the thickness in my throat. "Well, it is *my* shirt. Of course I like it."

A dark look crosses her eyes, and she toys with the hem, slipping it up higher and higher until a tiny hint of white fabric at the apex of her thighs appears.

My pants tighten around my groin, and I'm afraid to move for fear that any friction will only instigate my arousal.

"Soraya," I say hoarsely, "what are you doing?"

"Punishing you," she whispers, narrowing her eyes. My spine tingles. "After everything, you're still content to evade me."

A huff escapes me. Doesn't she know that her nearness is punishment enough?

I've never fully let myself admit it, for fear of losing my focus, but I've wanted her for a long time. Being close enough to smell her sweet skin and make out the flecks of darker green in her bright blue eyes... to see all the tiny freckles dotting her sun-tanned cheeks... to hear her throaty laugh...

It nearly kills me.

Being around her without getting distracted is a challenge in itself.

This punishment will send me overboard. It'll be the death of me entirely.

"I wasn't running from you," I croak, forcing my eyes to stay on hers. My joints ache from how rigid I've gone. "I was leading you."

She quirks a brow. "Are you sure about that? It felt like you were shutting me out again."

"I knew you'd follow me." The urge to finally spill everything on my brain tugs at me... but mischief glints in her eyes. The corner of her mouth tilts up into a smirk, and I focus on the soft curves of her lips.

A bolt of heat shoots below my waistband, and my mouth goes dry. Suddenly, all the words evaporate from my brain.

She steps closer to me, her movement slow and graceful like a deadly panther. I could stop this now. The Moon Priest should not indulge in pleasures or distractions.

Then again, a priest isn't supposed to fight—yet I did. A priest is supposed to hide during battle, but I didn't.

And our island is better for it.

So, how is this any different? Maybe I'll be better for letting her in.

My palms grow sweaty as she tugs the hem of her shirt higher, tugging it up and over her head. She stands before me practically nude—her chest bare, soft pink nipples hardening into desirable peaks, and just a tiny pair of nearly translucent white panties.

My eyes linger on the only bit of fabric left, desperate to see more of her—all of her.

Her fingers toy with the waistband, tempting me. "Are you uncomfortable?" she asks quietly, her hand pausing.

I shake my head, not once glancing away.

"Hm. I suppose I need to punish you further."

The seductive lilt of her voice shoots straight to my aching cock. Never in my life have I wanted anyone as badly as I *need* Soraya right now.

She strides past me haughtily, shoving the books off my table. The heavy thuds echo in the room.

My eyes widen, and I make a strangled sound. "Soraya—"

"Yeah." She recoils, facial features scrunched together. Kneeling, she gently fingers the books.

"That was utterly careless, disrespectful of—"

"I know." She stands on a sigh, shakes out her arms, then puts a finger to my lips. "Let's just ignore that. It was sexier in my head."

I grit my teeth, fighting the urge to pick the poor books up and right them.

"We can rebind them later."

"I never expected *you*, of all people, to be a destroyer of archives."

"Said like you know me," she challenges.

"I used to watch you, you know." It slips out before I can stop it.

Her lips part in surprise. "When?"

"When we were kids. I remember wondering who the bright-haired girl spending all her time with Kassia was."

Her features soften, her freckle-dusted cheeks turning pink. "Why do you call her by her first name? Rather than Priestess Nyx, like the rest of us?"

Floundering, I stare into the distance before replying. "She's retired."

"Hmm."

She doesn't push it, and I'm grateful.

"I used to wonder about you, too," she admits.

I laugh. "Didn't the entire island?" I realize how conceited that sounds, and I rub my jaw, quickly adding, "I mean, it was no secret I was training to take over Amos's position as High Priest one day. Everyone wanted to know about me."

It was overwhelming and invasive. And after what happened... it was more important than ever that I create space between them and me.

"It was more than that," she says, fingers caressing my arms. "You stopped coming to the classroom when we were kids. I rarely saw you in the village or at lunch. And on the rare occasions I saw you in the library, before you stopped going there too, you changed."

I raise an eyebrow at her. "Changed?"

"You stopped smiling at me," she whispers. "There was a day I saw your smile for the last time, and I didn't even know it until I never saw it again."

Her words simultaneously break and mend my heart, the guilt and apology battling the need to be *seen* by her. I soften against her, cupping her cheek and placing my forehead against hers. "I'm sorry," I whisper.

"Don't be. I understand now." Her fingers drag down my chest to the waistband of my pants.

A tidal wave of conflicting emotions—elation, sorrow, confusion—crashes over me, leaving me breathless. Goosebumps leave a trail where her skin meets mine, and I tense up, unsure of how to reciprocate.

I can't possibly give her what she wants from me. Can I?

She grabs my wrist, tugging me toward the desk before my thoughts spiral. "Stop me at any time."

Before I even register what I'm doing, I'm gripping her hips and lifting her onto the desk. She squeals in surprise, biting her bottom lip as she watches me with hunger. Her fingernails caress my bare shoulders, digging into my skin and dragging me toward her.

"Come closer," she whispers.

I obey, and she wraps her legs around me, locking me in place.

"Good boy," she rasps in my ear, causing a spark of lust to ignite deep in my core.

My hips thrust forward of their own accord, my erection rubbing against her thin fabric. I groan as the feel of her lips ignites me from within.

"Have you ever fucked before, Raziel?" she whispers, scratching me harder.

"No," I growl, ripping her hands off me. I secure both her wrists in one of my hands behind her back, and she gasps, her eyes lighting up. Leaning forward, it's my turn to whisper in her ear. "And I will never *fuck*."

She tightens her legs around me, squirming and rubbing herself desperately against me. "Moons, I love it when you talk dirty to me."

"Is this okay?" I murmur, pulling back to look her in the eye.

She smiles softly. "More than okay."

"I don't want to hurt you."

"Then don't run away from us anymore, Raziel, from *this*."

My lungs compress, and I turn away from her gaze, unable to weather the emotion there.

She sighs. "If I want you to stop, or if you want *me* to stop, we'll say coconut. How about that?" I give her a confused look, and she laughs softly. "It's a safe word, just in case."

I nod, leaning forward to nibble on her earlobe. The soft gasp she responds with has blood rushing into my impossibly hard cock.

I fear that if I don't get relief soon, I'll explode.

Of course, I've pleasured myself in private. But already, merely having her bare thighs wrapped around me brings me more excitement than anything I could've incited on my own.

Tightening my grip on her wrists, I continue to keep her from touching me. With my other hand, I weave my fingers into the back of her hair, tugging tightly and forcing her to look up at me. Her turquoise eyes glaze over with lust, and she pants with desire.

"Kiss me," she commands softly, not breaking our gaze.

Leaning forward, I hover my lips over hers, not quite giving her what she wants. "No," I whisper.

She groans against my mouth, seeking the affection I withhold. "*Please,* Raziel."

I smirk, swerving to her jaw and planting my lips there instead. "I like it when you beg."

Trailing my tongue down her neck, to her chest, I pause at one of her nipples, circling it gently. The noises she makes cause my balls to tighten, and I worry that I'm moving too fast —that I'll lose control long before my pants ever come off.

The thought has me releasing my grip on her and pulling free, to cool down.

Big mistake.

The moment she's free, she winds her arms around my neck, aggressively tugging me to her. Our mouths crash together, and it's like the rainstorm after a drought, filling up our wells of intimacy.

Kissing her is unlike anything I've ever experienced in my life.

The thrill of it sends shockwaves down my spine. A terrifying, exhilarating rush of adrenaline and fear fills the void inside me.

Just like that day we kissed in the jungle, we explore each other's mouths with fervor. Making up for lost time. Each moan and stroke and lick is barely restrained, birthed from years of silent lust.

When I can no longer breathe, I gently break away, panting. "Soraya," I murmur, resting my forehead on her shoulder.

"Do you want this?" she asks, voice thick.

"More than I can possibly put into words."

"Then show me." She grips the button on my pants, deftly undoing it.

I freeze. "We can't."

"We *can*," she whispers, wiggling her fingers into my underwear. Her soft fingers brush my flesh, and I hiss, my cock throbbing in response. Her brows rise, and she smiles softly. "Have you ever been touched here?"

My chest rises and falls vigorously. All I can do is stare, wishing she'll touch me forever. Instead, she pulls her hand out of my pants and loops her arms around my neck. She pulls my forehead to hers.

"Do you trust me?" she whispers against my lips.

I nod. "Much to my chagrin, I do."

She chuckles, trailing her fingers down my chest. I flinch at the feather-light touch, a pleasant, tingling sensation coursing through me. Her laughter builds until she reaches my erection again. Then, all her humor quickly fades.

"Moons," she says breathlessly. "I love the way you feel."

I move with her motions, allowing my pants to drop around my ankles. My manhood springs free, begging for her touch. She wastes no time, gripping me in her fist and pumping me cautiously.

Precum beads on the head of my cock, and she swipes her thumb through it. With a sly look, she brings it to her mouth, licking it away.

"I've been dying to taste you," she moans.

Unable to help myself, I tug her underwear aside and press my tip to her soft flesh. She's so damp that it nearly makes me combust as I drag myself up and down through her folds.

"I want this, Raziel," she murmurs, but she shifts her hips forward in an attempt to get me to slip in.

"I can't," I croak, but I make no move to pull away entirely.

"Yes, you can," she says softly, wiggling forward so my head presses against her slick center, threatening to enter. My chest heaves, my heart races, and my hands tighten around her hips to hold her in place.

I shake my head, sucking a breath in through my teeth. "No… this is wrong."

"Then why does it feel so right?" she whispers, and my vision goes spotty with desperation. "Just the tip… please, I need to feel you."

My pulse thunders, and adrenaline courses through me. All these years I've managed to avoid this, but for what? I'm not even inside her yet, and this is easily the most pleasurable experience I've ever had.

It's so easy to understand why people lose themselves to this.

More.

I need *more*.

She digs her heels into my backside, nudging me forward until I begin to ease inside her. Just the very end of my head prods her open, and my vision goes spotty. She inhales sharply, then exhales a soft puff against my shoulder.

"So… soft… wet," I croak stupidly. My eyes flick shut, and I groan, consumed by her. I fight against the innate urge to press deeper. "Don't move."

If she does, it's over, and I want this moment to last forever.

"Please, Raziel," she begs. "All the way."

I kiss her on the lips gently, then rest my forehead against hers. "It feels too good."

"I guess if you won't help me out, then I'll have to do it myself." Her tone is teasing, and before I can make sense of her words, she reaches between us, locating her clit.

Her first two fingers work in circular motions as she finds a rhythm, pleasuring herself on the head of my cock. She rocks back and forth, her tight opening squeezing the end of me.

It would be so easy to thrust forward, to submerge myself in her.

But I can't.

I need to control myself, to keep my wits.

It's not too late to back out now, but once I give in, it's over. I've lost.

Soraya keeps her eyes locked between us as she plays with herself, and I watch, enraptured. Soon, her breathing grows faster, coming in quick pants. She rocks more aggressively against me, her fingers working furiously.

Suddenly, she throws her head back and cries out my name.

Her walls squeeze the head of my cock, and I can't take it.

I shove all the way inside her, drowning in her sweetness. She screams, wrapping her arms and legs tightly around me, locking me in place as her muscles flutter around me.

It's too much.

It's overwhelming.

I groan, shifting my hips, pulling back slightly before pressing against her again and emptying every bit of pent-up pleasure deep between her thighs.

CHAPTER TWENTY-SEVEN

THE REALIZATION

SORAYA

*W*e lie in Raziel's bed, tangled in each other. I rest my head on his chest, listening to the repetitive *thud* of his heartbeat. At every point of contact, a delightful tingle spreads through my body. Our entwined legs practically melt into one another. Silky black sheets rest haphazardly over our naked bodies, and his fingers caress my back gently.

Without the lust fogging my thoughts, I sift through the day's events, processing.

The beach.

The intrusion.

Everyone knows my secret now.

Yet despite all the disruptions, I'm entirely at peace at this moment. We can't stay here forever. Soon, we should head down to the beach to help clean. At least all the injuries were tended to, and Kassia was feeding everyone. It eases the guilt of slipping away.

For now, I want to cherish every second with Raziel.

I snuggle closer to him, breathing in his musky scent. After our connection atop his desk, we showered together, then explored each other's bodies leisurely in his bed.

There's still so much we need to work out between us, but this is a huge milestone for our relationship. Moons, it's a massive step for Raziel. Finally, he's learning to ask for help not only with his work, but with his pleasure. He's loosening his control and learning to trust me.

The thought makes me smile.

A moment later, my stomach rumbles, and Raziel's fingers freeze. I tip my head up, smiling at him. He brushes my hair out of my face, studying me.

"We need to feed you," he murmurs.

"I won't argue with that."

We reluctantly disentangle ourselves. Raziel throws on a pair of tight underwear and black pants, then tosses me a clean shirt that's nearly identical to the one I was wearing before.

My stomach flutters with excitement, and hunger, as I slip it on. Then we head to the kitchen.

"Sit," he orders, turning away from me to assemble ingredients. I slide onto a stool at the island counter. "Don't even think about moving. I've got this."

I prop myself up on my elbows, watching as he prepares his ingredients on the counter that runs along the wall. His hands are confident and purposeful as he grabs an array of veggies, cleaning them in the sink and lining them up beside a bamboo cutting board.

The knife flashes as he chops with ease, a quick, rhythmic sound filling the room. He moves like he's done this a thousand times.

My eyes track his bare, muscular back as it flexes with the

motions. He sidesteps to the stove, lighting the flame and placing a pan on it. After drizzling coconut oil, he tosses in the veggies. The food roars, sizzling, and the scent of garlic fills my nose, causing my mouth to water.

He produces a bumpy, yellow-green fruit about the size of my head next. Holding it up, he cocks a brow at me.

"This," he says, his tone dropping low, "is the secret. Shred it, spice it, *savour* it."

I laugh, loving how alive he comes when he's cooking. "I see you have a thing for jackfruit."

"How could you not?" he asks, as he faces away and begins ripping into the fruit with his bare hands, fingers strong and dexterous. It shouldn't be as sexy as it is, but he makes it look decadent. "It's versatile, nutritious, abundant."

He uses a knife to dice the shreds into smaller bits.

Raziel glances over his shoulder, shooting me a cocky half-grin. The expression is so rare and lighthearted that it steals my breath.

"*Fucking* looks good on you, Raziel," I tease.

He pauses, his dark eyes sharpening. "I have never and will never *fuck*, Soraya."

I smirk. "Then what do you call what we did in there?"

He drops the knife and whirls toward the island counter, planting his hands on the surface and leaning forward until we're only a hair's breadth away. "Making love."

Then, without another word, he picks up his knife and continues to shred his jackfruit as if he didn't just send my heart tumbling down the mountainside.

"Is spicy okay?" he murmurs, entirely focused on his creation.

"Yes," I squeak out, wholly obsessed with the man before me.

He sprinkles an array of spices and salts, continuing to

walk me through the process. It goes in one ear and out the other because I'm wholly mesmerized by the ripples in his muscles and the deep, intimate tone of his voice.

At the end, he kisses his fingertips. "Perfection."

The fruit hits the pot, sizzling alongside the vegetables. He uses a wooden spoon to scrape the bottom, stirring it all up. Even though he's focused, he steals glances at me out of the corner of his eye. My cheeks hurt from smiling like a giddy child.

Finally, he covers the pot and leans his hip against the counter, crossing his arms over his bare chest and locking his gaze onto mine. "It needs to simmer for a bit. And we need to talk."

I perk up, sitting taller on the stool. "Yes, we do."

About so much.

About us, the island, our magic—

"Joss is a clever fella," Raziel says, halting my thoughts.

"Joss?" A confused chuckle escapes me.

"He pieced together the most obvious factor we've been missing."

"Two Moon Priests?" I arch a brow. "Just because I have the marking doesn't mean I'm equipped to lead the island. We only need one leader, and we have a great one—*you*."

A hint of color lines his cheeks as he glances away. "Two moons and one curse. Two moonstone markings and one curse; it's all connected, Soraya. *We're* connected."

"Yeah, but there's only *one* moonstone. How do you explain that?"

He zones out, deep in thought for a moment before shaking his head. "I don't know yet."

My fingers hover over the spot on my sternum, lightly caressing it through the fabric. Neither of us glow at the moment, but it's obvious now that our magic is interconnected. I don't know what it means, but he's on to something.

It's time to tell him the whole truth.

Clearing my throat, I quell myself for the impending awkwardness. "Speaking of Joss..." I force myself to hold Raziel's curious stare. "The reason he knows about my moonstone marking and magic is because he's... helped me with it."

He raises a curious eyebrow. "Helped how?"

Squirming, I ransack my brain for phrasing. It's a delicate situation, and I pray to the moons Raziel doesn't judge me for it. "Your curse is outward; mine is inward."

"I'm not following, Soraya."

"The magic, sometimes... is too much. You know how it comes to a head for you during the Union?"

He nods slowly, eyes narrowing.

"Mine does, too. It's not as destructive as yours is, just uncomfortable, but I've discovered I can... release some of the magic." Dragging in a slow, steadying breath, I continue before he can ask how. "Through intimacy."

At first, he says nothing. Then his brows scrunch together, and he gives me a strange look. "Is that why you just—"

"No," I cut in quickly. "I mean, yes, sex with you helped release me in more than one way, but I promise I *wanted*—no, I needed that with you, Raziel. With *you*," I add softly before he can assume incorrectly. "I should've told you before, but I just didn't know how to get it out."

He pauses. "I have a dozen questions, and I fear I don't want the answer to any of them." Spinning around, he snags bowls from the counter and busies himself at the stove. He shakes his head, sighing.

"That night you saw Joss and me in the woods—"

"Please, don't," he says hoarsely, gripping the counter and

tipping his head down. "I'm an intelligent adult. I understand what you're implying quite well. It doesn't mean I want to envision the woman I love being pleasured by another man."

My jaw drops, and I nearly topple off the stool.

The woman he loves?

"You love me?" I whisper, almost inaudibly.

A beat passes, and he doesn't reply. Despite being a mature adult myself, a hint of satisfaction blossoms in my chest at the thought that Raziel is *jealous*. Because that means he cares.

"Yes," he finally grits out, as if it pains him to admit.

"I never felt for him the way I do for you, Raziel," I add softly. He slowly turns, locking eyes with me. Relief flickers through his eyes. "I don't know what we are,"—I gesture between us—"but I do know it transcends friendship. And you're the only one I want to be intimate with."

"Thank the moons." His chest falls as he blows out a long breath. "We're *everything*, Soraya."

Dropping the bowls full of jackfruit jambalaya in front of me, he rounds the island and scoops me into his arms. I plaster myself to his bare chest as he rests his chin on my head.

"I pride myself in being good at many things, but I don't know how to do *this*," he murmurs into my hair.

I can't help but chuckle. "You're doing pretty damn good so far. Just be yourself and keep practicing your communication. Keep trusting me."

He cups my cheeks, pulling my mouth to his and kissing me gently. "I promise to do my best. For you. For us."

I smile against his lips. "That's all I ask. *That* is the man *I* fell for."

When we pull apart, Raziel gestures to the food and grabs the seat beside me. I take a hefty bite, and I'm gobsmacked. An explosion of flavorful spices steals my attention. "Wow," I murmur as I take another bite.

Raziel looks pleased, but he stays quiet as we eat. I relish his cooking, sending up silent thanks to the moons for this man.

"My monster appears during the Union," he says between bites. "It simmers down if I feed on blood, which I've learned the hard way." He uses his fork to push some food around. "That's why I lock myself away each Union when it appears until night passes."

Reaching out, I brush his pinky with mine. "Now that we know my moonblood counteracts it, you won't need to hide anymore. You won't have to worry about hurting anyone."

He goes quiet, stirring his food around.

"In exchange..." I pause dramatically, and he turns to me, so I waggle my brows at him seductively.

He tips his head back and laughs, the rich sound of his amusement softening my bones. "Your *curse* seems a lot less problematic than mine."

"I'll admit, it's easily managed right now. But when I was younger, without the... intimacy to ease it, I would get violently ill during the Union. At times, I felt like I was going to explode. Kassia hid me away when my skin would glow, and I feared the magic would swallow me whole."

He frowns. "Soraya..."

I put up a hand, shaking my head. "I don't want your pity. I just don't want you to think it's as simple as it seems."

"Or maybe it is that simple." He taps his jaw, eyes glossed over in thought. "Together, we form a symbiotic relationship."

Smiling, I shovel in another bite. "Always analyzing. Always logical. Just let yourself *feel*, Raziel."

"I feel plenty." His fork hovers over the bowl, and he shifts stiffly. "I know you're the one who healed Kassia."

I pause, my chest squeezing. "She wanted me to keep it a secret, but it was always to protect you," I admit. "I didn't know the details of the attack; I put it together recently. But I didn't want anyone to know I could heal like that anyway, for fear they'd want me to take your position."

"I thought Amos healed her... he was my father, you know." His words smack me in the face.

I whisper, voice pained, "Raziel..."

"Now it's my turn to say I don't want *your* pity." He laughs dryly. "He wasn't a very great father, nor a wonderful Moon Priest, but I need to accept that and stop blaming him for how I am today."

I tilt my head, reaching out to place my hand on his. "You're an amazing man, Raziel. Because of him or despite him, it doesn't matter. Either way, you are the best Moon Priest our island has ever had."

He rolls his eyes, turning his head bashfully, but not before I catch the whisper of a smile on his lips.

"Wait a second..." Something hits me, and I gasp, jerking my hand back. "That makes Kassia your grandmother."

Picking up his fork, he takes another bite and nods. "Yup."

"Moons have mercy, how many more secrets do you have?" I exclaim.

"I think you know them all now. Should I be asking you the same?"

I shake my head, chuckling as I dig back into my food. "If you had opened up in the beginning, we wouldn't be here right now."

Raziel shoots me a stern glance. "Exactly. We wouldn't be *here* right now: exactly where we need to be. Sometimes, secrets aren't a miscommunication, they're just us hiding from ourselves."

"You've come a long way, Raziel," I say, surprised by his words.

He clears his throat, dropping his voice an octave. "The reason I brought up Amos is... he died on his thirtieth birthday. As did the Moon Priest before him. I also found a journal from a priest decades ago who speculated the role was... cursed... and he stopped his entries after his thirtieth birthday."

I drop the fork. It splatters into my jambalaya as I whip my head to Raziel. "What are you saying?"

"I'm saying *that's* the real curse... dying at thirty, for the cycle to reset. We've only been distracted by the hiccups in the island's magic, but it's bigger than that. I think the cycle is nearing its end, and that's why the magic is acting up."

"Because your birthday is close," I whisper, shutting my eyes with a heavy sigh. But if we can break the curse, we can free the moons and thus the Moon Priest from the role.

Right?

Suddenly, I've lost my appetite. I push the bowl away, hating that I can't finish the divine meal Raziel prepared, but I can't fathom taking another bite with this information swirling through me. At least he was kind enough to let me eat most of it before bringing it up.

"Neridessa and Celandria were together thirty years before being torn apart. They spend twenty-nine days apart each month, uniting only on the thirtieth day," I muse. I'm familiar with the goddesses and their curse, having taught it to the children for years.

He sighs. "See? Death upon the thirtieth-year tracks for a curse."

"Now that we're together, with our moonstones and magic united, do you think we've broken the cycle?" I wonder hopefully.

"We'll find out during the next Union," he mutters.

I glance upward, taking in the two moons through the overhead window. He follows my line of sight, but neither of us voices the obvious issue: the smaller moon is still pale, its light less luminous than its larger counterpart.

If the moons are still separated, and the magic is still waning, does that mean the curse isn't broken?

"Raziel?" I ask quietly. "When do you turn thirty?"

He sighs, hanging his head. "Two days after the next Union."

CHAPTER TWENTY-EIGHT

THE OVATION

RAZIEL

I have twenty-eight days to live if the waning moon is any indicator. More importantly, I have twenty-eight days to figure out how to save Soraya's life. She might have a few years to go before approaching thirty, but one day, she inevitably will. Whether she's officially the Moon Priest or not, she has the cursed marking.

I don't care if *I* die, but I refuse to let her succumb to the same fate.

Yesterday, after eating, we returned to the beach to help with the cleanup. Though the villagers watched me with a mixture of wariness, shock, and confusion, they ultimately left me alone. I spent time with my thoughts, trying to make sense of everything.

We stored away any usable driftwood from the ship, burned their dead at sea, and combed away the bloodied sand. By the end, the beach was pristine, our skin unblemished, but the scent of charred flesh and the scars of battle will forever mark our souls.

I was disappointed Soraya didn't spend the night with me, but she said she had to speak with Mariel, which is understandable. It's admirable how she cares for her friends.

Now, I stand before my mirror, preparing for the assembly which was rescheduled for this afternoon.

I pull on my cloak and fasten it with the broach just below my throat. It feels heavier than it used to, suffocating in a way. With a sigh, I yank the neckline and tug it off; the material flutters to a heap at my feet.

I pause, dragging a hand down the row of stifling buttons adorning my silky shirt. Before I can overthink it, I let instinct guide me. Undoing the top few buttons, I make enough space to tug the top over my head. My hair skims my shoulders, tickling the skin there as I discard the shirt at my feet.

With deft fingers, I braid the sides of my hair out of my face. Sucking in a deep breath, I incline my head. The warm air caresses my bare skin, and instead of vulnerable, I feel free.

Deciding to lean into this newfound energy, I forgo my leather slippers and trek barefoot down the mountain to the village.

I'm starting to understand why the celestial servants dress the way they do. There's something liberating about unrestricted movement when you shed your clothes and shoes. My movements are swifter and more fluid, as if I'm one with the jungle rather than a stranger navigating it.

Steeling my spine, I head to the Assembly hut and brace myself for confrontation.

After a good night's rest, I know many questions will be flung my way. I won't be surprised if the islanders demand I step down and allow Soraya to take my place. They know she has the moon marking and magic.

If that's what she wants, they'll all be better for it.

Will she be there?

My heart flutters at the thought, and I keep my head up as I burst into the meeting hut.

The room is a few degrees warmer, filled with the salty, pungent scent of beach and bodies. The air buzzes with conversation. The benches are filled, and dozens of extra villagers cram themselves shoulder to shoulder around the room. The crowd is so dense that their breaths practically mingle.

The sight of so many people—touching—makes my skin crawl. I almost wish I had my cloak, or at least my shirt, to keep their skin from grazing mine as I pass.

As I wiggle my way to the front of the room, the conversations melt away. My face burns by the time I make it to the dais at the front.

Lachlan faces the crowd, with Joss and a few other wardens at his side. My eyes meet the chief's, and he tilts his head respectfully. Joss does the same; no scowling or irritation present on his face. Instead, he greets me with a genuine smile.

I try to return it, hoping it comes across as I intended. Lately, I've realized how foreign the expression is to me.

After watching Soraya laugh and smile so freely for so many years, I never thought it would be challenging to do so myself. She makes it look easy.

At the thought of her, I fight the urge to scan the crowd for her teal hair. Instead, I climb the few steps to the platform, ready to join the wardens.

The moment I step onto the platform, cheers erupt throughout the room.

I lean toward Joss, frowning. "What are they cheering for?"

He smirks at my bare feet, then arches a brow at me. "You, High Priest."

"What did I do?"

He shakes his head with a laugh. In a surprising move, he wraps an arm around my shoulders and tugs me to him, raising his opposite arm overhead. My muscles go rigid at the feel of his skin on mine. His body heat consumes me like a blanket, and I itch to pull away.

The ruckus grows louder as everyone stomps and claps. I wince, my ears ringing.

It isn't until my gaze falls onto Soraya that I finally relax. She raises her fingers to her mouth, whistling dramatically.

At that, a smile buds on my lips. This time, it comes more easily and naturally than the one I forced a few moments ago.

"Welcome," Lachlan greets, and the roars die down. "Blessed Union."

"*Blessed Union!*" the islanders practically sing back.

"Yesterday was a heavy day for us all, but Isle de Lunith does not yield. We protect our home, our people, our magic."

The stomping resumes, and the villagers break out into a cacophony of yells. Lachlan holds up a hand, and they quiet down again. The chief turns to me, moisture sparkling in his eyes.

"If it weren't for the Moon Priest, I wouldn't be here right now," he says, voice tinged with reverence. "He saved me. He saved *us.*"

As the crowd thunders with praise, I frown, my eyes meeting Soraya's.

"No," I say. When no one listens, I step away from Joss and clear my throat. I try again, louder this time. "No!" Turning toward Soraya, I gesture for her to join me.

She rises hesitantly, a wrinkle on her forehead, but she steps toward the dais. Her skirt shimmies around her deeply tanned legs. Dainty silver moon chains cinch at the waist. My eyes linger for a fraction on her chest, suddenly understanding why the fabric there is thicker—concealing the moonstone beneath.

When I draw my gaze to her face, her bright aquamarine eyes sparkle with affection.

She clasps my outstretched hand, gasping when a tingle of heat zips through where we meet.

"Soraya is the reason why Lachlan is standing before you today," I proclaim to the room. "*She* is why we have no fatalities from yesterday's scrimmage."

One by one, the onlookers rise, showering Soraya with the hollers and whoops she deserves. Her face turns redder than I've ever seen, but she beams.

"She might've healed them," someone shouts, "but you saved them. *You* stepped up as the leader we needed, High Priest!"

"Yeah!" another person yells.

They stay standing, continuing their onslaught of whistling and cheering. My cheeks burn, and my ears ring, but I watch, stunned, as they show their appreciation.

"But I didn't do anything," I murmur. "I've failed everyone."

Joss elbows me in the ribs, and I scowl at him.

"You were supposed to stay behind and hide," he points out. "*That's* what the High Priest usually does."

"You saved my life!" A familiar red-haired warden steps forward, and the crowd simmers down, straining to hear him. "I would've died, drowned in the waves, had you not pulled me to safety. I told you to leave me, but you didn't."

I recognize him. The warden who was shot in the leg with an arrow. It was all a blur, but I vaguely remember dragging him back to Mariel.

"You pulled me from harm's way," another warden says. She bows her head, her wispy bangs falling into her face.

Soraya places a hand softly on my bicep. "*You* saved them, Raziel. My moonblood doesn't bring people back from the dead. It only mends their wounds. Without *you*, they would've never made it long enough for me to help them."

I turn to Joss. "But you were with me. We both helped pull people ashore."

He shakes his head. "I only left my post to follow your lead."

Guilt rises in my throat. "If something happened to you, it would've been my fa—"

"I'm fine," he cut me off. "But my father would be dead if you hadn't decided to step in and help."

Lachlan leans around Joss, pride shining on his weathered face. "You proved yourself to be the leader this island needed, Raziel."

More cheers echo through the room, but my ears ring with a tinny noise.

I didn't do anything spectacular. I only did what was right. It could've gone bad in so many ways. I'm not the leader they think I am.

My pulse pounds in my temple as I face the crowd. My eyes catch on Kassia's, and she winks. The crow's feet around her eyes crinkle, representing a lifetime of joy. It only makes my frown deepen.

I almost killed her all those years ago. How can she possibly forgive me? If everyone knew the truth... they would never be cheering me on.

I'm seconds away from fleeing when Lachlan begins speaking again. I'm grateful for his public-facing persona because addressing the crowd is not for me. Merely standing here for a few minutes has left me feeling like an empty shell.

Soraya reaches for me, and I let her tug me back to the bench. I sit beside Kassia, with Soraya perched on my lap. She wraps her arms around me, nuzzling into my cheek. Kassia offers me a smile, patting my shoulder affectionately.

I clench my jaw as guilt climbs up my throat.

My head spins, still caught up in the moons and the curse, as Lachlan continues to cover the rest of the meeting. I'll have to speak with him separately to address the issue with the mainlanders, the insurgents, and the pollen.

But right now, I'm grateful he takes the point on our trade route with the wardens.

Plus, it leaves me with more time and space to focus on what truly matters: the woman in my arms.

CHAPTER TWENTY-NINE

THE MEAL

SORAYA

"*Y*ou should've seen him!" Mariel waves her arms around, eyes lighting up with excitement as she recounts how Raziel stormed across the beach on his rescue mission. "I had no idea he was hiding that powerhouse of a body. Now I get why you were checking out his ass before." She winks at me.

Embarrassment creeps up my neck, flushing my skin, and I avert my gaze back to the shelves in front of us. "He did the bare minimum, Mariel… The wardens were the ones who fought."

"Yeah, but that's *their* job. Raziel could've hidden away, but he stepped up. The other Moon Priests would have never done such a thing," she insists, her attention locked onto me instead of the titles we're supposed to be scanning. "They wouldn't have been capable! Raziel is going down in books just like these."

I bite my lip, staring at the dull leather spines until the letters blur into unreadable smudges. She already recounted her side of events to the scribes, who are meeting with the wardens to document accurate depictions of the beach invasion.

It's jarring how quickly we become a piece of history, a part of the very texts we study.

One day, so long as we do our jobs properly and protect these books, islanders will read about us. Or rather, about perceptions of us. Not even the most accurate of archives tell the full story. They only tell pieces of certain perspectives.

I eye the shelves, wondering how many sides of these stories are left out—how many voices we'll never hear.

"I'm just thankful you finally let me in," Mariel adds, lowering her voice and nudging me affectionately with her elbow. "I always felt you were keeping things from me... but I had no idea you were a Moon Priestess!"

I shake my head, glancing around to make sure no one's listening. "I'm not. I'm just a regular priestess."

"You have the marking." She narrows her eyes at the covered spot on my chest. "You and Raziel are equals. You should be—"

"No, *he* was trained for this role."

"And you weren't?" She gestures toward the library. "You were raised by Kassia here in the temple. You started lessons before any of us. You know this island like the back of your hand. You love our people, and they love *you*. You're every bit worthy of being the Moon Priest as Raziel."

"It's not a matter of worth," I whisper. "I don't want the isolation. I like being around my friends without the pressure."

"He isolates himself because he *chooses* to."

I shake my head. "It's just not the role I want."

"Okay." She shrugs, turning back to the books, but her stare is pensive. I know she has more to say, and after giving her a moment, she gives me a sideways glance. "I've been thinking... I know it's not the best time, but there will never be a good time, and..."

"What is it, Mar?" I reach out and squeeze her hand.

"I want to request time away from the temple to shadow the wardens," she rushes out on a single breath. "What happened was terrible, but I felt so alive—being down there in the action, able to help. I don't want to be the one writing it down."

She gestures toward the row of tables in the center of the room, where various celestial servants take notes as they speak with the wardens. Joss leans back in his chair, a cocky smirk on his face as he talks animatedly to a priest.

"I want to be in on the action," she murmurs. "If I could fight, if I had been properly trained, I wouldn't have had to hide away uselessly."

"You weren't useless." I shake my head. "But I understand. You're right."

She blinks, her shoulders tensing. "I am?"

"You're not happy here."

Her breath whooshes out. "You noticed."

"Of course I have. You've mentioned it before, and I hear you, Mariel," I whisper, offering a sad smile. I open my arms, and she steps into them as I wrap them around her. "Have you talked to Lachlan and Delores about it?"

She shakes her head, still clutching me tightly, and her curls tickle my cheek. "I love Ma; you know she's a great woman..."

"But?"

"But she checked out after my dad left for the mainland, Soraya. We never connected. If it wasn't for you..." She sniffles, and I rub her back in circular motions, trying to understand her implication.

"What do you mean?" I say softly. "I thought you and Delores were close?"

She sighs, and her muscles soften against me. "She loves me in her own way, but she's too busy drinking nectar or tending to everyone else to be there for *me*. It was lonely growing up with her. Especially before I came to the temple."

"Why didn't you tell me you felt this way, Mar?" I try to pull back and look at her, but she squeezes me tighter. A viny thorn winds its way around my heart, matching the grip of her arms. "I could've been there for you."

"You've always been there for me." Her voice cracks. "I didn't want to complain about my ma when you didn't even…"

Have a mother. The unsaid words carve straight through my chest.

I exhale slowly into her hair. "I had a Kassia."

"It's not the same."

"No," I agree. "It's not. Because *I* didn't feel lonely, and you never should've. I'm sorry your dad left you and that your ma let you down."

Her body tenses, and a stuttering breath escapes her. "Nope—I refuse to cry."

"You should probably let it out at some point, Mariel," I say softly. "Whether it's alone or with me, but don't hold it in. And maybe you should talk to Delores. Tell her how you feel. It's never too late."

Pulling back, she gives me a watery smile. "I will, but not—"

"Ladies!" Joss's loud voice causes us to jolt.

"Moons save me," Mariel mutters, wiping her eyes. But her lips twitch into a small smile. "Can we help you?"

He throws an arm around each of our necks, pulling us in. "Just glad to see two of my favorite priestesses upright and well."

"You, too, Joss." I pat his chest and duck out from under his arm.

Mariel laughs, and he playfully tugs on her hair.

She slaps his arm away. "Do *not* disrespect the curls!"

"I'd *never*. I like them." He grins, and they hold each other's stare for a beat.

I gape, sensing a spark between them that definitely wasn't there before—whether they admit it or not. Knowing them both, neither of them will accept it.

Clearing my throat, they whip their heads toward me. "Are you finished giving your account of events to the scribe?" I ask.

Joss nods. "Almost. We're going through a few more details. I have to head back down to the assembly hall this afternoon to meet with the High Priest and my father."

"What's the plan?"

"We're sending a few wardens to the mainland today. My father's going with them to sort out the insurgent issue."

"What about the silverdew?" I ask, feeling guilty, like it's somehow my fault that it hasn't opened.

He shrugs. "There's nothing we can do."

A silence lingers between us, but the faint sound of murmuring filters past from the other wardens. There's a minor relief in having everything out in the open.

Except the biggest thing of all is still secret: Raziel's thirtieth birthday is nearing.

With it marks the end.

A palpable sense of gloom settles over me, sucking the joy from the air and leaving me utterly deflated.

"I need to get back to work," I say quickly.

Joss and Mariel exchange a worried look, but I ignore them, turning back toward the shelves.

"We'll figure out the pollen trade," Mariel offers, placing a comforting arm on my shoulder. "It'll be okay."

No, it won't! I want to yell. *It's not about the pollen! Raziel's going to die if we don't break the curse!* But instead, I merely nod and continue to scan the shelves, collecting books on the original goddess lore.

"I'll finish with the scribes and find you two for lunch after," Joss replies. I'm vaguely aware of him shuffling away.

Mariel and I work in quiet tandem for an hour or so, the collection of books between us growing. We've been through them many times before, but primarily for mindless work or distracting fun. Now, we're seeking specific insights.

"I'll be right back," I tell Mariel, leaving her to read about silverdew.

I make my way to a back row of shelves, secretly searching for anything to help with Raziel's curse. My eyes roam familiar titles, and I huff. I've scoured these shelves for months now.

There's nowhere else to turn, nowhere else to look for answers.

Everything about our island, its moons, and our magic is recorded here in the archival library. If the answer isn't here, then where is it?

A warm, nutty aroma of food hits me. It mingles with the musty scent of aged paper. I sniff deeply, and a surprising burst of citrus fills my nostrils.

A throat clears behind me, and I glance over my shoulder

Raziel stands shirtless and shoeless, his handsome features pinched tight. My breath catches as I take him in. His dark pants sit low on his hips, snug against his powerful thighs.

Despite skin being the prominent uniform on the island,

Raziel's exposed muscles make my heart skip a beat. My fingers ache to trail the ridges and smooth swaths of skin.

"Scandalous," I tease, pointing to his bare feet. I can almost swear a faint blush crosses his cheeks.

He holds up the small wicker basket he's carrying. The divine, savory scent wafts over me again. "I brought lunch. Can you take a break?" he offers.

The indirect reminder of what we're searching for—a way to break the curse and keep him alive—slams into me. My smile falters, and any hints of hunger I previously had melt away.

How can I eat at a time like this?

Raziel holds his head high, shoulders back and rigid. He studies me, his brow arching slightly. I'm ready to refuse, but it's impossible to decline him. The challenge in his eyes tells me he knows this.

"You need to eat," he murmurs.

"Okay." I nod, leading us to a table near the side windows, away from the books.

Mariel spots us, skipping over. "Hey, priesty!"

A muscle in Raziel's jaw tics. He blinks once, twice. "Priestess Nyx, hello."

Despite the solemn energy between us, a soft laugh bubbles out of my throat.

"I brought enough for you, too," he says, setting the basket down and unloading the goods. "Coconut rice, lemon-glazed lunar fish, and mashed isle-beans."

Mariel squeals, helping Raziel serve three plates. He pulls out a palm leaf-wrapped loaf, catching my eye as he slowly sets it on the table.

Kassia's cinnamon bread.

I offer him a smile, and my heart rate doesn't slow until he finally—*finally*—softens his tight jaw muscles. It's not quite a smile back, but I'll take it.

"Damn, something smells amazing." Joss strides up to the table, scratching his chest. He smirks at the food laid out before us.

"I didn't realize you were still here," Raziel retorts, giving me an unamused look.

I chuckle. "He's like a sea barnacle; he clings relentlessly."

"Your celestial servants are *very* thorough with their historical accounts. A good thing, I suppose." Joss plops into the chair on the other side of Raziel, glaring at me. "If I'm a sea barnacle, you're a—"

"Finish that sentence at the cost of that pretty smirk of yours," Raziel warns with a growl.

Mariel snorts, covering her mouth with her hand.

Joss pulls back, eyes wide, then he laughs and claps Raziel on the back. "I think I'm the only one on this island who's ever been punched, insulted, *and* called pretty by the Moon Priest."

"He punched you?" Mariel gasps, eyes widening.

Joss leans in scandalously. His eyebrows waggle. "Many times. In fact, he—"

"Here," Raziel grunts, shoving his plate toward Joss. "Take mine. I have more upstairs; I'll eat when I return."

"If this is a pity meal—"

"It's not. I need to get back to work anyway." Raziel stands, his eyes locking on mine in silent conversation. The gravity of the situation between us grows heavier. "Eat," he whispers, breaking our stare and planting a kiss on my head. "Enjoy, ladies." He frowns at Joss. "Warden."

"Thank you!" Joss beams, flashing a smile, and snatching the plate. He lifts it to his nose, flicks his eyes shut, and inhales greedily. "This smells divine. Could even rival Delores's cooking, Mar."

Mariel rolls her eyes. "I wouldn't go that far."

Raziel's lips curl into a smile, but he leaves without another word. I track his movements, desperate to milk every second of his presence for as long as possible. It takes everything in me to stay put and reach for my fork, but my heart aches to go after him.

I'm finally understanding his fears about *pleasure* being a distraction. If I follow him upstairs, we won't get anything done.

A seam splits me in two. One part of me wants to ignore all this and spend every last second with him, soaking him up. The other part stubbornly refuses to give up the search for a moons-damned answer!

I clench my fork, angrily shoveling food in my mouth. Raziel can *cook*, but the tastes fall flat and dry on my tongue, given the turmoil in my mind.

"We just had a broment," Joss says between bites. He puffs his chest out and jerks a thumb over his shoulder.

"A what?" I share a confused look with Mariel.

"A brother-moment. A broment."

"Moons." Mariel shakes her head. "I can't believe he punched you... I mean, then again..."

"Keep going, Mar, and I'll tell Delores on you." He lowers his voice. "Or should I say I'll tell *Ma?*"

She reaches over the table and flicks his nose. "Shut your mouth, barnacle boy."

They break out into another fit of laughter, then continue eating. My heart squeezes tighter with each bite, knowing this lightheartedness won't last for long. My friends and Raziel just started getting along, and it means the world to me.

He just made up with Kassia after all these years.

Seeing Raziel come out of his shell to engage with others, to become a part of this island... It's indescribably beautiful.

And it's also far too late.

My eyes burn as I force the next bite of food down, hoping I don't choke.

"Why'd he run off?" Joss kicks me gently under the table to get my attention. "I hope I didn't make him uncomfortable."

I shake my head. They have both been plenty respectful to one another. Lately, at least.

"He likes you in his own way. He's just very focused on... finding answers right now." I drop my gaze to my food, swallowing down the lump in my throat.

"The silverdew will open again," he reassures me with a smile. "I know it. I *feel* it."

"Yeah," Mariel adds. She nudges me in jest. "None of that matters. What *does* matter is that we have each other."

I nod, forcing a smile that I hope is convincing.

It's the one thing I haven't told Mariel, or Joss, or anyone. If I tell them about Raziel's theory about his thirtieth birthday, it would only cause them stress, and I don't want them consumed with worry over me.

Because if the curse takes Raziel... it's only a matter of time before it takes me, too.

Instead, I work hard to keep my stormy mood at bay so I don't alarm them.

But in the back of my mind, that little voice reminds me that as perfect as things seem right now, they're swiftly approaching an end.

FOURTH UNION MONTH

CHAPTER THIRTY

THE REVEAL

RAZIEL

*T*he weeks fly by, and we quickly draw closer to the next Union.

Scouring the archives during the day gets me nowhere. However, my nights exploring Soraya are everything. For once in my cursed life, I welcome the damn distraction. Ironically, it's not nearly distracting enough from my impending doom. There's a twisted humor there.

We eat together often; I cook all her favorite meals. I keep Kassia wordless company some afternoons, sipping tea that I don't like, just to spend time with her before it's too late. I even spar a few times with Joss and Lachlan as we discuss the trade with the mainland, working hard to pretend everything is fine.

But it's not.

Every time Soraya looks at me, I can see fear in her eyes, even when she tries to smile it away or pepper me with kisses.

That layer of apprehension hovers over us like a storm cloud. We make love—slow, fast, and on every surface in my residence. She teaches me how she likes to be touched and helps me discover what I like, too.

Even though soon, none of it will matter.

Because I'm the failure I always feared I'd be. And now, I've made it to my final Union.

I stand at the edge of the River of Rest with my hands in my pockets, staring grimly at the gently flowing water. Soon, my forever-resting body will float down the river on a pyre, out to sea.

My bare toes sink into the muddy bank. The humid night air sits heavy on my bare shoulders, representing the weight of the island I carry.

"Amos—*Father*," I mumble, floundering for what to say. If the legends are true, I suppose our souls will meet again in the afterlife. "I don't know if you knew about the curse or if that's why you indulged recklessly, but regardless, I wish you had been more of a guiding light for me."

I clear my throat, hating the lump of emotion that sticks there.

"I don't know. Maybe I should've voiced my needs sooner and asked for help. Maybe closing myself off wasn't the answer. I'm filled with a thousand *maybes,* but none of them matter."

Hell, *none* of it matters.

I've tried so hard to be a great Moon Priest, and look where it's gotten me. Days before my thirtieth birthday, before my impending death, and I've done nothing to stave off the curse. I'm just now getting to know the villagers and making friends.

I've finally experienced *her.*

I want to lie to myself and say I'll die a happy man, but I can't.

Soft, musical flute notes ring through the air, followed by strings and drums: the start of the Union.

I glance up, catching sight of the two moons nestled into the dark turquoise sky. They've already begun their slow shift towards one another. The smaller moon is dimmer still than it has been, a reminder of my failures.

At one point, I thought the villagers were ignorant or careless, not having noticed the changes in the island's magic. Now, I realize they didn't notice because they didn't have to. Because they trusted me implicitly to safeguard their magic.

They never had a reason to doubt.

My skin itches on the inside. I'm tempted to run away, to flee back to the temple and hide, but it's the last Union I'll ever experience—the first one I'll celebrate with my people. A haunting irony.

"Raziel?" A whisper reaches my ears. "May I touch you?"

At the sound of Soraya's voice, my muscles go lax. My emotions churn and change, like grinding gears, until my heart opens up.

Without turning, I give a single, brief nod.

Soft hands wind their way around my sides, clutching my abs. I sink back into her hold automatically, filled with a sense of peace only she brings me. After so many years of avoiding touch, I don't know how I survived as long as I did without her.

"Come with me to the Union?" Soraya whispers, resting her head between my shoulder blades. "Maybe that's the key to breaking your curse."

I turn, tucking her against my chest and cupping her head. "How do you figure?"

She shrugs. "You haven't been... Well, maybe you need to

worship the moons. Maybe that's why your curse is so much worse than mine."

Sighing, I squeeze her tighter. "Sounds too easy."

"Then you have nothing to lose." Her voice cracks, and my heart aches knowing this situation hurts her, too.

"It's not going to be the magic fix to everything, Soraya."

She winces at my harsh tone. "It's worth a try."

Pulling back, I stroke her jaw with my thumb, trying to ease the tension there. "I'll try anything with you by my side, little star."

The silver moonlight washes over her face, highlighting the soft blush on her cheeks. Her vivid hair shines, waves cascading down around her shoulders, as magical as the sky's hues overhead.

"That's what Kassia calls me," she murmurs.

My mouth softens into an almost-grin. "I know."

"I'm glad you've been spending time with her."

I nod. "Yeah. Do you know why she calls you her little star?" I pause, giving her a chance to shake her head. "She believes you belong to the magic of the moons; that you're meant for the skies. A little fallen star. You saved her."

She bites her lower lip and glances down, taking a long breath. My thumb caresses her jaw, and I gently coax her gaze back to mine. The floor fades away for a moment, and I lose myself to her iridescent, breathtakingly ethereal eyes.

My grandmother isn't wrong. Soraya *is* made of magic.

"You saved *me*, too," I whisper.

Her eyes well with tears. She shakes her head, pulling free from me. "I didn't." Her voice cracks. "I couldn't."

"You did, Soraya. Every life ends in death eventually, but you saved me while I was still living. You freed me in my final months."

Her gaze shifts behind me to the river, and the way her expression falls clues me in on where her thoughts have gone.

"Hey, look at me," I command gently.

She does, blinking rapidly to keep her tears at bay.

"Promise me you won't give up after I'm gone." When she doesn't reply, I continue, "On the island. On the temple. On the curse. On *yourself.*"

Wrapping her arms around herself, she turns abruptly. "Raziel…" Her tone is strained. "I can't do this. We can't… it's not…"

I snake my arms around her waist, tucking her to my front. We're silent, lost in the trees to the sound of the gurgling river and not-so-distant music. We sway together, taking a moment to exist.

The song fades to an end. Soraya sniffles and shifts away, linking her fingers with mine. "We should go."

"There's something I want to do first… Before…" I clear my throat, almost embarrassed to request my desire, but the way she gazes at me with patience and adoration gives me confidence.

I wind through a thicket of trees, finding a good spot. My hand trembles in hers, but I steel my spine, leaning into the momentary courage I've summoned. Gently, I press her against a tree.

She squints in confusion, but then her mouth drops open, and a soft breath escapes. "Raziel—"

I lean down and press my mouth to hers, swallowing her words. She grips the back of my neck, holding me in place. Our mouths move in tandem, lazily tasting each other while her fingers slide up the back of my neck, tangling in my hair. Her nails scratch my scalp, and I moan into the kiss.

She smiles in response, arching her back. "I love the noises you make."

Each touch and kiss is liquid heat, thawing the burning lust deep within me. I drop to my knees, gripping the hem of her dress and glancing up at her.

"May I?" My words come out as a plea, a prayer.

She gasps. "Are you sure? Now?"

"If not now, then when?"

A shudder wracks her body. She nods rapidly, her cheeks tinted pink. Her ragged breathing tells me she's just as affected by this as I am.

I smile up at her and then bury my head under her skirt, kissing a trail up her leg. It's a fantasy I've wanted to fulfill ever since I stumbled upon her and Joss. The thought of *him* doing this to her makes me angry. An envious beast bursts to life within me, fueling my lust.

She is *mine*.

The thought of any other man in this position, praying between her thighs, eviscerates me.

My fingers loop around the waistband of her underwear, and I tug them down. She steps out of them, and I stuff them into my pocket. Guiding her with my hands, I widen her stance until she's opened up enough to let me in.

"I love this," I whisper, so quietly that I doubt she can hear me.

Grabbing an ankle, I place it on my shoulder. She shifts, clutching onto my hair to keep her balance.

"Is this okay?" I ask from beneath the light fabric.

"Yes," she urges. "Keep going."

I grip her ass, growling as my fingers dig into the soft flesh. She squeaks, jerking her hips forward. Her heat settles on my face, and I soak it up.

"Yes!" Her short exclamations of pleasure spur me on.

What a stupid man I've been to miss out on this for so long. I've unknowingly punished myself for years.

Fueled by carnal desperation, I press my lips to her most sensitive bits. My tongue works out of habit, recently trained to hit her in the specific little place she likes—the place that makes her buck against me and scrape her nails against my scalp.

She was honest about being a good teacher, and now she reaps the benefits.

"Raziel!" she gasps, her legs trembling as she grabs me tighter.

I don't relent until she's panting, thrusting her hips against my mouth to chase the high. When a violent tremor wracks through her, and she moans, I stop my onslaught.

I gently place her foot back on the ground. She smiles, hearts in her eyes.

"I'm not done with you yet," I murmur, working the button on my pants.

She chuckles, giving me a smug look. "I thought you didn't like being touched," she teases.

"I'm touching *you*," I point out, dropping my pants and kicking them off.

My hardness springs out as if it's reaching for Soraya. My pulse intensifies, and I glance over my shoulder to ensure we're alone. Never in a thousand years would I have imagined *this* as my reality. She brings out a new side of me.

Or perhaps my impending doom gives me a sense of fearlessness.

I swallow the dark thought, focusing on the present moment with Soraya instead. Silver light washes over her, and that luscious hair glows as if it's part of the jungle itself.

Her eyes roam my bare skin, and a look of pure amazement crosses her features. When she reaches for me, I grasp her wrists, pinning them to the tree overhead. I shake my head slowly and repeat myself. "*I'm* touching *you*."

Her head tilts back, and she watches me with intrigue.

"I don't want to hurt you," I murmur, eyeing the rough bark she's plastered against.

My erection is as hard as the tree behind her, already weeping for her. I line my head up with her opening, sliding it through her warm desire.

"Raziel," she warns, narrowing her eyes. She undulates her hips, brushing against me.

I pull back, teasing her this time. She groans in annoyance.

Releasing her wrists, I slip my hand through the opening of her top, covering her marking with my own. A soft glow emanates from below the fabric, and she gasps, melting against me.

Unable to wait any longer, I slowly press into her, relishing the way her pussy wraps tight around me. The moonstone light between us grows brighter, sending an indescribable comfort through my veins.

"Wrap your legs around me," I murmur.

She obeys immediately. I hoist her up, freeing my hand to clutch her against me. My cock stays inserted in her as I move carefully, reluctant to have her slip free, as I lay her down on the jungle floor beneath me. The ground is much softer than the tree: a blanket of fallen leaves and dirt.

I prop myself up with a hand on either side of her head, gazing down at her. She's so beautiful it hurts. All I want from now until the end of time is to gaze upon her stunning face. To be inside her—body, heart, and spirit.

Her eyes well with tears.

"Don't cry, darling," I say, gently stroking her cheek.

"Distract me," she begs, wrapping her ankles around me and drawing me closer. "Please." The raw desperation in her voice has me nodding like a man possessed.

I pull my hips back and drive them forward, burrowing

deeper into her. At first, it's a steady, slow pace, and I angle my hips just right until her eyes roll back. When the pressure builds in my balls, I hiss through my teeth.

Soraya tugs me to her, and I bury my face in her neck, breathing in her scent.

"Harder," she whispers in my ear, making my skin prickle.

Picking up speed, I bury myself in her over and over again. Soon, she's latching onto me like a boa, desperate to suffocate me. Her walls squeeze—once, twice—a tell of her impending orgasm, I've quickly learned.

Studying the archives for years was merely practice for when it came time to study *her*. She's the most interesting story I've ever memorized.

And when she gasps in my ear, her warm breath hitting the sensitive part of my lobe, my balls tighten, and pressure courses through my spine.

"I'm coming," I gasp, thrusting deeper into her and filling her up.

She moans, her muscles spasming as she milks every last drop. We reach our pleasure together, the pinnacle of intimate connection, here on the jungle floor.

I collapse onto her, gently stroking her hair. Her fingers dance up and down my back muscles, caressing me.

"I need you to know, Soraya, that—"

"Oh, for sea's sake!" Joss's very unwelcome voice cuts through the intimate moment. Heat blasts through my face. "This is *not* the moon I was expecting to see tonight."

Sighing, I glance over my shoulder, seeing red. "Give us privacy, will you, Thalor?"

"Guess this is payback, isn't it?" Joss says with a smirk.

Red spots of rage infiltrate my vision. I'm disgusted with myself at the vulnerable scene he's stumbled upon—me, fully nude, atop Soraya. At least her dress and my body cover her.

"Get lost!" I yell, gritting my teeth.

"Nice ass, High Priest!"

Soraya's body shakes with laughter beneath me. Joss stomps away, and I wait until I'm sure he's gone before slowly sliding out.

"See? You *do* have a nice ass." She winks.

We clean up and head to the beach. By the time we arrive, the party is bustling. A string band plays music on a small bamboo stage at the edge of the sand, in tune with the rhythmic lapping of the waves against the shore. The sounds mingle together, rather than competing for dominance.

A long line wraps around the small hut, serving drinks beside it.

Villagers sip from their coconuts, faces bright with delight.

There must be at least two hundred people here, and as we walk, conversations taper off and eyes track me.

"Is it always this... busy?" I clutch Soraya's hand tighter, allowing her to lead me through the throng.

She chuckles, tugging me closer to her. "Always."

I meet another priest's eyes, and he smiles, but I quickly look away. Shame floods me. I know I was doing the right thing by hiding during the Union, to protect everyone, but I can't help but feel like I've let my people down.

Groups of celestial servants laugh loudly, swirling in circles and sipping from coconuts. I wince at all the noises. It's the opposite of the library's quiet rigidness.

But... nearly everyone wears a smile on their face. And instead of those smiles fading away at the sight of me, they only grow.

Shame quickly gives way to regret and misery, and my

mind replays the last few Union Nights. How isolating and lonely they were.

Mariel bounces over to us a moment later, thrusting a coconut at me. "Here, Razzy!"

My face scrunches at the nickname. Before I can comment on it, Soraya grabs the coconut and hands it to me. It's heavier than it looks. I shift the weight, trying to balance it so it doesn't tip over. The little hairs tickle my palm.

"Thanks, Mar," Soraya says with a smile. But it's strained and doesn't quite reach her eyes.

My heart dips, knowing I'm the reason for her pain. However, her friend doesn't seem to notice as she cracks a joke and throws her head back with laughter.

The two chatter, but I stare into the coconut. The clear liquid shimmers, and its fruity scent wafts to my nose.

I can't bring myself to drink it. If it's my last Union, and my first time celebrating on the beach since I was a child, I want to keep a clear head.

People approach us in groups. Some exchange pleasantries with me, but most engage with Soraya and Mariel, throwing me curious glances. My neck heats, and I pass the nectar between my hands without drinking it.

Lachlan and Delores join us, and the former offers me a paternal pat on the shoulder. Despite the hurricane of unease inside me, I smile and pretend to be relaxed.

Joss waves as he passes, surrounded by a few wardens I'm unfamiliar with. Soraya greets them all by name.

My eyes lock on the dual moons situated high overhead. Acid roils in my stomach. I've failed my duties as the High Priest. If I could go back in time, there's so much I'd do differently. Such as make an effort to learn my fellow islanders.

"—right, Raziel?" Soraya asks, nudging me.

"Hmm?" I quickly shift my gaze to her, trying not to let my emotions show on my face. She doesn't need to be burdened by my pain.

She glances from me to the coconut, then back up. Her smile slips, but she quickly forces it back into place. "Never mind. How about we dance, huh?"

I run a hand over the braid along the side of my head, exhaling heavily. "I can't dance."

"It's easy. Here, I'll show you." She takes my drink, passing it back to Mariel wordlessly, and then she grabs my hand and leads me closer to the water, where the crowd thins out a bit and the shadows play.

I swallow the knot in my throat, trying not to stumble over my own feet in the sand. How can I possibly dance when I can't even *walk*?

This isn't something I'd ever volunteer to learn. But... perhaps it's the final opportunity I'll ever have to choose differently; to be different than the Raziel I've been for nearly thirty years.

Soraya squeezes my hand and leans in. "You look uncomfortable."

"I am," I admit. "But perhaps not for the reasons you might think."

"Do you want to talk about it?"

I stew on the question for a moment before settling on an answer. Shaking my head, I smile. "No. I want to take you up on your offer and learn how to dance."

Her smile mirrors mine, and she steps toward me, reaching for my free hand. I place it in hers with ease.

"It's all about the hips," she says, her body swaying rhythmically to the music. She moves like the river with a natural, fluid grace.

I try to copy her, shifting my hips from side to side. She

chuckles, and her face lights up with joy. Despite the acknowledgment that I'm butchering the dance, I continue to move my body in response to hers.

At first, it's incredibly unnatural. My body is stiff, and the movements feel awkward. But soon, I find myself laughing alongside her, lost to the freedom of being at the edge of the sea beneath the twin moons.

"I'm sorry you must teach me how to do everything," I say when we finally take a break.

"I like it," she whispers, kissing my jaw. "Teaching is my passion... and you make a divine student."

Silver moonlight washes over the sea, brightening as it highlights the dark cyan waters. Soraya sighs, glancing beyond me. I follow her gaze into the jungle, where wildlife glitters with the kiss of magic.

"It's almost time," she whispers.

My throat closes as I turn skyward. The two moons brighten as they begin to overlap. An echo of violent power courses through my body, a threat of what's to come.

The surge grows stronger, like a tidal wave of magic within me. I shudder, my skin prickling. My fingers ripple, threatening to elongate into claws. My eyes widen, and I ball them into fists to hide the impending transformation.

"No," I hiss, my chest caving in. "Not here."

The music fades out, and excited chatter litters the beach as the islanders prepare for the merging of moons. I stay facing the sea, with the islanders at my back.

"You don't want to watch with your people?" Soraya asks softly, placing a hand on my shoulder.

"I can't bear to face them, Soraya," I admit, nearly choking on my fear.

"Hey." She cups my face. "Look at me, Raziel... Please keep your eyes on mine. I've got you, okay?"

"Soraya," I croak, "I can't shift here… not in front of them."

Instead of flinching at my words, she stands taller, her narrowed eyes fierce. "I'm here. You won't hurt anyone."

My skin stretches taut to contain the viciousness deep inside me. Sweat beads on my spine. The urge to run is overwhelming.

"Stay," Soraya whispers. "Let them see *you*."

"They won't… Understand," I croak as another threatening tremor moves through me.

"They will—"

She continues to speak, offering reassurances, but her voice is lost to the ringing in my ears. With a growl, I drop to my knees.

Run.

Run.

Run.

Whether the words are directed at her or me, I can't tell.

All I know is that it's too late.

My biggest fear is coming true, and everyone will see me for the failure of a Moon Priest that I am.

CHAPTER THIRTY-ONE

THE FAILURE

SORAYA

*F*rom the corner of my eye, I catch the glittering light blaze across the sky as the moons merge. Screams ring through the air, right on cue.

But instead of the cheers and prayers of happy islanders, there are ear-splitting shrieks of terror.

"Raziel!" I drop to my knees, sinking into the sand beside him.

He groans, his eyes glowing an ethereal silver. Claws sprout from fingertips, his knuckles cracking unnaturally. My throat grows thick, but I swallow through it, focusing on calming breaths.

This is my fault.

Perhaps, for some reason, I thought love would be enough to break the curse: love of each other, love of himself, love of his people. I was stupid to think that attending a Union would be the fix.

Instead, I've put his vulnerability on display for everyone to see.

"Soraya!" Joss bolts toward me, sand spraying everywhere. He halts to a stop a few paces away, eyes wide and jaw slack. "Get away from him!"

Behind him, I spot Kassia watching, a trembling hand at her mouth. Coconuts thud to the ground as people bolt from the beach, presumably for safety. But the old priestess stands frozen as she watches her grandson.

"Move, Soraya," Joss yells. "We need to go."

I shake my head, focusing on Raziel. "I'm not leaving him," I retort, reaching for him. "You're okay, darling."

An ear-splitting roar rips from his lungs, and I rip my hand back. My heart pounds, but I force myself to stay at his side. He's still Raziel, still human, but with added animalistic attributes. Sharp claws dig into the sand, as if he's fighting to ground himself. With each grunt and snarl, elongated canine teeth glint in the moonlight.

"Joss!" I say steadily, without taking my eyes off Raziel. "I need something to cut myself with."

"You stubborn shell of a—"

"*Now!*"

"Okay, *fuck*," Joss says, panic lining his voice.

If he bites me, my moonblood will neutralize his transformation. But if he doesn't go for me...

I can't allow him to hurt anyone else. It needs to be me.

A second later, something thuds into the sand beside me. The shining blade catches my eye—a warden's dagger. There's no time to thank Joss.

I snatch it up and quickly drag the blade down my arm. Thick, silver rivulets pour out. Ignoring the chaos erupting around me, I grip Raziel's hair and yank his head back. He fights against me, spitting and snarling, but I shove my arm against his mouth while I have the opportunity.

His warm tongue caresses my skin, lapping up the liquid pooling there. I practically melt with relief.

"That's right," I whisper. "Drink up. Good boy."

A haunting silence quickly replaces the clamoring. Dozens of eyes needle my back. The confusion is palpable, but I push it to the back of my mind.

Raziel's muscles go lax, and he tears his lips from my arm to gulp in air. He closes his eyes, tilting his head back.

Carefully, I cup his face. "I love you, Raziel, and you are not alone."

He doesn't reply.

A soft groan bursts from him as his body seizes. He slumps forward, faceplanting into the sand. Gasps go up around me, and the remaining villagers rush forward.

For a moment, I expect them to rip me away from Raziel— or to restrain him.

"The Moon Priest..." someone whispers urgently. "Is he okay?"

"How can we help?"

"Get him out of the sand!" A flurry of hands move, rolling Raziel onto his back and checking his pulse.

"Where should we take him?"

I blink a few times, then I realize the question is directed at me. Glancing up, I meet Kassia's eyes. She nods slowly, then turns and strolls in the direction of her hut.

"Kassia's," I croak. "Take him to Kassia's, please."

There's no hesitation as a couple of wardens lift Raziel's limp body, carrying him away with ease. The crowd watches, concern pinching their faces. More questions are thrown at me—mostly people wondering how they can help.

I don't know how to answer.

All I can think about is how Raziel's fate is sealed. He might be alive tonight... but soon, he won't be. We didn't break the curse. It was pathetic to hope it was so simple.

Strong arms wrap around me, hoisting me up.

"He'll be okay, Soraya," Joss murmurs. I allow him to guide me to my feet and lead me from the beach. "Come on."

"You don't understand..." I trail off, voice thick with emotion.

"No, I don't." Joss sighs. "You priests and your sea-damned secrets."

My eyes burn with tears. "You have no idea."

CHAPTER THIRTY-TWO

THE FAMILY

RAZIEL

*M*y throat screams, begging for water. I hesitantly crack an eye open. An unfamiliar bamboo ceiling greets me, and dread floods my body.

My last memory assaults my mind—the transformation on the beach.

What did I do?

Who did I hurt?

"No," I croak, pinching my eyes shut.

"Raziel?" a soft voice whispers into my ear.

The weight of her body plastered against my side hits me. My eyes flit back open, and I turn my head. Soraya's forehead wrinkles as her eyes roam my features. She reaches up, pushing the hair out of my face.

"How are you feeling?" she whispers.

A door creaks open, followed by the slap of bare feet on wood.

"Is he up?" a familiar, feminine voice asks.

Soraya nods, sitting up and leaning against the headboard.

"Good. Ma!" the intruder yells. "He's up!"

I wince at the ear-splitting yell and slowly sit up. My gaze lands on the sassy, curly-haired priestess who has the personality of a protective jaguar when it comes to Soraya.

"Mariel?" I mutter in confusion. "Where am I?"

A second later, an older spitting image of Mariel peers into the cramped room. Her dark curls are tied up into the shape of a pineapple, held back by a bandana. The pale apron is marred with stains, and some sort of powder cakes her hands and cheeks.

"Delores?" I frown, confused as hell. I turn to Soraya. "What's going on?"

She smiles, gripping my hand. "We're taking care of you."

Delores barks orders to Mariel, instructing her to bring bread and water. "Kassia has a kettle on for cacao tea. I figure you two might need something soothing."

"Thank you," Soraya says to the women, squeezing my hand tightly. They leave, shutting the door behind them.

"Kassia's here too?" I run a hand over my head, blowing out a breath.

Soraya chuckles, pulling her knees to her chest and leaning toward me. "We're at her hut. Delores and Mariel came to check on you and help.

My frown deepens. "Why?"

"Why not get up and find out for yourself?"

She stands, and the thin nightgown she wears falls awkwardly to her ankles, appearing a size too big. Kassia's surely. With a yawn, she stretches her arms overhead. Then, she beckons for me to join. I follow her out the door into the hallway.

The sweet, rich aroma of cacao and the warm fragrance of fresh bread washes over me.

The moment we enter the kitchen, I halt. My eyes land on Kassia and Delores laughing together at the counter as they work together to prep food. Joss and Lachlan sit at the table, heads bowed over a couple of mugs as they talk. Mariel holds a pitcher of water and immediately smirks when she spots me.

"Welcome back to life, Razzy!" she says dramatically.

All movement in the kitchen halts. Something clatters onto the counter, and everyone's attention lands on me.

I shift awkwardly, my face heating. I turn toward Soraya. "What is this?"

"*This*," Soraya says, lacing her fingers through mine and leaning in to whisper in my ear, "is what Isle de Lunith looks like beyond your tower, beast."

Overwhelming emotion clogs my throat. "I almost killed you last night,"—I turn my gaze to each person individually—"all of you."

"Darling, you didn't," Delores says lightly, unfazed. "Not even close."

Joss runs a hand through his hair, his mouth in a grim line. "I knew something was wrong with you."

"Jossidian!" Lachlan scolds, pinching the bridge of his nose.

"He's not wrong," I mutter, stroking my jaw and averting my gaze to the floor.

"If you weren't as stubborn as a frozen clam, we could've helped you with this a long time ago," Joss points out.

"Help?" My nose scrunches, and my eyes slowly raise back up.

"We're glad you're okay," Lachlan adds, shooting his son a stern look. "You're important to us, kiddo." He stands and steps toward me, planting a hand affectionately on my shoulder.

"No one ever wanted you to be perfect, Raziel," Kassia says, slowly striding toward me. She stands just behind Lachlan, her hands trembling as she clasps them in front of her. "We just wanted *you*."

Mariel thrusts a mug of water at me, and I accept it.

An unfamiliar feeling prickles at my eyes, and my nose burns. I blink rapidly, shoving the emotion down. Not now. Not here.

The unexpected kindness clogs me up, and I nod dumbly.

The only thing I can think to say is the truth before it's too late. As much as I hate to admit it, Joss is right. Again.

Perhaps the islanders could've helped if I had been honest with them and allowed them to come together. I just never imagined they'd care like this.

"I'm going to die tomorrow." My voice cracks as the admission spills. "This marking,"—I hold up my hand—"isn't a blessing. It's a curse."

Gasps rise, and everyone freezes once again. Soraya gives me a sad look, and her hand flies to her chest, hovering over her marking.

Regret floods me.

I've failed her. But maybe the rest of Isle de Lunith won't.

"I might not live beyond tomorrow, but you need to figure out how to break the curse before it's too late for *her*."

Kassia's hand flies to her mouth. "No, honey. Why would you believe in such a terrible fate?" she cries.

"Because Amos died when he turned thirty—"

"That was a fluke. He lived a rather unhealthy lifestyle." Kassia shakes her head. "It's no surprise he succumbed to his ways young. It doesn't mean you will, too."

I sigh. "There was another High Priest, Demetrius, who disappeared on his thirtieth birthday. He wasn't the only one."

I pause, letting it sink in. "Do you know what happened to the Moon Priest before Amos?"

"Yes. He stepped down and retired to the mainland, to let Amos lead." Kassia's eyes fill with tears. "It was time."

"He *retired* at thirty?" I ask skeptically. "And did anyone see him after he left? Do you have proof he lived beyond?"

At this, Kassia's face pales. Tears streak down her face. "No, I—I never realized the coincidence, Raziel... that the Moon Priests step down on their thirtieth year."

"Because they *die*," I say flatly.

Mariel nearly drops the pitcher of water, slamming it on the counter and gripping the edge to steady herself. Joss plants a hand on his head, staring at Soraya with concern. Lachlan gapes at nothing, his mouth a grim line.

A haunting silence stretches through the room as the words sink in.

Delores clears her throat, cutting through the thick tension. "Let's eat." She uses a wooden spoon to scrape something into a bowl. "Ain't nothing anybody can do on an empty stomach, and ain't no one dying today."

The world stands frozen for a moment. Then, at once, everyone resumes their previous activities. We move stiffly, following Delores's orders and pretending the previous conversation never happened.

I chug the water Mariel gave me. Then I follow Soraya to the counter in a trance and accept a bowl of food from Delores.

I can't meet anyone's eyes as I take a seat beside Lachlan.

"You know what?" Joss asks thoughtfully. "I thought Soraya was lying at the assembly when she said you had magic." He gives a humorless laugh. "Thought she was covering for you, because that's what she does. She's a lover. A giver."

Soraya sighs, taking the seat across from me and stirring her food dejectedly. "I told you."

Joss shakes his head and leans back. "Who would've thought. In the end, you really were protecting him because he's so much more than just a conduit, huh?"

I open my mouth to question what he means, but then I remember what Soraya told everyone that day. There's no sense in calling her out on lying at this point, so I opt for shoveling food into my mouth instead.

When I finally glance up, Soraya is completely still, studying me with an intensity that makes me squirm.

"Yeah," she says, her voice tight. "He's so much more than that."

CHAPTER THIRTY-THREE

THE MERGING

SORAYA

*C*onduit.

I wake with a gasp. Joss's words replay in my mind.

My skin is damp and clammy, the sheets tangled around my legs. I glance at Raziel, and I exhale a long breath at the sight of his chest rising and falling in his sleep. Moonlight highlights the ridges of his muscles, as he lies on his back with his head cocked. Dark hair fans out around his head, tangled from a night of tossing and turning.

The lie about Raziel being a conduit came from a good place. Like Joss said, I wanted to protect him. And, in many ways, it wasn't a lie. He *is* a conduit of information, after all.

My eyes linger on the two moons, which have drifted apart after their Union the night prior. That means when first light washes over the island in the morning, it'll officially be Raziel's thirtieth birthday.

His final birthday.

My chest tightens, and I jolt up. I can't just sit here and sleep.

I reach for Raziel's palm, fingering the textured lines there. A buzz courses through my skin where we meet, but I don't pull away. Instead, I simmer in sensation. It's almost a vibration, a soft, static-like feeling humming through my veins. It frightened me the first couple of times, but I've come to learn it's harmless.

It's our magic responding to one another. My magic is steadier than his, but his comes and goes in waves. His power builds and builds until it overpowers him. Only I can neutralize his magic with my moonblood.

It's almost like it's too much for his body to handle.

It's nearly the opposite of the moonstone, which drains of magic and requires more to replenish the island.

An image of Raziel in the moonstone pond flits to my mind. If only there were some way for Raziel to drain his magic into the stone... to power the island. It would benefit them both.

Almost like a—

Conduit.

The word rings in my mind, and I freeze.

"Raziel," I hiss, shaking his shoulder. "Wake up!"

He sucks in a sharp breath, and his eyes whip open. "What's going on?"

"Come on!" I jump out of bed, yanking his hand. He jerks up, squinting in confusion as he glances around.

I don't know if my idea will work, but I mentally kick myself for not trying it sooner.

Gripping a half-sleeping Raziel's hand, I fly through the hallways, tugging him along. The echo of our feet on the stone thunders around us. We spill out into the warm night air, and I don't stop until we're at the edge of the moonstone pool.

"What are we doing?" Raziel asks, eyebrows pinched tight.

His tight sleeping shorts highlight strong quads, and his muscles flex as he scratches his bare stomach. I keep my eyes locked on his face, unwilling to allow myself to get distracted.

The night is quiet, save for the gentle trickling of the water down the sides of the temple.

"Trying one last thing."

He sighs, shaking his head. "Soraya—"

Before he can continue, I lean up and press my lips to his, swallowing his next words. His mouth quickly mirrors my movements, and his tongue enters my lips with newly acquired skill. We kiss until we're breathless.

I pull back, cupping his cheeks and leveling him with a serious look. "It's not over until it's over."

He places his hand atop mine, caressing it gently. His gaze softens. "What do you need me to do?"

Turning my attention to the moonstone at the center of the pool, I point. "Get in."

Without another word, he lifts himself over the wall and into the pool. Clear water ripples around him as he moves, wading toward the moonstone.

I follow suit, hopping over the wall. The water splashes, sending waves surging out around me. Raziel glances at me, face stern, but then he continues heading toward the center where the stone sits—a pale shadow of what it once was.

Sorrow floods me at the sight. Its once vibrant beauty has nearly faded entirely.

Halting beside Raziel and the stone, I incline my head and square my shoulders. "Moons, I hope this works."

Raziel stays silent, watching me with curiosity. I slip the

straps of my dress down, exposing my bare chest. His eyes flit to my breasts, and he sucks in a sharp breath.

"Place your hand on my chest," I instruct. He reaches up, palming a breast. I can't help but chuckle. "No, not my tit— and use your other hand."

He pauses, blinking at his hand before quickly understanding what I mean and switching hands. As soon as he touches the place where the moonstone rests in my skin, a shock courses through me.

"Good," I murmur. "Now place your other hand on the moonstone."

Slowly, he lifts his opposite hand, doing as I say. I do the same, planting both hands against the cool, rough surface of the stone.

A sudden burst of buzzing energy flits through me, and I gasp. It's static at first, like the first time we ever touched in the stairwell, and it spreads throughout my entire body.

Instinct guides me. Squeezing my eyes shut, I focus on forcing the magic out into the stone.

The energy builds and builds, but it stirs within me, not coming out. After a few moments, I open my eyes. The moonstone remains unchanged.

"No!" I slap the water. My shoulders slump.

In the distant horizon, a faint orange light begins to spill across the sea. We've run out of time.

Raziel's expression is crestfallen as he stares at the same view. "It's okay, Soraya. We tried."

"Trying isn't enough!"

He throws his hands up in defeat. "It's just the way—"

"Wait." I grip his wrist, pulling his left hand toward me. "Look!" Soft, pulsing light emanates from his palm. "Something's happening."

His eyes lock onto my chest. "You're glowing, too," he murmurs, a muscle in his jaw tightening. Slowly, he drags his gaze back to mine. His head tilts, and then he steps closer to me. A renewed vigor brightens his face. "Can we try one more thing?"

I nod stiffly, unable to find any last drops of hope.

"Do you trust me?"

"Always," I choke out, my throat thick with emotion.

"Good," he says. Then he presses my back against the moonstone and bends, wrapping his hands around the backs of my thighs. "Wrap your legs around me."

He hoists me up, and I do what he says. I don't have time to question his movements, because he presses me against the moonstone, eliminating all space between our bodies.

His mouth descends on my jaw, trailing a kiss to my neck. Goosebumps decorate my arms as I arch into him.

One last time. That's what he wants for his last day—I can give him that.

"Kiss me," I demand. "On my lips."

He nods, frantically meeting me where I desire. I groan into the kiss, my nails digging into his back. He's hard in an instant, rocking his erection against me.

"I need you, Soraya," he says when he breaks free for air. "I love you."

My hands drop to his waistband underwater, and I make awkward work of tugging his trunks down. They slip down his thighs, and he's able to wiggle them down his legs and step out of them. Once he's free, I grip his stiff shaft and guide him to my opening.

"Wait," he says, giving me a pained look. "We can't rush. We need to warm you up."

My eyes flit over his shoulder, catching the fiery ascent in the distance. I don't know how long he has. Death is guaranteed on his thirtieth birthday, but whether that's at first light or last light, I am uncertain.

"There's no time," I whisper, a tear falling from my eye. "Make love to me one last time, please."

He huffs a breath, planting his forehead on my shoulder. When I tug his cock toward me, he thrusts his hips, sinking the tip into me.

"Happy birthday, Raziel Kasper," I choke out, tears clouding my vision. "I love you."

He crashes his mouth against mine, pressing all the way inside me at the same time. I nearly yell from the shock of it, but he devours the sound. Instead of the patient, reserved, attentive lover I've gotten over the previous weeks, Raziel takes me in an animalistic manner.

Grunting and groaning, he rhythmically thrusts inside me. Water splashes around us, and my back slams against the moonstone.

The heightened adrenaline, the fear, and the passion mix into a flurry of emotion inside me. I close my eyes, clutching Raziel as I ride him toward release.

One of his hands releases my thighs, but the water and moonstone help keep me in place. I grip him tighter, and he reaches between us with his glowing hand. I meet his eyes, confused, and a small smirk plays on his lips.

The moment his skin meets mine beneath the water, I nearly combust.

Silver streams of light spread from his palm, covering my clit. The ribbons vibrate with magic, caressing me in just the right spot. They wrap around his cock, forming a ribbed effect.

"How?" I gasp.

A laugh escapes Raziel. I wish we had discovered *this* perk of his magic sooner.

The thought doesn't last long, as the intense pleasure from his ribbed, vibrating moonlit cock takes me to the brink.

A gasp escapes my lips, swallowed by the urgent rhythm of our bodies. The world shrinks as exquisite friction consumes me. My heart beats frantically, a drum against my ribs.

Like a lightning strike, release comes crashing down through me. My breath hitches, and my muscles tense as pleasure rips through me, unlike anything I've felt before.

My senses overload as the friction ignites. A wildfire moves through my core, devastating me in the most delightful of ways. I moan, gasping in pleasure. The noises grow to screams, and I clamp my teeth down on my bottom lip.

A beautiful, blinding silver light grows between us— brighter and brighter until I'm nearly blind.

Somewhere in the distance, I hear Raziel grunt his own release, and his movements slow. He collapses against me, pressing me against the stone.

I can't see.

I can't hear.

I can only *feel* the vigor with which his chest rises and falls.

As quickly as it came, the moonlight magic fades away. Raziel gently sets me on my feet with a small splash. My head swims with a lightness, and I nearly topple over. A strange, unfamiliar metallic taste fills my mouth.

"Are you okay?" He frowns down at me, planting a hand on my arm to steady me.

I nod, eyeing the harsh red marks on his shoulders from where I scratched him. "I'm sorry," I whisper.

"Soraya," he says, eyes wide. His thumb comes up to my lower lip. He swipes it, and I wince from the tenderness there.

But when he holds his thumb up for me to see, it's lined with crimson.

My heart stalls. For a moment, I can't speak. My tongue darts out, tasting the source of the strange coppery taste.

"Blood?" I gasp. "But..."

"Have you ever bled red before?"

I shake my head, jaw slack. My hand comes up to my chest, the spot where the magic usually roils and irritates me. But there's no feeling there, only a foreign numbness.

"Soraya," Raziel repeats, his tone strained. His eyes flit behind me, locked on the moonstone.

I whirl around, and my legs nearly buckle at the sight.

Moonlight dances on the iridescent surface, sparkling vibrantly. Depending on the angle of light, it gleams with a dazzling array of colors: silver, blue, green, and a hint of purple.

A sob rips from me, and my hands fly to my mouth. "The magic... the moonstone... Fixed?" The words escape me in short bursts. I spin toward Raziel, gaping. "The curse?"

His shoulders lift into a lazy shrug. "I don't know... but I think maybe we broke it. It feels different this time." Hope lines his words.

I nod rapidly, licking my bloodied lip again. "We did it," I murmur, the words not feeling real. "How?"

He blinks a few times, then, ever so slowly, his face brightens into a dazzling smile. "You. *You're* the conduit, Soraya."

Before I can ask him to elaborate, something dark floats by, snagging my attention. At the sight of his abandoned shorts, the reality of our situation sinks in, and we both burst out into delirious laughter.

CHAPTER THIRTY-FOUR

THE BIRTHDAY

RAZIEL

*a*fter the longest day of my life, hoping and praying to the goddesses that the curse is finally broken, I sit on the beach to watch the day fade. Water laps gently at the shore, a calm lover. A couple of wardens yell and splash in the water, just a little further down the beach.

The sky's light disappears bit by bit, giving way to night.

I can't help but think of it as a metaphor for my own time running out. Fate will come for me any second now.

Soraya leans against me, her finger drawing circles on my knee. "It was a good idea—the best one you've had yet. It's bound to work."

My throat tightens. I nod wordlessly. I wish I shared her optimism that my idea broke the curse, but it's impossible to tell until my birthday passes entirely.

"I dispel my excess magic through pleasure. I should've

thought of it first." She chuckles, shaking her head and nudging me.

Making love against the moonstone certainly changed something for us. Even if it didn't break the curse, it brought the moonstone back to life.

And the silverdew opened again.

I find solace in leaving behind those fixes for the islanders.

Excited chatter fills the air around us, telling me they're equally as happy with the recent turn of events. I hadn't expected the entire island to show up to *celebrate* my birthday, or potential death, but here we are. Someone's high-pitched laughter rings out, piercing my brain. I grimace.

"At least they aren't playing music," I mutter.

"Hm?" Soraya's fingers pause, and she shakes with silent laughter. "Is it music you hate, or just joy in general?"

"Neither... Just the noises are too much at once."

"Overstimulating?" she offers.

I nod, studying her stunning face for what might be one of the last times. "Exactly."

She nudges me with her shoulder. "I'm proud of you."

My muscles tense up. "For what? I've failed at everything."

"For coming out of your shell and *trying*. You've overcome so much in the last few months, Raziel," she says softly.

Glancing down at my swim shorts and excess of exposed skin, a flicker of pride alights in my chest. She's right. I almost don't recognize the man I've become... and I kind of enjoy him.

"Hey, buddy!" Joss plops down into the sand beside me, a little too close for my liking. "Wanna go for a swim?"

My nose scrunches instinctively.

"Can we have some alone time?" Soraya asks, saving me.

"Whatever tickles your pickle," Joss drawls, shooting to his feet. "Come find me if you two get bored of brooding." He waves at someone, then bolts off, yelling, "Mariel! Come swim with—"

I tune him out, focusing back on the beauty beside me. "I suppose I should thank him, if I survive the night."

"Joss?"

Snorting, I shake my head with disbelief. "It was his random string of oblivious commentary that helped me put things together."

"*Joss?*" Soraya repeats, confused.

Sighing, I lean back in the sand with my hands under my head. "Yes. I know." Staring at the rapidly darkening sky, I brace myself for whatever happens next.

All the terror and urgency have dissipated, leaving a strange, numb acceptance in their wake.

"It's almost like a Union Night," Soraya says wistfully.

"Except we're waiting to see if I *die*."

She leans over me, blocking my view of the sky. My breath hitches at her thick waves tumbling down around us, but it's her intense stare that pierces my heart. "You won't die."

We stay like that for a while, silently challenging one another.

A scream shatters the moment. I lurch up so quickly that I accidentally knock my forehead into Soraya's.

"Ouch," she hisses, falling backward into the sand.

"I'm so sorry." I reach for her, gently cupping her chin and inspecting her flawless skin. "Are you okay?"

Her response is swallowed by the storm of noise overtaking the beach. A wave of adrenaline floods my system as I leap up. My heart drums violently against my ribs. I whirl, desperate to locate the source of the chaos.

Instead of pain and destruction like I initially expected, the cries and gasps turn to glee.

Dozens of villagers stand nearby, their heads tilted toward the sky.

"Raziel!" Soraya yells, grasping my hand in a death grip. "Look!"

Afraid of what I might find in the newly darkened sky, I slowly raise my gaze. The moons' edges touch, much closer than they should be, mere nights after a Union.

My eyes widen. "Are they…"

"Yes!" Soraya bounces beside me, screeching with glee.

I wince at the noise but keep my attention locked overhead. The smaller moon, as bright as ever, crawls toward its larger counterpart. The moment they merge, an uproar of celebratory cheers and confused conversation pollutes the night.

Opalescent aquamarine and turquoise streaks ripple through the sky, and the entire island mirrors it. The plants and water come to life, sparkling with the promise of *magic*.

Villagers rush toward me, peppering me with questions. I can't hear them over one another, and my palms begin to sweat.

Soraya steps in front of me, putting her fingers to her mouth and letting out a loud whistle. It cuts through the mayhem, and a wave of silence washes over the villagers.

"Moon Priest," someone asks, stepping forward. "What's happening?"

A murmur rises through the crowd, but they all stare expectantly at me. I'm not sure how to answer them, because I have no concrete answers.

Instead of running, I decide to give them the best answer I have: "I don't know exactly, but I think we might've freed the moons, the goddesses, from their curse… I think this is a good thing."

I'm met with varying looks of confusion and concern at

first. To combat that, I try my hardest to relax my posture. Swallowing down my nerves, I force my lips into a smile, showing my teeth and all.

"Blessed Union!" I yell in my most lighthearted tone.

The man who asked the question seems appeased. He barks a laugh and claps his hands dramatically. "Let's celebrate!"

The islanders, satisfied with my pathetic reassurance, reanimate.

Off to the side, I catch Kassia watching me. When I meet her eyes, she offers a sad smile. I wave, and instantly the smile reaches her eyes, brightening her face. I wish I were as open and loving as everyone else; I'd approach her with a hug and an apology, but it's just not me.

Instead, I make a silent vow to try harder with Kassia. With *everyone*.

My eyes flit upward to the sky, and for the first time, I feel a sense of relief.

I made it to the night of my thirtieth birthday.

Alive.

SIX MONTHS LATER

EPILOGUE

THE PLEASURE

RAZIEL

*S*oraya drags the dagger across her palm, giggling as bright red streams from the wound.

"Holy moons," she says, aghast. A disbelieving laugh escapes her. "That day at the Assembly... I *wasn't* lying after all." Reaching up, she cups my cheek. "Turns out you really are the conduit of magic—the key to this island's magic."

I turn, kissing her bloodied palm. "Will you *please* stop cutting yourself? You're starting to scar."

My eyes wander over the pale white criss-cross markings along her palms.

"So what? I'm able to scar now." She pulls back, staring at the cut in awe.

I watch her the same way she watches her bloody hand—with butterflies flitting through my chest. Rivulets stream down the side of her wrist. My pulse picks up, pounding in my temples.

"Moons save me," I grumble, reaching for the gauze resting on the bedside table.

She pouts at me, jutting out her lower lip. "I'm just checking that it's still red."

"You don't need to go that deep!" I work with familiarity, having done this more than a few times over the last several months.

Soraya nuzzles into my lap, letting me wrap her hand. "Thank you."

A growl escapes before I can stop it. "You can thank me by keeping your blood inside you."

Giggling, she lifts herself and throws a leg over my waist, straddling me. She plants her hands on my chest and pushes me backward. "Perhaps I can thank you by keeping something else inside me."

My face heats at the implication, but I can't help the small twitch of my lips... and something else.

"One day, you'll admit you find me funny," she says, waggling her brows and leaning forward. "Until then, I'll keep pestering you."

She hops off me, humming to herself as she stretches her arms overhead. We've spent an absurd amount of time together in my bed lately, but I suppose we're making up for years and years of missed pleasure.

My brush with death was rather eye-opening.

I shift beneath the silky sheets, glancing at the stunning night sky through the overhead window.

"Would you like to go down to the beach?" Soraya asks.

"No. I want to stay here. With you."

"But the Union—"

"Isn't even necessary anymore." I turn to study her.

Her eyes stay locked on the supermoon overhead. The two

moons have remained conjoined ever since we broke the curse six months ago.

"We might not be celebrating the same way, but we're still celebrating." She pouts, puffing out her lower lip and crossing her arms.

I roll my body weight over hers, propping myself up on my elbows. I gently caress her bottom lip, tucking it away. "We go to the beach almost every night. Let us celebrate alone tonight, my darling."

Soraya smiles. "Fine. You win."

She guides my hand right where she wants it, unashamed to direct me. My thumb lands on her clit, and she bucks her hips. Her eyes roll back, and her head tilts up.

"Look at me, Soraya," I command. "Look me in the eyes while I make you come on my fingers."

She does as I say, lifting her head and allowing her gaze to connect with mine. Her pupils are blown out, her cheeks flushed.

"You're such a good student," she whispers breathlessly.

Moons, she's too beautiful like this.

Naked. Vulnerable.

At my mercy.

All *mine*.

"Remember who makes you scream like this," I croon against her pussy before allowing my tongue to replace my thumb. I slowly slip two fingers inside her to add pressure while I lick her with a steady rhythm.

Her strong thighs wrap around my head, locking me in place. My cock strains at my pants, desperate to be touched— to be tasted like this.

My hips move of their own accord, thrusting into the bed as the taste of her nearly causes me to explode.

When her muscles tense and her back arches, I know I'm

close. Instead of changing a thing, I continue like the patient man I am, knowing she needs me to keep steady so she can—

She yells my name, her thighs gripping me. Her walls flutter and pulse around my finger, and a tremble wracks through her body.

Smiling against her flesh, I slowly pull back and gaze down at her.

"Raziel," she whispers, a lazy smile on her face, "how could I ever forget how *you* make me feel?"

She grabs my head, pulling my lips down to hers. Using her feet, she shoves her toes in the waistband of my pants and tries to shuffle them down my legs. My cock springs out, heavy and hard.

Suddenly, her soft fingers latch onto my shaft, and I nearly combust. My tip weeps with precum, and she runs her thumb across it.

"You feel so good," she mumbles, biting her bottom lip as she gazes up at me. "But you feel even better inside me."

In a trance, I allow her to guide me to her opening.

The moment I push myself into her, I shudder from the onslaught of pleasure. Her soft warmth welcomes me, hugging my cock tightly. It's unlike anything I've ever imagined.

"Raziel," she whispers, pressing her hips up, attempting to find friction.

Intense heat builds at the base of my spine, and I hiss. Fear flits through me.

"Don't. Move," I mutter into her neck. My eyes shut, and I breathe in her scent, which does nothing to help me fight the incoming pleasure.

Chuckling softly, she wraps her legs around my waist and draws me closer. I groan as her walls clench around me, as if gripping tightly and refusing to let go.

"Feels too good," I whisper on a moan, loving how she shudders under my words.

She wiggles, trying to get me to move.

"Soraya," I hiss. Pulling back onto my elbows, I give her a warning look. Her beautiful blue-green eyes twinkle with mischief. "If you don't stop moving... I won't last."

"That's the point," she says with a smirk.

Her fingers grip my ass, digging into the meaty flesh there. Heat consumes me, and the urge to move explodes within me.

"*Fuck.*" Unable to hold back anymore, I pull my hips back, then buck them forward, reentering her with a controlled motion. But when she moans my name again, I lose any semblance of control I had.

My vision wavers, and the intense pressure in my spine builds until we explode together. Our hearts and bodies merge like the moons overhead.

"Blessed Union," Soraya whispers with a lazy smile. "You and I are made of sea and sky. Our souls are intertwined."

ABOUT THE AUTHOR

Miranda is a fan of all things magical and romantic. She believes some of the best heroes come from dark pasts, and family is more than blood. She loves writing about strong characters who overcome unpleasant situations and find love along the way.

LOOKING FOR MORE STEAMY ROMANTASY? CHECK OUT THE REST OF THE ROMANCING THE REALMS COLLECTION!

COURTING THE DRAGON MAGE

My head slammed against the floor, and the shouting became distant.

Still, I'd never felt more alive.

Get up, Lyra.

"No one told me the Pit Viper was little more than a weedy little cunt. It's almost unfair, beating on a woman like that..." My opponent's words were invigorating as my anger sang through me like a numbing drug. The taste of copper was thick on my tongue as blood flowed through my mouth, and I spat it out as I forced myself to my feet. People surrounded me, shouting, though I could not discern their words. The man who had struck me waved his hands as if he had already won. I wanted to groan; the world swayed, but I refused to fall again as I launched myself at him. The people around me gasped, but I was quick and had my legs wrapped around his waist and my arm across his neck before he could turn to see me coming. I pulled my arm taut against his neck, crushing his windpipe, and he flung us around in a panic, scrambling with blunt fingers to pry me from his back. If I could just get him to pass out…

I cried out as he threw himself back. I hit the ground hard, and my vision went spotty as the air was ripped from my lungs. Gods, had he broken my rib? No, no, I could still breathe.

"Submit," I whispered, forcing my arm to tighten around his neck. I had managed to keep my arm across his neck by Nymera's miracle. My fingers locked around my wrist, and though he struggled, his thrashing was beginning to fade. I was lucky; they'd put me against someone suited to my size in this fight.

After a few tense moments, the man slumped against me, allowing my hold on him to lessen. The fighting rings of Kraeva were not to the death, and though my blood sang for violence, I yielded. I used what strength I possessed to push the man off of me, allowing the one in charge of enforcing fair fighting to drag me to my feet. My hearing was distorted; the crowd cheered as he lifted my arm, their screams distant and too loud all at once. Still, I smiled.

This was why I came down here.

"The Pit Viper takes another prey!"

"Thank *fuck*. I put a lot of sandyms down on her victory."

"Fucking bitch cheated!"

Their words surrounded me as my head thundered painfully. The headache I was about to have would be merciless, but I won, which was all that mattered.

"A small spitfire as always, my little viper." A man in noble silks approached with a large bag of sandyms. My head throbbed again, and the motion jarred against my swelling cheek. My tongue darted out, tasting blood on my lip, which had split on the right side. My opponent had done a number on me before I knocked him out.

"Some of us have to earn our suppers." The lie came to me quickly. I had more than enough sandyms to fill my belly, but the fewer underlings who recognized me, the better. The last thing I wanted was to get my father or brother involved with the fighting pits in the belly of Kraeva. Hence, I paid a local mage handsomely for a potion that would mask my features for a few hours.

The bag of sandyms in Faeva's plump hand was for potions I could only find in the lower districts, districts my father was too proud to purchase from, even if it was for medicine for his son.

The magic was beginning to wear off, though. It prickled against my skin, a warning that if I didn't hurry away, my cover would shatter.

I attempted to keep calm as I held my hand out, hoping, for once, that Faeva would be merciful and give me my dues with little trouble.

He was not.

"Come and speak with the others. They wish to celebrate your recent accomplishments. It's not common to have someone of your stature go undefeated in the rings." His eyes raked over me, and I suppressed the urge to shudder in disgust.

"I'm afraid I have other business to attend." Now that the fighting had won, my lust for the fight had diminished and slunk away to the hollow of my chest to slumber until it woke again and demanded blood. I had no time for the squabbles of nobles, no time to pretend to give a shit about their praises. I didn't do this for the validation. I did this to calm the ache in my chest. I did this to try to save my brother from the Blooming Dahlia, a plague that had swept through the streets of Kraeva in recent months. My brother had fallen ill with it a week or so ago, and my desire to seek his cure had consumed all of my efforts.

Faeva frowned but relented with little trouble, passing over the bag of sandyms and simply nodding. The weight felt good in my palm, and I made a mental note to stop by the bakery nearby in the morning to buy some warm gyras. They were my brother's favorite. He may be well enough tomorrow to eat one. His appetite came and went, and he hadn't been able to enjoy his favorite treat since before he got sick.

"Next time, then," Faeva said, and I agreed with a feigned smile. He said that every time. Sometimes, I indulged him, but not tonight. Not as my skin itched, and the magic began to liberate itself from my skin.

People murmured quietly around me as I made my way towards the door. Another fight was getting ready to happen, so most people paid me little mind, which I was grateful for. The room was small, and sweat collected on my brow from so many bodies pressed closely together.

The nape of my neck prickled like I was being watched. I glanced up from where my eyes had been trained mainly on the floor and met the gaze of a faerie.

She was of Eirwyn's Court. I knew that much. The fae from Neferíl's Court did not come here, not while they warred with the humans of the north. If the fae were here, it was from the Elven King of Southern Elvira, the forest of the fae.

She stared at me, her hair almost ethereal as it wove around her, embellished with intricate braids. Her eyes were cat-like, her ears as pointed as her canines when she flashed a wicked smile my way. It wasn't uncommon for the fair folk to attend these fights; they had a simple curiosity for human affairs and could only breach the forest's edge at night.

Another faerie stood next to her, a male. He was tall and

lanky, with dark hair that was longer than hers and draped over his shoulders. He was pale, eerily so, his eyes dark voids of black.

I ducked my head, ignoring the anxious patter in my chest, and strode past him.

The male faerie said something, but I couldn't understand him. Some folk from Kraeva braved the faerie food and wine to understand the fae, diluting it to avoid the consequences of too much of its consumption. I was not one of those people, and I smiled apologetically as I met the faerie's gaze.

He didn't say anything else, and I barreled into someone in my eagerness to escape them.

"*Shit*. I'm sor—" My words died as the stranger flinched away from me in disgust.

It was the crowned prince, Nasir, someone I was all too familiar with during my time growing up in the castle. His hair was slicked back, and his dark eyes raked over me in disgust. Luckily, he didn't seem to recognize me. His attention turned towards the front of his shirt, now covered in ale. I must have knocked his glass from his grasp.

What was Prince Nasir doing at the fighting pits?

"Stupid cunt—these silks cost more than your worthless life. They could throw you back in the pits, you know—all it would take is a snap of my pretty little fingers." He raised his hand, his fingers poised at the ready. Like a snake, ready to strike. "Next time, I'll see you fight someone you cannot win against."

I sneered, but my words lodged in the back of my throat as my skin prickled again. *Last warning. I need to get out of here before the prince recognizes me.*

"My apologies, Your Royal Highness." I curtsied and then turned on my heel, fleeing before the prince could rebut.

I spilled out into the alleyway. The air, while warm, was a

welcome relief against my aching skin as I pressed myself against the wall and sighed.

That was too close. I would time things better next time.

Still, the thrill of it all sang through me, and breathless laughter escaped my lips as I pressed a hand to my face. I clutched the bag of sandyms in my other hand as I hurried from the alley, eager to be home. The fighting pits were located in the lower districts of Kraeva, but I had learned which alleys and side roads to take to reach the royal districts more quickly as I tucked my sandyms inside my shirt, hiding the bag from wandering eyes. I knew better than to flash currency in the struggling parts of the city.

Wind trailed through the deserted streets as I stayed within shadows, hidden from anyone who might be out. Knights patrolled the city in their light leather armor and khopeshes, but I managed to stay out of their observant gaze as I hurried up the cliffs towards the Royal Keep.

A low whimper echoed to my right as I passed by an alley. It was so soft it could have been the wind, but as my eyes adjusted to the dark, I flinched and ducked away as a fist swung past my left shoulder.

"Beat it, little rat," a man hissed, his eyes glowing in the darkness. Fae, perhaps? I couldn't tell as I scrambled away, my heart a wild, untamed thing in my chest. I couldn't see well enough in the dark, but it looked like there were two of them, and one had someone pinned up against the wall further in the alley, their shirt wrapped around his fingers. "Before you end up in'a sit'a'tion you don' wanna be in."

"What did he do?" I asked, gesturing to the man pinned to the wall. "Because if there's something I hate, it's pricks that think they can beat on someone half their size."

The man who had nearly punched me growled and lunged,

his bald head gleaming in the moon's light. I swung out of the way just in time and then let go. Headache be damned.

The ache in my chest rekindled as it sang in excitement. I swept to the side and turned, instantly swinging out to grab the man's wrist as he lashed out at me with a curled fist.

Dodging the man's attack, I sank low. I needed to take him out quickly. I was already exhausted from my last fight.

He was quicker than I thought, though, and he laughed. "Tired, street rat?" His words were meant to poke at me, tug at my resolve, and make me reckless, but I had learned long ago that anger only led to mistakes and loss.

Somehow, I managed to get behind him as he darted past me.

Gotcha. Like the man from the pits, I latched myself onto the man's back, wrapped my legs around his waist, and slipped my arm across his windpipe. Tugging, I did not hold back as I had in the fighting pits. Here, there was no one telling me to show mercy.

The man struggled for several moments before he eventually gave up, his body slumping. I released him and managed to stay on my feet, my attention turning towards the others in the alley.

The other man cursed in a language I did not recognize and spit on the ground. "Not worth the trouble," he said in a heavily accented tone, pushing the man towards me and bolting.

Chest heaving, my legs gave out. I had borrowed too much time tonight and fought the odds stacked against me. The man they'd been bullying rushed over and knelt, his face swimming in my blurry vision. Oh gods, I was going to pass out. I couldn't pass out, not here. Not now. Someone would find me. Someone would…

"Breathe." The man's voice washed over me, and I inhaled sharply, forcing the darkness encroaching at my vision's edge to retreat. It was as if by magic, and I blinked rapidly as my eyes fell upon the stranger.

"Thank you for saving me," the stranger said, his eyes burning with the flourish of magic. It was otherworldly, and I immediately flushed as he smiled at me. The alley was too dark to reveal his features, but I knew he wasn't human. No human looked as he did now, with the soft glow of magic brushed against his skin.

"You shouldn't be out at night unless you know how to handle yourself. Or at least keep away from dark alleys. There's a fucking war going on," I scolded, but my voice was weak, wavering from exhaustion.

"Yes, well..." the stranger's thumb brushed against the sharp line of my jaw, and the tingle of magic returned. Suddenly, I didn't feel quite so weak, as if I could stand if I tried. Pain pulsed through my face, a reminder that I had taken quite the beating *before* I had fought the men in the alley. "They caught me off guard as I was leaving."

"What were they bothering you for anyway?" I trailed off, distracted by the man's thumb against my cheek.

He pulled away, adjusting his jacket as he rose and offered me a hand. "Wrong place, wrong time, I gather," he muttered as I allowed him to pull me to my feet. Yes, I could make it home now, and a startling clarity overcame me.

Not many knew how to wield magic, which meant this man was either a fae or a mage.

Both prospects made me uneasy, and I watched the man limp over and pick something up off the ground. A cane, one he leaned heavily against as he turned to meet my nervous gaze.

I shouldn't have been so frightened; I had seen him

incapable of defending himself, but the idea of what he was capable of magically didn't sit right in my stomach, and I sidled towards the lip of the alley and cleared my throat.

"I'm glad I could help, but I should get home."

"Let me accompany you. As you said, it's dangerous at night."

I sneered, trying to tame the flurry of my racing heart in my chest. "And as you saw, I know how to care for myself. Good night..."

A low, breathy laughter escaped the man's lips. "Alistair."

I turned and fled the alley, sticking to the main roads towards my flower shop. The magic had worn from my face, freeing it from its disguise, and while I was usually one to stick to the shadows to avoid recognition, the whole night had left me rattled.

No one was out anyway. The warring kingdoms had left the streets of Kraeva silent; everyone was too fearful of Bracaea flying their dragons to lay waste to the cities and villages to dare brave the nightlife. No one knew of the sickness that festered in the belly of their city. Not yet. I knew it was only a matter of time, though. The Crown couldn't silence it forever.

Chilly sea air brushed my face as I rounded the corner, and my flower shop appeared. It was near the keep, which loomed high up on a cliffside edging the ocean, and relief overcame me. Everything that had transpired tonight left me rattled. It was becoming increasingly dangerous to travel the city at night.

A shadow blotted out the moon, and my blood ran cold as I looked up and met the sight of a dragon soaring overhead. It wasn't close enough to discern its size or what it looked like, but there was no mistaking it as it sailed over the city and bells began to sound, an alarm signaling that the city was under attack.

I quickened my pace and did not look up again as I found myself safely inside my shop, my heart thundering in my ears.

What the fuck was a dragon doing in Kraeva?

Continue reading now on Kindle Unlimited: https://mybook.to/6lFQ1

COURTING THE TIGER KING

"Fucking fuck!" He shook out his hand to ease the sting, squinting against the dusty darkness in the tunnels that had them all stumbling around like blind idiots. If the witch would hold still for just two seconds, then maybe she'd know that they weren't there to harm her.

It was difficult to communicate that while being struck with her sparks of silver lightning though.

They'd hunted her down over the course of weeks until his men had received word that the witch had been spotted in the forest that precluded the shore. If she left his kingdom now there was no telling when they'd be able to find her again, and he didn't have time to waste. Not with the curse breathing down his neck.

"I don't have time for this," he muttered, following the sound of the witch up ahead around the curve in the tunnel. How she'd known the tunnels were here, he wasn't sure. There were not many secrets that his kingdom held that he did not know about and yet she'd managed to evade them for an impressive amount of time. Louder, he called, "For the last time, Sonnet. We're here to—*Ouch!*" The pain sparked his anger, the beast within snapping at the reins and Wren decided he had no reason to hold it back.

The change was a warm cascade over his skin. Heavy paws hit the dirt floor as his senses sharpened, the tunnel no longer appearing pitch black. A metallic scent tickled his nose and he chuffed, suddenly understanding why the witch hadn't utilised anything more than sparks to dissuade them from following. She was injured, which meant she likely didn't have much more magic in her reserves since it depended on the life energy of the user.

He moved quickly, his stride long between his paws, and he caught up to the witch easily. She spun, silver eyes widening as she lifted her hands between them and only the faintest flicker of magic answered her call. Blood coated her side and the pallor of her face was chalky, panic overtaking any logic she may have had until Wren knocked her to the ground with the press of one large paw.

Perhaps it was the pain that jolted her out of the panic, or maybe being face-to-face with a tiger knocked the sense back into her, because she stopped trying to fight and instead breathed a sigh of relief. "Your Majesty."

Sensing it was safe and that the witch was at last in her right mind, Wren let his beast fade away in favour of the man. With barely a thought, the magic of the change reproduced his clothes and he offered the witch a hand, frowning when she grasped it weakly. She couldn't die. Not when he needed her. She was the only known lunar witch left of her line and, consequently, the only one who could perform the spell he needed.

"Sonnet," he acknowledged. "What trouble have you got yourself into now?"

The infirmary was largely empty, affording the witch privacy as his team of healers worked to cleanse and erase the wound that stretched from her hip to her ribcage. Sonnet had fallen unconscious on the journey back to the palace and Wren could only pray to the goddess that the witch pulled through.

"Thank Selene you found her when you did. The worst is over now." Gabe clapped a hand on Wren's shoulder, making him grunt. He wished he could believe that his friend was right, but the ceremony he needed Sonnet to perform was only the first step in thwarting his curse. Gabe sighed, like he could see the doubt churning in Wren's mind behind his eyes. "Come, let her rest. There's nothing you can do here while the healers work."

That much was true at least.

Wren accepted Gabe's hand up as he stood from the uncomfortable wooden bench that lined the outside wall of the infirmary. He'd been out on the hunt for weeks and was desperate for a bath, whiskey, and bed. Not necessarily in that order. He didn't like to spend so much time away from court, but needs-must and this wasn't a task he could let fall to anyone else. Only his most trusted soldiers had accompanied him in an effort to keep their task under wraps.

He followed Gabe out of the room and into the stone corridor, their footsteps muffled by the green runner that wound through the halls. Wren must have looked worse than he'd thought if the unusual tightness of Gabe's jaw was anything to go by.

"Tell me," he said quietly and Gabe nodded, scrubbing a hand over the blond stubble on his jaw before heaving a sigh. His amber eyes were weary when they met Wren's.

"More of the same. Whispers mostly, that the king would

rather be out fucking and hunting than looking after his court."

Wren snorted. If only that were true.

The hour was early, most of the castle hadn't yet stirred as the sun began to stream weakly in through the windows that lined the corridor. But still, he was careful to guard his words lest someone be lurking unseen. In a kingdom full of shifters, you couldn't trust anything you saw—sometimes the fly on the wall was a grown man in disguise.

"Someone is going to a lot of trouble to sow discord," Gabe continued, the early morning light washing over him and dyeing his white skin momentarily gold. "But whoever it is, they're being careful."

"Well, hopefully this should be the last hunt I'll have to go on for a while." Then they would have no reason to complain or spread rumours.

The entrance to his chambers was a welcome sight and he nodded in greeting to the two guards who stood sentry before he turned to clasp Gabe's shoulder.

"I need to rest, will you and Skye—"

"We'll keep an eye on your witch," Gabe confirmed, voice pitched low enough that the human guards wouldn't have picked up the words. "Rest, brother."

Wren smiled, the look fleeting as Gabe nodded and walked back the way they'd come. Gabe wasn't a brother by blood, but he had grown up with him and Skye and the three of them were close. The doors opened quietly beneath Wren's palm and the familiar scent of his rooms tickled his nose and relaxed his body automatically.

The hearth was cold but Wren couldn't be bothered to heat it, instead he wandered to the small golden cart in one corner of the room and poured a healthy measure of the amber liquid into a crystal glass. He sat down heavily into one of the plush armchairs arranged around the low, large oak table as he sipped.

He had his witch and had collected all but one of the ingredients Sonnet would need for her spellwork. This curse had been in his family for generations, so he was well versed in what it would entail. Lunar witches like Sonnet were beyond rare, they specialised in matters of the soul—a magic that many felt was too powerful to be allowed to exist. As a result, they had been hunted. His family had done what they could to protect the witches, but they were a stubborn lot and Wren was forced into secrecy; any hint of his curse could be perceived as a weakness that the court and their adversaries may pounce upon.

Worse, Wren wasn't sure that he could blame them for questioning his fitness for the throne if they discovered the truth. He'd only learned of the curse himself that same year. The ceremony Sonnet would perform could only be done during the cursed's twenty-fifth year. Now he had less than a year to find and bond with his mate, or the curse would take effect.

The only comfort was that Wren wouldn't know that he'd failed if that happened. Trapped in his animal form, Wren wouldn't know much of anything. He couldn't say the same for the kingdom and the throne. The chaos would leave them weak, scrambling for his replacement, perfectly poised for their enemies to close in.

He swallowed back the last of the drink, frowning in the darkness at the morbid turn his thoughts had taken. The glass thunked as he set it on the table, the sound loud in the quiet of the room as he stood and walked to the drapes and tugged them open until a small slither of light cut through the gloom.

His parlour space was where he did his best thinking, aside from when he was in the bath, it was also where he spent the most time with Gabe and Skye. Normally accompanied by drink and cards as they worked to clean out his coffers.

Dust motes swirled in the small beam of light, returning some warmth and brightness to the room as he turned and walked into his adjoining bedroom. A balcony waited to his left, the drapes shut to keep the sun out while he slept, but despite the security risk he often liked to sleep with the doors open, enjoying the smell of fresh air that carried the scents of the forest below up to his room. He pulled open one drape, leaving the one closest to the bed closed to keep it in shadow, and opened the door, breathing deeply and enjoying the hint of earth on the air.

The bed took up most of the room, carved wooden posts forming the vague shape of trees and birds guarding the bed below like a woodland canopy. A copper tub sat in front of the empty hearth, steam curling up from the water within and he hesitated, gaze flitting between the promise of the bed and the heat of the bath calling to him.

His simple tunic and trousers hit the ground, discarded next to his boots and the small horde of weapons he'd had hidden on his person. The need to be clean was too strong to be ignored and he slipped into the water with a groan. After the rough sleeping of the hunt, endless days spent in the underbrush of the forest and the odd tavern, the opportunity to soak in the bath was heavenly. One of his attendants had even added his favourite jasmine oil to the water and the scent had his eyes falling closed.

Water slipped over his nose and he spluttered, jerking upright and blinking the moisture out of his eyes. Fuck. He'd spent all this time trying to break the curse, only to nearly drown in his bath.

Wren dunked his head and reached for a bar of soap, lathering his hair and body and rinsing quickly in the rapidly cooling water. How long had he been asleep for? He wasn't too pruney yet so he had to assume it hadn't been a long time.

A large towel had been placed onto the fabric seat of the wooden chair beside the hearth and he reached for it as he stood, toweling off roughly and pushing the dark fabric over his hair so the semi-long strands wouldn't drip down his back. There was also a small pot of cream on the chair, scented similarly to his favored jasmine, and he scooped up a portion with two fingers before working it across his face and hands. Spending so much time outside would leave him with weathered skin as thick as a bore's hide if he wasn't careful.

Mostly dry, he stumbled over to the bed and promptly collapsed atop the sheets face first. He was asleep before the sun finished rising.

Continue reading now on Kindle Unlimited: https://books2read.com/u/4EjdZl?store=amazon&format=EBOOK

COURTING THE SWAN PRINCE

The air is heavy with the Autumn Realm's constant amber haze, sunlight filtering through the oak trees' branches. I close my eyes, relishing in the warmth as it seeps into my skin. It's a perfect day for archery practice with my best friends. Best friends who are the princes of the kingdom.

"Ready to lose, Odette?" Odin asks, taunting me with his playful voice. He knows just how to provoke me. Ever since our earlier years in primary school, he was always teasing and toying with me, relentless in his pursuit to make me laugh or get a rise out of me. Ever the troublemaker, but I love him for it.

I open my eyes and shoot him a glance. "You only wish," I say, pressing my shoulders back and adjusting my bow. The target stands across the clearing, bark chipped where we've already missed a few times. "Besides, we all know Siegfried is the best shot," I say, looking over my shoulder at Odin's twin. Siegfried's cheeks flush after I wink at him. If Odin is the jester, Siegfried is like the royal librarian, wise and quiet.

Odin's smirk deepens, his gaze flicking between Siegfried

and me. "Well, then let's make it interesting," he says. "Whoever lands a bullseye first gets to marry Odette someday."

Freezing in my spot with heat rising in my cheeks, I glance toward Siegfried. His face is turning red too, but he tries to laugh it off, rubbing the back of his neck. I know it's just a silly game, but I'm baffled he'd wager such a bet. We're just friends, and to suggest we'd be more someday makes my stomach flutter with a thousand butterflies. Neither prince has ever dared to even hold my hand, let alone kiss me. Although, I've daydreamed of Seigfried doing those very things.

"Odin, that's..." Siegfried says, rubbing his temples. "Odette's too good for either of us."

"That may be true, but one of us will be king someday, so maybe she'll want to be queen. Besides, it's just a bit of fun, right?" Odin asks, flashing that charming, dangerous, gorgeous smile of his.

The twins couldn't be more different in personality or looks. Odin, with his dark, curly locks, wide jaw, and dimples, and Siegfried with blonde hair, a long nose, and high cheekbones. Their only similarity is in their stunning blue eyes that are now staring each other down. "Or are you too afraid to compete?"

Siegfried stiffens, the flicker of rivalry between them sparking as it always does when we do anything competitive. Neither wanting ever to appear weak, especially not in front of me. I'm not sure when things became this tense between them, this shift in their relationship to prove themselves. It's hard sometimes, balancing between them. Odin and Siegfried —they're like fire and water, and I'm caught right in the middle, tugged between their differences. But I don't want to choose. I prefer things to remain unchanged.

It infuriates me, especially when they should know they

have nothing to prove. I'll always be their friend and refuse to be something that comes between them.

Siegfried squares his shoulders, staring at me for a moment before nodding. "Fine," he says, tightening his grip on his bow.

My heart stutters at that, and my face burns at the idea that they would bet on me. This is silly, and we all know it's not serious. They could never marry me anyway. I'm just a simple elven villager and not future queen material, I remind myself. It's expected that their future partners will hail from the royal families from the other kingdoms.

"Hey!" I say, my voice rising to match their intensity. "And if I win? What then?"

Odin cocks his head, a glint in his eye. "If you win, Odette, both of us will give you a kiss."

"A kiss?"

My voice comes out in a squeak, and Odin grins wider, pleased with himself. Siegfried's face goes pale. We've always been close friends, but never outright flirted. My stomach twists and the sun feels too hot. If I'm being honest, I've daydreamed of what it would be like to mean more to Sig, but Odin? We might kill each other with how we argue about the silliest things. Besides, it's inevitable we won't see one another once they turn eighteen and go off to the royal college. I want to enjoy their friendship while I can and not complicate things.

"Well?" Odin asks, gesturing to the target. "Ladies first."

I shake off the nerves, focus my eyes, and raise my bow. It's just a game, I tell myself again as I steady my breathing and let the arrow fly. It sails through the air, swift and true, and lands…just outside the bullseye.

"Close, but not close enough!" Odin taunts, chuckling to himself, before setting up his own shot.

I roll my eyes and step back, pretending I don't care, but I feel my pulse quicken. Odin pulls the string back, his eyes narrowing as he lines up his shot. There's a confidence in his stance that makes me flustered, as if he already knows he'll win.

He lets the arrow fly, and with a dull thud, it sinks into the bullseye, dead center.

"Woo!" Odin shouts, throwing his hands up in victory. "Looks like I've won myself a bride."

"Just a lucky shot," Siegfried says, muttering under his breath.

"Luck?" Odin asks with a scoff. "Maybe you're just jealous because you're not as good as I am."

Siegfried's jaw clenches as he stares at the target. I see the way his hands grip his bow, his knuckles turning white as he lets go and his arrow soars towards the target. It misses its mark, just outside the center circle. He glares at Odin, and for a moment, it's as if there's nothing playful left in their rivalry. His eyes flick toward me, but he doesn't meet my gaze.

Siegfried's face darkens, and before I can say anything, he breaks his bow in half, turning and walking away, his steps quick and tense.

"Siegfried!" I yell, calling after him, but he doesn't slow down.

I round on Odin, fists clenched. "Why did you have to say that?"

Odin shrugs, unfazed. "It's just a bit of fun, Odette."

"Fun?" I glare at him, heart pounding with frustration. "You're being a jerk."

Odin raises an eyebrow, crossing his arms. "He'll get over it."

"You'd better hope so," I say, shaking my head. "I'm going to go find him." Without waiting for his response, I turn and hurry off in the direction Siegfried went, leaving Odin alone in the clearing. The sun dips lower, casting long shadows as I follow the path toward Siegfried's favorite spot—a tranquil lake where he goes whenever he wants to be alone.

I find him there, tossing stones into the water, each one making a ripple that spreads out across the glassy surface. His back is to me, shoulders hunched, his posture radiating frustration.

"Hey," I say as I approach him. He doesn't look at me, but I can tell he knows I'm here. "You shouldn't let him get to you."

He's silent for a moment, watching the ripples fade, and then he sighs, picking up another stone and hurling it into the pond. "Odin always wins, Odette. Always."

I step closer, reaching out but stopping just short of touching his shoulder. "It doesn't matter. It was just a joke. Besides, I'm not some prize to be won. And we both know I'm no one's future queen."

Siegfried's jaw tightens, and he stares down at his hands, as if the stone he holds contains all the words he can't seem to say out loud.

After chucking it into the lake, he meets my eyes. "You don't realize how special you are, do you?" he asks, shaking his head. "Odin always gets what he wants, Odette, especially if he thinks it's something I want."

I'm surprised by his omission. Does that mean Seigfried likes me more than a friend? I feel warm all over and bite my lip, searching for the right words. "Odin wasn't being serious. We all know neither of you can marry me," I say firmly. "We will be lucky to be able to stay friends. You both will move on to bigger and better things without me."

Siegfried glances at me, his eyes dark and full of something I can't quite place. "It won't be long before everything changes, and I dread it."

I shake my head, trying to brush off his words, but a small part of me feels unsettled knowing that they'll leave for the Royal College when they turn eighteen in a couple of years. "I don't want things to be different, but I know you're right."

He almost smiles at that, but it fades. "I wish... I wish I weren't a prince."

"How can you say that?"

Siegfried glances back at the pond, silent again. He tosses the last stone into the water, and I watch it skip once, twice, before sinking beneath the surface. "Compared to Odin, I just don't feel cut out for royal life. I'd much rather live in the village, like you. Enjoy a simple existence."

"That's why you'd make a great king. You understand your people and our way of life, and I know you'd fight to protect it."

He looks me in the eye as he takes my hand in his. "Thank you, Odette. You always know the words to say to make me feel better." He squeezes my hand before releasing it.

"Come on," I say, tugging his sleeve. "Let's go back. We can make Odin charm Madame Fallow for cookies as punishment for being an arse."

That earns me a genuine smile, and he follows me away from the lake, leaving the ripples to settle in our wake.

Two Years Later

"I wish you were coming with me," Siegfried says as he packs the last of his favorite books into his trunk. "You could fit in here and I'll sneak you into the college."

I let out a sad laugh at the visual of that. "Tempting, but

what would I do once we've arrived? Hide in your room all day while you're attending your courses?"

Sig lets out a frustrated grunt, grumbling under his breath about stupid royal rules. "I should have pushed my mother harder about convincing your uncle to let you enroll."

"It would have been no use. My uncle tested my abilities, and I'm not powerful enough to study further. Besides, I'm content with making teas and elixirs with my flora magic. You are meant for more. You'll have an amazing time, even if I'm not there."

"Doubtful," he says as he latches the trunk closed and turns to face me. His eyes are full of sorrow, and it breaks the false bravado I've been mustering up today. Despite trying to be happy for him, I'm hating this. I don't want him to leave; I want us to stay in our happy little bubble that we've been in the past year. Somewhere along the way, our friendship evolved into something more. Something deeper. Something I think might be love. But alas, all royals and nobles' elflings must go away to the Royal College at eighteen.

"You know this is hard for me too. I'm going to miss you so much, but it would be selfish of me not to want you to learn to harness your moon magic." Siegfried's powers emerged a couple of years ago, but it's been difficult for him to learn to wield them due to how strong they are. The moon's energy can flow into him, which he says will allow him to use it as a weapon and a shield. So far, he's only been able to use it to create light orbs and small beams. He needs to go to college.

"It's going to be the worst four years of my life. Every moment away from you will be absolute torture," he says as he steps closer, reaching a hand out to cup my face. I lean into the warmth, savoring his touch while I can. "But, I vow I will write to you every day, so expect a hawk delivery daily."

I smile up at him, bringing my hand up and resting it on

his chest. "And I'll write back just as often, but I don't want you to feel pressure to keep in touch. You need to focus on your studies and advance your magic. Don't worry about me." We've known this day was always coming, and sometimes I wish I hadn't let myself fall for him. Everyone knows there's an expectation that the royals find a suitable match while at the college. As deeply as I care for Sig, I know it's futile to hope he'd wait for me.

He drops his hand and frowns down at me. I'm much shorter than him, my head coming up to his chest. He's gotten so tall over the past couple of years, and so handsome, even when he looks at me in dismay.

"You really think I could forget you?"

"I'm just trying to be realistic, Sig. Our paths are going in different directions, and I don't want to hold you back. Our kingdom needs you — you could be the future king someday, and I'll just be making tea."

"But, I need *you*," he says with a hint of desperation in his voice. "Odette, maybe I haven't made this clear, but I... I love you. I always have. Going away to college will not change my feelings. You're what I want. All I want."

I gasp at the words I've been longing to hear, but a little voice deep inside me reminds me he's leaving and we're too young to be making such claims.

I reach out and clasp his hands in my own. "Sig, you know I love you too, but it may not be enough. You must make the kingdom a priority, and I won't ever blame you for that. Promise me you'll focus on yourself while you're there."

He looks away from me, his jaw ticking. "I don't agree, but I will promise you that, if you promise me one thing before I leave?"

"Okay... what?"

"Just tonight, let us be enough. Stay with me. Let me love you fully, wholly."

"Okay."

"Are you sure? You want me as much as I want you, right?" he asks, and I can't help but blush. We've come close so many times to letting ourselves go all the way, but something has always made it nearly impossible to get enough alone time. If this is our chance, I'm taking it.

"Of course I do, Sig, you know that. I'd regret it if we didn't, but I'm also scared it'll make telling you goodbye that much harder," I admit, looking down, trying to hold back the tears that threaten to spill out.

He lifts my chin with his fingers, forcing me to meet his beautiful icy blue eyes. I think they might be what I'll miss the most.

"I know, and you may be right, but I can't leave without showing you just how much you mean to me. My heart, my body, my soul — they all burn for you," he says before crashing his lips to mine. I let him pour all his love and angst into me as I kiss him back with everything I have. He may not be mine forever, but he's mine in this perfect moment, and I'm going to savor it.

We kiss. And kiss. And kiss some more, before he lifts me into his arms, my legs wrapping around his waist as he carries me over to his bed. He lays me down so gently that my chest aches. I try to steady my breath so that I can commit every touch, every kiss to memory.

"You are the loveliest elf in all the realm, Odette," Siegfried says, standing over me. "I'm the luckiest elf in all the realm to be loved by you. I'll never take your love for granted." A tear falls from the corner of my eye and slides down into my hair. He wipes it away with his thumb and then takes his time undressing me. First, taking off my leather slippers, then rolling down my stockings and tossing them on the floor. He kisses his way up my legs, teasing me with one quick press of his lips to that magic spot above my entrance before pulling my pantaloons off. I can't help but groan in both frustration and need. My middle feels like it's burning up in anticipation, and I'm sure he can see the evidence of my desire.

Just when I'm about to demand he hurry, he leans over me, our bodies perfectly aligned. I moan at the delicious feel of the weight of him against me. He hikes up my chemise and dress, teasing my core with his fingers. We've done this part so many times that he knows how to make me explode, playing me like an instrument.

"That's my girl, soak my hand so that you're ready for me," he croons over me, making my toes curl.

"Oh stars, Sig. I'm so close, don't stop," I say, my breathing turning ragged as I lose myself to his touch. It doesn't take long before I'm shaking and coming undone beneath him. He bends lower, kissing me hard to cover my cries as waves of pleasure flow through me, eventually ebbing away into mere ripples. And yet, I'm ready for more. Craving it. Craving him.

Siegfried rolls onto his back, pulling me with him. Sitting, straddling his hips, I lean down to kiss him while holding his face in my hands before trailing kisses down his neck. I push myself up, sitting atop him, so I can unbutton his trousers and slide them off. He sits up to take off his shirt, and I help pull it off. Then he does the same to my dress, loosening the tie in the back and lifting it over my head. There's nothing left, just our burning bodies, begging for each other.

"Are you sure you're ready?" he asks as he brushes my wild red curls back behind my shoulders.

"I've been ready. Make me yours," I tell him.

"You've always been mine, and you always will be," he says right before he lines himself up and nudges my entrance. I'm still so wet and warm that he slides in easily. There's a pinch of pain as he stretches me wider than I've ever felt before, but it dissipates into pleasure as Sigfried moves slowly in and out of me.

"You feel better than I could have ever imagined," he groans above me, as he pinches his eyes closed and bites his bottom lip.

It feels so good that I can't form words, so all I do is nod in agreement. Chasing the friction I'm craving, I lose all sense of time getting lost in the electric feel of him. Our bodies collide over and over as I ride him. When Sigfried brings his lips to my breasts, zings of lightning zap through my body. His teeth pull at my hard peak, and I come undone once again. "Yes, yes, yes," is all I can say as I get lost in the pleasure flowing through me.

Next thing I know, Siegfried flips us over and pulls my hips up, pressing into me from behind. "You have the most perfect body," he says as he caresses my backside before holding onto my waist. He feels so deep at this angle that I think for a moment maybe I can't take it. I grip the sheets beneath me and hold on for dear life as Siegfried enters me faster and harder.

Nothing has ever felt this good and this right. I squeeze around him, eliciting moans from his mouth before his movements get erratic. "Odette," he whispers like a prayer over and over, except it's me he's worshipping instead of the woodland spirits. Turning my head to look over my shoulder, I watch in fascination as he stills inside of me, only feeling a slight twitching before he wraps an arm around my middle and collapses against me.

We both roll onto our sides, facing each other with heaving chests, trying to catch our breath. Siegfried interlaces my fingers with his and kisses the back of my hand.

"Thank you," he says and kisses me. He stares into my eyes so reverently, like I'm the most precious thing in the world. I've never felt so cherished, so adored, so worshipped. "Do you feel okay? I didn't hurt you, did I?"

"I'm perfect. I'm sure I'll be sore, but that's to be expected, I think. Don't worry," I tell him and I mean it wholeheartedly.

"I hate that I'm leaving in the morning. I want to stay here with you and love you over and over and over again."

"I hate it too," I whisper, my voice beginning to shake with all the emotions I've been holding in. I've never felt so happy and sorrowful at once. Burying my head in the crook of his neck, I try to breathe him in and fight back the tears. But as he pulls me into his embrace and runs his hand down my locks, I can't hold them back.

"I know, I know," he says into my ear, consoling me. "It will be pure torture being apart from you. I swear to you that when I return, we will be together again."

"I hate their stupid rules. How can they keep you secluded for four years and not let anyone visit? It seems cruel to keep everyone away from their family and friends."

"I'll see if I can get my mother to get them to allow me visits, but it may not happen. That has been the rule for centuries upon centuries, unfortunately. Are you sure you don't want to hide in my trunk?"

"Wishful thinking won't get us anywhere. I'm just not ready to say goodbye," I tell him, wiping my eyes.

"Stay the night then. Let me show you the depth of my love until the sun rises."

"I'd like that," I say, as we crash our lips together once again. This time, our movements are not slow and sweet, but frantic and full of the desperation we feel to cling to each other.

We stay tangled up together, loving each other with

everything we have until we are both too spent for more. When the first rays of sunlight stream through the cracks of the drapes, I can't bear the thought of saying goodbye. So, I kiss him one last time before slipping out of his arms. Out of the castle. Out of his life for the unforeseeable future.

Every step away from him feels like wading through mud. I know he'll be upset that I left, but I refuse to say goodbye. My heart already feels like it's shattering, and I don't want him to feel any worse about leaving than he already does. He needs to focus on honing his power and not have me as a distraction.

So, I'll do the same. I'll build my life here, contributing what I can to our kingdom. And I'll hope that the next four years go by like a flash of lightning and pray he'll come back to me.

Continue reading now on Kindle Unlimited: https://mybook.to/NKPMHD

COURTING THE FAE CAPTAIN

'The Mithrian Fae are among the most ruthless species recorded. Unlike their elemental brethren across the seas, theirs is a race that reveres bloodshed and darker power. If you cross them on a bad day, don't expect to see another.'
-*The Trials and Traditions of a Mithrian Fae*

I had always known I'd never outrun fate ... that didn't mean I couldn't try.

Lightning forked through the sky as I made my way inch by careful inch down the rain-slick slate beneath my bedroom balcony. Thunder roiled; a large crack making me flinch so violently I nearly lost my grip and tumbled to the precarious drop below.

My heart bashed against my ribs. I'd done the climb many times before and was no stranger to the risk, but my fingers were so cold, it was an effort to curl them into the narrow ridges of stone. One wrong move and this foolhardy endeavour would all be for nothing.

But I had to go. My father would ship me off to Domeratt

tomorrow to join a host of other would-be-wives hellbent on marrying the city lord's son—a captain of the Shadow Court's vast naval army, or so I had heard.

Frankly, I couldn't care less what the male's titles and achievements were. I had no desire to vie for his attention. Stories of how highborn fae treated their wives in the Shadow Court had often floated past my ears. The servants in my home liked to gossip over juicy scandals or female misfortune. And, seemingly, there was a lot of that in my homeland. When one was born into a world of immortal necromancers and dark magic wielders, one was bound to get a little more comfortable with death or other ill-fated fortunes.

There were four courts in the fae land of Mithria, each with their own class of magic wielders–Spell Weavers, Soul Speakers, Bone Cleavers or Blood Mages. I belonged to the Shadow Court, though my magic had yet to reveal itself.

I frowned, pressing myself flat against the stone as one of the castle servants reached out to tackle the banging shutters of a bedroom window beside me.

Halfway there. Just a few more balconies to navigate and castle guards to avoid. I'd prepared for this, though. This was a climb I'd timed more than once, considering patrols, guard rotations, and any other disturbances one might find when scaling a damn building as tall as this one.

Ironic, that I was the damsel locked atop my father's tallest tower. Only, he had no idea of the kind of extracurricular activities I got up to when he wasn't looking. Take rock climbing, for example. Not very demure. Not very ladylike.

A slow smile spread across my face. The conditions were less than favourable, but I'd trained enough times in hazardous weather to know the grooves and footholds as well as the back of my hand. Besides, this was just the kind of challenge that made me feel *alive*. The only other time I felt like this was when tinkering with potions and brews.

Alchemy. *That* was my true passion. Something I had done under my father's nose since I was a little girl, and something I had no plans of stopping. Which was exactly why marrying some pompous noble who thought of females only as breeding vessels was not on my list of things to do.

I was nearing the lower levels now. My fingers were turning blue with the cold, but I'd have time to lament the stiffness later. Just a little further and—I froze. Because just below me, bundled up in furs and staring out from the balcony edge, was one of the ladies of court. Melania, judging by the ginger hair wisping out of her braid. And that female? The only thing she loved more than herself was money and power. Or any means in which to get it. If she spotted me …

I sucked down a breath and forced my teeth to stop chattering as I waited. All she had to do was look up. Why in hells was she outside anyway? The winds were bitter and howling, the cold sinking deep beneath my bones. No one in their right mind would be out here unless … oh.

A male strode onto the balcony, gathering Melania in his arms as he turned her and claimed her lips. My body went taut. It wouldn't be any real scandal or surprise to see a noble getting cosy with another member of the court, but this was not a male any female had a right to covet.

That was Declan James, Blood Sword of my father's and, more importantly, a married male. Scandal, indeed. If word got out about this affair Melania would be finished. Declan would receive no real punishment, but that's the way it always went with the male fae in Mithria. Bastards.

My muscles were screaming as I held onto the wall for dear life. Sweat bubbled over my back, forming little rivulets that dribbled down my spine. *Please, please just go inside and go back to bed.*

He whispered something in her ear that made her laugh and blush prettily, then he was pulling her back towards his chambers. She protested coyishly, and it took everything in me not to roll my eyes. I'd bet my left tit she was already naked beneath those furs.

Five steps.

Four.

hree.

Two.

I almost heaved a sigh of relief when they took one last step, their heads nearly disappearing beneath the threshold.

Maybe I'd done something to piss off the gods. Maybe it was the boot that slipped ever so slightly out of the groove it was jammed in, but right before that last step, Melania fucking Harron raised those pretty blue eyes and gasped as she found me staring right back at her.

She took in my clothes, the braid, the gaiter pulled up over my face before her eyes slowly moved to my own. Recognition set in before the bitch smiled like it was the best day in her miserable little life.

Melania whispered to Declan, who looked up with piercing blue eyes of his own. He'd always given me the creeps. That male was colder than the deepest frost or the most bitter of winds. And I knew when he looked at me that I was as good as dead.

He swore and stepped indoors briskly, though his face remained a mask of calm. I fucking moved, hightailing it across the wall as fast as I could go. My shot at escaping this hellhole just dropped by half, and the odds were never great to begin with. Declan was not a forgiving male, nor would he forget. Even if I made it safely back to my rooms, I knew he'd eventually come for me and make it look like an accident. Maybe even pay some lowlifes to do the job for him.

My heart thumped; my palms slick and clammy. I could either continue down the wall and run, or find a public place to lay low in. There was no way he could harm me in plain sight of the castle patrons.

I looked longingly at the ground. My future was at stake. My freedom. But what chance did I have of making it out now? My father would be furious with me if I returned and Declan informed him what had happened, but he wouldn't do much more. Not when the Rite was coming up tomorrow. Everything would be swept under a rug and kept hushed. I'd have my life, yes, but what was that really worth if I was never free?

Fuck it. I bypassed the closest balcony and kept descending. The heavens opened, and rain poured down in a sudden torrent of rage. My hair was sodden within seconds, my visibility drastically decreased.

I blinked back the water in my eyes just as Declan reappeared and nocked an arrow to a bow. My heart dropped into my stomach. He wouldn't take me out on the wall, surely? His arrow could be traced back to him, and then where would he be? That evil male looked down at me, took aim, and *smiled*. Terrible and cold, and joyful with the hunt. Oh yes, he fucking would. Perhaps he was a greater asset to my father than I'd realised. Perhaps my father would turn a blind eye for his precious Bloodhound. Declan had never liked me. Maybe covering the affair was just an excuse to shoot me down.

The arrow flew, speeding through the air towards me. And as a scream tore from my lungs, thunder cracked in answer, swallowing any sound. I took one look at that arrow, prayed to any god who might be listening ... then jumped.

Continue reading now on Kindle Unlimited: https://
mybook.to/EunI